A
VINTAGE
FRIENDSHIP

Cathy lives in Bath with her husband and three cats. In her spare time, she is happiest digging, planting or reading in the garden or on a walk with friends in the local countryside – usually ending in a pub. For more about Cathy, find her on Twitter, Facebook or on her website:

CathyHopkins1
CathyHopkins
www.cathyhopkins.com

Also by Cathy Hopkins

The Kicking the Bucket List
Dancing Over the Hill
Blast From the Past

A VINTAGE FRIENDSHIP

CATHY HOPKINS

HarperCollins*Publishers*

HarperCollins*Publishers*
The News Building,
1 London Bridge Street,
London SE1 9GF

www.harpercollins.co.uk

HarperCollins*Publishers*
1st Floor, Watermarque Building, Ringsend Road
Dublin 4, Ireland

First published by HarperCollins*Publishers* 2020

1

Copyright © Cathy Hopkins 2020

Cathy Hopkins asserts the moral right to
be identified as the author of this work

A catalogue record for this book
is available from the British Library

ISBN: 978-0-00-829500-4

Set in Birka by Palimpsest Book Production Limited,
Falkirk, Stirlingshire

Printed and bound in Great Britain by CPI Group (UK) Ltd, Croydon CR0 4YY

There is nothing on this earth more to be prized than true friendship.

Thomas Aquinas

That awkward moment when you think you're someone's close friend, and . . . you're not.

Anonymous

Sara

1972

'We have to do something,' said Jo, 'like a ceremony or ritual where we make a promise that, no matter what, we'll stay best friends.'

It was July, our last day of school, and we were waiting at the bus stop outside Woolworths on the High Street in Hulme, Manchester. Ally, Jo, Mitch and me. We called ourselves the Fab Four, but today we were feeling more weird than fab. Our A-levels were done, the familiarity and routine of lessons over, tearful farewells made to classmates and the summer holidays were stretching before us. I knew we shared the same thoughts. Our lives ahead. Would we be OK? What would become of us? Jobs? Homes? Love affairs? Would we meet The One? Get married? Have children? We would be going out into the big unknown and, for the first time in seven years, going our separate ways. It was unimaginable to think of days and nights without my three closest chums – no more sleepovers, no more discussing every intimate detail of our lives, no more being there on each other's

1

doorsteps to share, support, laugh or cry. It was Oxford to study English literature for Ally, Exeter for me to do social sciences, art college in Brighton for Jo. Only Mitch would be staying put and getting a job, having put off college for a year.

'A ceremony to mark our friendship?' said Ally. 'For better for worse, for richer for poorer, to love and to cherish, til death do us part.'

Mitch sang the opening lines of 'Going to the Chapel of Love', and the rest of us joined in with gusto.

'I'm serious,' said Jo. 'This really matters to me.'

'Me too,' I said. I looked at my three friends and felt a surge of affection. I loved these girls more than anybody in the world: more than my brothers, more than any boy I'd had a crush on. We knew each other so well. Soft-hearted Jo who was so pretty but didn't know it or believe it, no matter how many times we told her. She had soulful brown eyes and a full mouth with a perfect Cupid's bow. The fashion at the time was for boyish figures and straight hair; Jo, with her curves and wild, curly hair, was the polar opposite.

Only Mitch looked as if she'd stepped out of one of the magazines. With her long lean limbs, high cheekbones and straight, long blonde hair, she was the beauty of the four of us: easily the most confident and a boy-magnet wherever we went. She was the leader of our small group, the coolest girl in school, too, endlessly curious, the first to come back to the rest of us with a music track or a lipstick, or to suggest we experiment with our parents' drinks cabinet when they were out. In later years she would roll up a quid deal of Red Leb to smoke while listening to Pink Floyd or the Grateful Dead.

Ally was the smallest of the four of us. Neat and petite, with brown shoulder-length hair and grey, intelligent eyes. She was confident, too, but in a different way to Mitch. She had a calm about her; she seemed unruffled, always sure about who she was and what she wanted to do, the first of us to have a steady boyfriend, a boy she'd been with since fifth form. And then there was me, Sara Meyers, somewhere in the middle on the confidence scale. I had to work at how I looked. I scrubbed up OK, but only if I battled with my wavy chestnut hair by, much to my mother's horror, ironing it under brown paper. Plus I'd been the last to lose any pubescent chubbiness, and I still didn't really know what I wanted to do when I left college.

'We could go out to the woods and dance naked under a full moon,' said Mitch.

'In Manchester? Even in July we'd freeze,' said Ally.

'We could get tattoos?' Jo suggested.

'Yeah. Where?' said Mitch. 'On our bums? Or boobs? What would it say? What's the symbol for friendship?'

'A heart? Two hands holding?' I said.

'No way,' said Ally. 'I'm not doing that. Too painful. What about we plant a tree? Or name a star?'

'Nah,' the rest of us chorused.

'Why not? If we named a star, every time we looked in the sky at night, we'd think of each other.'

'True,' said Jo. 'That's sweet. Or . . . I know! My mum's still got all my milk teeth. If you've got yours somewhere, we could have them made into jewellery then give it to each other.'

There was a brief silence before Ally, Mitch and I cracked up.

'No words, Jo,' said Mitch. 'I can tell you now that I am not wearing a bracelet or necklace made from your old teeth.'

'How about we become blood sisters?' I said. 'All we have to do is prick a finger at the same time then press it against each other's to mix the blood.'

'You lot are seriously weird,' said Ally. 'Sharing blood is too creepy and – like the tattoo – it would hurt.'

'OK, so let's just make a promise to stay friends then go and get pissed down the student's union. We've earned it,' said Mitch. She looked up at the bus stop. 'The promise is that today, right here, at this magnificent, significant and noble bus stop—'

'Noble?' asked Ally.

I put my hand on Ally's arm. 'She's on a roll, best let her finish.'

'This place where we've stood a thousand times,' Mitch continued, 'in rain and snow and wind and sun; this place that has been a constant part of our lives since first year, we will swear here, at this landmark, that we will be friends for ever and always. Stand on one leg.'

Jo and I did as we were told. We were used to obeying Mitch's mad instructions.

'We're eighteen,' said Ally. 'Oughtn't we to act more grown-up now?'

'Never, it's very important that we don't grow old and boring,' said Mitch, to which Ally nodded and joined the rest of us on one leg. 'Repeat after me.'

'After me,' I said. Mitch gave me a warning look. I grinned back at her.

'I swear,' Mitch continued.

'I swear,' said Ally, Jo and I.

'That I.'

'That I.'

'Mitch, Ally, Jo and Sara.'

'Mitch, Ally, Jo and Sara.'

'Will never grow old.'

'Will never grow old.'

'And be friends for ever.'

'And be friends for ever.'

'Come what may.'

'Come what may,' we repeated.

'Amen.'

'Amen.'

We put our legs down but Mitch hadn't finished. She put her left hand on the bus stop, Jo put hers on top, then Ally, then me. 'Friends for ever,' she said.

'Friends for ever,' we chorused.

'And we promise to be each other's bridesmaids,' said Jo.

'And name our children after each other if we have girls,' I said.

'Or boys,' said Mitch.

Ally rolled her eyes. 'OK, you could probably get away with a boy called Mitch, Jo or Al, but Sara? I don't think so. The main thing is that we stay in touch and continue to be there for each other. That's the main rule of friendship.'

'And real friends keep their promises to each other,' I said.

For a moment, Mitch looked tearful. 'You really do promise? I'm the one being left behind here while you all swan off to college life and bright new futures.'

I put my arm around her. 'We would never leave you behind, ever and you'll have a bright future whatever you do because you are Michelle Blake and a force to be reckoned with. Anyway, it won't be long before you're off too, and in the meantime we'll write and call with all our news and you must do the same.'

'Deal,' said Mitch.

'Deal,' said Ally, Jo and I.

Chapter One

Sara

2018

I was walking down the stairs towards the exit after the screening of our company's latest drama production, *The Rat*, at BAFTA, when I noticed my boss Chris Lindsay. He was putting on his jacket ready to head out. It had been a glamorous night, the reception held upstairs in the David Lean room, where leafless trees in pots had been lit with white fairy lights creating a magical atmosphere. The area had been hot and noisy with chatter, the scent of perfumes and colognes wafting in the air as the TV crowd mingled after the viewing, picked at delicate canapés, sipped Prosecco and eyed each other up. I, being older than most there, was ready for my bed.

'Hey Chris,' I called. As he turned and saw me, I gave him my most winning smile. He didn't return it. He looked away and walked towards the doors and out into the late summer night.

What the . . .?

Behind me, my agent Nicholas tripped and stumbled into

me. I caught and steadied him, then we both almost fell down the last steps just as Rhys Logan, my arch rival and super bitch appeared at the top of the stairs. He looked as well groomed and smooth as ever.

'Bit squiffy are we, Sara?' he asked.

I took a deep breath. Rhys, of course, would have only drunk mineral water all night. 'You know us,' I replied with a grin. 'Party party party. Can't take us anywhere.' I'd learnt long ago not to be defensive when Rhys was trying to wrong-foot me and I prayed he hadn't seen Chris blank me. Rhys would have loved that, and it would have been all round the office by lunchtime tomorrow.

'And what were *you* doing here?' Rhys asked. Nicholas ignored his question and breezed out through the door on to Piccadilly.

'Same as you, I'd imagine.'

'Maybe. *I* was personally invited by the PR team.'

I'd been personally invited too, by the director who was an old boyfriend, but didn't feel it necessary to say so.

'Anyway, got to dash, early morning start,' said Rhys.

'I know. Way past your bedtime.'

Rhys shrugged. 'The price of looking good.'

We both leant forward, air-kissed, and he was gone.

'Did you see that?' I asked Nicholas once we were outside and out of Rhys's earshot.

'See what?'

'Chris Lindsay, he just blanked me.'

'Nonsense,' said Nicholas. 'You're Sara Meyers. He wouldn't dare.'

'You just blanked Rhys, and very few people dare do that.'

'That's different. Rhys is a tosser. You're being paranoid, imagining Chris blanked you.'

'No, he did.' I put the back of my hand up to my forehead

in a mock-tragic posture and sighed. 'It's over. I tell you, my career is over.'

Nicholas laughed. 'Drama queen.'

We got into our waiting cab. As we drove away into the warm night, Nicholas closed his eyes and was soon snoring softly. Dear man. In his late seventies, bald as a coot, debonair and dapper, he was impeccably dressed as always in a suit and socks from Paul Smith, his shoes handmade in Italy. He'd been my agent and friend for over thirty years, a charming, kind and funny man, but with a core of steel when negotiating terms and well respected in the industry, something I had been grateful for over the decades.

I stared out of the window as we headed west past the familiar landmarks of Fortnum & Mason, The Wolseley (my and Nicholas's favourite watering hole), The Ritz hotel, past Green Park on our left and into the flow of traffic around Hyde Park corner. I was puzzled by Chris's behaviour. Fifteen years ago, he had been the man who was 'thrilled and delighted', his words, to have me on board. His team had put on a hell of a show at the time, pitching to me why I should join them and leave the magazine where I'd worked in my thirties and forties. I'd done a bit of TV work before then; I'd often been brought in as a guest writer and broadcaster on various lifestyle programmes, or to review the papers on a Sunday, but nothing permanent until spotted by Chris Lindsay. It had been seductive and flattering, and I'd accepted, and I'd had a very happy time since, coming up with programme ideas as well as presenting. For years, I'd hosted the morning show, then more recently the mid-morning programme, with a few extra appearances on shows covering everything from gardening to antique finds, the type shown in the early evenings. I'd particularly enjoyed the fact that my ideas were respected and often taken through to production.

For years, I'd been the face of Calcot morning TV, my face on posters, social media, even buses. 'Face *on* the back of a bus, not *like* the back of the bus,' I gaily told friends at the time. I was recognized wherever I went, got good seats in restaurants, was invited to everything. It was a golden era, but I'd had a feeling these last few months that something had changed. The extra appearances were starting to dwindle. It didn't look as if I was going to be given back my usual slot on the early morning show.

Nicholas opened one bleary eye. 'Are we there yet?'

'Almost. Nicholas, my inner drama queen aside, what would I do if work dried up? I'm fifty-eight. Am I too old to be presenting?' Actually, I wasn't fifty-eight. I was sixty-four, a fact that Nicholas knew all too well, but kindly ignored.

'Don't talk tosh. There are plenty of women your age going strong on our screens, all still working. Have a facelift if you're really worried about your age.'

'I will if you will,' I said. I knew he wasn't serious. We'd discussed it at length after one of the directors had suggested it last year. I wouldn't go that way. Why should I? I looked years younger than I was, something I worked hard at. A ten-minute routine every morning with my facial toner, an hour's Pilates every other day, wheatgrass in smoothies, probiotics for my gut, six to eight glasses of mineral water whatever the weather. I maintained a size eight, despite the more than occasional night on the fizz. Luckily I'd inherited my mother's good bone structure and my father's slim build and, thanks to the talented Damian Ward, hairdresser to the celebs, no one would ever know that my shoulder-length hair, once chestnut brown, was now white under the blonde and fudge-coloured highlights. 'And did you hear Rhys ask what I was doing there and not in a friendly way?'

Nicholas's soft snoring told me that he'd dropped off again.

When we reached his house in Holland Park, I gently shook him awake. He opened his eyes, got out cash, waved away my refusal to take it and tucked the money in my handbag. 'Sleep well, dear Sara. Your career isn't over. Rhys isn't your friend so don't worry about how he acts or what he says. He's an ass and all will be well.'

He had been listening, after all. I watched him as he got out and walked up the steps to a white teraced town house. A welcome glow from lamps lit on the ground floor showed that his partner, James, and their shepadoodle Atticus would be waiting up for him.

The taxi went on to Notting Hill and into a cobbled mews where I had lived for the past ten years. Home. No lights on. No dog, cat or partner waiting. My choice. No regrets. In I went and was upstairs, make-up off, in bed in less than ten minutes. Sadly, although exhausted, sleep wouldn't come. My mind had gone into overdrive, going through my budget. How long could I survive without work? How would I pay the mortgage with no regular income? What else could I do? Is there a care home for celebrities where we'd all gather together in a communal area and sing 'Memories' from *Cats*? I finally dropped off as the lyrics about 'better days gone' droned on in my head.

Chapter Two

The following week, I'd just finished a piece for a series looking into the true value of health spas, when Chris's secretary called to say he'd like to see me. Deep breath. Good posture. Ready to smile. Try to block out 'Memories' from *Cats* and singing has-beens in my head and replace them with Gloria Gaynor and 'I Will Survive'.

Chris got up to greet me when I entered his office (floor-to-ceiling windows looking out over the canal at Camden). Peck peck on each cheek. *The Judas kiss*, I thought as I took a seat and he settled himself behind his desk. I looked at him directly, confidently. What I saw was a man was in his fifties, grey hair worn too long considering it was thinning, dressed in jeans, checked flannel shirt and red Converse sneakers. No mention of the other week and blanking me.

'How are you, Sara?'

'Excellent,' I said, giving him the Meyers smile (wide, dazzling and bright according to *Hello!* magazine eight years ago). 'You?'

'Good, yes, thanks.' I noticed he wasn't making eye contact. Never a good sign. 'So. Sara. Bit awkward this. No easy way to tell you but we're going to be making some changes round here. I . . . er . . .'

I let him squirm. I stopped smiling.

'Well . . . thing is, direction from above,' he continued. 'They want a fresh look for the morning show . . .'

As if I didn't already know, I thought. 'Ah.' A couple of months ago, there had been some changes in management and a young chap in tight skinny jeans and designer sneakers had been brought in. I'd only met him a couple of times but the rumours were that he'd been head-hunted to take Carlton TV into the next decade.

'New faces . . .'

'Younger faces.'

'Some, not all. This isn't about your age, Sara, but the programme formula is getting a bit tired . . .'

'I get it. So you won't be renewing my contract.'

Chris looked very uncomfortable. 'I'm so sorry, if it was up to me—'

'Not a problem, Chris. I've already had some offers,' I lied. 'One that looks very promising actually.'

'Really? Who?'

'You know I can't say.' I stood up. I didn't want to prolong the meeting. No point. At least I'd be leaving with my dignity intact, and Chris would tell others that I'd had offers. I'd learnt long ago not to let anyone see when you're sinking. This had been coming a while, moved from the prime morning show to mid-morning; only a dummy wouldn't have seen what was happening. I offered Chris my hand.

Chris stood and we shook hands. 'Best of luck, Sara. I really mean that.'

'And to you too. I really mean that.' I didn't.

As I came out of Chris's room, I spotted Rhys by a coffee machine on the other side of the open-plan office. He was staring at me to see how I'd taken it. I put on my most cheerful face and gave him a friendly wave.

What now? I asked myself once I was in the lift. I needed to talk to someone who would understand. The first person I used to call in situations like this was my close friend Anita, but she'd died five years ago. She'd have known what to say but she'd gone. So . . . what to do? Alcohol. Nicholas.

*

An hour later, Nicholas and I were ensconced in a comfy pew in a bar on Ladbroke Grove. In front of us was an ice bucket and an almost-empty bottle of Chablis.

'Told you so,' I said.

Nicholas rolled his eyes. 'You told me your career was over. As your agent, I can't possibly agree with that.'

'So what now then?'

'I'm often asked if you'll do commercials.'

'What for? Equity release? Stair lifts? Retirement homes?'

'No, of course not, Sara, nothing like that, so you can stop that right now. Commercials can be quite lucrative.'

'And everyone who sees them knows you need the money.'

'So? Everyone needs money. No shame there. Want me to put some feelers out?'

I shrugged. 'Beggars can't be choosers.'

'Again, enough with the "woe is me" attitude. It's not like you and it's pathetic and self-indulgent.'

I laughed. 'OK, being realistic. I'm past my sell-by date. Is it over for me now in TV? What other opportunities are there out there?'

'Of course you're not past it – you're being over-dramatic. There are lots of women on TV who are your age.'

'So you keep saying, but usually fronting programmes about pension fraud and care homes in crisis.'

He sighed. 'Then write a thriller like one of those that are so popular now; they have to have "girl" in the title: *Gone Girl*, *Girl on a Train*, *Girl with a Dragon Tattoo*.'

'Mine would be *Girl with a Bus Pass* or *Girl with a Hearing Aid*.'

He sighed again. 'Stop wallowing. How about you write a children's book? Loads of celebrities are doing it—'

'I can't write,' I pointed out.

'You don't always have to. Some of them use a ghost writer to do the bulk of the work then add their voice with a few tweaks at the end.'

I shook my head. 'I haven't a clue what children like to read now.'

'That hasn't stopped the others, and don't forget you were a child once. What did you read to Elliott when he was small?'

'Charles used to read him the *Financial Times*. That's why he ended up in banking.' Elliott is my son, currently living in New York.

Nicholas laughed. 'Write one of those guide-to-life books, or how to entertain or decorate your house.'

'No, thanks. It would be in the bargain-basement bin before you could say Pippa Middleton.'

'Can you afford to take some time off? Think about things? Let me see what's out there while you tread water for a while?'

'I could for a few months, not more. I hadn't planned for this, as you know. My divorce cleaned me out, then, before she died, Mum's care-home costs ate up most of what was left of my income.' My dear mum had suffered from dementia and had needed care for the last eight years of her life. I found her a fantastic place, not that she really knew where she was, or even who I was some days, but she was safe and looked after, with doctors and nurses on call twenty-four hours a day. It cost all her savings, just about everything I earned to keep her there, plus I'd remortgaged my house but I wouldn't have had it any other way. No regrets. She died last year but, in truth, I'd lost the mother I'd known years before that.

'You should have got more when you divorced Charles.'

'I didn't want his money. I just wanted to move on, not get caught in some lengthy battle between lawyers.'

Nicholas sighed. 'He was the guilty party, so it wouldn't have been a long battle. He didn't deserve you. Many women in your situation would have taken him for everything he had.'

'Not my style – anyway, let's not talk about him.'.

Nicholas reached out and put his hand over mine. 'Something will turn up. Careers have ups and downs; you've had to change direction before and you can do it again. Wait and see.'

Chapter Three

I did wait and see if Nicholas's 'something' turned up. It didn't. It was odd not having to get up, rush out, work long days.

I spent the first weeks hiding away, watching TV and reruns of *Frasier* and my all-time favourite, *The Bonnets of Bath*, a series about a group of feisty and funny friends in their sixties.

In the mornings, I had a few cursory glances over job opportunities advertised on the industry websites. Waste of time. Nothing for me. It was a younger person's market, the openings were for people starting out, willing to do anything, go anywhere to get their foot in the door. I was over-qualified and too well known for anyone to hire me for what would appear to be a backwards step on the career path.

Nicholas called from time to time, sounding cheerful. 'Nil desperandum. Chins up. I have a few meetings. I'll let you know if anything comes of them; it's got to be the right thing.' He and James were great, supportive, cooking supper frequently and pouring the wine, but then they went off to the south of France for a week in early September and the phone went quiet.

Network, I thought, *that's what I must do.* And I did.

Launches, lunches, I was willing to go to everything and not to hide away. *My motto is to say yes to all invites*, I told myself in an attempt to be positive. I went through my book of contacts, renewing acquaintances, people I'd worked with, people I swore I'd never work with again. It was obvious that many of them had heard that I was no longer with Calcot TV and no one had any openings.

A book launch party at The Ivy in Covent Garden was the last straw. With its dark wood interior and beautiful stained-glass windows, it was usually one of my favourite venues, but I could see people looking at me then turning away, whispering to friends who'd then look over. It wasn't me being paranoid. *That's it*, I decided. No more. I felt my inner Greta Garbo coming on and wanted to be alone.

I left early and hopped on the tube to get home. An elderly man kept staring at me. When he stood up to get off, he leant over. 'Didn't you used to be Sara Meyers?' he asked.

'I did,' I replied.

*

At home, I went into my sitting room, lit a candle and flicked through my contact list to see if there was anyone I had missed. I knew I was lucky that I had such a place to come back to. Normally I am a positive person who likes a challenge but there was no doubt that my confidence had taken a knock and I was glad to have somewhere as lovely to retreat to. My shelter from the storm was a three-bedroom two-storey house with bi-folding doors at the back of the kitchen that opened out onto a small courtyard garden, presently alive with night-scented jasmine. Best of all, it was within walking distance of the cafés and shops in Notting Hill, so I never felt isolated. James had found it for me after Charles and I had split up and we'd sold our family home in Richmond. James's mastermind subject is

Rightmove, and both he and Nicholas advised that I go for the house, not only to live in, but as an investment. I'd decorated it in neutral colours and added texture in shades of pale lilac with linen and velvet cushions and soft wool throws. James, who worked as an art dealer (when he wasn't looking at property porn), helped me choose rugs, artifacts and antiques to complement the look and stop it looking bland. It was a light and lovely space, but the truth was that I'd spent little time there over the last years. I was always either working or out most evenings. The house was comfy, uncluttered and tasteful but something was missing. I needed people on those stylish sofas, round the elegant dining table – friends, those dear ones you could turn to when the chips were down. The ones who had been with me through thick and thin, who knew me before I was Sara Meyers, celebrity. Where were they? And why weren't they calling to commiserate?

In the many years my career had been booming, I'd lost touch with some of the good old folk I'd known for ever, so maybe they didn't even know what had happened. As is the way for so many in the industry, I'd hung out with the people I worked with. I have 400K followers on Twitter, more on Instagram and my public Facebook page has thousands of likes. Supportive messages had been pouring in since the news of my leaving Carlton had hit some of the papers. Not that the press knew what had really happened. Sara Meyers is moving on, the journalists had said, and I'd played along with that with lots of jolly posts on social media about new opportunities beckoning. But were these cyber-followers my real friends? People I could confide my anxieties to? Never. Not in a million years.

Nicholas and James: there was no doubt they were great and kind friends. I spent Christmases with them, they made a fuss on my birthday, they took me with them sometimes when they holidayed in France, but I was aware that I was the singleton and they needed space and time alone as a couple as well.

Jo and Ally were the next who came to mind. My oldest friends from school days. We spoke on the phone or emailed but due to geography, distance and busy lives, now I only saw them once a year, if that. It was my fault, I knew; especially in the last decade, I'd put my career first at the expense of letting my friendship with them fade. I felt a sudden ache for what we'd had as girls when Mitch, the fourth member of our group, was still around too. When one of us felt down over a boy, or something that had happened at school or with a parent or sibling, it would be treated with the same seriousness as if we were facing the end of the world. We'd gather in whoever's bedroom it was, bringing company and consolation, then maybe go into the sitting room and watch TV, listen to music or just talk it through, squashed on a sofa, our arms draped around each other. If at Jo's, she'd make bowls of butterscotch Angel Delight or cheese toasties to take away the pain. Overall there was love, and I knew that each one of them had my back as I had theirs. I had no idea where Mitch was any more but I knew where Jo and Ally were. I could contact them, but they lived too far away to troop round as they used to and be sitting with me at my table half an hour later, plus it was probably unreasonable to call out of the blue after so long and expect things to be as they were.

I went to my computer, looked through my contacts list, and realized I had loads of 'friends' going back years: friends from work, friends from when Elliott was at school and from whom I grew apart once the shared bond of the school gate had gone; local friends in the neighbourhood who I liked but always felt I had to be on my best behaviour with. Those who 'got me', with whom I could completely be myself, were few and far between.

Anita Carling. My lovely friend from university days. Was. When she died, it broke my heart. We'd hit it off from the day we met and had stayed friends right to the end. She was like family to me, lived in London so we could always drop in on each other and her passing had left an almighty big hole. She would have been round in a flash, making me laugh, coming up with mad suggestions to retrain as a stripper or such like.

It was sobering when friends and family died and the familiar landscape of life shifted. My world had changed. Losing a close friend, and some time later my mum, had hit me hard. They say people deal with grief in different ways. Some weep until there are no more tears, others block it out. I went for distraction. I felt their loss daily, so took every opportunity to work or be occupied, accepting every invite to a party for a movie, art show, launch of a new play; anything to escape from the reality of Mum and Anita not being there any more.

Of course there were others. Lyn and Val. Friends from work. Both gone from London and despite promises to stay in touch, we hadn't. Martha. Ah. A great mate for two decades when I was in my thirties and forties until a demanding and prestigious job took up her time. Jen Beecham? A strong older woman, a mentor for me when I first got into TV. She moved to the States over twelve years ago and although we FaceTimed, I needed someone in this country, preferably this city, even better in my street.

As I went down the list, I saw there were so many others I'd drifted apart from over the years. Jane Ewing. Susan Lewis. Erica Peters. Sophie Jenson and Karen Wood. Sandy Jenson. Josie. Caz, Suse, Alice, Kate – great fun, good-time girls. Hadn't seen them in ages.

Friends. They can heal but also hurt. Some can build you up, support you and help you face the world, others can also bring you down and leave you wondering what happened. *Friendships change*, I thought, *evolve. Some you outgrow, some have different expectations, some come to a hard and painful end* – which brought me to Ruth. Another good friend for many years, up there with Anita, Jo and Ally. For a long time, she was one of my go-to people in a crisis, one of my share-everything girls, one of my thank-god-for-girlfriends type of pals. She was a petite woman with dark Spanish looks, although she was Sussex-born. I'd known her thirty years, since I started working in television and she was a casting director. We hit it off immediately, same sense of humour, same hang-ups, same liking for a good Chablis or two. She had a son, Ethan, the same age as Elliott, so as they'd grown we'd shared all the ups and downs of their childhood, teenage tantrums, exams, university days, getting them ready to fly the nest and then the emptiness when they'd gone.

When she lost her husband Brian to cancer just over ten years ago, I'd persuaded her to have a spa day, a bit of pampering to take her mind off probate and the endless tasks of the newly widowed. We were in the sauna when she gave me the news that ended our friendship.

Charles and I had been married for thirty years; in fact, it had been at a garden party at Ruth's that I'd met him. They'd been friends since their university days, even dated, apparently. They both used to laugh it off but it was clear she adored him and I, fool that I was, didn't think there was anything to worry about. Most people adored Charles. God, he was, is, a handsome man: tall, fair-haired, high forehead, aquiline nose. He could have been a lead actor with his looks. Women always stared at him in restaurants, on the street. I enjoyed that, proud to be seen with him. At home, he was a gentle man, considerate, easy to get along with. We were happy. He was my safe place. It was he who pursued me, wooed and won me, not that I put up much resistance. I knew straight off he was the One; there was an ease there, a sense of the familiar, a feeling of coming home as well as a strong physical attraction.

We soon settled into married life, did all the usual couple things: country weekends with friends. He met and got on well with Ally and Jo and their husbands. We went to farmers' markets on Saturdays, walks by the river on Sundays, cooked for each other, talked a lot about books, politics, life, made each other laugh. I was sure he'd always be there for me, as I was for him. We liked each other, looked out for each other. We had history, had seen each other through the death of my father fifteen years ago, and then his a year later. We had done exactly what the marriage vow says – for richer and poorer, better and worse – and, of course, we had Elliott, who'd sealed and strengthened our bond from the moment he was conceived. OK, the sex had faded a little (a lot) towards the end, but didn't it with all couples? We even bought a book with exercises to do at home to resurrect the passion, but then agreed it didn't matter, we had plenty of other things going for us. The bottom line was that he was my best friend, and I his.

Ruth and I were talking about a mutual friend, whose husband had had an affair. One morning he'd come down and told her that he no longer loved her and was leaving her for a work colleague, a woman who looked just like her, only fifteen years younger. She was devastated, and I was saying that we should be there for her, take her out, be supportive friends, when I noticed Ruth had gone quiet.

'Look . . . no easy way to say this. I've been having one with Charles,' she blurted. I laughed. She didn't. 'No seriously, Sara, for five years. We've been waiting for the right moment to tell you, but of course there never is one.'

I studied her face, puzzled as to where this bizarre claim was coming from. We'd been on holiday with her and Brian many times. We were close. I knew all her secrets, didn't I? She went on to fill me in on more details. I listened, not taking it in. Five years? That meant it had started when Brian was still alive, before he got ill. It couldn't possibly be true but it was. I got home that evening to find Charles had already packed his bags. 'I am sorry,' he said. 'I never wanted to hurt you.'

For once in my life, I was speechless.

After he'd gone, I knelt on the floor in front of his empty wardrobe and howled like a wounded animal. Nothing had ever hurt so much. As deep as grief but a different kind of loss. He was still alive but gone from my life. I'd always thought Charles was mine. *My* husband, my go-to person, pick me up at the station ride, accompany me to a hospital scan and be there in the waiting room, holiday companion, my mow the lawn, take out the bins man, presence in the bed next to me, person to look over at and smile at a funny moment on TV, man to tell a piece of news or gossip to, put his feet on my knee for a foot massage. Part of my life. All my life. Always been there and would be until death do us part. *My* husband.

Not any more. The shock was overwhelming. I hadn't seen it coming, hadn't suspected, not for a moment. I'd left them alone so many times. Why wouldn't I? We were all such good friends. I'd trusted him, and her. But then it made sense – Ruth's over-concern when Charles was unwell. I'd been touched by it. Her defence of him on the odd day I was having a groan. She always took his side. I'd thought it was her just trying to show me what a good marriage I had. And it was good. I knew he loved and liked me. Was it the sex? I pushed away the mental picture of him making love to Ruth. The thought made me ill but of course it was there – what did she offer that I didn't? Adoration? Notable appreciation of him? Probably. Perhaps I'd taken what we had for granted, not expressed my true feelings enough and had expected him to know how I felt? Company? She didn't work the hours I did but Charles, who was also in the TV industry, albeit behind the camera, had always seemed to understand, even support me in the demands my job made. 'I'll be here with a cooked meal when you get back,' he'd often say when I was away from home a lot. He could have been the one that pushed and climbed the career ladder, even been a director, but he never had the ambition, he was a team player rather than a leader, a man who said he preferred a simpler, quieter life. He was my rock. My place to return to. Although . . . as a cameraman, there had been occasions when he'd had to be away shooting a programme. As Ruth made her confession, I began to wonder if he actually had been working all those times.

So, Ruth as a person, a friend to call at this moment of crisis in my life. I think not.

Sara Meyers. Me. What kind of friend had I been to some of these people? A good one at times, I liked to think, but a distant one who hadn't made the effort in the past years, so basically a pretty crap one. I used to value my friendships highly, had rules I tried to adhere to about staying in touch, being there for the ones I cared for but I'd fallen short of my own standards. No regrets? That was usually one of my mottos but I did have regrets: I regretted that Mum had gone. Before her illness took hold, we used to have long chats about our lives, hopes, relationships, news, books and gossip. Although there physically for many years before she died, the mother I knew disappeared to the point she didn't recognize me any more and often thought I was her sister. I missed the woman she had been – capable, curious and engaged with the world. I missed her maternal care and concern.

That Anita had died. She was still alive when Charles left and was there with endless support and sympathy, as I was for her through her illness. It was our unspoken code that we had each other's backs.

Charles, also gone. When we were together, our table had always been full of mutual friends for long Sunday lunches, summer barbecues, cosy winter suppers. We made a good team, sharing the shopping, him doing the mains, me on starters and puddings. When he left, friends divided like guests at a wedding, taking sides – his and hers – and I lost the heart for entertaining. It never felt the same.

Three of the closest people to me had gone from my life in a decade and a part of me had closed off, unable to deal with the reality of losing those I had loved and being left behind.

Ally and Jo were still there, good friends and, though not in London, not really too far away. I should make a lot more effort to stay in touch.

So regrets, yes, I have a few, as the song goes. I could see, looking back, that I had hardly been the model friend, maybe not even the model wife. There were times when I'd done that typical TV personality trick of disappearing up my own backside. How were my next chapters going to be as I sailed into my late sixties, seventies and eighties and didn't have the distraction of work? And no real pals to hang out with? I didn't want to be alone, and yet who would be there for company and care? To laugh and cry with? I sensed a tsunami of gloom about to rise up and consume me, so I did what I often do when doom threatens. I got out my laptop, found a 'dance along to Bollywood' clip, pressed play and shimmied round the sitting room for ten minutes. Despite the uplifting music, though, I couldn't escape the underlying feeling that I'd made a mess. I was in my sixties and a Billy No-mates. Friendship is a two-way street, one of my old rules, I reminded myself. Both make equal effort. You get in touch, they get in touch. I should do just that. True friends don't let distance or work get in the way, so I should pick up the phone and let those I care about know that I'm still here and haven't forgotten them.

Chapter Four

'Some of those people weren't your real friends,' said Nicholas the next day, after we'd caught up with our news. 'Plus people grow apart, move on when you find you suddenly have nothing in common any more. Sometimes it's not personal.'

We were sitting at a popular breakfast spot just off Ladbroke Grove, enjoying the autumn sunshine on an outside table where we could people-watch as well as chat.

'Yes but thinking about various friendships and why we're no longer close, I know some of it has been my fault.'

'Then do something about it. It was tough for you to lose one of your best friends to illness and another to—'

'Charles.'

'To Charles, and OK, so you don't currently have a Thelma to your Louise, but you've got the time now, you can start again.'

'Thank god for you,' I replied. 'At least you like me.'

He made a mock-puzzled face. 'Whatever gave you that idea?' he asked, then laughed. 'What about your brothers?'

It was my turn to laugh. 'Patrick and Henry? Not people to turn to in a time of crisis, and anyway, they live so far away. Henry's in Norfolk and Patrick is in Iverness. It's very much a one-way street – you know what it's like with blokes. I call them and we have a catch-up at Christmas and birthday and that's about it.'

Nicholas sighed. 'That's why friends are essential. As the saying goes, they are the family you choose. Old friends then? What about those school friends I've heard you talk about?'

'Jo, Ally and Mitch. I was thinking about them the other night – well, Jo and Ally anyway, I have no idea where Mitch is now.'

'What happened to them? Where are they now?'

'Jo's in Wiltshire, Ally in Devon. Jo has a big family and menagerie of animals living with her. Ally married her soul mate. We've been through phases, sometimes seeing little of each other then a lot then less again. After Charles left, I was the single one, I guess that changed things a fair bit, for me anyway.'

'You've been very focused, had a fantastic career, not many people can say that.'

'True and I worked hard to get where I am but success could be problematic sometimes.'

'How so?'

'Earning more than some friends, being able to eat out in nice places. Do I offer to pay or is that patronizing?'

'Was that a problem with Ally and Jo?'

'There was a time I was earning a lot more than them. One year I bought them expensive gifts at Christmas, lovely things. I wanted to. It made me feel really happy to spoil them both a little and share my good fortune. The next year Ally suggested we had a limit and not to go over it because Jo had felt she couldn't match my presents and she had so many of her own family to buy for. But then, she gave gorgeous things like home-made chutney or jam. I'd loved getting her presents. It cast a cloud over the whole gift-giving caboodle so in the end we just stopped completely.'

'You could have talked it through.'

'I could have. I should have. They're my oldest friends and probably would have teased me about it, told me to get over myself and that would have been the end of it.'

'It's good to agree on a figure for gifts sometimes, makes it easier all round or do Secret Santa. They both worked, didn't they?'

'Oh yes, they had careers too. Jo was always a great cook, had her own café, deli and farm shop for a while. She was struggling in the early days but she's more comfortable now as her parents left her a tidy sum. Ally went into publishing then became a literary agent. Her and her husband were quite the golden couple. He's a very successful writer—'

'Name?'

'Michael Conway.'

'Writes thrillers. Course I know him.'

'Ally was his agent. That's how they met. She retired some years ago though.'

'And what about the third one? You said you have no idea where she is.'

'Mitch? Ah, we had a falling out . . . actually, no, more a parting of the ways.'

'Why?'

'She changed and Ally, Jo and I couldn't relate to the lifestyle she chose. None of us know where she is any more. Actually, I'd *love* to know what happened to her now.'

'When did you last see the other two?'

'Jo last year and, oh god, I can't even remember when I last saw Ally. Jo's on Facebook so I can always see what she's up to and I never feel too out of touch. Ally doesn't do any social media. I owe her a call in fact, now I have more time, I could visit both of them.'

'When was the last time you spoke on the phone?'

I groaned. 'Months ago, maybe longer. I know, I've been a crap friend recently.'

Nicholas raised an eyebrow. 'Sounds like it. It has to work both ways.'

'I know, and I believe that too. I should get in touch, find out their news.'

'How come you don't know where Mitch is?'

'Good question. I was closest to her at school. She was quite the beauty. As well as being my friend, I admired her. Everyone did. She had charisma, cheek and charm, and she ran at life with both arms open, embraced new experiences, always a glass-half-full type of person, endlessly curious about life and other cultures.' As I described her I felt a stab of regret. Why *had* I let her go from my life? 'She was a rare bird, the original wild child. She disappeared after Jo, Ally and I had gone off to university and . . . well, we all went our separate ways – careers, men, the freedom of being away from home., it was a time of exploration for all of us. I didn't see much of Ally or Jo then either. Work and climbing the career ladder were my main priority, and they were busy finding their way in the world too.'

'And you really have no idea where Mitch is?'

'Not now. She got in with a strange bunch, went to live in a commune. I'm not sure after that . . . Don't forget that back then there were no mobiles, no texting, no social media.'

'So what's the story? Has she ever tried to contact you? Or you her?'

'She did at first, mainly to try and get me involved with the group that she'd joined. She was adamant that I should, in fact, but it wasn't for me. I guess we forgot the rule that friends should be open to each other's discoveries. I did try to do that in the early days. I made an effort to stay in touch, to understand what she'd got into, but I felt that she pushed me away once it was clear that I wasn't going to join her group. Gradually she seemed less and less interested in my new life, and our friendship didn't appear to mean as much to her as it had done – plus, if I'm honest, I was enjoying being single, exploring what was out there. She distanced herself from Jo and Ally too, and then life took over and we drifted apart, you know how it is.'

'No, I don't know how it is. I make an effort to stay in touch with most of my old friends, the ones that matter anyway. You have to. Doesn't everyone make an effort with the people who are important in your life? Even if it's just once or twice a year, you know where they are.'

'God, you can be so stern sometimes.'

'Tell me more about her. When's the last time you actually saw her?'

'Mid- or late twenties? I wouldn't even know what she looks like now. As I said, she was a great-looking girl back in the day, but we all look different now. I was tall for my age with unruly hair—'

'Photos?'

'Hah! Hidden away somewhere you'll never see them.'

'Do Jo or Ally know where Mitch might be?'

'I doubt it. I'm sure they'd have mentioned it if they did. Mitch had a boyfriend in London, a musician – quite famous I seem to remember, though none of us ever met him so perhaps it wasn't that serious. Jo went to art college in Brighton, Ally – she was always the clever one – went to Oxford, and I went to Exeter. We saw each other in some of the breaks but I only remember Mitch being back up north once in our first year when we went back and met up briefly. After uni, I got my first job with a local newspaper in Plymouth and, of course, that took up all my time. Mitch went into a commune, and I seem to remember hearing she went on the hippie trail to India. She could still be there, for all I know. The group she was with were out to save the world – that's when she became a bit weird. In fact, it was in that phase, or not long after, that I last spoke to her.'

'Maybe she died, ever thought of that?'

'I'd have heard. Someone would have let one of us know.'

'Not necessarily. Sounds intriguing,' said Nicholas. 'Aren't you curious?'

'To be truthful, I haven't given her much thought for a long time, but now I'm talking about her, yes, I suppose I am curious.' *Had she tried to contact me?* I wondered. Perhaps a message from her got lost in the black hole of social media?

'She's possibly not in the UK then,' said Nicholas, 'because you would've been hard to miss for the last few decades, unless she's not got a TV. But people don't just disappear in this day and age, unless she ran off with Lord Lucan.'

'Sounds about right for Mitch. She'd have done something exceptional. Even the commune, austere as it sounded, was out of the ordinary.'

'Why don't you use your newly won spare time to track her down as well as visit Ally and Jo? There are no friends as precious as old ones, and I can't keep an eye on you every day.' He sighed, slumped his shoulders and looked weary. 'I need to share the load.'

I thumped him. 'Stop it.'

He sat back up and smiled. 'Seriously, are you coping OK?'

'Trying not to panic. I have to find something soon or I won't be able to make the mortage payments, but it's not just that, what's happened has given me time to reflect on the fact that I'm going into a new period of life. What do I want now? Who am I now?'

'Look up your old friends,' said Nicholas, 'and ditch the existential crisis, it's so last century.'

I laughed. 'OK, it's ditched. Top of the list – call Ally and Jo and start to track down Mitch.' These old friends had been my morning, noon and night in my younger days. I knew I'd let things slip, but I was going to try and change that, starting now.

Chapter Five

As I walked home, I thought back to when I first met Ally, Jo and Mitch.

We went to the same convent grammar school and quickly found each other as like-minded spirits amongst the other new girls. Mitch stood out from the beginning; she wore her skirts too short and was always in trouble with the nuns for wearing lip-gloss or mascara. Ally stood out too. She seemed older than the rest of us, the grown-up in our gang, so composed, feet firmly on the ground and always self-assured. She never worried about fitting in and the latest fads or fashions. She was the middle child to two sisters, both boisterous: the elder one sarcastic, the younger beautiful. Ally, being more reserved, escaped from the pair of them into the world of books from an early age. Jo was a sweetheart from day one, one of life's givers, too much so, in fact – she was always a sucker for a sob story, a puppy in need of rescue or an abandoned kitten. She cried if she came across a bird with a broken wing, couldn't bear to think anyone was lonely or sad. She was funny too. All were good friends to have.

Those were innocent days. We used to hold sleepovers at each other's houses, though mainly at Jo's. We were always welcome there because she was an only child, and her parents were more than happy that she had friends. We spent hours talking about music and boy bands. My favourites were the Small Faces, Jo had a crush on Marc Bolan from Tyrannosaurus Rex, Mitch had a poster of Jim Morrison from The Doors on her wall, and in our first year at school, Ally liked Davy Jones from The Monkees, whom she claimed to love with a love that was true. We told her to keep quiet about that but she didn't care. Mitch always seemed to be a few steps ahead – first to get her period, first to get a bra, then later a love bite, which got her into trouble when Mother Christina discovered it when checking name tags sewn in on the back of our school uniform.

Saturdays we'd go into town, hang out in Miss Selfridge and Chelsea Girl, trying on clothes that none of us could afford because our parents weren't rich; then we'd head off to the wig department to try new hairstyles and hats and drive the shop assistants mad. Next was the perfume department to sample all the scents and, lastly, the lingerie department, where the lace and silk looked so much more appealing than the navy blue knickers we had to wear for school.

Once past puberty, we began to think about boys; there were endless earnest discussions about love and what we were going to do with our lives – careers or children? We got little sex education from the nuns. They told us two things about relationships. Firstly, if a boy wanted you to sit on his knee at a party, it was permissible as long as you placed a book at least the thickness of a telephone directory between his legs and your bottom. Secondly, again at a party, if anyone switched the lights off, we were to go to the nearest corner and shout, 'I'm a Catholic.' We thought that was hilarious because convent girls had a reputation as goers back then and shouting, 'I'm a Catholic' would only have alerted all the lads to where the game girls were. In my case, the racy reputation was unfounded. I was as green as anything, although not lacking in curiosity. We spent many hours discussing when we'd lose our virginity, how, where and with whom – which led on to meeting The One, how to recognize your soul mate, what fellatio was (not a character in *Hamlet* as Jo thought) and cunnilingus (not an exotic flower as I thought), and whether or not we'd do it. I have an image of Jo's face during a discussion about blow jobs. 'You *what?* You . . .? Ew. That's disgusting.'

On Friday nights, we'd troop along to St Bernadette's youth club, which was in the basement hall of the local church. There we'd dance in long lines to Tamla Motown and soul music. Afterwards it was back to one of our houses to discuss who'd kissed whom, which boys were gropers, which were to be admired and sought after. We rarely went back to Mitch's house. Her dad was so strict and would complain if we played music too loudly or stayed out too late. Mitch always had some boy or other after her. She was a natural flirt and had her pick of the local talent. Most of them never lasted past two weeks, then she'd get bored and move on. Ally settled with a boy called Steven in the fifth form and went out with him until university and geography separated them. Jo and I were in awe of her having a proper grown-up relationship. It went way past anything Jo and I had experienced; we were late starters when it came to serious boyfriends. I was taller than most of the local lads and Jo was lacking in confidence. We both had a few admirers, we just weren't sure what to do with them.

Our late school years were hard work, lots of homework, studying for A-levels that we all took seriously – we had no choice when the nuns ran the school – but there were respites between the studying, experimenting with drink at one of our houses. No one taught us that valuable lesson – don't mix your drinks – and I would often end up lying behind the sofa with the room spinning, my head swirling after having sampled crème de menthe and lemonade, port and lemon, and – what we thought was the height of sophistication – vodka and orange.

Other nights, we'd discuss the state of the world. The Beatles went to India to see the long-haired Maharishi. A Buddhist centre opened locally. In 1972 when we were in sixth form, a hippie shop appeared on Oxford Road selling mung beans and muesli. We'd go in there and buy herbal teas and sit at our table, feeling ever so 'with it'. Mitch's sister Fi was always off to a demonstration of one sort or another. We asked ourselves if we should go that way too, get into politics, or should we learn to meditate and take the spiritual path?

I smiled to myself at the recollection of those days. Ally, Jo and Mitch were my best buddies, we'd sworn we'd be friends for life and, at that time, I couldn't imagine existing without them. We shared everything: make-up, clothes, books, records, kissing tips, feelings – and god, there were lots of those, from angst, self-doubt, elation, frustration, to moments of just pure laughter because we were young and had the whole of our lives ahead of us.

I will get in touch with Ally and Jo, I told myself as I reached home. See if we can resurrect something of what we had and show them that I do still think of them and care. Ally's probably in some chic little restaurant with Michael in the south of France sharing a bottle of good red wine. And Earth Mother Jo? I can envisage her in her kitchen, concocting something delicious for a houseful of family and friends, or on her land feeding chickens or ducks or sheep. I felt a sudden pang of envy for the lives that they'd created and a stab of regret for how mine had turned out. My fault. I'd been too reliant on Charles before he left, then too busy escaping into my career to keep up meaningful relationships.

Still . . . Ally, Jo and I went back a long way, knew each other before we hit the world or the world hit us. Nicholas was right, old friends are precious. It was time to pick up the phone.

Chapter Six

Ally

Present day

I awoke to find my husband Michael sitting on my side of the bed, shaking me. 'What time is it?' I asked.

'About six,' he said.

I groaned. 'What is it?'

'I don't feel right.'

'You probably had too much to drink last night,' I said as I pulled the duvet up and turned over. 'Go back to bed and sleep it off.'

'No, Ally, something feels wrong.'

I sat up immediately. 'Why? Are you in pain? What hurts?'

'I feel weird—'

'Breathless?'

He nodded.

'Chest pains?'

'Yes.' I raced into the bathroom and got the blood-pressure machine. Something had been brewing for a few months now so I always kept a monitor nearby. At first Michael thought it was hay fever, an allergy causing a tightness in his chest. He'd suffered from allergies before, pollens causing asthma, shortness of breath, but it was now October and long past the pollen season in England. I'd finally persuaded him to see the GP, who told him it could be angina and organized for him to have tests. We were due at the hospital next week for a stress test. Friends made the joke about having a cute angina. We looked the condition up on the Internet and learnt that there were two types: stable and unstable. If the feeling of breathlessness came on after exertion but subsided on resting, it was stable angina and could be treated with rest and medication. If it came on randomly, not after exertion, it was unstable and more dangerous. Michael had just been asleep, hardly exerting himself.

I wrapped the blood-pressure cuff around his arm, pressed start and we waited. I glanced at Michael. He looked strained and anxious as the machine whirred, let out a puff of air and up came the result: 195/135.

Holy shit, that's high, I thought. 'I'm calling an ambulance,' I said. 'You stay here. Deep long breaths. I'll get you a couple of aspirin.'

The rest of the morning was a blur. Two short fat bald men looking like Tweedledum and Tweedledee arrived at the door. Joe and Kev. Ambulance men. I'd no idea how long they had taken to reach us. I was in a daze, trying to remain calm, not panic, be practical. Nothing felt real. Joe and Kev were lovely. They made Michael laugh, reassured him, did tests, took his blood pressure again, glanced at each other in a way that confirmed to me that it was not good. They told me to pack a bag in case they needed to keep Michael in, carried him out to the road as if he was as light as a feather and into the ambulance. *This can't be happening*, I thought. Michael was over six foot, fit as a fiddle, ex-rugby player, played cricket, tennis, went hiking, rarely ill.

'I'll follow on in the car,' I said, 'so I can bring him home.'

'Good idea,' said Kev, 'though I expect they'll keep him in until his blood pressure comes down. Bring what you need too.'

I gathered a few things and drove to the hospital, though I have no recollection of roads or traffic. When I got there, I found Michael in a cubicle in A&E, connected up to a heart monitor. He looked relieved to see me. I glanced over at the machine behind him. BP 200/135.

'How is it?' he asked.

'I can't see from here,' I lied.

A young female doctor with dark hair in bunches came in, sat opposite and explained what was happening. She looked about fifteen years old. None of it was going in until I heard. '. . . heart attack.'

Michael and I were both shocked. We knew something was wrong but neither had suspected a heart attack. He hadn't fallen on the floor clutching his chest. 'Are you sure?' Michael asked.

The doctor nodded. 'We can tell from the blood test we did when you first came in.'

Michael glanced anxiously at me. 'So what now?'

'First thing is to get your blood pressure down, run a few more tests, then we can decide on the best course of treatment.' She carried on talking and I tried my best to listen, take it in, '. . . take you up to ward, angiogram to see what's going on.'

Michael reached out, took my hand. 'Looks like I won't be home today. Don't worry. I'm feeling OK now. Could you bring me a couple of things in case I have to stay in a few days? Books, my laptop.'

'Sure. I brought clothes, your wash bag. But I'll wait. See you up to the ward. See where you're going to be.'

*

The rest of the week went by in a haze. My dear friend Philippa, on hearing of Michael's condition, was straight over. 'You won't drive, we won't let you,' she said and, true to her word, she organized a rota of friends to ferry me back and forth to the hospital. At first, I felt embarrassed. I could drive, there was nothing wrong with me, but Philippa insisted. 'People want to help, let us. It won't be for long.'

As the days went on, I was overwhelmed by friends' kindness to the point of tears. Every day, another one would arrive at the door, then drive and drop me at the hospital. It was a relief not to have to go round in circles looking for parking spaces or worry if I'd gone over the meter time. Most friends came in, said hi to Michael, then diplomatically disappeared to give us time alone. 'We are blessed, lucky,' I told him. 'We have the best friends in the world.'

In between hospital visits, I went into a cleaning frenzy at home, took every item out of the fridge-freezer, dusted, polished, wiped. The house had never been so spotless. I couldn't sit. Something compelled me to keep busy because I didn't want to face or hear the voices that appeared in the wee small hours, when friends had gone, the house was quiet and sleep hadn't come. The voices saying, what if he doesn't make it? What if he never comes home? And the reality would sink in. This was serious. Potentially life-changing. Maybe he'd make it this time but there might be another time when . . .

Some friends I expected to hear from, I didn't. Others I didn't expect to hear from, I did, like Sara Meyers, my old friend from school days. She called out of the blue, said she'd been thinking of old times and me. As soon as I told her the news, she offered to come down and stay. We had been close once, a long time ago, but we weren't really part of each other's lives any more, apart from Christmas cards and the occasional catch-up call. I'd see her on TV from time to time, of course, but less so lately, now I came to think of it. I'd missed her when she first drifted away; she was an upbeat person with a big smile and a bounce in her step, but her career had taken her away and I'd got used to living without her after all these years. The same went for our other school friend, Mitch, who had disappeared even earlier and seemingly dropped off the face of the earth, though Jo and I had never lost that bond. 'No need. He'll be home soon,' I told her. I was touched by her offer, I'd always enjoyed her company, but I had my team around me and my daughter Alice, who had arrived from Sheffield, where she lived now. My son Anthony had also offered to come over from Hong Kong, where he lived and worked. I told him to wait, reassured him that his father was in good hands. There would be time for longer visits when Michael was out of the hospital.

As I left the ward on the fifth night of Michael's hospital stay, I said goodbye, kissed him. 'You'll be home soon,' I said. When I got to the door, I turned back. He was sitting up, watching me, the expression on his face unguarded and infinitely sad. It hit my heart. It was as if he was saying, here we are, my love, not in control of our lives at the moment. We're in the hands of others now, of others who tell me what I can eat and drink, what pillow I lie on, what time I am woken, when I must sleep and when you can come and go. In the hands of others.

*

When I arrived on the cardiac ward at the hospital the next day, Michael's bed was empty. I looked around for someone to ask where he was. One of the young nurses, Yaz, noticed me and dashed forward. She had poppy red hair and tattoos on her arms. I liked her and her cheeky nature and knew that Michael did too. She had a bit of banter going with all the patients, and was one of those many people for whom you feel so grateful that they work in the NHS. She looked anxious.

'Can I have a word?' she said, and led me into a small room at the top of the ward where she closed the door behind us.

'Where's Michael?' I asked.

She took a deep breath. 'I'm so sorry, Mrs Conway. He was a lovely man.'

Was a lovely man, *was?* 'But where is he?' I presumed that he had been taken for his angiogram or some test or other.

'The doctor will come and see you in a moment.'

'Has something happened?'

'A massive heart attack about half an hour ago,' she said as she reached out a hand to steady me.

'Heart attack? No. Another one? But I just spoke to him on the phone this morning. He sounded fine. Is he all right?'

She shook her head. 'We tried to call you but you must have been on your way here and there was no answer from your mobile phone. I'm so sorry. He didn't make it. We did everything we could. Is there someone you can call?'

This time I got what she was saying. Michael had died. I felt my knees give way and I sat heavily on a chair in the corner. 'My friend Philippa. She's in the car park. I'll call her now.' With shaky hands, I fished my mobile phone out from the bottom of my handbag, where I noticed six missed calls from the hospital and the volume turned down too low to hear it.

This can't be happening, I thought. *Can't be right. Can't cope with this*. I felt as if some malevolent force had blown a hole in my abdomen. The expression, hit by a train, came to mind. I couldn't think, breathe or move. I was frozen.

Yaz brought me water in a plastic cup from the unit in the corner, then went to talk to Michael's consultant who had appeared outside the glass partition separating the small office from the ward. He glanced at me then came in.

Philippa arrived I don't know how many minutes later. She was out of breath from rushing. She sat and held my hand as various staff came in and gave us information or instructions. I wasn't sure what. When the doctor came back to tell me something, I remember thinking, I don't want to hear what you're saying. I don't want to hear this. I kept glancing at the bed on the ward, now empty, willing Michael to appear, be there again, sitting up, making cracks about the food and being given everything he didn't get at home, like apple crumble and custard.

When Philippa drove us home some time later, I recalled the last time I'd seen Michael. Last night. Of course, I hadn't known then that I'd never see him alive again. That look he'd given me, so tender, so sad. Had he known it was the final time he'd see me? End of. Date of expiration Thursday 25th October, a day in the calendar unmarked for the sixty-eight years he'd lived. We'd passed over it so many times, never suspecting for a moment that it would become a date to remember.

Chapter Seven

Jo

Present day, October

'So what's the problem?' I asked Mr Richard as I sat in his consulting room at our local hospital. I'd had to wait twelve weeks for the appointment with him, despite my GP chasing it up. It was a warm day for October and I felt clammy and slightly breathless, something I'd been feeling more and more frequently of late.

Is this going to be it? I wondered. *Bad news?* My friend Ally's husband had died of a heart attack, just a few days ago. Big shock. He'd appeared so fit, played sport, didn't smoke, yada, yada. If someone like him can pop his rugby boots, what hope is there for a lazy lard-arse like me? Naturally, Ally's devastated. He was the love of her life, her best friend; they had a wonderful relationship, unlike my late husband and me. Doug died over seven years ago and, even after all these years, I haven't admitted it out loud to anyone, but god, it was a relief when he went. What's that song by Bette Midler? You are the wind beneath my wings. Not in Doug's case. He was the weight around my neck.

He was a miserable sod and a crap lover. Oh, we'd go through the motions and all that, but making love with Doug was like trying to get a nicotine hit from one of those ultra-light cigarettes after years of smoking full strength. It all looked the same but didn't reach the spot.

Doug never hit the spot. I doubt if he even knew there was a spot. When I confided in Ally, she said we just needed some fire to fan the flame. *More like a case of dynamite*, I thought. According to some statistics, the average couple have sex two to three times a week; latterly with Doug, it was more like three times a year – if there was nothing on telly – and even those times faded to nothing. Neither of us could be bothered. 'Blessed is she who has no expectations, for she is not disappointed' became my motto.

I'd stayed because I felt sorry for him, he'd have been hopeless on his own. He was often ill and suffered from depression, and couldn't keep a job down in the end. I was his north star. Quite a responsibility. He tried in his own way, and he was good with the kids, but I'd left it too late to leave. I couldn't do it, and in the end I found a way to live with him, mainly by pursuing interests out of the house and keeping busy, volunteer work at the hospital, looking after my parents before they died, kids, grandkids, pets. All the same, I had to do the grieving widow bit in case people thought I was heartless. They didn't have to live with him. As well as his ill-health, he was a moody bastard, and so critical when there was no one around but us. Mr Smarmy Charm in public, Mr Nit-Picker in private. He wore away at my self-esteem and he drained any joy from my life, like a Dyson vacuum on supersuck. Liberated, that was what I was when he went. I got my life back, my bed back and my space.

Anyway, back in the room. Test results.

'The problem is obvious,' said Mr Richard. 'You're fat.'

'Pardon?'

'Fat, obese. Severely overweight. Simple. Blood pressure's high, cholesterol's high, you're a heart attack waiting to happen.'

'OK, now tell me what you really think, doctor,' I said. He didn't laugh. 'But can't you give me medication?'

'Certainly, pills, pills, the answer to everything. If you shifted a few stone, people like you might not need them and would save the NHS a lot of money.'

'People like me?'

'Fat people.'

'Yes, I got that. But the breathlessness I've been feeling? This tight feeling across my chest . . .'

He looked me up and down in such a way that he didn't need to say the 'f' word again.

'Do you smoke?' he asked.

'No,' I lied. I do. Socially. Every now and then. I have lots of friends who keep a sneaky pack in a drawer somewhere. I hide mine at the back of the cupboard, behind the organic coconut oil and decaffinated green tea.

'Exercise?'

I nodded. Not a lie. 'I walk the dogs every day. Miles.'

'Good. So walk more. How many units do you drink a week?'

'About ten,' I lied again. I don't know anyone who drinks within their units or even knows what the units are. Fourteen a week for women, according to the leaflet that I'd just read in the waiting room. One glass of wine is about one and a half units. Not the way I pour them, more like four units per glass, so three and a half glasses in an evening and that's your lot for the week.

'I'll double that,' said Mr Richard. 'Everyone lies. I'm going to give you a prescription for tablets to try and regulate your blood pressure, which you need to take straight away. Come back in two weeks and for goodness' sake lose some weight.'

'I don't think you're very nice, Mr Richard.'

'Cruel to be kind.'

'That's what my late husband used to say,' I said as I stood to leave, 'and it was never kind.'

'I'll put your name down for some tests, an ECG, stress test, possibly an angiogram, though I have to warn you, there's a long waiting list. In the meantime—'

'Don't worry, doctor, I've got what you're saying. Lose weight.' I went to the door. *I shall be dignified*, I thought, *and then I'll show him, this Dr Smug, I'll lose the weight. I can do it. I've done it before*. There's not a diet I don't know about. Lean for Life. Slimming World. Zest4life. Food Doctor Diet. I have two book-shelves full of manuals on how to shift the pounds. And a cupboard packed with diet food and shakes. All work. Just have to stick to them.

I swept out of the room, along the corridor, and climbed the steps to the café where I'd arranged to meet my friend Jane. *The cheek of the man*, I thought as I felt the familiar tightness in my chest, took a deep breath and put a hand out to steady myself on the banister. Once in the café, I couldn't see Jane, so I got a cup of green tea (new diet starts here) and texted her to let her know that I had finished. As I sat there, I was aware that the feeling across my chest wasn't going away; in fact, it was getting worse, as though someone had put a rope around my ribcage and was tightening it, causing severe pain, like really bad indigestion. It began spreading up to my jaw, my left arm. Uh oh. I felt nauseous and dizzy. *Deep breaths. Chill*, I told myself. The pain still wasn't going away, my back hurt. I felt myself starting to fall and reached out to grip the table. *Jane, where the hell are you? Oh, here we go,* I thought as I keeled over, taking the table, tea and saucer with me.

Next thing I knew, I heard a buzzing, a ringing in my ears,

then I was floating, floating . . . out of my body. *What?* I felt as if I was a balloon, wafting gently, softly upwards. *Hold on a moment. This is strange*, I thought. *Nice but weird.*

I looked down. I could see myself on the floor. *Uh? How can that be if I'm up here looking down?* People in the café were staring at the body on the ground. They looked shocked. I saw a medic run towards my body. 'Clear the space, give her some room,' he said to the few onlookers who'd gathered around. *Nosey sods.* I felt like laughing and waving – woohoo, I'm up here. I'm fine.

Another medic came running, she was carrying a bag. She knelt beside me, or rather my body, not me because I was floating around up here in the air. Not sure how. My own version of the lyrics to *The Snowman* began to play in my mind. I'm floating in the air . . . I'm floating in the hospital sky, I'm also down below, oh bollocks am I go-ing to die? I wasn't bothered if I was. Being out of my body didn't feel uncomfortable; in fact, the pain in my chest had gone. I felt light, weightless. *Oh! Am I actually dead?* I asked myself. *Have I died?* I watched the medics work on me; loosen clothing, the woman calling someone on her phone. 'Urgent.'

I wanted to tell them, it's OK. I'm up here, perfectly fine, really. The woman was injecting something into my arm. I didn't feel anything from my place as spectator. I wasn't sure what to do, though. Did it matter? Didn't seem to. *But what next?*

Suddenly I felt a jolt, a pull upwards, away from the hospital café, away from the area, and I found myself hurtling through a dark tunnel, top speed, a sort of shunting sensation. It wasn't unpleasant, just unusual. I was travelling very fast then I was out, like a ball out of a cannon, flying, expanding into a sea of light, white light and oh . . . what a beautiful feeling. Calm. Pure. Love. Warmth. Joy. *I know this place*, I thought as I felt myself dissolving, like salt in water. So *so* peaceful. *I know the feel of this place. I belong here. This is my true home.*

Somewhere, a long way away, I could hear someone calling my name. I knew the voice. It was Jane's. When did she arrive at the café? It was peculiar. I was aware of the sea of light but also the scene in the café. I wasn't sure how long I'd been up wherever it was. I didn't want to reply to Jane or go back down there. I liked where I was, floating, warm, so very *very* comfortable. But . . . oh *no*, I felt a pull in my solar plexus, I was going back, something was calling me back, back, back.

Then I realized what was happening. I probably wasn't dead. I was having one of those out-of-body, near-death experiences. I had seen a documentary about it and thought it was a load of tosh, but hallelujah, now it was happening to me. How cool. *Not tosh after all*, I thought as I watched my body being put on a stretcher then hoiked up onto a bed, one of those with wheels. The female medic had a long plait and the man had a tattoo of a dove just behind his left ear. *Bet that hurt*, I thought. I wasn't in the slightest bit afraid which was odd considering the circumstances. God, I felt good. *I am soooooo chilled*, I thought as I watched my body being wheeled away. *Mr Richard was right, though: I am fat.* It's not often you see yourself from all sides, three dimensionally.

I heard a voice beside me. 'Do you want to go back?'

I turned. Who was that? I sensed a presence, though couldn't see anything or anyone. It was more like the sensation of a being, an energy, but whoever it was, they felt like my very best friend ever, full of love, warmth and humour. I got the feeling that this being shared my sense of the absurdity of it all. I was glad it was there. I couldn't tell whether it was male or female, but I knew somehow that it had my best interests at heart. The presence seemed kind. 'Do you want to go back?' it asked again.

'Well I don't think I do,' I somehow communicated telepathically. 'I like it here, weightless, timeless.'

'Have you finished with your life?'

As I pondered the big question, my life or parts of my life began to stream in front of me, like a film. I saw myself as a toddler, learning to walk, a child growing up in Manchester, walking to school in the rain, digging in the back garden, fast-forwarding to being a teen at school with Ally, Mitch and Sara, in chapel, our shoulders shaking in silent laughter before getting detention, me as a young woman studying, a stream of friends. Doug, the kids, happy times, sad times, me rushing about a lot. Did I ever sit still? Always working. Getting married, having children, cooking, gardening, driving, cleaning, working, caring for my parents, caring for the neighbourhood. Busy, busy, busy. I'd been a human doing, not a human being. I felt the presence next to me, not judging, though a few memories left me embarrassed, like the time I was pissed and managed to pull the fridge-freezer on top of me, then had to lie on the floor with a frozen chicken and pack of garden peas in my hair until someone rescued me soon after.

'Does whoever's editing this film that is my life *have* to show that?' I asked.

'All part of the whole,' said my new astral pal. 'You learnt from the good and the bad and that was what it was all about.'

And then I saw more recent times. My grandkids. Oliver, Holly, Jason, Annie. My children, Kirsty and Graham, and their partners, Will and Saskia. My dear ones. All struggling with jobs, trying to get by, not able to buy their own properties. The lovely sensation I had been experiencing changed. I felt in the middle of a tug-of-war: my family on one side, the pull of the light on the other.

'Darn it, damn it. I have to go back,' I said. 'It's not my time. I still have stuff to do.'

'Your choice,' I heard the voice say.

'Hey, but before I go, where am I? Who are you? What's it all been about?'

'Love,' was all I heard, as suddenly I was being pulled, hurtled, catapulted back into that fat piece of blubber that was me. Oomph. Landed. Back in the body. Back in the room. It felt so heavy after the sensation of weightlessness, like being in wet sand. Hurt too.

'I think she's coming back,' said a voice. Not the kind one up above, not my astral chum. I opened my eyes. It was the medic with the plait. 'Jo, are you OK?'

'We thought we'd lost you for a moment,' said the man with the topknot.

'You did. I was watching.'

Jane was at the end of the bed. 'Jo. It's me. Thank god.'

'It's OK. I felt like I died but I was watching the whole thing from up there.' I pointed at the ceiling.

The two medics exchanged glances, as if to say we've got a cuckoo one here.

'I was,' I said. 'I could see you working on me. You've got a tattoo of a dove on your neck just behind your left ear.'

The male medic looked shocked and put his hand up to his neck. 'I do.'

'So how was it?' asked Jane.

Suddenly, I felt drained. They were all staring at me, Jane and the two medics, with expressions on their faces as if they were indulging a fanciful child, but I knew what I'd experienced and it had been real. I closed my eyes and tried to will myself back to the sea of light, but all I could feel was a throbbing pain in my head, my chest, and my shoulder where I'd hit the floor. Damn it.

Chapter Eight

Sara

Present day, November

Iflicked on the TV and watched Rhys for thirty seconds. He was in the bright studio kitchen watching Antonio, a celebrity chef, cook risotto. 'Oo,' he oozed as Antonio spooned food into his mouth, 'aah, fabulous.' *Ew,* I thought as the camera zoomed into a close-up of him masticating the food. In the press of a button, he was gone. Thank god for remotes. If only they worked in real life.

Back to my quest to reunite with my old friends. I hadn't got far. I planned to visit both Jo and Ally and make steps to reconnecting, but there had been shocking news from both of them. Jo was now recovering in hospital from a heart attack, and Ally was reeling with grief over the death of her beloved husband. I'd sent cards and flowers and would travel to see them when they were both up for visitors. So much for my assumption that they were living happy, idyllic lives. The recent events had served to show how out of touch I really was and I wanted to make up for that when the time was right.

Next on the list was Mitch.

I went to my computer, found Facebook and typed 'Michelle Blake' into the search box. Hundreds with that name came up, pages and pages; some with profile photos, some without. I made myself a cup of tea and sat down to go through them properly. Depending on the privacy settings, I was able to look at some and eliminate them – too young, too old or nothing like her. Other pages I couldn't get into but could see photos. There were no pictures of anyone looking as I'd imagine Mitch would now. Once I had been through all pages with the name Michelle Blake, I typed in Mitch Blake.

Next I tried Twitter. As with Facebook, there were plenty to choose from, all around the world, but none looking like my Mitch. It felt hopeless. She might have married, changed her name. It was like looking for a needle in a haystack. As a last resort, I found an old photo of us from our school days, took a picture on my phone then posted it on my page with a tweet saying: Michelle Blake from Manchester. Where are you now? Responses were immediate, mainly from pervs who clearly liked the look of us in school uniform. I took the post down after a private message from a man who'd sent a close-up of his willie. Bleurgh.

Deli. An almond croissant was calling me. It had been calling me for years but I'd always resisted. TV can put weight on a person, so I could never take the risk of anything so indulgent. But I was no longer on TV. I had some catching up to do in the 'piling on the pounds' department.

*

I was at the cash desk at the deli waiting to pay.

'Sara Meyers!'

I turned to see Gary Parsons from Little Dog Productions. He used to work at Calcot TV but had left years ago to start his own independent company and had been very successful in doing so. He was a cuddly bear of man with a bushy beard. He was wearing clothes that made him look as if he was about to go hiking: jeans and a red checked flannel shirt, probably Oxfam's finest; army boots on his feet. I'd always liked him and he was one of the few people I didn't mind catching me with no make-up wearing an old jacket, my slouchy pants and trainers. He had two Portuguese custard tarts in hand. 'Hey!'

'Just the person I wanted to see. This is synchronicity.'

'I am? It is?'

He glanced at my croissant. 'Let me pay for that. Time for a coffee?'

'Absolutely.'

We found a table by the window and caught up on gossip for a while. Who was doing what. Who was working where.

'So. Synchronicity?' I asked, once we'd exhausted the gossip.

'I was only talking about you this morning.'

'Good, bad or bitchy?'

He smiled. 'All good. We have a gap in our programming. A gap I believe you could help us with.'

I felt my spirits rise.

'We want to develop a new reality show.'

I felt my spirits fall. 'Reality show?'

'For the over-fifties. There's a whole new market out there for—'

'People my age?'

'Exactly. We call it the Second Marigold Hotel market.'

'You mean the Saga Louts? The Silver Surfers? You're right, they're finally being acknowledged.'

'I know. The over-fifties have money, they read books, they watch TV, they go to the movies, the theatre. People are cottoning on that there's a whole generation that are only just beginning to be catered for in the media in the last decade.'

'And where would I fit in?'

'Ah, well, that's the question.' He laughed. 'We haven't actually got an idea as yet. That's why we were talking about you. If you could come up with something that would appeal, you of course could front the series.'

'OK. So what kind of areas were you thinking about?'

Gary finished off his tarts, then combed the crumbs out of his beard with his fingers. 'Something that hasn't been done before.'

I laughed. 'No pressure there then. Isn't that what everyone's looking for?'

'It is, but I remember working with you. You were never short of ideas and often had more than the production team you were working with.'

'You know I'm no longer at Calcot?'

'I had heard. Idiots to have let someone like you go.'

'I knew there was a reason I liked you.'

'So, how about it? Have you got other commitments yet?'

'Honestly, nothing. I could lie and say I had offers coming out of my ears, but the truth is, I haven't.'

'Well, that's great news. I'll send you over a brief but truth is, we haven't got much so far. All I can tell you is we want something upbeat, an angle to draw in our more mature viewers, something relevant to that time of life. You still with your agent Nicholas?'

'I am.'

'I can sort out the details with him.'

'Sounds great.' I looked down at my half-eaten croissant. 'And here was me thinking I could have one of these. If I'm to be fronting a show again, these will have to go.'

'You look great. Too thin, if you ask me. Have a tart as well. They're truly excellent.'

'I've got an idea for your show. *Love Island* for older folk who like their food. We could call it *Love Handle Island.*'

Gary laughed so hard, he spat coffee.

'Or *Bus Pass to Love Island*, for the over-sixties?'

Gary laughed again. 'I knew I could count on you.'

'How soon do you need realistic proposals?'

'Next few weeks. We'd like to get started as soon as possible. So are you in?'

'I'm in.'

I couldn't wait to get started. I felt as if I'd been given a shot of adrenalin and, as I left the café, my mind was already firing off ideas.

I went straight round to see Nicholas at his office, which was in the basement of his house.

'Sounds promising,' he said, after I'd made a fuss of his shepadoodle Atticus and filled Nicholas in on my meeting with Gary. 'Any ideas so far?'

'No serious ones. First I thought I'd have a look at what's been done so far. I googled on the way here. Gary was right. It has all been done. *I'm a Celebrity, Get Me Out of Here*, *Big Brother*, talent shows, cooking shows, health shows, travel shows, *Strictly*. How about a version of that for the elderly?'

'With zimmer frames? *Strictly Come Hobbling* for people who've had knee and hip replacements.' Nicholas screwed up his face. 'Dating shows? *Naked Attraction* for the elderly? Can you imagine?'

I screwed up my face. 'I'd rather not.'

'OK, let's think about this. You're the age that they want to attract, so what's important to you at this time of life? What concerns you? People your age?'

I sighed. 'I remember turning thirty and feeling that I was old then, and now . . .'

Nicholas held up his palm. 'You're as young as you feel. We don't need figures.'

'Priorities change as you get older, don't they? Elderly parents, looking after them and losing them, sometimes divorce, seeing some friends battle with illness, some lose that battle, others coming to terms with becoming empty-nesters or grandparents.'

'What about for you?'

'Presently my main concern is: will I ever work again? Finances. How much I might need to survive depending on how long I live. It's weird to think about how much I might need if I live to ninety, or that maybe it would be better if I popped off before.'

'Cheerful. It would help if when we're born we got a date of issue and a date of expiration.'

'Like a driving licence.'

'Programme about finding work in your fifties?' Nicholas suggested.

'Sounds dull. Gary said he wanted uplifting. What about a makeover show? Everyone loves a good before-and-after programme.'

'Like *Queer Eye for the Straight Guy*? Hard to top that.'

'Or what about *Snog, Marry or Avoid* for the elderly? We could call it *Medicate, Resuscitate or Pull the Plug*?'

Nicholas eyes twinkled. 'What you have to do, Sara, is really get into the mind of a fifty-year-old,' he said with a grin.

'If I can remember how that was. Gary still thinks I'm in my fifties.'

'No one need know you're not. What I mean is – you're the

target market. Come on, think. What is relevant? Sex? Men? Relationships? Cooking? Gardening? Retirement?'

We sat in silence for a moment.

'I think I may have bitten off more than I can chew,' I said.

'Sleep on it, dear Sara. You have a few weeks.'

I left the office with my mind in a spin, generating and rejecting ideas one after the other as I tried to rise to the challenge of creating the next big thing. Did I still have it in me and why had I agreed to come up with the impossible so quickly?

Chapter Nine

Ally

Present day, November

Philippa had stayed over with me in the week following Michael's death. 'I can stay longer,' she said as she made coffee one morning. 'John can bring me some more clean things over.'

'Look, I have to get used to it some time, plus he must be missing you.'

'It's your call, but I am happy to be here longer. We don't need to talk if you don't feel like it. I can get on with things, make a list of what needs to be done and not be in your way.'

I went into the hall and opened the travel case I'd brought back from the hospital. I'd been putting off looking at it and it had been sitting there untouched since the day Michael died. I retrieved the plastic bag that the ward nurse had given me. It contained Michael's wedding ring, his watch, his mobile and his wallet. There was also a copy of *Private Eye*, a few clothes, clean pyjamas and the jeans and jumper I'd taken in for him ready for his return. He wouldn't be needing those now.

I wondered what he was wearing now in the funeral home and who, which of the nurses, had been with him when he died? Who was it? Yaz? Or someone else? Was he aware of what was happening? Did Yaz or the consultant tell me? They had but I hadn't taken it in, only that he'd gone. I think the consultant said it was sudden, I think he did. Michael hadn't suffered. Could I go back and ask them to go over it all again? I decided not to. It wouldn't bring him back.

A fresh wave of grief erupted. When alone, I'd cried until there were no more tears and I felt physically sick, but then something would catch me, a reminder of the man I'd spent so many years with – his shaving kit in the bathroom, a jumper over the back of a chair, the brand of tea he liked, his coffee mug – and I'd be off again, unable to contain the torrent deep inside.

In the past, Michael and I had shared everything – books, TV shows, newspaper articles, new recipes, new restaurants; any new experience we had was told to the other. We'd even talked about how death was a taboo subject in our society although it was going to happen to all of us. We joked that we'd send each other signs from the beyond. If Michael could, he would want to tell me how it was. *How's he going to do that now then?* I wondered. And how could it be that my husband went to the hospital but all that came back was a plastic bag containing a few personal items? It felt unspeakably cruel, so final. He had been a big man in every respect, a larger-than-life character with a hundred interests and opinions, my best friend and lover. How could someone so vibrant, so present, be now in the past?

I went back into the kitchen. 'Do you believe in life after death, Pip?'

She shrugged. 'I'd like to think that the soul lives on, but I guess we'll never know for definite until it happens to us.'

'My friend Jo, the one who had a heart attack, she was on about having a near-death experience, leaving her body and watching everyone down below attending to her physical body while she floated about on the hospital ceiling.'

'Sounds a bit wild.'

'Does, doesn't it? I'm not sure what to think of it. But if the spirit does live on, people should be allowed to send one text after they die, don't you think?'

'Except you don't get to take your mobile, or anything else for that matter. And what would you say? Arrived safely, then an emoji with angel wings? But I agree, it would be good to get some sort of message.'

'Jo's experience sounds like wishful thinking to me.'

'That's what I thought . . . OK, I'm going to tell you something I've never told anyone and you must promise not to laugh.'

'I won't.'

'After my father died, I was very distressed that I wasn't there to say one last goodbye, plus I wished there was some way of knowing that he was OK. I remember confiding all this to a friend. Ask for a feather, she advised me, and told me about the white feather theory.'

'The white feather theory?'

'Is that people who have died send them to let you know that they're OK.'

I burst out laughing. 'A feather? Sorry but . . . you *believed* her?'

'Not at the time. We were on a beach in Dorset and, just to appease her, I opened my arms up to the sky and said, "OK Dad, send me a feather to let me know you're all right." I thought the idea was crazy, we see so many feathers every day, on the pavement, in the garden, they can't always be signs from the spirit world. Anyway, John and I had a laugh about it as we drove home, but when we got back to the house, there – lying on the mat inside the porch at the front door – was a large white feather with a black marking in the shape of a W at the lower end of it. I took it inside and wept. My father's name was William, and in all the thirty years we had lived there, I can't recall ever having picked up a feather from inside the porch, never mind such a large one. Since then, often when I am upset about something, white feathers appear in the strangest places. Before a job interview that I was stressing about, I found one in the glove compartment of my car. Another time, I was worried about a medical test that John was having and I found a feather in the fruit bowl. It was reassuring finding them, like Dad saying: hey, I'm still looking out for you. And now you will think I am mad, grasping at straws . . . or, rather, feathers.' Philippa shook her head and sighed. 'You definitely think I'm mad, I can tell. Apart from John, you're the first person I've told that story about my father.'

'Why not? You never know.' I gave her a hug. I didn't think she was mad but to me, the idea was highly unlikely. I thought it was coincidence, that's all, but I wasn't going to pour water on something that had obviously comforted her.

*

For the following days, it felt as though someone had pressed fast-forward on the film of my life. The house was full of people: my daughter Alice, who was pale with grief (she'd been close to her father); my son Anthony; my elder sister Susan who took over running the household from Philippa. She was a control freak and normally I objected to her barging in and rearranging things, but this time, I was grateful. She made a list of family, friends, ex-colleagues who hadn't already been contacted, got death certificates printed, booked the church for the funeral, organized the service – though Michael had specified in his will what he wanted. We searched for photos for the order of service, sourced the music he wanted, readings I knew he liked. I kept busy alongside her but felt removed from it all, hollow, as people came and went.

Alice's husband Ethan arrived from Sheffield the day before the funeral. My younger sister Jess came from London, as well as one of my authors, Katie Brookfield. I was touched by her effort and glad she'd come. She was now in her eighties and as sprightly and sharp as ever. I'd become extremely fond of her over the years I'd represented her books.

I was grateful for the distraction of guests staying, beds to make, linen to wash, food to prepare, endless cups of tea to make; anything to take my mind off the reality of what had happened. Philippa was over most days with other close friends who lived locally, and my old school friend Sara arrived from London on the morning of the funeral, as did Lawrence Carmichael, Michael's oldest and dearest friend. His presence was a comfort because he'd known Michael so well and had been a big part of our lives together. Before his wife died two years ago, we'd holidayed with them most years and had always got on well. I felt he understood what I was feeling more than anyone.

The day of the funeral was a dark day, with black clouds that lashed down rain, as if the sky was angry. It felt like a manifestation of my feelings.

'Couldn't have staged this better,' I said to Philippa when there was a loud rumble in the sky as we dashed from the car into the church. 'Michael appreciated a bit of drama.'

Philippa squeezed my arm as we went inside. 'Yes, a mild summer day wouldn't have been right for him at all.'

The service took an hour. I knew that because I'd been told when we booked the church, but it felt like two minutes. *Adagio* played as the coffin came in. The priest said something about Michael, which struck me as odd because he'd never even met him. Michael's younger brother Neill read from *The Prophet*. Lawrence read a poem that I barely heard. Alice wept quietly all the way through. I kept my arm around her but no tears came from me. I was numb, sore, sad and – for the time being – cried out. There would be time for more tears later when Alice and Anthony had gone. As people filed out, the Liverpool football anthem, Michael's team, played; there was a smile as everyone remembered Michael's humour and the man.

Next it was over to the Horse and Jockey pub for drinks and ham and mustard sandwiches. There were hands to shake, people hugged me, commiserated, told me what a lovely service it had been and that was it. Done. Over.

I sorely missed Michael to lean on, to gossip with, about who was there and how they looked; how the men had been checking out Sara, the women too, a celebrity in our midst. I noticed that she'd made a beeline for Katie Brookfield and they seemed deep in conversation with each other for a while, and then Lawrence Carmichael, who was Katie's editor as well as Michael's, joined them.

It was strange to see Sara after so long; it must have been a few years since we'd met up. She was as glamorous as ever, looking ten years younger than our sixty-four years, and I was touched that she'd come and by her offer to stay over if needed. Her presence reminded me that we had been close at various points in our lives. When first married, we'd spent many happy weekends together. Things had cooled off a bit when we'd had our kids. It should have been a bonding time, but we had different ways of bringing them up, Jo and I working from home when we could so that we could spend as much time with them as possible; Sara with a nanny and a home help. Even on the times we met up and Jo and I brought our children, Sara came on her own and left her son with a babysitter. Our relationship had particularly faded in the last decade. After her divorce, by her own admission, she'd gone into a frenzy of work. It was her way of dealing with things, and I'd tried to respect that, even though it meant she barely had time to see Michael and me. I also wondered if part of the reason we hadn't seen her was that we were a painful reminder of the early days with Charles when we'd all hang out. Once upon a time, we'd have talked about what happened with him, had a proper heart to heart about it but she'd appeared to want to move on from all that reminded her of him, us included.

She broke off from her conversation and came over to me. 'Can I do anything? I could stay as long as you like if you need company after today.'

'I . . . thank you, but I have Philippa and my family here for the moment. I appreciate the offer, though, really I do. We'll catch up properly once things are more settled.'

'Of course, whenever,' she said. 'I . . . I can't imagine—'

Lawrence interrupted our conversation and handed me a drink. 'This too shall pass,' he said as he put his arm around me and kissed the top of my head. I hugged him. With so many of our mutual friends present at the funeral, I knew it would be bringing back memories of his own loss. Sara hovered for a moment as if she wanted to say more, but then drifted away and I lost sight of her.

Back at the house later, Alice and Ethan absented themselves and went up to Alice's old room. Anthony got caught up with relatives he hadn't seen in a while. Katie and Susan poured more wine.

At last they were all gone away to their beds, apart from Lawrence who helped with the clearing up. Before heading off to the B & B he was staying in nearby, he gave me a sleeping tablet. I took it with gratitude, welcoming the temporary oblivion that it brought.

*

The next stage followed swiftly on as house guests left and Lawrence and Philippa helped with shopping, feeding, washing, cancelling bank cards, subscriptions, Michael's gym membership, letting his dentist, doctor, pension people know, the DVLA, tax office, passport office . . . The list seemed endless and, at the back of my mind, there was always the feeling that Michael would be back soon. I'd hear his keys in the door, my name called and then there he'd be. But no. His absence had a presence all of its own and it filled the house. The phone calls stopped. The bereavement cards ceased. Silence.

No one prepares you for this, I thought as I looked through his wardrobes, buried my face in an old jacket, breathed in his scent. Susan advised me I'd have to clear his clothes out but not yet . . . not yet.

Chapter Ten

Sara

Present day, November

I'd researched every reality show I could find, in this country, in the States, around the world. I wrote down words that I thought were relevant to the over-fifties.

Health.

Mortality.

Finances.

Support tights.

Whatever this original idea was that was going to save my career, it wouldn't come. I was getting desperate.

My mind drifted to Ally and Jo. Ally was understandably quiet at Michael's funeral and I knew it wasn't the time to reconnect, but she had sounded so subdued when I spoke to her on the phone afterwards too. Also understandable, but I wished that there was something I could do to let her know I was there for her and help her through her grief, if that's possible. There'd been a great turnout of people at the church and I'd met Katie Brookfield when I was there. She was the author of my favourite books and TV series, *The Bonnets of Bath*, and I couldn't help but be a little starstruck, despite the circumstances.

Jo, on the other hand, sounded as high as a kite when I called her. Probably from the post-cardiac medication. She didn't make the funeral because she was still recovering from her heart scare. She kept on about seeing a light and floating down a tunnel and how it had changed everything. One thing that struck me when I spoke to both of them was that they had a good network of friends who had been there through their troubled times. It made me realize all the more that friends were what was really missing from my life, how rare and precious the old ones were. I wanted to be there for mine, if they'd let me, as much as renew our closeness.

I headed out to the shops to find another gift or something to send to them both. I was aware that I couldn't expect either Jo or Ally to just pick up on our friendship and that we'd be back with the ease we used to have, especially at a traumatic time like this for both of them, but I could make inroads. While I was at the shop, I flicked through the racks to find a Get Well Soon card to send to Jo. I opened one with a picture of a cake on the front. Inside it said, 'Friends are the fruitcakes of our lives. Some contain nuts, some are soaked in alcohol, some firm, some sweet but altogether, they make a great cake and are good to have in your life.' I smiled. That summed our old gang up. Mitch was nuts, I was soaked in alcohol, least I was these days, Ally was firm and Jo was sweet.

Ping. A light-bulb moment. I had it. An idea for the TV series. Friends. Programmes about friends. That's it. It had been staring me in the face the whole time.

I dashed back to the house where I spent the next couple of hours scribbling like a madwoman. By the end of it, I had a format worked out for six programmes.

I FaceTimed Nicholas. 'I think I've got it – the idea for a programme.'

On the screen on my phone, Nicholas looked expectant. 'OK, what's the pitch?'

'You know that programme *Lost Lost Family*?'

'The one where people hunt down family members, find sisters and brothers they have never known?'

'That's the one. Well my series wouldn't be looking for family, it would be looking for friends. Most people have that one friend in their life, maybe two or three, who they have lost touch with, in my case Mitch, Ally and Jo. People you grew up with, shared experiences with, loved, swore eternal friendship with, but then somehow lost along the way. So . . . a series about finding these friends. Partners will come and go, leave you, die, move on, children fly the nest, so the programme will focus on the importance of enduring and lasting friendships to see you through. It will also look at those friendships that haven't worked, or that have let you down.'

'I'm getting interested now. I would imagine some reconnections would be good, heart-warming; others would bring up all sorts of buried resentments and open old wounds.'

'Exactly.'

'Could make great TV.'

'Each programme, we take someone—'

'A celebrity,' said Nicholas.

'Exactly, they would bring in more viewers. Each week there'd be a sports person, an actor, musician, rock star, maybe a politician or an author. We can see who's out there who might like to take part. Get some researchers on it.'

'And of course you'd front it.'

'I'd love to, and Gary seemed keen if I had the right idea. The more I thought about it, the more I realized there's so much material. Friends can heal but also hurt, men's friendships can be different to women's, plus the series could look at advice from counsellors on the importance of friendships, how to make them, where to find them.'

'Sounds good. Keep it varied.' Nicholas grinned. 'Sara, I love it, and I can tell you're fired up. I think you have something here. Write it up as a proposal, a few pages, and I'll look it over then we can send it to Gary. Well done, I knew you could do it. And, on a more personal note, where are you up to with your search for your friend? I assume that you're going to ask the two friends you are in touch with about the programme—'

'Jo and Ally.'

'Yes, see if they'd be up for taking part.'

'Taking part?'

'Of course. As well as fronting, you could be one of the celebrities looking for an old friend.'

'Mitch?'

'Mitch. Rope the other two in and see if they might be game.'

I shook my head. 'I doubt it. I've been in touch with them recently and both are going through difficult times. Ally has just lost her husband, so it's maybe not the time to broach it but . . . I do wonder what she's going to do now.'

'Maybe this could be just the thing – a distraction, an adventure. And Jo?'

'Jo's recovering from a heart procedure, so she may be reluctant too.'

'You can always ask them. Nothing ventured and all that. Sometimes losing a partner or something like a hospital stay can be one hell of a wake-up call. Was for me when I came close to losing James when he had his scare, and the same for him when I was unwell. It might be perfect timing for both of them. They can always say no. Where are you up to in looking for Mitch?'

'Still no further forward. I looked on Facebook and Twitter and couldn't find her, at least not with the surname I knew, but I'm sure there are other ways. If Gary does go for the programme idea, then no doubt he'll get top researchers in and Jo, Ally and I can do what we can to try and find her in our own way.'

'Get on it, Sara. And it's made me think too. Some of my old friends, where are they now? Probably in rehab or in their graves.'

'Cheerful.'

'My middle name.'

*

I did what Nicholas advised and spent the next week working on the proposal. It went off to Gary and he loved it, put it to his committee who gave it the thumbs up and assigned a budget to put it into development. He asked me to front it and potentially have my search for Mitch as part of one of the programmes.

Next on the agenda was to go and see Jo and Ally, see how they were and, if it felt appropriate, maybe try and persuade them to take part.

Happy days. I was back in employment. Back in the game.

Chapter Eleven

Jo

Present day, November

A prophet has no honour in his own country, so the Bible says. Yeah, tell me about it. I told my nearest and dearest about my out-of-body experience at the hospital, seeing the light, my astral pal. Hah! The looks on their faces.

'Not out of your body, you were out of your mind,' said my daughter Kirsty.

'Must have been the drugs,' said her husband Will.

'But I wasn't on any then,' I replied.

'Whatever you were on, can you get me some?' said Jason, my sixteen-year-old grandson as he checked out my medication. 'Hey, this looks interesting.' I had to grab the Glyceryl Trinitrate out of his hand before he sprayed some on his tongue.

'You weren't well. Clearly whatever you experienced was a result of your medical condition,' said my son Graham.

Apart from Jason, they looked at me with the same expression, as if I'd lost my marbles. It was very frustrating. What I'd experienced had been real, not imagined, not drug induced, not a hallucination.

As well as having seen the light, I am now bionic or robo-woman, as Jason called me. I had a couple of stents put in during my hospital stay. Amazing things, tiny metal mesh tubes that open up any blockages in the arteries. Angioplasty. 'Saved your life,' said the nurse in charge. 'Ten years ago, you wouldn't have made it.'

So, all good, apart from my family and friends thinking I am away with the fairies. Six to twelve weeks recovery time, that will be nice, and apparently I'll be fit to go for another thirty years. And I've shed seven pounds already. It's the new 'have a heart attack diet'. I might market it and write a book. A radical if not extreme method to lose weight – chest pain, hospital food and no appetite.

While I'd been lying in my bed, I thought a lot about my old school friend Mitch Blake. She'd talked about seeing the inner light, and the need to find calm, when she joined a commune back when we were in our early twenties. I thought she'd lost the plot but she was talking about what they now call 'mindful-ness'. It's everywhere – in books, magazines, classes springing up all over the place; the hospital even recommended it to reduce stress – as if it's all new, but Mitch was on about it a long time ago. She was always ahead of the rest of us. I'd give anything to talk to her about it now.

Curiously, another of my old friends from back then, Sara Meyers, called out of the blue recently. She'd lost her job, a big blow to someone like her who lived to work. She certainly hadn't had much time for me in the last few years, but she sounded different when we spoke on the phone. On the few occasions that we'd been in touch over the last years, she'd always sounded in a rush, distracted, impatient to be off to some place more glamorous, with more interesting people, and when we met up either on our own or with Ally, she was notoriously late. It drove Ally and me mad, especially in our younger days. She could act a bit 'I'm so fucking fabulous' when things took off for her in our thirties and forties, like she'd started to believe her own publicity, but Ally and I had known her too long and could usually tease her back to earth when we saw her. One time, when she was flying high in her career and I was still struggling, we'd gone out for lunch with Ally. Sara ordered two bottles of Cristal champagne to celebrate some promotion. When the bill came, Sara suggested we split it as we had always done, but that champagne would have wiped out my budget for the rest of that month. She hadn't stopped to think that we weren't all earning the big bucks that she was. Ally took one look at my face and got it straight away, and to be fair Sara cottoned on pretty fast, insisting on picking up the whole bill as her treat. 'In that case, let's get another bottle,' I joked, but I felt bad about not being able to pay my way. Since then life has dealt Sara some knocks – her mum's illness, losing Charles, her son Elliott going abroad to work, one of her good friends dying and now she's lost her job. I got the feeling that behind her cheerful act she was rather unhappy, a bit lonely too. I tried to let her know I was here for her, invited her to stay numerous times. She came less and less in recent years, always too involved with her job to venture down to Wiltshire, though part of me suspected that the busy, busy lifestyle was an escape for her from what was really going on. The other day, when we spoke, she was like the old Sara; she listened to what I had to say and seemed genuinely concerned about me. It was nice, reminded me of what close friends we used to be. She had been a good person to have as a mate, despite her occasional thoughtlessness, and her intentions had always been well meaning. She was a sunny, open soul who wore her heart on her sleeve and liked to chat, chat, chat. I liked that because I always knew where I was with her and she laughed at all my jokes, even the rubbish ones. She said she'd been thinking about Mitch too.

'Any idea where she might be?' she asked after I'd told her about my floating into a sea of light and wanting to talk to Mitch about it.

'Not a clue. I'd love to talk to her about my near-death experience.' Like my family, I could tell that Sara wasn't convinced that what I'd been through was anything other than due to medication.

'Yes, I wonder if she's still into all that "peace and love" stuff.'

'Me too. I feel bad I dismissed it at the time. She must have been frustrated that none of us were that interested. I certainly know how she feels now.'

'Oh Jo, I'm sorry. I don't mean to dismiss what happened to you, just it sounds . . .'

'I know, bonkers. You can say it. So, let me think. Mitch was in London for a while, we knew that; then Devon, I seem to remember. It was so long ago, it's all a bit of a blur. I was too busy trying to survive as a new wife and mother to think about seeing the light and saving the world like she was.'

'Anyone you can think of who might know where she is?'

'Not that comes to mind, but there's bound to be someone back in Manchester you could ask. I saw her when I did the flash review of my life while I was having the heart attack, and she's been on my mind a lot. Strange that we're both thinking about her after so long. Do you think we were bad friends? Should have made more of an effort to stay in touch?'

'That's what I've been asking myself. Maybe, maybe not. Works both ways. She didn't exactly try to stay in touch with us either, once she knew we weren't going to join her way of life.'

'Fair point. Shame though.'

'And . . . I've been as bad as her at not staying in touch with my real friends, not lately that is.'

'Well, you've had a lot going on. But you're in touch now, Sara, and that's what counts.'

'You and I could meet up if you like.'

'I'd love to, but I'm not exactly ready for house guests just yet.'

'I wouldn't stay long. I have something I'd like to run by you.'

'Sure. Shoot.'

'Er . . . not now. Not on the phone, it's sort of about Mitch as well.'

'Intriguing.'

'I'll see if Ally'd like to come too. This period post-funeral must be hard for her – so quiet now that everyone will have gone. The house will feel empty. She might like a change of scenery. What do you say?'

'I say great.' I'd stayed in touch with Ally more than Sara had in recent years. I had a lot of respect for Ally. She was the thoughtful one of our group, quieter and less inclined to blurt out all her feelings the way the rest of us did sometimes, but there was a lot going on behind her grey, intelligent eyes, and when she did let some of it out, I always wanted to hear what she had to say. I also knew she had great affection for our old gang. We brought her out of herself and made her laugh with all our teenage dramas and declarations of love or loyalty. If it hadn't been for the heart attack, I'd have been up there cooking her hearty chicken soups and making sure she was looked after.

So. Size eight Sara wants to be back in my life. In the past few years when we'd meet up, I always felt like a large lump of whale meat next to her 'not an ounce of fat' frame, but curiously, since meeting my astral pal and experiencing the sea of light, none of that seemed to matter any more. I'd spent my whole life criticizing myself and my body, hating the way I looked. Such a waste. I wanted weight loss for health reasons and curiously, now I wasn't so down on myself, the pounds were melting off. Plus, there was something else. Whilst lying in my hospital bed, I'd realized I'd spent the majority of my time looking after everyone else – family, friends, animals, waifs and strays – and look where it had got me. Heart attack hotel. My health had suffered. It was time to look after me for a change, and to have some fun whilst doing so. Sara had always been excellent company. It would be good to see her and renew our friendship.

Chapter Twelve

Ally

Present day, December

Finally I was on my own. I didn't like it at all. Night-time was the worst. I'd never thought about intruders before. Michael was always there, either in his study or watching TV, then later, a reassuring shape in the bed beside me. Now I heard every creak of the floorboards, every bump of a radiator once the heating went off or came on again, every sound outside. The house had six bedrooms, all empty now. Michael liked to entertain so wanted a place with space for guests, as well as for his vast collection of books. Michael also liked quiet so he could write without disturbances, so we'd bought a detached manor house with a large garden down a lane a short distance away from the village. Anyone could try and break in as there were no neighbours to hear. I was on high alert, unable to let go and sink into deep sleep. I was listening to noises that the house had probably always made but that I was never aware of before. For the first time, I felt uncomfortable; aware I was a woman alone.

On the Sunday a few weeks after the funeral, I'd been invited to lunch with my nearest and dearest. Philippa and John, Jane and Ray, Geoffrey and Maris, Becca and her partner Angie. Over the years we'd shared our Christmases, New Years, weekends, birthdays, summer barbecues. I loved them and they loved me but, as the meal went on, I knew something had changed. There was no denying it. Someone was missing: Michael. He'd been the one with all the hilarious anecdotes, making people laugh, pouring the wine, drinking a lot of it, staying up until the early hours, putting the world to rights. When he'd tell one of the many stories that I'd heard a hundred times from his repertoire, I used to catch Philippa's eye. 'Number forty-four,' I'd mouth. She'd laugh. Her husband was the same, with a list of tales to tell that we as spouses had heard over and over again. If Michael caught me, he'd pull a face of mock offence and carry on regardless. I didn't mind listening to the repeat performances. I was the moon to his sun. Our roles had been long established. I knew what was expected of me, but today and from now on, there would only be me at social occasions and I was aware more than ever of how much quieter I was than he had been. Plus I felt my friends were walking on eggshells, unsure whether to mention Michael or not, wrapping me in cotton wool. As Philippa served cheese and her home-made chutney, I wished that Lawrence lived closer so that I wouldn't be the only singleton at gatherings, but he'd gone home to Sussex a few days after the funeral.

I realized that I needed to cultivate some single friends, people like me who'd maybe lost their partner but still wanted company. Sara Meyers had been in touch again. She'd suggested that we go and visit Jo, who was recuperating from a heart attack. Sara'd been working on a programme idea and I'd listened to her talk about it, but not a lot of it had really gone in. My head had been full of fog.

As soon as I got home from the lunch, I called her.

'Tell me more about what you're up to,' I said. 'Your new programme.'

'God, Ally, I'm so sorry about that,' she said at the other end of the phone. 'I shouldn't have gone on about it last time we spoke but, you know me, I never did know when to shut up. Inappropriate is my middle name.'

'Nonsense. I did ask you and you talking about it was exactly what I needed. It was refreshing to hear about life beyond death and now probate.'

'How's that going?'

'Long and arduous, endless papers, far too boring to talk about. Tell me about you.'

'I've been busy working on the new programme idea, plus I've been thinking about our time of life, how things change, priorities shift. Like for you, what you've just been through, or rather are going through: it's a huge and unexpected life change. You're lucky you have such good friends around you.'

'True, I am, and I'm having to revaluate so many things, that's for sure, but there's no question about it, friends are crucial. I wouldn't have got through these last weeks if not for mine, and no doubt I will need them even more in the weeks to come.'

'I've been coming to that conclusion too. Friends *are* important, and I know we haven't been in touch properly for a long time. Let me be one of yours again.'

I was touched by her offer, but not sure we could just pick up where we used to be. It had been a while since we'd shared our true feelings. She sounded so earnest, though, that I didn't want to make her feel dejected. If nothing else, she meant well.

'Sure because, actually, the other thing I've realized is that most my friends are couples and suddenly I'm the single one.

I need a few friends who are outside the couple bubble, see what they're up to.'

'Have you been in touch with Jo?' Sara asked.

'Only on the phone, which is why I thought I might go and visit with you. She sounded a bit weird, though, if I'm honest, going on about floating up to the hospital ceiling and how she's not the same person any more.'

'I guess something like a heart attack is life changing – to be suddenly confronted with your own mortality . . . oh god, sorry, I'll change the subject.'

'No need. I'd prefer people just acted normal, say what they normally would. Let's go and see Jo. A trip to take my mind off things here would be great. It's far too quiet. This house was meant to have people in it.'

'Deal. I'll get it organized. Any dates you can't do?'

'None that can't be changed.'

'Excellent. I'll be in touch. I have something I want to put to you both.'

'Sounds intriguing.'

'That's exactly what Jo said. I'll tell you all when I see you.'

After I'd put the phone down, I felt a wave of grief threatening. Some days, I felt numb, but others, like today, the sense of loss hit me like a tsunami. Where was my husband? I kept questioning – had he had an experience like the one Jo talked about? Seen a light? And was there anything in my friend Philippa's idea of the parted sending white feathers to let those left behind know that they are OK. I opened my arms and spoke to the ceiling. 'OK, Michael, if you can, just send me a sign to let me know you're all right.'

There was no reply. I didn't expect one. 'Keep busy, keep busy,' I chanted my mantra for coping.

I went upstairs to begin the dreaded task of clearing out

Michael's things. I'd start with the bathroom cabinet and cupboard under the sink, where he kept toiletries and various medications. I still wasn't ready to face the wardrobes, his clothes and more personal items. I opened a drawer. Toothpaste, razors, Nurofen all thrown in there. He was never one for being tidy.

As I pulled out a few things, I heard a crash from downstairs. My heart began to pound in my chest. *Intruder*, was my first thought. Our village is small; word would be out that the man of the house was no longer here. I crept down and into the back room where the noise had come from, but there was no one there and all was silent. As I looked out into the garden, I noticed that on the outside of the glass pane in the middle of the French window was the imprint of a bird, like a tiny angel with wings outspread, the feather markings perfectly visible. I went over to look closer. Outside, on the ground beneath the window, a white pigeon was looking very dazed and shaken and there were feathers from the crash floating around the poor thing. Clearly it had seen the reflection of sky and trees in the window and, not realizing it was glass, thought that there was a way through.

I began to laugh. Only five minutes ago, I had asked for a sign from Michael. Was this it? It would be typical of him to have sent a kamikaze pigeon, much more his style and sense of humor than leaving one delicate feather lying about in a fruit bowl. I felt strangely comforted by the angel-shaped imprint on my window and watched as the bird fluttered for a few moments then flew away, leaving the scatter of feathers behind it. Timing, Philippa had said when she'd told me her story. I knew what she meant and went back into the hall chuckling to myself.

Chapter Thirteen

Sara

Present day, December

'I'm a changed woman,' said Jo as she bustled around her kitchen.

And looking great, I thought as I watched her. She had a glow of health about her that had been missing the last time I'd seen her. That had been a while ago. She must have been struggling with her health even then, and I cursed myself for not having taken more notice.

We were sitting at the kitchen table by an ancient-looking red Aga in Jo's old farmhouse on the outskirts of Calne in Wiltshire. All the walls in the house had exposed brickwork that complemented the open beams above on both floors. A tall dresser was weighed down with rows of mismatched colourful china, some of which looked like Clarice Cliff. Jo had always had a good eye. Under the long wooden table lay one of her black Labradors, Arthur, and on a seat in the corner, Dusty the grey cat watched us with suspicion. Everywhere in the house there was evidence of people and interests, guitars and open books in the sitting room, toys stacked in a box by the TV, a jigsaw on a table, a chess set on another smaller one. Every wall in the house was covered in groups of paintings and photographs by family or local artists, making it a fascinating place to wander round. I felt as if I was viewing a private art collection. I'd always loved Jo's house; it dated back to the sixteenth century and was full of character and charm.

Outside was equally as lovely and spacious, with mature shrubs, fruit trees, a wooden summerhouse, outbuildings, workshop, greenhouse and vegetable garden, ducks and chickens and a few sheep in the paddock at the back. The house also had an annexe that Jo had converted into a guest suite, which was presently occupied by her son and family. I noted that the house was everything my home wasn't – lived-in; a place where people worked, played and rested. As an only child, when Jo's parents had died, she'd inherited a tidy sum of money which, along with what she'd earned from her shop and deli, she'd used to buy the property.

'Should you be out of bed?' Ally asked.

'Sure,' said Jo. 'I have to do a little activity every day, and build on that day by day until I'm functioning normally again. I can do most things, just not heavy lifting or ironing. I feel fine, better than fine.'

Jo had filled us in about her time in hospital, and her near-death experience. 'I know it sounds far-fetched but, believe me, it was real enough,' Jo said as she brought a teapot to the table and sat down to join us. 'I didn't want to leave the place where I went. Such peace, I can't describe it, and it's left me with a feeling that, if that's dying, I haven't had as much fun in years.'

'But you didn't die,' said Ally.

Jo's face clouded. 'Oh god. I hope I haven't offended you with Michael . . .'

Ally waved her hand. 'It's OK, just there's no proof, is there?'

'I knew you'd be sceptical,' said Jo, 'and I would have been too if it hadn't happened to me. I can remember everything. I told the medics exactly what they were doing when I was supposedly out cold.'

'So why did you come back if it was so wonderful up there?' asked Ally.

Jo grinned. 'I was given a choice and I knew I had unfinished business. I had to get back to my family and friends . . . and who was going to feed the hens whilst I was lying in bed?'

I glanced over at Ally. I wondered if the conversation was upsetting her. Michael hadn't come back.

Jo continued, 'I somehow knew it wasn't my time. I still have things to learn and things to do. I knew I couldn't leave my family yet. All of them need me.'

'I needed Michael. He had loads of things to do as well. He didn't come back. Are you saying that if he'd been given a choice, he chose to leave.'

Jo clamped her hand over her mouth. 'Oh god, Ally, I am so sorry. I'll shut up now although . . . if Michael is where I went, he's in a good place. It was like being home, not in the physical sense, but in the sense of a feeling of belonging somewhere.'

'Thing is, we just don't know, do we? We don't know much at all, in fact,' I said. I gave Jo a look to say 'change the subject' but it didn't register.

'Remember how Mitch used to go on about the light as well?' said Jo.

'We thought she'd lost it,' said Ally.

'Are you saying I've lost it?' asked Jo.

'No, *no*,' I said. 'Actually, truth is, you lost it years ago, you've always been bonkers. Ally and I didn't want to say.'

Jo laughed.

'It might just be chemicals that were released in the brain at the time of your heart attack that made you feel so euphoric,' said Ally.

'Could be, but that doesn't explain me witnessing the whole procedure—'

I could see that Ally was uncomfortable so I decided to butt in. 'Let's change the subject for now . . . tell us about your family, Jo, how are they all?' There were a lot of them presently camped out with her: her daughter Kirsty and son-in-law Will, along with their two children, Jason who was sixteen and Holly who was fifteen. Her son Graham, his wife Saskia and their twelve-year-old, Annie, and son, Oliver, who was eight, were staying in the annexe. In another room was a student, Lucas, who was eighteen and studying at a nearby college. Luckily she had four bedrooms in the house as well as the two-bedroomed annexe. 'How do you cope?'

'I have very strict house rules,' she said, and pointed at a rota on the wall. 'The idea was that we should all take turns in cooking, and everyone has their chores but, if I'm honest, I usually end up doing it all.'

'Seems like you've taken on a lot of responsibility with them all here.'

Jo shrugged. 'It is what it is, but I'm aware that I have to make some changes. When Kirsty left home, then Graham . . . god, the house felt quiet. I even considered selling it, but then, like many young people, they struggled with high rents and were unable to save for their own houses, so one after the other, they came back with the idea of saving up whilst staying here. Then Lucas turned up on the doorstep, needing a home. I was happy to provide one and it's meant I've never been lonely. One thing I realized,' she said as she pointed skyward, 'when I was up with Astral . . . that's the name I gave the presence that was with me . . .' Ally raised an eyebrow and shot me a glance, which eagle eyes Jo noticed. 'I saw that. There *was* a presence . . .'

I laughed. The old dynamic was still there. Ally still the sensible one, Jo unsure, always testing the water, me trying to keep the peace.

'What I realized though,' Jo continued, 'was that I want to change my life. I have been rushing about for forty years, working nonstop all that time, and why? For what? I barely get a moment to myself. I want to make more time for friends and more time for me, to do what I want, whatever that is. I want to allow more time to be happy.'

'Have you not been happy?' I asked. I was surprised to hear this. Jo had always struck me as one of the most contented people I knew.

'I've been too busy to notice if I was happy or not, and maybe there was a reason for that. As long as I didn't have time to think, I wouldn't have to acknowledge it.'

'I can relate to that,' I said.

Jo looked thoughtful. 'I wasn't happy with Doug.'

'But I always thought you were solid,' I said.

'Maybe in the beginning, but he changed, grew grumpy, critical—'

'Why didn't you ever say?' I asked, and glanced at Ally. She had clearly known.

'A few reasons. I dunno . . . I felt I'd failed and I thought you would advise me to leave. Ally did. I thought about it, believe me, many times but . . . there was also a part of me that felt sorry for him. No one else would have put up with him. What my heart-attack experience made me realize was that I'd made myself too busy to notice how I really felt about anything. Now I want to slow down. Express myself more. Some of the peace

I experienced up there, wherever I was, has stayed with me, like a stillness. I don't want to lose it by resuming my old life of running around after people.'

'You mean let go taking care of family?' asked Ally.

'That and other things. I'm not sure yet.'

'What about people your own age?' I asked. 'You have lots of friends here, don't you?'

'I do. There's a wonderful community here and I do have some really good friends but, if I'm honest, not exactly like we were back in the day.' She looked at me. 'I know we've had phases when we haven't seen or even spoken to each other, but we always seem to pick up where we left off. No one knows me better than you two.'

'Sara's TV series idea is about friends,' said Ally.

I nodded. 'Looking for old friends and their importance.'

'Nooooo. I get it. Is that why you wanted to see us?' asked Jo.

'Not just that, no, please don't think that.'

'You can't possibly want us to take part,' said Ally.

'Maybe, in fact yes, if you were up for it, but only if you want to and it feels right.'

'I'd need to know more about what's involved,' said Jo.

'And it's a "no" from me,' said Ally.

'Tell me more,' said Jo.

I'd already filled Ally in on the idea for the programme, so I quickly outlined it for Jo to bring her up to speed. 'You don't have to decide immediately . . . in ten minutes will do.' I laughed. 'No, seriously, think about it. Take your time – but finding Mitch would be part of it too.'

'That I would be interested to do,' said Jo. 'I'd love to see her again, not just to discover what she's been up to all these years, but also because,' she glanced at Ally, 'I'd like to talk to her about her experiences with that group she joined. Remember them?

The Rainbow People, or was it Rainbow Children? I dismissed it at the time but now I wonder if she was on to something and experienced the same inner peace that I did. I don't care what you think.' She folded her arms defiantly.

Ally reached out and put her hand over Jo's. 'Sorry. I didn't mean to dismiss what you experienced. Floating about on the ceiling with an astral being sounds perfectly normal.' Jo laughed. 'And yes, I'd love to find out what happened to Mitch too. I've thought about her many times over the years and wondered what became of her.'

'I did try to reach out to her once,' said Jo. 'I went to one of the Rainbow Children's meetings in the early days in Brighton, then wrote to her afterwards asking why she felt she had to join the commune. Not everyone involved did. She didn't reply and, as you know, she didn't come to my wedding either, but like you, Ally, I was never sure if my letter got to her. I tried Friends Reunited years ago and I regularly trawl through Facebook. I reckon she's not in the UK any more, and hasn't been for a long time. Otherwise I think I'd have found some trace of her.'

'Or . . .' said Ally.

'I know,' I said. 'Not here any more at all.'

'You mean dead?' Jo looked shocked.

'We have to allow for the possibility of that,' I said.

'Someone we know would have heard, surely?'

Ally nodded. 'I just think she's abroad somewhere, especially as you've been all over the media, Sara. If she was in the UK, or her sister was, remember her? Fi? Well, they couldn't have missed you.'

'Unless she didn't want to get in touch.'

Ally shook her head. 'Why wouldn't she? We were such good friends. I can't imagine why she wouldn't. Let's think back. When did you last hear from her, Sara?'

'About the same time as you both, when we were in our mid-twenties. She wanted me to go to the Rainbow Children meetings, but to me it sounded as if she'd got involved in some kind of cult. Not my thing at all. I don't know why I didn't do more about it at the time. I feel bad about it now. I spoke to her a few times on the phone and she sounded evangelical, not at all like the Mitch we knew. And didn't she go to India at one point? A lot of people did around that time, the hippie trail, the search for God and all that. And I seem to remember she was briefly in Devon. I can't believe no one has heard anything since.'

Jo shook her head. 'It would make sense that she was in a different country. We could try her parents' address; rule that out before we go any further. Has anyone still got it?'

Ally and I shook our heads. 'But I remember exactly where it was in Manchester,' said Ally. 'We spent enough time there when we were at school.'

'And her sister Fi has to be somewhere, though I always felt she disapproved of us,' I said.

Ally nodded. 'The original Queen Green. Remember we used to call her that? She was always off on marches, ahead of her time when it came to the environment and global warming.'

'She thought we were all boy-mad and shallow,' said Ally.

I laughed. 'We probably were.'

'Mitch's dad disapproved of us too,' said Jo. 'He was so strict; Mitch was always in trouble with him. Remember? Mitch used to say that when he went out, it was like the whole house sighed with relief, spared a few hours of his criticism. We rarely had our sleepovers at hers because it was never comfortable there. I wonder what her dad made of her joining a commune.'

'Probably same as us,' I said. 'Disbelief. Of the four of us, I would have said she would have been the least likely to choose that path. She loved life so much and she liked men. It sounded as if she'd moved into a monastery, the people who lived in those houses—'

'Communes,' said Jo.

'They were celibate.'

'I can't imagine why Mitch would choose that way to live,' said Jo. 'Wasn't there some guy she hooked up with? I can't remember his name but I remember her telling me about someone she really liked.'

'A musician,' said Ally. 'John, or Jake, something like that. Yeah, she was really into him, then suddenly never spoke of him, so I assumed it hadn't come to anything. What happened to him? I'd love to know, and if he had anything to do with her going into the Rainbow commune.'

'I looked for her on Facebook too,' I said, 'but couldn't see her on there, but of course, she might have changed her name too. People who joined the Rajneesh group got new names, so maybe people in her group did too.'

'She could be living in India or Australia for all we know,' said Jo. 'I always thought she'd do something interesting. She was never one to settle for a life of routine.'

'Something different, that would be for sure,' said Ally. 'She was never going to go the boring way so – a farm in the Masai Mara? A palace in India? She could be anywhere, and now we're all here and actually talking about her, I can't believe we've let it go so long. Let's try and find her. We have to.'

'Fantastic,' I said. 'I hoped you'd say that.'

'But not for your TV programme,' said Ally. 'That's not for me.'

'Nor me,' said Jo. 'I don't need time to think about it.'

'Please, don't decide just yet,' I said. 'There might not even be a story there to tell because we might not find Mitch, but then again, there might be.'

'We've nothing to lose by starting to look for her ourselves,' said Jo. 'I'd like that.'

Ally nodded. 'Me too.'

'OK,' said Jo. 'I'll start by looking for her parents' address in Manchester. I've still got relatives up there and I'm sure one of them would find the house if I give them directions and tell them which road it's on.'

'And my sister Susan used to hang out with Mitch's sister, Fi. She might know where she is. If we could find Fi, she's bound to know where Mitch is,' said Ally.

'Sounds like a plan,' I said.

'So, who have you got for the series so far?' asked Jo.

I pulled my laptop from my bag, put it on the table and opened the file titled *Bus Pass to Love Island*.

Ally laughed. 'Are you going to call it that?'

'Doubt it. It's a working title while we see what unfolds. The researchers are still looking at options. Whoever takes part; it has to be someone who has an interesting story to tell. In the meantime, while you both give taking part some thought, we start the search for Mitch.'

'Deal,' chorused Ally and Jo.

Chapter Fourteen

Mitch

Spring 1973

Worst year of my life. Didn't start out that way. Oh no. I'd fallen in love – truly, madly, deeply. Thank God, because my nearest and dearest, Jo, Sara and Ally, had gone to university the previous September and virtually disappeared from my life. After a glorious last summer together, I missed them like hell. OK, yes, there were phone calls and even a few letters as they settled in, and then they all came home for Christmas for a reunion, but it wasn't like having them around the corner, come rain or shine. Off they went again as soon as the holiday was over. I still had mates, people to hang out with, but not like them. We'd been friends since day one at secondary school and had seen each other through the rollercoaster of teen life until sixth form, then 'poof', they were gone.

My plan had been to go to college too, to study dance, but due to faffing about trying to decide which course was best, I'd missed the final date for applications for the place I'd finally decided on. They said I could start the following year, but it meant I had to tread water in the meantime, in Manchester, without my best buddies, working temporary jobs to make some cash. It was hard. I'd always been seen as the cool one, the leader of our group. Suddenly I'd been left behind.

The sense of abandonment didn't last long because I met Jack Saunders at the Banshee Bar in Deansgate, where his band Black Rose were playing just before the Easter holidays. Up and coming, the *Melody Maker* said about them, ones to watch. Jack was the bass player, a mane of dark shaggy hair, a lean and muscular physique, black jeans, black T-shirt, sexy as hell. It was love at first sight, or rather lust. I didn't expect him to notice me, as every other girl in the room was drooling over him, but he did. I was with a friend from work and we danced our socks off in front of the stage, showing all our best moves. When the band slowed down to do a ballad, Jack stared right at me all the way through the song, like it was meant for me. I felt it right down to my toes and back again. A few more numbers and the band were gone and I wasn't the type to go acting like a groupie and hang around the stage door.

However, as I was leaving, I spotted him in the alleyway next to the bar. He was loading equipment into the back of a van. I went straight over and told him how much I'd loved the set.

'And I liked your dancing? Are you pro?'

I was flattered. 'Maybe some day. So you, where next?'

He grinned, eyes twinkling. 'You're very forward.'

'I meant gig, your next gig?'

He laughed. 'I know. Blackburn tomorrow night but where next this evening? Fancy a drink?'

I did, and that was the beginning. I took a few days off work from the health store I'd been working in. I'd been covering while someone was on leave so I didn't care if they sacked me. Mum and Dad went mental but I didn't care about that either. I couldn't ever do anything right in Dad's eyes, anyway. I was such a disappointment to him, and all my life he'd been overly critical. He was from a working-class background and had studied hard all his life to get a good job working in a tax office, his whole life focused on getting the best for Fi and me so that we could have the chances he never had. I was disappointed that I hadn't gone to college too, but decided to make the most of it and take up my place the following year. In the meantime, there was Jack, so I went to Blackburn with him then Bolton, and back to London where he and the band had temporary digs in a squalid terrace in Dulwich. It didn't matter. I was with the band. The bass player's girlfriend. It was heady stuff. We talked into the early hours, made each other laugh, made love day and night, became inseparable. He was as infatuated as I was, and we both declared that we had found a soul mate in each other; we were in it for life.

I got pregnant after we'd been together just over three months. Not planned. It was August. We'd been using condoms. They were ninety-eight per cent effective if used properly, the statistics said. I was one of the two per cent. To my surprise, Jack was over the moon. Said it was meant to be. Asked me to marry him. I accepted, no hesitation. I knew he was The One. However, a producer wanted to promote the band and had arranged a trip to America, then an extended tour of Europe. It was happening for them. He wanted me to go with him, though he hadn't broken it to the band yet. I knew they weren't keen. Jack was the only one with a steady girlfriend and the other band members didn't like it; in fact one of them, the lead guitarist Lou, had taken to calling me Yoko. Neither of us wanted to rock the boat while they were all so fired up about the upcoming tour, so we kept things quiet about our plans and how much time we spent together. Privately, we discussed a wedding in the States. Las Vegas maybe. We'd tell them then.

Jack planned to come up to Manchester and break it to my parents with me. I was still living at home when not with him – couldn't afford not to – so Jack and I agreed that we'd tell Mum and Dad before anyone else, before friends, before the band. I was dying to tell Jo, Sara and Ally, talk wedding plans with them all as my bridesmaids, but Jack was adamant that we wait. He called before he set off from London and was coming up on his motorbike. I cooked supper for the four of us. I set the table. Cooked the meal, tuna pasta, lit candles. I hoped it would be a celebration once Mum and Dad got over the shock that they were to be grandparents.

We waited and waited. Six o'clock, seven, eight. No Jack.

'I don't think your boyfriend's coming,' said Dad as I blew out the candles at around nine.

I tried calling the number of his digs. No answer. No one home. I couldn't understand it. No phone call from him since the one before he set out. No nothing. I was gutted. Had he had second thoughts? Had his band mates talked him out of it? *Something must have happened*, I thought, and gave him time to get in touch, explain, apologize, but a day went by, then another. I called the number of the digs in London again, only to be told by a grumpy landlord that the band had left for the States. I couldn't believe it. My heart broke into pieces. He'd gone without me and I had no way of knowing where he would be staying. I hadn't got as far as looking into all the details of the trip. Jack had done that. I'd trusted him completely and had been content just to know that I was going with him. I didn't even have a contact for his mum, although she had been next on the list to tell our news to. His dad had passed away when Jack was twelve, I knew that, so there was only her, and all I knew was that she lived somewhere in Wales. I didn't even know her first name, or if Saunders was her maiden or married name. Wales was a big place to look for someone with so little to go on.

My parents didn't take it well that I was pregnant. Dad couldn't look me in the eye. Mum just cried, as did I. In the end, I had to speak to one of my friends. I needed their support, so I called Sara first.

After a few failed attempts ringing her student digs, I finally got through. 'Mitch,' she said. 'How are you? I've been meaning to call but it's been mad here. I've been missing you so much. Can you come and stay? I've met loads of people I want you to meet . . .'

She was so eager to share the world that was opening up, her course, her new friends. I couldn't bring myself to blurt out that I was up the duff and what a mess I'd made of things.

I tried calling Jo in Brighton the next day; big-hearted Jo, she was bound to be sympathetic, but she was never in. Same with Ally. Out whenever I tried, and what could they have done anyway? I left messages for them but was never really sure that they got them. They were in those halls of residence for students, so who knew who took the phone call and if they passed on the message.

After a few weeks, Ally finally got in touch.

'I got a message you called, so tell me everything,' she said. 'What have you been up to? And how many hearts have you broken since we left?'

Only my own, I thought. But the moment to unburden had passed. I'd started to close that part of me off and now I couldn't bring myself to tell her what had happened. I felt like a failure. We'd shared everything to do with boys, first kisses, first dates – who'd done what with whom. We'd laughed our socks off at confessions of our teenage fumblings in shop doorways, the back seat of a car or a bedroom whilst parents were down below, but I couldn't tell her this. Pride? Shame? Embarrassment? All three.

I felt my friends had moved on, had bright futures. Mine was to be broke, pregnant, abandoned and jobless. I'd contact them again when I was back on an even keel, whenever that might be. At the same time, I felt angry that they hadn't been there for me when I needed them, but also confused. How were Ally, Jo and Sara to know what I was going through if I didn't tell them? I'd made out to them that I was doing fine, that I'd moved on too; and, if I was honest, when Jack had been alive and we'd been wrapped up in each other, I'd hardly given Ally, Jo or Sara a second thought. Mixed up, that's what I was.

Mum and Dad were so angry; well, Dad mainly, said I'd ruined my chances, wasted my opportunities, let him down. Although they said I could stay in the house, the atmosphere was so miserable and heavy with disappointment, I couldn't bear it. I got out. My elder sister Fi was in her second year at university in London studying politics. Mum had told her my news. At least she wasn't judgemental. She shared a flat in Notting Hill and had a couch I could crash on, so there I went.

It was a hard pregnancy. Fi didn't really want me there. A pregnant sister trailing round after her cramped her style. We were such different people and had never been great friends growing up. Fi was much more serious and academic than I ever was. I was always too girlie and frivolous in her eyes. In London, she had her new-found community, her own life to live and so, grateful as I was to be there, I kept out of her way. It was a lonely time. Every ache and kick from the baby was a reminder of someone I wanted to forget. I worked as a waitress in an Italian café for as long as I could. Then I had the baby. Fi was with me on the day of her birth, and held me when I sobbed my heart out on the day I gave her up for adoption, but she was with me in believing that I was doing the right thing. I had seventeen pounds in my purse, barely enough to pay any rent – how would I ever look after a baby on my own? I wanted the child to have a fighting chance, so I agreed to let her go. Plus, I wanted no reminders of Jack. I'd move on, see if I could still go to college, turn the page and resume life as it had been before him.

The day the adoption services arrived, I faltered. My baby was a darling thing, a fairy angel with chubby cheeks and a fuzz of dark hair. I loved her from her first breath, and the idea of giving her away was ripping me apart, but I had no home of my own, no money, no man, nothing to offer, and a sister who didn't really want me – never mind a child – around. Mum and Dad knew I planned on adoption. They never offered an alternative. 'For the best,' said Mum. So I let her go, but the pain of doing so was a knife-cut to my heart, deep and hurtful, leaving a wound inside that I could barely deal with.

I grew up that day, shut the pain away, closed and locked the door, not to be opened. I told myself I must move on, make a new life, keep busy. I'd named her Sara Rose. Sara after my friend Sara Meyers, because we'd sworn one night that if we ever had baby girls I'd name mine Sara, she'd name hers Michelle. Rose was for Jack after his band, Black Rose. I knew her new parents would probably rename her, but she'd always be Sara Rose to me. I toyed with the idea of calling Sara – she'd want to know; would be thrilled about the baby's name – but then I'd have to reveal everything and she'd question why I hadn't told her I was pregnant and everything that had gone on. No. I'd blown it and left it too late.

After Sara Rose had gone, as soon as I could, I went back to waitressing. One weekend, I had a brief visit back to Manchester, where I met up with my old friends who were home for the holidays. If it felt right, I'd tell them what had happened.

We met in a pub in West Didsbury, and at first it was great to see them, all brimming over with excitement about their new lives and aspirations for when they'd finished their courses.

'So, Mitch,' said Jo, 'what happened to your going-to-college plan?'

'Er . . . not sure. To tell the truth I've been so caught up in London, I didn't confirm my place and . . .' They all looked surprised and it was partly true. College plans had been the last thing on my agenda.

'I can't say I blame you,' said Sara. 'Must be amazing being there, in the big city. It's all happening in London, isn't it?'

'But don't you get bored waitressing?' Ally asked. 'I mean, wasn't it meant to be a stopgap year for you?'

'More than a year now though isn't it?' said Jo.

'It is but I'm . . . I'm not sure what I want to do any more. I'm not sure there's much of a long-term future in dancing. A lot—'

'I can understand that,' said Jo. 'I bet there are so many opportunities down in London. I say no harm in waiting, experience the world a bit, then I'm sure you'll be clearer what direction you want to take.'

As I listened to Jo trying to be supportive in her way, I thought about one of our unspoken rules of friendship – that true friends don't judge and can trust each other with painful secrets. These were my oldest friends. I could surely confide in them. 'I er . . . I've been meaning to tell—' I started.

'Can't see you waiting on tables for long,' Sara interrupted. 'You're Michelle Blake, meant for better things. Watch out world, when you do decide what you want to do.' She put her hand over mine. 'Whatever it is, I know you'll be amazing. You are amazing. Always were.'

I felt tears prick the back of my eyes. They were still seeing the old Mitch, but that girl had gone. I felt older than them. I couldn't tell them about Sara Rose or Jack for fear that I'd break down and cry so, for me, it was an odd and uncomfortable reunion. Had I changed or was it them? Whichever, I didn't feel I could be honest about the year I'd had, and I went back to my parents' house later in the evening, feeling that, more than ever, we'd gone our separate ways.

Chapter Fifteen

Sara

2019, January

The *Long Lost Friends* series was well into development by the New Year, and research had thrown up some interesting results. There was a young and enthusiastic team working on programme possibilities, headed up by lead researcher Lauren Haines, whom Gary had asked to come along to give me an update at the offices. She was a pretty young thing in her twenties, long honey-coloured wavy hair, dressed in jeans, grey T-shirt and pink sparkly Converse sneakers. We met at the production company office in Soho one bright afternoon in February.

'A few of the celebrities we'd hoped to get, turned us down, not interested,' she said, 'but there were enough on board who either liked the idea—'

'Or want to keep their public profile alive,' Gary interrupted. 'First to be confirmed is sports personality and ex-cricketer Simon Redburn for the programme about men's friendships.'

It was going to be called 'Let's Hear It for the Boys', a look at men's friendships and how they communicate, how they bond, that sort of thing. Nicholas had told me that when he'd had heart problems and had his stent put in, he'd got to hear about others who'd had the same. They called themselves The Stent Gents, and another, even older group he'd met in cardiac rehab had called themselves The Dicky Tickers, and had bonded over medical problems and gallows humour.

'Fantastic,' I said. I'd met him a few times – at six foot four, he was a great handsome hunk of a man. Although retired from sports for many a year, he was a regular on panel shows and fronted a series about fishing.

'He wants to find his old friend Steve Barnett,' said Lauren. 'Hasn't seen him since university, apparently.'

'I'll read you what Simon said,' said Gary. '"Steve was a force to be reckoned with. I met him at university and we were the best of mates. We lost touch when he became hugely successful and travelled all over the world with his business ventures. Curiously, he's been on my mind of late, so it's timely that you have suggested a reunion. I'd like to reconnect. I want to know what happened to him. Where is he now? And how has he dealt with what life has thrown at him? Also, I'd like to see if we still connect the way we did. Can't imagine we wouldn't, no matter what he's been through."'

'Sounds good to me,' I said. Simon was a good choice, easy on the eye, charming and articulate, and his friendship sounded straightforward enough.

'TV gold,' Gary said. 'And Simon's presently single, a widower of four years.'

'Stop that now, Gary. Nicholas and James are forever trying to pair me off, so I don't need you on the case too. I am not interested in Simon.' That was a lie. Who wouldn't be interested in Simon Redburn? He was extremely attractive on many levels, but I wanted to make my own choices when it came to men and I certainly didn't want half the production crew watching for a romance when it came to filming with him.

'Word has got around about the series,' said Gary. 'Rhys Logan's agent has been in touch to say that he'd be very happy to take part in the men's programme and, to quote his agent, "give the series a touch of class".'

'How very kind of him. Let me think about that . . . So Simon it is.'

Gary grinned. He didn't think much of Rhys either.

'So. One down, four to go – or five if Ally and Jo refuse to take part or if we don't find Mitch.'

'Have your friends refused?' Lauren asked.

'So far, but I'm going to work on them. Christmas was especially hard for Ally, she spent it with her daughter as it's her first one without her husband. I don't want to pressure her, and it's still early days in looking for our missing friend.'

'And how was your Christmas?'

'Same as always. Lovely. I was with Nicholas and James who love to host and cook.' I didn't add that most of the festive period had been a lonely time and I couldn't wait to get back to work. My son Elliott had a new girlfriend over in the States, so his Christmas had been spent meeting her parents in Colorado. We'd had a cyber visit on Christmas Eve and I called my brothers, and that was it as far as family time went. The holiday had only served to strengthen my determination to reignite my friendship with Jo and Ally and do what I could to find Mitch.

'Any news at all on Mitch?'

I shook my head. 'So far, fruitless. My friend Jo got on the case before Christmas and asked her cousin in Manchester to go and find the house where Mitch had grown up. We hoped her parents would still be there. He sent back word that he had been round to the house in person and that there was no one of that name there any more and that the owners said, according to the house record showing previous residents, that Mitch's parents, the Blakes, had moved out long ago. They had no idea where to, and the house had been sold three times since they last lived there.'

'Oh, that's a shame,' said Gary.

'Jo's undeterred. She said she'll try the Records Office to see if she can find anything there. Mitch's parents could have moved locally. We just have to find out where. My other friend's search has led nowhere either. Ally offered to see if she could find Fi, Mitch's sister, through her sister Susan, as they used to be friends at school. She came back with the news that Susan had lost touch with Fi years ago. Basically, we've come to a dead end for now.'

'We can help,' said Lauren, 'just say the word when you'd like us to step in.'

'Will do. Once I know Ally and Jo are properly on board for the series, not just looking for Mitch. In the meantime, what's next?'

'For the "Let's Hear It for the Girls" programme, featuring groups of women,' said Lauren, 'we've had no shortage of people willing to take part. It's hard to choose. All are a testament to the strength and support women give each other; some are pretty wild, some wonderful. Gary and my team have spent ages looking through and making a short list, though it's still undecided.'

'There are The Pink Ladies, a group of cancer survivors,' said Gary. 'Inspiring stuff. They all met whilst having their various treatments and supported each other through.'

'And the celebrity?' I asked.

'Erica Domas. Used to do the weather, remember? Now retired. She got the all clear from breast cancer last year.'

'I like the sound of them, so definitely a possibility,' I said. 'Keep them on the short list. Who would be the long-lost friend?'

Gary grimaced, 'Ah well, this is the interesting part. See what you think. The long-lost friend didn't make it through the treatment. She died.'

'So they can't search for her.'

'Ah, but they say they can,' said Lauren. 'The proposal is that they *do* search for her, starting with a visit to a spiritualist church to see if they can reach her through a medium.'

'What? Like a séance?' I asked.

'A séance, then continue on through all the different churches asking spiritualists and mediums where they might think their friend has gone,' said Gary.

'Wow. The big question. Where do you go after death?' I said. 'So – it would be a look at different beliefs and philosophies.' *Jo would love this*, I thought.

'As well as visits to mediums,' said Lauren.

'Could be a bit spooky,' I said. 'Interesting, yes, but it might not appeal to some people and we're trying to keep the series commercial with the focus on friendships.'

'True,' said Gary. 'But we also want the programmes within the series to contrast, the good, the bad and—'

'The spooktastic,' I said. 'It sounds to me like subject matter for a separate programme.'

'There is much in life that we don't understand. Have to stay open-minded.'

'I agree. You should meet my friend Jo, you'd get on.' *And maybe we could go to see a medium to see if they might know where Mitch is*, I thought.

We continued leafing through the proposals that the researchers had got so far. There were many groups of women who came together for charity events, sponsored walking, baking, even shaving their heads to raise money.

'I know loads of groups of girls who have given themselves nicknames. The Ratpack. The Hens. The Stalkers . . .' I said.

'The Stalkers?' Gary's eyebrows shot up.

'They were at my university. They all fancied the same guy and used to follow him about. The Quality Street gang were another, all top-notch.'

'These look like fun,' said Lauren as she held up a sheet of paper showing a group of women dressed in white. 'White witches. They call themselves The Coven and they meet in sacred locations all over the world: Stonehenge, the Pyramids . . .'

'We don't want to be too supernatural, I don't think. I envisaged a strong group of women, and their programme would be testimony to their friendship rather than their interests or hobbies. Friendship is the key here.'

Lauren nodded. 'OK. I get what you're saying.'

'So. Third programme? The one about pets?'

Lauren grinned. 'My favourite so far. "A Man's Best Friend". It's progressing nicely. We've an abundance of material.'

'We have lots of touching tales of people who were in hospital but reunited with their pets in their last weeks. Some of the clips have brought a tear to my eye,' said Gary. 'Many people who have guide dogs and rely on them. And there's a fascinating story about a man whose cat alerted him to a poisonous leak, carbon monoxide. The cat saved his life by patting his cheek until he woke up.'

'And there's a dog that dived in, rescued a drowning boy and pulled him to safety,' said Lauren. 'And some dogs can apparently smell illness or when their owner needs insulin. Another story is of a dog who ran to a child and knocked him out the way of a poisonous snake.'

'Or the one about a man in a car crash. His dog managed to get out of the car and went to alert a neighbour,' said Gary. 'Another about a Scottish farmer who was attempting to relocate a dairy cow and her calf to a different paddock one afternoon. The territorial mum began attacking the farmer, rushing up to him and knocking him to the ground. Just when the farmer thought he was about to be smashed by the big cow, his horse marched up and kicked the cow away.'

'This programme's going to be a tear-jerker,' I said. 'Can we use all those stories?'

'As many as we can. It's going to be hard to choose because they're all—'

Lauren and I chorused. 'TV gold.'

'After all the feel-good stuff, we need a contrast for the next one, which is why I thought it could be about the downside of friendship,' I said. 'What have the researchers come up with so far about how friends can hurt as well as heal, Lauren? Murder? Espionage? Betrayal? Revenge?'

'We're still working on that one,' Lauren replied. 'Oh, there's plenty out there, but not so many people willing to stand up in public and talk about it. A number of them are musicians who were in bands together, then one moved on, the friendship broken; but, as I say, some are reluctant to discuss it on camera. One possibility is Jojo Manning, who back in the day was an Emmy-award-winning singer-songwriter. She retired from the public eye over twenty years ago but still has a strong base of fans and followers.'

'What's the story?'

'Agent and friend swiped all her money.'

'No!'

'There are also a few examples of people using social media to destroy friendships, hate mail, nasty tweets,' said Lauren. 'Cyber-bullying is a big thing now, particularly prevalent in schools. Teenage girls can be really mean to each other, and of course now the internet allows them to do that anonymously.'

'I think that's a definite,' I said. 'Friendships are so important when you're young, the need to fit in, be liked, but kids can be vicious to each other. It would be good to cover bullying with some positive input from counsellors or anti-bullying groups on how to deal with it.'

'And programme five?'

'Also still in development. Friends of different religions, cultures, politics. Not decided yet. Then, of course, programme six with your good self.'

'I have been thinking about something else too. If there was a list of rules for friendship, it might help some friendships stay on track. Some dos and don'ts if you like.'

'Do you mean a handbook, something tangible?' Gary asked.

'Maybe, I'm not sure yet. But real advice, practical things friends can do for each other.'

'I like your thinking.' Gary seemed to be mulling it over. 'It could be an amalgam of everything learnt from the programme . . . So, back to the search for Mitch?'

'I need a bit more time. So far, we've not got anywhere.'

'Let us help,' said Lauren, 'if you give me everything you have about your friend, I can get the team on to it and . . . don't dismiss the psychics. We wouldn't be doing a séance to find Mitch, just seeing if any of them could give us an idea of what country she's in, that sort of thing.'

'Just what I'd been thinking,' I said.

Lauren laughed. 'See, we're psychic ourselves.'

'Could be fun,' said Gary. 'See what your friends think.'

'Oh, I know already. Jo would love it. Ally will pronounce it rubbish.'

'You wouldn't have to go yourself,' said Lauren. 'I could get one of the researcher team to go.'

'Tell you what; I'll see if Jo would like to come along. She likes all that stuff and it might just swing things to get her on board.'

'Can we film it?'

I grimaced. 'She's not said yes yet. Give me some more time.'

Chapter Sixteen

Mitch

Summer 1974

Back in London, I never gave up looking for Jack's band in the music papers, but it was as if they had disappeared off the planet. Then, one day in July, I was looking through *Time Out* and there it was, a piece announcing that Black Rose would be on tour in the UK. The boys were back in town.

I took note of where and when the next gig was and, when the day came, I headed off there. They were playing at The Forum in Kentish Town, a venue I knew well.

When I got there, I asked the man in the ticket office if I could speak to one of the band. He laughed in my face. 'You buy a ticket like everyone else if you want to see them,' he said, before directing me to the back of the queue.

I bought a ticket, got inside and waited. A warm-up band came on, did their set and then on came Black Rose. I felt a rush of anticipation. Lou, Barry, Jon . . . no Jack. How could that be? Jack had started the band with Lou. Could there have been a falling out? The band struck up their first number and a man with ginger hair was playing bass. *Why isn't Jack playing bass?* I asked myself. Maybe he was ill?

In the interval, I waited and watched. As soon as I saw the security man go to the bar, I took my chance and headed backstage to the dressing room. I took a deep breath as I stood outside the door, unsure of what I'd say. I was a cauldron of mixed emotions: angry, sad, hurt, confused, most of all curious. I needed to know why. Why had he dumped me? I needed to find him, hear it from him, look him in the eyes and see what was there.

I knocked on the door. 'Come in,' said a voice I recognized as Lou's. I opened the door and he was sitting on a stool in front of a mirror, guitar in hand. He went white when he saw me and I heard him say 'shit' under his breath.

'I need to speak to Jack,' I said.

He looked around as if for help, a man in a corner with nowhere to escape to.

'Where is he? Why isn't he here? Why's he not with the band tonight?'

'You don't know?'

'Know what?'

'Oh Christ. Jack. He was killed last year, before we left for the States. Motorbike crash on the M1, on his way to see you, I believe. A lorry went into him, skidded, he didn't stand a chance. Not Jack's fault. It was a filthy night.' Lou looked angry, as if he blamed me.

I felt as if I'd been hit full force in the abdomen, a body blow. '*Killed?* But . . . why didn't anyone let me know?'

'No one had your number. We looked through his things, honest, searched everywhere but he . . . he must have had your number on him or in his head and then we had to go to the States and leave it all in the hands of Dave, our producer over here.'

'So why didn't anyone tell him to contact me?'

Lou gave me a look I'll never forget. It said, why would we? You weren't important. Just another girl chasing after a bass player, one of many. Lou would have had no idea what we meant to each other, and why should he? We'd done our best to play our relationship down.

'I am sorry, Mitch. I think Dave tried to find you but none of us even knew your surname.'

'You *left* to go to the States? Didn't go to his funeral?'

Lou looked sheepish. 'We had to go. It's what Jack would have wanted.' He sounded irritated. 'We all agreed on that and we did a tribute night to him in San Francisco.'

'Did you? How big of you.' I turned and left. I wanted to strangle him but it wasn't his fault. Jack and I had agreed not to tell the band what we were to each other. I stumbled out of the venue onto the street, trying to take in the enormity of what he'd told me. Jack killed on the night he was coming to me. He *hadn't* given up on us. All that anger and hate I'd directed to him had been wrong, all wrong. I found a shop doorway, collapsed down to the cold concrete where I sat and cried like a wounded animal. Sara Rose. I'd let her go. Would I have kept her if I'd known what had really happened? One hundred per cent I would. I would have found a way. She wouldn't have been a reminder of a bad time, of being let down, she would have been a reminder of the best man and best time I'd ever known.

Chapter Seventeen

Jo

Present day, January

Another three pounds down, not bad going seeing as we've just had Christmas. I had a programme worked out. Jogging. Pilates. Yoga. The 5:2. I was seeing a nutritionist. My body is a temple and, seeing as mine had turned into the Parthenon, I had some rebuilding to do. So far, so good. Since my experience in hospital, I had renewed energy, and after being nose to nose with my mortality, the world looked a brighter place. What had worried me before was now like water off a duck's back.

My daughter Kirsty doesn't like her job so goes in late, gets reprimanded, then wants to retrain, again. I've already forked out for three different courses since college. Not this time, amigo. The bank of Mum is closed.

My son Graham got done for speeding and has had his driving licence taken away. No, I will not be ferrying you about.

My grandson, Jason, is smoking dope. Get over it, kid. I am not going to spend more sleepless nights worrying over you or trying to talk sense into you because you never listen to me and are going to do what you want anyway.

My granddaughter Holly's been dumped by her arse of a boyfriend. Tough, I know. I've been there. Turn the page, move on. Find a boy worthy of you.

And while you're all at it, start looking for your own place to live, do your own laundry, cook your own meals, make your own beds, do your own grocery shopping, stack the dishwasher, and clean out the shower after use. That ship – of having me as your unpaid servant, babysitter and all-round mug – has sailed.

I picked an angel card from the pack this morning, bought for me by a neighbour when I got out of hospital. It said, 'Spread your wings and say yes to invites'.

Bend stretch, bend stretch, morning exercise.

Saved by the phone ringing. It was Sara Meyers.

'Simon Redburn is doing the second programme about men's friendships,' she said.

'Simon Redburn the cricketer?'

'Ex-cricketer.'

'God, I love him.' If meeting Simon was on the agenda, it was beginning to sound tempting. 'If we did take part, would we meet people in the other programmes?'

'Possibly, there's usually an end-of-recording party which everyone goes to.'

'Let me think about it,' I said. 'Ally is still insistent she won't take part, though.'

'Maybe she fancies Simon so could be persuaded if she could meet him.'

'Doubt it. It was only ever Michael for her.'

'Sorry. Course. Inappropriate of me to have said that. And um . . . if you're up for taking part in the programme, I know this might sound a bit offbeat . . .'

'Spit it out, Sara.'

'How about a visit to a medium or psychic? Our researcher Lauren suggested it. She said some of them help the police with looking for missing persons. We could see if we can find one who can give us any clues about finding Mitch. You could stay with me in Notting Hill, if you'd like.'

The angel card lay on the table next to the phone. Say yes to invites.

'Great idea. Yes. Let's do it, give my lot a chance to fend for themselves. They won't know what's hit them. Talking about friends and all your research into different angles, have you thought about a feature in one of them about learning to be your own friend? That's what I'm learning how to do for the first time in my life.'

'Excellent idea, Jo. Sounds good to me.'

Chapter Eighteen

Sara

Present day, January

I drove down to see Ally, take her out and see how she was doing. The house seemed quiet and Ally subdued and diminished. At five foot six, she appeared to have shrunk and, though I could see she was making an effort to be fine, it was clear that behind the mask she was hurting.

'So how are you doing?' I asked, as we sat on the leather Chesterfields in her sage-green sitting room, where the walls were lined with shelves heavy with books. 'I know, stupid question but . . .'

She lifted her arms indicating the house. 'I'm rattling around in here,' she replied.

'I suppose it's too early to know what you want to do,' I said.

'It is. I can't think straight. I doubt I'll stay here, though. It's way too big for just me. It's so weird; you trundle along a particular path for a while then, with Michael not being here, it doesn't make sense any more. Suddenly single again. I don't know where I want to go or how I want to live, but I don't think it will be on my own.'

'Alice?'

Ally laughed. 'I wouldn't move in with either of my kids. They have their own way of living and I have mine. Spending Christmas with my daughter and family was lovely for the first two days, and they clearly wanted to take care of me, but it didn't take long before I felt like a spare part. I value my independence and I'm not used to being waited on.'

'Come and stay with me for a while,' I said. 'That's if you'd like. I have a spare room, so you'd have some company and you can do your own thing there. I think Jo may be coming too. Stay as long as you like, until you have a better idea of where you'd like to be.'

'That's kind, Sara. Let me think about it. So how's the series coming along?'

'OK – good, in fact, but we're still looking for the right group of women for programme one. Our lovely young researcher Lauren has come up with some unusual choices: witches, a group of cancer survivors who want to get in touch with a friend who passed away—'

'But you want something more normal?'

'We do. A group of strong women, ordinary but extra-ordinary. The heart of the series must be friendship.'

'I know a group that might work,' said Ally as she got up. She returned a few moments later with some papers and a photo of an elderly and stylish woman.

'That's Katie Brookfield,' I said, recognizing her as soon as I looked at the picture. 'I met her briefly at Michael's funeral. God, I love her books. I've read them all and I loved the TV series too. It saw me through my first weeks of redundancy.'

'So you know that the TV adaptation of her books was about

a group of women, what they got up to and the letters they wrote to each other, signing off with funny pseudo-names.'

'I do. *The Bonnets of Bath.*'

'How about using them for your programme?'

'They'd be just the sort of group I'm looking for, but the women in it are fictional.'

Ally shook her head. 'That's where you're wrong. They're all real. The characters in *The Bonnets of Bath* were based on living women. I know that for a fact because I've met most of them, though they're older than the women portrayed on TV.'

'Wow. So The Bonnets were based on people she knew?'

Ally nodded. 'Remember the characters in the show?'

'Of course. There were five.'

'Katie Brookfield, Gabrielle Bise, Rebecca Fraser, Bridget O'Mara and Jenny Harkin. They're all in their eighties now, but they've known each other most of their lives. In the books, Katie wrote about them when they were in their fifties, then of course the books were adapted for TV. Be great if you could get them to take part, because how they live now could be of interest as well.'

'How come they called themselves The Bonnets?' I asked.

'It came about when Katie moved to Bath over thirty years ago. Part of the reason she moved to the area was that Gabrielle, Rebecca, Bridget and Jenny, her closest friends, were living in the area. I remember Katie saying that life had changed for her in London and there had been a great exodus of people she knew, heading for pastures new, to the point she found she'd lost all her group. She came into my office one day and said, "Acquaintances, I have many. True friends, apart from you dear Ally, all gone."'

I can relate to that, I thought. 'So she moved to Bath?'

'She did. She would have been in her early fifties then. On

the day the removal trucks arrived at her new house, her friends turned up with their husbands, the women wearing brightly coloured bonnets with feathers, ribbons and flowers that they'd made especially for the occasion. They'd even made one for her.'

'I remember that scene on the TV, with the new neighbours peeking out from behind their curtains. They must have thought, oh god, who are these mad people moving in? When I was watching the programme, I thought I'd love to know women like that. They gave Katie such a welcome.'

'They did. They're a bright bunch, and continue to be so. I can only pray that I have half their energy when I'm their age. Anyway, after that day, when they helped Katie move in, they began to call themselves The Bonnets of Bath and, as Bath is a Georgian city, they began to assume pseudo-names that fitted the period. Kate signed letters and emails as Lady Muck, Gabrielle became Lady Eyre, Rebecca was The Duchess, Bridget's pseudo-name was Lady Bottom, and Jenny was simply known as Rosamund.'

'I remember, they wrote in a sort of Jane Austen-style language. Some of the letters they featured on TV were hilarious.'

'What's interesting is how they live now. Most of them are still around the Bath area and, as they got older, they bought properties within five minutes of each other in the same village, so that they can watch over each other as they sail into their old age. They did toy with buying a big house and dividing it into apartments, but they felt that might cause problems because they all value their independence so highly.'

'What a great idea.' I felt a rush of excitement. If we could get these women, the programme would be, as Gary liked to say, 'TV gold'. *The Bonnets of Bath* series had got millions of viewers; most of them would surely tune in to learn about the real Bonnets behind the fictional ones played by actresses. 'I like the idea of doing something like The Bonnets did – old friends living nearby to each other.'

'I read that it's becoming more popular.'

'You and Jo are lucky that you already have such good friends close by.'

Ally looked thoughtful. 'Luck doesn't come into it, Sara. Friendship is a two-way street and I've been there for my friends at times they needed me to be.'

I felt Ally was making a point about my prolonged absence, and it was fair enough. I deserved it. I looked her in the eye. 'I'm sorry I wasn't around more, I truly am,' I told her. 'I don't know what I was thinking, and it was selfish of me but . . . I'd like to right that if you'll let me.'

Ally reached over and put her hand over mine. 'Of course, we go back a long way.'

I smiled. 'We do and I really do value that – our history and our friendship. And all that's happened recently has made me realize that I don't want to be on my own when I'm old, I don't want you to be alone either. I'm not talking about men. I don't think I have it in me to have another long-term relationship.'

'Me neither,' said Ally. 'No one could ever replace Michael.'

'Of course not, and, at our age, no one comes without some baggage. Plus all that learning to be with someone, and getting to know their ways of doing things. I like my space. I like not having anyone to tell me what to do.'

'Do you ever get lonely?' Ally asked.

'If I'm honest, I do, but I'm not sure a man is necessarily the answer. You can be lonely in a relationship, anyway, if it's not right. Feeling lonely is what got me thinking about how import-ant friends are, which led on to the idea about the series.'

'It's a good idea, Sara.'

'It also made me think about Mitch. What was really going on in her life that she chose to cut herself off from us? I didn't see it at the time but I have a feeling something happened. For me, it was losing Charles, Mum and Anita. My way of dealing with it was *not* to deal with it, if you know what I mean. I hid myself in work and made sure I was so busy that I wasn't aware that I was lonely. I wonder now if Mitch had some sort of loss and that's why she felt a need to escape from mainstream life.'

'I've often wondered the same. Hopefully we can find her and ask.'

'Do you think Katie and her friends would take part in the series? I can't imagine that they haven't been asked to do something like this before.'

'They were asked before, but either the time wasn't right or they were suspicious of how they would be represented but . . . it could be good for them now.' For a moment, Ally looked sheepish.

'What? I know that look, Ally. What are you up to?'

'Well . . . Katie asked if I would help her put together a book of their correspondence.'

'The Bonnets' letters?'

'Yes, their letters, and later their emails, plus a bit about them all in real life. The truth is, some of them need to earn some money – to travel, to do whatever it is they want to do, and to cover healthcare too, which is why I need the book to do well for them.'

'Ah. I get it.' I laughed. 'You're thinking that if The Bonnets featured on our TV programme, it would also help sales of their book.'

'Exactly.'

'Always the literary agent.'

Ally shrugged and laughed.

'I'm pretty sure our producer Gary would go for it,' I said. 'We'd have a guaranteed audience because people already know of the group from the TV but, like me, most people thought the characters were pure fiction. But . . . the idea of our series is that the celebrity in each programme would be looking for an old friend they have lost touch with. If Katie was our chosen celebrity, who would she be looking for? Has she lost touch with one of the group?'

'Yes, sort of. Rebecca. She took off to live in the Italian lakes and, as the rest of the group grew older and less inclined to travel, the only communication they've had has been their letters and emails. You need to see friends in person from time to time to keep things alive.'

I laughed. 'I know. I've got the message.'

Ally laughed too. 'Rebecca has a big birthday coming up and I know Katie wants the others to don their bonnets and do something special for her. That could maybe take care of the "finding an old friend" part of the programme, and if the party they plan is anything like ones they've had in the past, it will be a hoot. Their celebrations are legendary.'

'They sound perfect for the programme. Do you have clips of their performances?'

'Some. I also have a lot of the original correspondence if you'd like to see it. I think that writing with a pseudo-name allowed them to express many things they maybe wouldn't have been able to say otherwise. I also have photos of some of the hilarious outfits they wore for various birthdays.'

I felt a rush of adrenalin. I couldn't wait to tell Gary. He'd fall over himself to get them to sign up for the programme, as would I. But I decided to play it cool. Ally wanted this to help promote *The Bonnets of Bath* book as much as I wanted it, and I had an idea of how I could make it work for both of us.

'I will put The Bonnets on the short list,' I said.

'Short list?'

'We have a few possibilities. I'd have to put The Bonnets to the team.'

I saw that Ally's face had dropped.

'Unless . . .'

'Unless what?' asked Ally.

'Unless you agree to take part in programme six and the search for Mitch.'

Ally narrowed her eyes. 'Sneaky.'

'No more than you wanting your group put forward in order to promote their book.'

'Always the TV producer,' said Ally.

I shrugged and grinned, just as she had minutes earlier. I put out my hand. 'Deal?'

She let out a deep breath then shook. 'Deal.' I felt a sensation of warmth at the beginning of our renewed bond and thought that a good rule to remember is that it's never too late to reconnect with those who mean something to you.

'It will be an adventure, Ally, and maybe just what you need at this point in your life.'

Ally nodded. 'Maybe. I know Michael wouldn't want me moping.'

'So all we have to do now is find Mitch.'

'Any more leads?'

'Jo said she'd look into records to try and trace Mitch's family and see if they're still in Manchester or indeed the UK. Er . . . and Jo and I are going to see a psychic detective to see if they can shed any light.'

'A what?'

'Psychic detective. Too late. You shook on the deal. Jo's going to come with me.'

Ally rolled her eyes. 'Ever thought of just getting a normal detective to help? Someone who specializes in finding missing people.'

'And ruin all the fun? Want to come with us?'

Ally laughed. 'No way. I won't come and see the psychic but . . . I might take you up on your offer to come and stay with you. Here, every room, every surface is a reminder of Michael. He was such a presence in this house and now such an absence.'

'I'd love to have you,' I said. 'How about we do a trip up north? Revisit some of our old haunts and see if there are any clues about Mitch while we're there.'

'I'd be up for that. Since we've been talking about her so much, Mitch has been on my mind a lot these last few days. I mean, look at us three, you, Jo and me. So many changes in our lives since we were those young girls in Manchester. I'd love to know her story.'

'Me too.'

Chapter Nineteen

Mitch

Summer 1974

It was about a month after I'd learnt that Jack had died that I came across the Rainbow Children. A sweet-faced man – wearing a red bandana wrapped around wavy dark hair, dressed in jeans and an orange-coloured kaftan – handed me a leaflet in Portobello Road. I was coming out of The Seventh Star, a shop that sold incense, vegetarian food and hippie clothing. I'd got a job working there four days a week with Fi's flatmate Lesley, and Fi worked there too on Saturdays to help subsidize her student grant. It reminded me of On the Eighth Day, a shop back home in Manchester where I used to hang out with Ally, Jo and Sara when we were in the sixth form.

The outside of The Seventh Star was painted in psychedelic colours and the shop assistants were unlike anywhere else, Woodstock wannabes drawn to the hippie style of dress and way of life. You could wear what you like and we did – the men wore their hair long and dressed in jeans and T-shirts, the women in colourful Eastern-style clothing; apart from Fi, who wore her hair short and went around in shapeless dungarees. Lesley, with her big blue eyes and fine blonde hair, wore flowing lace or velvet dresses from the many vintage stalls in the area. We all had a lot of admirers, but since learning about what had happened to Jack, I wasn't interested in men. No one I met came anywhere near him, and that part of me seemed to have shut down. I was still nursing my broken heart and trying to cope with the loss of Sara Rose as well; she was constantly on my mind. I daily questioned where she was, how she would be coping with her new family, what she might look like day by day as she grew. Most importantly, was she happy? I worked long hours, always eager to do overtime, anything to distract from the emptiness I felt inside.

The top floor of the shop was where the clothes were sold and was my territory. It smelt of patchouli and sandalwood oil. The middle floor sold herbs and spices and was pungent with their scent, the ground floor, where the café was situated, of garlic and onions. The herbs were Fi's area on the Saturdays she worked there. Her space was like an old-fashioned sweet shop, with floor-to-ceiling shelves with tall glass jars full of exotic-sounding leaves and powders. I'd never heard of basil or oregano until I worked there, and would drop the new words into conversation whenever I could to show that I too was hip when it came to herbs. All the music played was a nod to the Sixties: Grateful Dead, Richie Havens, Jefferson Airplane, Crosby, Stills and Nash, The Doors, Carole King and Joni Mitchell played on a loop on the sound system. I ate lentil stew, drank chamomile tea – though I thought it tasted like cat's pee, even with honey. I spent what money I had on clothes from Biba, a great shop in Kensington, and felt as if I was right at the centre of the London scene. I had found a new tribe with the people I worked with and did my best to fit in and forget the past year.

On the bus home, I glanced at the leaflet that the sweet-looking man in the street had handed me. 'Change is coming. You can be a part of it. To discover how to have peace of mind and live on a more harmonious planet, come to meet the Rainbow Children at St Luke's Church, Notting Hill Gate. Every Friday night 7 p.m.'

I put the leaflet in my bag. I liked what it said; in fact everyone who worked at The Seventh Star believed in creating a more harmonious world. I'd often thought that I'd like to put something back into the planet, but I had no intention of going to the meeting. There was always something happening on a Friday night – a movie, a band on locally, or a party where I could hang out with the crowd from the shop.

Around this time, my parents went to live in New Zealand. It had been on the cards for a long time, ever since Mum's sister Maggie had emigrated out there five years before. The plan had always been that Mum and Dad would join Aunt Maggie and her husband once Fi and I had left home and were established. We were invited to go with them.

No way, I thought. A million miles away, trapped with my parents, hearing my father's disappointment and my mother's regret? Not high on my life plan. Fi didn't want to go either. She was well into her course, didn't want to change halfway through, or leave her friends and fellow students. We both declined the offer and away they went, Dad in an almighty sulk about Fi's and my decision, to the other side of the world.

Weeks went by and I forgot all about the peace meetings. However, one Friday evening, the flat was quiet. Fi and Lesley had gone to a gig in Camden and I came across the leaflet in my bag. *It's the sort of thing I'd have gone to with Sara, Ally and Jo*, I thought as I was about to put it in the bin. When in sixth form, we'd prided ourselves on being open-minded about other cultures, philosophies and beliefs. But those girls were gone from my life for the time being, all busy doing their degrees, meeting new people. We chatted on the phone occasionally, caught up on news, but I still couldn't bring myself to talk about Jack or the loss of Sara Rose and the calls only confirmed that we'd all moved on; not just them from me but, from what I could make out, from each other too. So much for our promises to be friends for ever. Ally's life was Oxford, Jo's Brighton and Sara was at Exeter. They'd made new friends, as had I, so I thought, why not go and listen to what these Rainbow Children have to say? If nothing else, it was a way to fill an empty evening.

*

The meeting was held in a church hall. The scent of incense wafting out into the warm summer evening announced to the public that they'd found the right place. Inside, a crowd of people were already seated, many dressed in bright colours or with rainbow-coloured scarves or jumpers, some with eyes closed, a look of contentment on their faces as though gazing on some beatific vision. I was struck by how peaceful it felt in there.

I took a seat at the back so I could make a quick escape if I needed to and, so as not to look out of place, I closed my eyes as well. I was just nodding off when I heard someone begin to speak. I opened my eyes to see that a man with sandy-coloured hair was at a microphone at the front. He looked to be in his early twenties and was dressed in a green suit with a fabulous rainbow scarf around his neck. He had a radiance about him as if he'd been polished inside out and had found a shampoo that actually did what the ad claimed – gave shine and gloss. His looks were such a contrast to the usual men I met of his age, many of whom had a pasty look about them, as if they didn't get enough fresh air. This man looked all-American bright though his accent was northern. He introduced himself as Andrew.

'Everything in this life is changing,' he began, and went on to talk about change being the nature of our universe. The message resonated. This man was speaking my experience. It was true; everything had changed for me – Jack, my family home, my friends.

Other speakers followed him, highlighting the imbalance of wealth on the planet. There was so much I agreed with as I listened.

'The peace you are looking for lies within you,' said a dark-haired woman who was dressed in orange and without make-up. *Could have fooled me*, I thought. *Not within me, anyway. Inside me feels lost and at sea.*

I went back the following week, and the week after, and the week after that. I didn't tell Fi or Lesley where I was going and they didn't ask. We all did our own thing – off out to yoga or dance classes, to a concert or the cinema, plus I didn't want to cramp Fi's style by following her round. She'd been good enough letting me come and live with her.

I felt soothed in the hall, welcomed and wanted. I liked what the speakers said. They talked about the need for change on the planet. They talked about respect for others. I began to recognize the regulars, among them a tall, Byronesque-looking man with a mane of dark wavy hair who I recognized from the café at The Seventh Star where he worked. He stood out from the others in their rainbow-coloured attire because he dressed in jeans and a three-quarter-length red chenille coat. We got talking on the way out one night, and I told him that I had a bedspread made from the same fabric as his coat. He laughed at that. We didn't speak for long though. No one did. People were there to listen.

It was a place where I could go and sit; soak up the atmosphere, with no demands made. I didn't feel alone when I was there. I didn't feel the loss of Jack or Sara Rose. Everything that the strangely intense people said started to make more and more sense, and I felt I might have found somewhere I could belong. I sat, thirsty for the words I was hearing. I wanted the peace they had and was prepared to do whatever it took to get it.

Chapter Twenty

Sara

Present day, January

As the train drew in to Manchester Piccadilly Station, Jo got out her lipstick and a mirror and applied a red smear to her lips.

I felt a stab of nostalgia as I gazed out over familiar red-brick landmarks and remembered a time when the city had been my home. Work on the programme was well under way. Katie Brookfield was signed up, and the plan today was for Ally, Jo and me to visit old haunts, to bring to life the times we had spent as friends with each other and with Mitch in our teens. Already they'd helped me compile some more rules of friendship on the train journey.

'How long is it since you've been here?' I asked Ally and Jo as we got up and gathered our coats and bags from the overhead rack.

'Decades,' said Jo.

'Same,' said Ally.

'I haven't been back for a long time either,' I added. 'After Dad died and Mum moved closer to me, then into the care home, there was no reason to come back.'

Jo grinned. 'Until now. I'm looking forward to our trip down memory lane,' she said. I noticed she had lipstick on her teeth.

I pointed at her mouth. 'Lipstick,' I said.

'Oo, thanks.' She quickly rubbed it off as the train stopped and we alighted. 'Add that to your rules of friendship. Good mates tell each other when they look a prat and have lipstick or spinach on their teeth—'

'Or chin hairs that need plucking,' Ally added.

I laughed. 'Noted.'

Our new pal Ajay, a tall man with a dark goatee beard, had travelled up the day before and was waiting at the end of the platform to greet us. 'I thought we'd start the filming at St Mary's, your old school,' he said as we headed for the escalators down to the car park. 'We've got a car and driver for the day, so we can go on from there to places you used to hang out. Then finally we'll head for the street where Mitch used to live.'

Yesterday, Gary had come up with the additional idea that we should go knocking on doors on Mitch's road. 'Even though her parents have gone, there's bound to be one neighbour who remembers them and might know where they are or even where your friend is,' he'd said.

Minutes later, we were on our way in a people carrier with Peter, our driver at the wheel.

'I hardly recognize this place,' said Ally, staring out of the window as we rode through the streets towards Hulme and our old school. Blocks of flats had gone up, familiar shops replaced with curry houses, cafés, grocery stores with fruits and vegetables spilling out onto the pavement, the atmosphere much more cosmopolitan than it had been when we lived there.

'Me neither,' said Jo.

'What happened here?' I asked when we reached a road lined with houses on either side. I remember this being a busy high street. Where are all the old shops?'

'Yes,' said Jo, 'there was a Boots, a hardware shop, and there was a handy newsagent's there. I used to get Black Jacks . . .'

'And I'd buy Coconut Mushrooms,' said Ally. 'I loved them.'

'My favourites were those Rhubarb and Custard sweets that cut the roof of your mouth—' I started.

'And those Sherbet Fountains and Fizzers,' Jo interrupted. 'God knows what was in them, they used to fizz for ages.'

'All demolished to make room for new housing,' said Ally as she continued to stare out. 'Hey, isn't that where Woolworths used to be?'

'It is! Peter, please stop here,' I called to the driver. 'Ajay, we need footage of the bus stop . . .'

'Bus stop?' Ajay asked as the car stopped and we piled out.

'God, it's still here,' said Ally as she approached the stop.

I turned to Ajay who had started filming. 'This is where we waited for the bus home, every night for seven—'

'Years, yes! Where Mitch made that speech on our last day of school—'

'And we all made our promises,' Jo added.

Ally laughed. 'This magnificent and noble bus stop – that's what she called it, or something like that . . .'

'And we promised to stay in touch, be friends for ever,' I said.

We were all quiet for a moment as we remembered that day. It felt odd to be standing on the same spot decades later, a place so familiar and yet unrecognizable. I looked over at my two friends. Behind the signs of ageing, I could still see those eighteen-year-old girls who had stood there with me so long ago.

'Friends for ever,' said Jo. 'We didn't keep our promise to her, did we?'

'It's not too late,' I said as I glanced at Ally. 'And there's another rule for the list: it's never too late to make a new start and make changes.'

'It took my experience in hospital to kickstart that,' said Jo. 'Anything is possible, and finding Mitch is one of those things.'

We took one last look at the old landmark, then got back in the car and headed off again.

'Apparently, even our old school has changed, it's now a sixth-form college,' said Jo as we drove along.

'I wonder if they still have to wear that same disgusting uniform,' said Ally. 'Remember those purple felt hats we used to wear? Like plant pots turned upside down.'

'And boaters in the summer,' said Jo. 'I doubt they have to wear them if it's a sixth-form college now. They can probably wear their own clothes. We looked a right load of ninnies in those hats. You got detention if you were ever caught not wearing one.'

'Or if your skirt was too short. It had to be exactly on the knee,' said Ally.

'Mitch used to turn her skirt over at the waist as soon as she got out of the school gates, and her hat went straight in her bag,' I said.

'Probably why she was always in detention,' said Jo. 'She was the rebel in our group.'

'A pretty well-behaved rebel,' said Jo. 'None of us could be anything more with those nuns who taught us.'

'Same old gates,' I said as we drew up outside a pair of tall, wide wrought-iron gates with a long brick wall on either side. 'I always thought it looked like a prison from the outside.'

'Felt like one on the inside,' said Jo and groaned.

The car stopped and we got out onto the pavement.

'Oh god,' said Ally as she pointed inside through the railings to the neatly manicured garden in front of a chapel on the left and the red-brick building at the back. 'Doesn't look much different in there, though, does it?'

'I feel fourteen years old,' said Jo, 'and worried I haven't done my homework. Those nuns were terrifying. I was always in trouble. I remember Mother Christina summoning me, looking at my feet and telling me that untidy shoes were a sign of an untidy mind. I was mortified.'

'And Mitch getting detention when Mrs O'Riley saw all the love bites on her neck when checking for name tags,' I said.

'We were an innocent bunch really, though, not a clue about the wider world, or boys, or what was to come,' said Ally.

'Remember how we used to do our Diana Ross and the Supremes routine at lunchtimes?' Ally asked.

'And Mitch was always Diana Ross,' said Jo.

'She had the best voice,' I said.

'Baby love . . .' Jo started.

Ally and I joined in and we went straight in to our age-old dance-step routine as Ajay grinned from behind his camera.

'TV gold,' he said.

'I don't think I've laughed as much since we left,' I said. 'Another rule should be to take every opportunity to embrace our inner child with friends, laugh our heads off and act like idiots. There are far too many times in life when you have to be serious and responsible.'

'Exactly,' said Jo. 'And acting like an idiot is something you're very good at.'

'Ow,' I said, but Jo had been grinning when she'd said it so I grinned back at her, happy that the easy familiarity and teasing we used to do with each other was starting to return.

The school gates were locked and there didn't seem to be anyone around to ask to let us in, but we could see enough through the rails to remind us of the many years spent there.

'I still remember the smell in there,' said Jo. 'All those dark polished wooden floors, the scent of lavender beeswax . . .'

'And school dinners, yuk,' I said. 'The food was disgusting, that sponge with hundreds and thousands sprinkled all over it.'

'And semolina pudding that looked like frogspawn,' said Jo.

'And pans and pans of cabbage that had turned to slime,' said Ally. 'God I hated that stuff. The dining hall always stank of it.'

I did remember. So much of it came flooding back – years of lining up for assemblies, classes, masses where we'd sit on the back row in chapel, shoulders shaking as we tried to suppress the giggles we always got in there, working hard for exams. But, most of all, I recalled our friendship. Despite the discipline, detentions and fear of the nuns, I'd loved going to school because it meant days spent with Ally, Jo and Mitch. Each morning, we'd discuss details of what was going on in our lives, from homework, what was on telly, to make-up, our hair, new bands, boys. As long as I had my friends, my world back then was a good one.

'When you searched for Mitch on Facebook, did you look to see if the school has a page?' asked Ally.

'I didn't. Good idea,' I said. 'Most schools have one so that old pupils can post messages or memories. There might be someone on there who could help. At the very least, we could leave a message on there.'

Jo got out her phone and did a search. 'Yep. Found it. There is a page . . .' she scrolled down. 'I can't see anything dating back further than when it turned into a sixth-form college, though.'

'Maybe there's another page or site or something for old pupils,' I said.

'Worth a look,' said Ally, 'though I wouldn't get your hopes up too high. We three were the people closest to her, and if we don't know where she is, I don't imagine anyone else from our old class does.'

Ally wasn't going to put me off. Cruising around Manchester, remembering times together, had only reinforced my determination to find Mitch and reunite the four of us.

Chapter Twenty-One

Ally

Present day

Our second stop on the trip down memory lane was St Bernadette's on Princess Parkway. They'd had a youth club in the basement hall where every Friday night, there was a dance. We'd set off there when we were fourteen and fifteen, our first foray into the world of boys, kissing them and fighting them off, mainly fighting them off because they were a horny lot, all eager to gain experience and get into our clothes, particularly Mitch's.

Jo laughed when we arrived in the car park. 'There should be a blue plaque on a wall here to commemorate all the gropings in the car park in the freezing cold as the boys battled with bra straps, desperate to cop a feel and we tried to shove them off. I remember the first time I felt an erection. Some boy, Jim or Stuart, I can't remember which, pushed my hand down his trousers and it was like, *woah*, what the *fuck* is that? I'd never seen a penis before, never mind felt one; it was like a warm firm silky rubber tube, with a life of its own, jabbing its way into my thigh. What was I supposed to do with it? I hadn't a clue.' She sighed. 'I haven't had enough sex in my life, good sex. I want that written on my gravestone. Here lies Jo. She didn't have enough sex.'

'But you were married for years,' said Sara. 'What about Doug?'

Dear Jo. She'd confided in me through the years that she hadn't been happy with Doug but, being who she was, she'd always put a brave face on it and had never discussed their sex life in detail.

Jo pulled a face. 'He wasn't that into it after the flush of the first years wore off and the kids came. He was never great shakes in bed. He wasn't the love of my life like Michael was for you, Ally, or Charles for you, Sara. And romance? He didn't know the meaning of the word. He was tight. For birthdays, if I was lucky, he'd buy me an economy-sized bottle of bubble bath from a supermarket. He was always one for a discount or sale, but I longed to – just once – get a beautifully packaged parcel from Jo Malone or Chanel or a romantic weekend away, booked by him, a candlelit supper somewhere lovely. But no, I booked the treats. I even bought my own birthday fizz most years. It wouldn't occur to him. He'd say, I thought you were on a diet, or something that would let him off the hook.'

'So why did you stay with him?' asked Sara.

'They say you get the partner you think you deserve. I guess I didn't believe that I deserved better. I always thought who'd want me? A great lump of lard.'

'Now stop that,' said Sara. 'You're very attractive, always have been, bigger or slimmer. You have sex appeal, how could you not know that? But I had no idea you weren't happy with Doug. I thought you were Mother Earth with your perfect family.'

Jo gave a wry laugh. 'Fooled ya.'

'I wish you'd said.'

'I always thought you were so happy too,' said Jo, 'with the beautiful Charles.'

'Well, we all know what happened there. Believe me, the sex faded for us too as the years went on. Before he left, we often slept in separate bedrooms. He said it was because he snored and didn't want to keep me awake. Now I know it was because he was plotting his escape with Ruth.'

I put my hand on her arm. 'I am sorry about Charles, Sara. I wish I'd been there for you more over that time.' I meant it. I'd been there for Jo when she needed someone to talk to, but had always assumed that Sara was doing fine with her job, her large circle of friends. Now I realized she'd been lonelier than I'd assumed.

I shrugged. 'Hey, I survived, so did you, Jo.'

'And now so must I,' I said.

We'd all forgotten for a moment that Ajay was with us, but when I looked over, I saw that he'd taken himself off a distance, aware that we were having an intimate conversation, not one for the programme.

'We were very green, weren't we?' Jo commented. 'It might have helped if we'd had some proper sex education. I seem to remember we did something in biology about how rabbits made babies, but that was it. No wonder a real-life willie came as a shock.'

'And it's not over yet,' I said. 'Jo, I wish you more men, great sex and some monstrously expensive presents.'

'Fat chance,' said Jo.

After a bit of filming in the car park of the church, we moved on to locate the Top of the Town disco near the centre, only to find it was now a stationery shop. We drove on and went past

Sara's old house, Jo's then mine. We'd lived nearby to each other so it didn't take long. I felt a wave of sadness flood through me, those dearest to me – my parents gone, Michael gone. All of us were quiet as we stared out, lost in memories of another era when we'd been so much younger, our whole life in front of us waiting to be discovered.

'Central library next,' I said to Ajay as the driver took us towards town.

'What happened there?' he asked.

'We'd go under the pretext of studying, but the main purpose was to eye up the students working there and see who was hanging out in the basement café,' said Jo.

'Mitch's sister Fi was right when she said we were all boy-mad,' Sara added. 'We were. Each of us looking for our Heathcliff, our Mr Rochester, our Darcy. Sadly, most of the lads were pale, a bit spotty, and as inexperienced as we were.'

'We may as well head over to Mitch's road,' said Ajay, 'or we're going to run out of time.'

We drove past the library then turned back down Oxford Road and passed another familiar landmark, a shop called On the Eighth Day.

'Oh my god, it's still there,' said Jo as she pointed out of the window.

Back the day, it had been a cool hippie shop, and many of the students and musicians in the city used to hang out there. It was now a food emporium and vegetarian café. We stopped off to buy some sandwiches to eat en route. Once inside, we were dismayed to see that there was no trace of the colourful and bohemian place it used to be.

'Mitch worked in a similar place in London, didn't she?' said Jo. 'I seem to remember her telling me about it. Her sister worked there too. Sixth Star—'

'Seventh Star,' I said. 'I went there once when I happened to be in London and thought I'd look Mitch up. I found Fi there and she gave me a number to call Mitch in one of the communes, I forget which one.'

'Is The Seventh Star still there, Sara?' Ally asked.

'It is, but like The Eighth Day, it's a food shop and café now. I never thought to ask about Fi or Mitch because all the people who work there look so young. It was so long ago that Mitch worked there, over forty years.'

'You never know,' said Jo. 'Some people never move around, so there might be someone there who knows where she went.'

'Doubt it,' said Jo as we got back in the car. 'Hey, remember Karl Twigg's antique market in Deansgate? We'd buy vintage dresses from the 1940s and 1950s, or bits of lace and velvet.'

'You did,' I said. 'I was never into that hippie look.'

'The antique market has long gone too,' said Sara. 'I did go and have a look once when I was up here working.'

Jo sighed. 'The look I aspired to then was Pre-Raphaelite—'

'Inspired by the collection at Manchester City Art Gallery in town,' said Ally. 'You had that fabulous ankle-length velvet cape, Jo.'

'We'd spend many a wet Saturday afternoon gazing at the beautiful women painted by Edward Burne-Jones or Rossetti,' I told Ajay. 'We were all looking for a knight to come and rescue us, then carry us away into the sunset on his trusty steed.'

'More like a rusty bike,' I said, 'or moped.'

'I mourn that lost girl,' said Jo.

'Why? She's still inside you.'

'Just more wrinkly on the outside,' I said. Jo punched me gently on the arm. 'We all are, Jo, not just you.'

'I mean I mourn the innocent Jo, the girl before the

responsibilities, the disappointments, the losses that life has dealt along the way. Jo back then was so full of hope, dreams, ambitions.'

'We're older and wiser,' I said.

'Older, but not much wiser in my case,' said Sara.

'But look at us,' said Jo, 'here we are, still friends, still with that bond we had back then.'

I put an arm around Jo, the other around Sara and gave them a hug. 'Indeed. Here we still are.'

'It would be amazing if we could find Mitch, wouldn't it?' said Jo. 'Being here, remembering so much from those days, she was such a part of it all, an essential part of our gang.'

'Exactly what I think,' said Sara.

I had my doubts. Our trip down memory lane had only served to show that Manchester was no longer the place I knew or belonged. *Everything changes, places evolve to the point they're unrecognizable*, I thought, *but maybe some elements remain. My old friends from that time are still here in the present day, older but still as dear. They are part of that lost past that I can take with me into the future.*

Chapter Twenty-Two

Jo

Present day

The car took us down towards Withington and Mercury Drive, where Mitch's parents used to live. We piled out and looked around.

God, I was having a good time. A day out looking at old haunts with my best old mates, away from the chores back at home. Ally was subdued, which was understandable; Sara more enthusiastic, especially about finding Mitch. I was with her on that. We'd been the Fab Four, not the Fab Three. Mooching around Manchester and going back to our roots was interesting, and yes the place had changed, but the city I knew was still there underneath and it was stirring something inside me – the memory of a girl I used to be before I became the mug who married Doug. She was still in there. OK, so I'd not been very confident back then but I was carefree with hopes and dreams and a life of possibilities. Maybe, as Sara said, it wasn't too late. I'd spent so many years thinking exactly that – too late, too late – but of course it wasn't. I wasn't doomed quite yet. The surgeon who'd put the stents in had said, 'You're good to go for another thirty years.' Since the experience in the hospital when I was floating about on the ceiling, I'd felt different – renewed and more determined to live life to the fullest. I could have a resurgence. A resurrection. I could rise like a phoenix out of the ashes. And maybe, when the time was right, I could help Ally back to a place where she didn't feel it was all over for her with Michael's death. I wanted to spend more time with Sara, too, so that she would realize she wasn't alone either. Together we could go forward.

'Doesn't look that different,' said Ally, as we surveyed the quiet tree-lined street of semi-detached houses, some mock Tudor, with small front gardens. She pointed down to the right. 'Mitch's was down there, wasn't it?'

'Number thirty-six,' said Jo. 'So what do we do now? Go together to knock on doors, or shall I take one side, you two the other?'

'Stick together,' said Ajay. 'There's only one of me and I have to record it all.'

We set off with Ajay behind us and rang the first door bell. A middle-aged lady came to the door. The moment she saw Ajay and the camera, she closed the door. 'Excuse me, madam, we're looking for someone who used to live on the street,' Sara called through the door.

'Why the camera?' she called back.

'We're making a TV programme about looking for lost friends,' Ajay replied.

She opened the door again but looked at us suspiciously.

'I am sorry to intrude,' said Sara. 'We're looking to find the Blake family, who used to live at number thirty-six back in the 1960s and 70s.'

'I've only been here three years. You want number forty-three.

Eric Simmons. He's been here all his life.' She put her hands to her hair to tidy it then smiled at Ajay. 'So will I be on the telly then?'

'Yes, madam. You will.'

We went back onto the pavement, crossed the road and found number forty-three. I went and knocked on the door but there was no reply.

'Let's try next door,' said Sara, who marched over there and rang the bell.

The door was opened by a teenager, who went pink as soon as she saw the camera and Sara. 'Oh my god, like, oh my god, you're that woman off the telly? Am I on the telly? Have we won something? Mam, mam, the telly's here. We're on the telly.'

'We're just looking for someone who used to live on this street. Blake family,' I said.

'Mam, mam, do you know the Blake family?' the girl called back and looked around the street. 'Are we on Michael McIntyre? Where is he? I love his Midnight Gameshow.'

An older blonde woman came out from the back of the house. 'Do we get paid?'

'No,' said Sara. 'We're just trying to find someone. We only want to know if you remember the Blake family who used to live at number thirty six.'

'Can't say I do. Eric. Number forty-three. He's lived here the longest.'

Just at that moment, a car drew up outside the house she was pointing at and an elderly gentleman got out.

I went rushing over. 'Excuse me. Are you Eric Simmons?'

'Who wants to know?'

I gestured to Ally, Ajay and Sara. 'We're making a programme, searching for an old friend, Mitch Blake, her family used to live at—'

'Number thirty-six. Left years ago.'

'Do you know where they went?'

'Young 'uns went to London, Fiona and Michelle.'

'That's right. And her parents?'

'Claire and Howard. Moved away some time in the 1970s. Went to New Zealand. Claire had a sister out there. Howard died not long after they moved, don't remember the year.'

'Do you know if Mrs Blake, Claire, is still out there?'

'You need to ask Eileen Morrison at number fifty-nine. She's a cousin or some relative. She might know.'

'Have Fiona or Michelle ever been back?'

'I've never seen either of them. Ask Eileen.'

I thanked Eric, then trooped over to number fifty-nine. A lady with a tight perm and sour expression opened the door. 'Sorry to bother you,' said Sara and indicated Ajay behind us. 'We're making a film about tracing old friends. I went to school with Michelle Blake. Eric at number forty-three, said you might be related to the family.'

'That's right. Third cousin. Is it for *Who Do You Think You Are?* I like that. I've watched all of them. The one with Danny Dyer was my favourite. He's royalty, you know.'

'Er no, we're not that programme. Ours is about tracking down old friends.'

'Do they owe you money? That's why most people come looking for people they haven't seen in ages.'

'No. They don't owe me money. I'm just trying to find my old friend.'

'Mitch owes me a tenner,' I said. 'I've been waiting all these years.'

Ally shushed me.

'Blake family?' Sara persisted.

'They went a long time ago.'

'Might you have an address? Eric said that Mitch's parents went to New Zealand.'

'We weren't close and we're a big family. Catholics. I can't say I know half the cousins, only the local ones. As I say, Claire and Howard moved a long time ago. New Zealand. He died not soon after . . .'

'Did Claire stay over there?' I asked.

'She did that. Anyroad, I never saw her again.'

'And the daughters? Michelle and Fiona?'

'No idea, though that younger one was in trouble last I saw.'

'What kind of trouble?' I asked.

'Not for me to say but . . . she was well down the wrong road and only nineteen.'

'Wrong road?'

'No father.'

'What do you mean no father? Mitch did have a father, you just told me he went to New Zealand.'

'Not Michelle's father, he was Howard. No, the father of her child.'

'Child? At nineteen. Mitch didn't have a child then.'

'Well then, maybe something happened. I don't know. She left for London and wasn't seen again up this way, 's'all I know.'

'And you think she was pregnant?'

'All very hush-hush but of course, I'm family.'

The three of us looked at each other.

'Are you in touch with anyone who might know where Mitch is?'

Eileen pursed her lips and folded her arms. 'Nope.'

Sara gave her a business card. 'Well, if you do remember anything, please could you give me a ring?'

'Right,' she said, and closed the door.

We went back to join Ajay and Ally who were at the gate. 'Not much luck but . . . She seemed to be saying that Mitch was pregnant when she was nineteen . . .'

'No way,' said Ally. 'We'd have known.'

'Would we?' I asked. I glanced back at the house. 'Course we would. I reckon that old bird must have got her wires crossed. We met up in the summer holidays after our first year at college. Don't you remember? She did seem a bit lost and unsure of what to do . . .'

'I do remember,' said Sara. 'She'd put off going back to college again.'

'Maybe she lost the baby?' said Ally. 'A miscarriage? Abortion? If she'd had a child, she'd have told us.'

'When exactly did she join the Rainbow Children? I wish I could remember,' I said. 'She wouldn't have been able to go into the commune with a child. The communes were for unmarried followers. I reckon Eileen's talking about someone else.'

'And if there was no sex in the communes,' said Ally, 'she wouldn't have got pregnant then.'

'Maybe it was Fi who was pregnant?' Sara suggested.

Ally shrugged. 'I saw her in London at The Seventh Star place. She would have mentioned it, surely?'

'At least we know what happened to Mitch's parents and why we couldn't find them here in the UK.'

'So where do we go from here?' I asked.

'Back to London,' said Sara. 'See if Lauren has had any luck.'

'She's working with two companies that claim to be able to find anyone anywhere in the globe,' said Ajay. 'Nothing to report as yet but it's still early days.'

'Maybe Fi and Mitch went over to New Zealand to join their parents. That would explain why Mitch seems to have disappeared.'

'I doubt it. She was never that close to either of her parents. Don't you remember her dad and how scary he could be?'

Ally and Jo nodded.

'Lauren will find out,' said Ajay.

I hoped so. People don't just disappear. *The Fab Four will ride again*, I thought as we got into the car and headed back to the station.

Chapter Twenty-Three

Mitch

Autumn 1974

The vision of Paul and his ensuing conversion took place on the road to Damascus. Mine took place just off the A406, behind World of Leather.

I learnt that the man in the chenille coat was called Tom Riley.

I learnt that the teachings of the group were devised by four Americans, John, Robert, Maya and Debra who'd done the hippie trail in the sixties. On their journey, they had studied the philosophy of a guru from Kerala in India. The guru was old and didn't travel but he did provide advice and direction to American founders.

'Indigos' were members who had been trained to pass on the teachings. They had been members since the beginning and spent their lives travelling wherever they were told to go by John, Robert, Maya and Debra.

We heard that there would be an introductory session to the meditation side of the teachings in October, led by one of these indigos. When I learnt that Tom Riley was going, I decided to go with him.

As we drove to the venue in his clapped-out van, we discovered we had a lot in common. We were both twenty years of age. We'd both been reading Carlos Castaneda and Herman Hesse but *The Prophet* by Kahlil Gibran was our favourite. We both liked Captain Beefheart and His Magic Band and had both been affected and inspired by what we had heard from the Rainbow Children. As I got to know him, I discovered that he had a lust for life and all its pleasures – food, women, wine and music – and was an all-or-nothing man, presently aspiring to a higher path. Although he was attractive, there was no chemistry and I didn't fancy him, but I felt comfortable with him and could tell we were going to be friends.

The meditation session was to take place in Harlesden in northwest London in a commune where a number of the followers lived. I'd imagined some hippie-type place, a bit like The Seventh Star where I worked, but when we got there it looked like an ordinary semi-detached house. We took off our shoes and left them on the pile outside, then were ushered into a front room where there was no furniture and nothing on the walls apart from a rainbow mural on one wall. The house smelt of curry, incense and unwashed socks. All sorts of people packed in, about thirty of us – old, young, different cultures. We sat cross-legged on the floor and waited for the arrival of the indigo.

'Do we have to pay?' I whispered to Tom.

He shook his head. 'The message is given freely. They accept donations, though.'

As we waited, I thought back to when Sara and I had attempted to learn to meditate a couple of years ago. We'd sat on the floor of my bedroom with our 'How to' book open, and attempted to do the lotus position. In a flash, Sara had folded her legs and sat with her feet resting on her knees, a smug look on her face. My legs wouldn't go beyond cross-legged. 'Obviously easy for me because I'm a superior soul on my thousandth incarnation,' she'd said, 'whereas you're obviously just a low-life and it's your first time on the planet.'

'Not true,' I had told her, 'because superior souls don't judge and you just cast me as a low life.' She'd laughed. 'Fair point.' The book had told us to say Om Shanti over and over until it became a vibration of sound. We'd closed our eyes and given it a try. It felt nice and I'd got into it. Ommmmmmm shantiiiiiiiii. When I'd reopened my eyes, Sara had been asleep on the floor. 'Superior soul?' I'd said when she woke up. She'd grinned sheepishly. We had discovered cannabis soon after so we never tried the Om Shanti Express again.

My reverie was disturbed by the entrance of a plump middle-aged woman dressed in an indigo-colored kaftan. She looked in her thirties, Italian or Spanish, and reminded me of Jo with her brown eyes and dark hair. She introduced herself as Francesca then she sat on the floor in silence with closed eyes. I'd never seen anyone so still or serene.

After a few minutes, she opened her eyes and began to speak. 'Today we're going to learn a breathing meditation. Like a radio, you have to turn the radio on and tune into the right frequency. The human body can be likened to a radio in that it is the perfect instrument to tune into the life force that is everywhere and the nature of it is peace. Meditation is the key, and now I will show you how to do that so that you can experience it for yourselves.' She got up to dim the lights and I felt a rush of excitement. I also felt a rush of something else – adrenalin, fear. Was I about to be brainwashed? The atmosphere in the room felt intense. One part of me wanted to stay, another to get up and walk out, but there were so many people between me and the door, there was no way I could do that without disturbing everyone. My curiosity got the better of me and I told myself that Tom seemed like a normal bloke; if anything weird happened, he'd get us out. I stayed.

'There are many methods to bring the focus within. Today we will learn a very popular one that many people find easy to do,' said Francesca. 'Put your right hand up to your face and rest your thumb on the right side of your nose, index finger on the left. Now close off the right nostril with your thumb. Breathe in through the left nostril. One two three. Good. Now close the left nostril with your index finger and breathe out. Now breathe in through the right, one two three, close the right nostril with the thumb, breathe out through the left. Continue in this way, changing sides.'

OK, I can do that, I thought as I followed her instructions.

'Ignore your thoughts, let them be there, imagine them to be like clouds floating by overhead but don't go with them, imagine you are the land underneath, still, completely in the moment. Feel your body seated on the floor, don't worry if you lose track, just start again,' she continued.

I did as I was told. At first I found it difficult to remember which nostril I was meant to be closing, where my thumb was supposed to be and which side I was meant to be breathing out of, but after a few minutes of listening to Francesca repeating the process, I got the hang of it. I began to feel calm and was surprised to discover that something was starting to happen in my inner forehead. First a pinprick of light, then stars and geometric patterns getting brighter and brighter in intensity. Wave after wave of pure white light was flowing into me, and with it came the sensation of stillness. As I continued, I felt as if my consciousness was expanding until I was totally unaware of my body or my thoughts, only a silence that was ringing and an endless ocean of light where nothing mattered.

I don't know how long we sat there but, after some time, I realized that Francesca was speaking. I opened my eyes and someone turned up the lights. I looked at my watch. We had been there for an hour. For the first time in months I felt at peace. I glanced at Tom; he looked as dazed as I felt. Francesca spoke a little longer but I can't remember anything she said. My mind felt utterly refreshed. Later, as we picked up our shoes and filed out into the evening air, I felt as though I was floating. All around me looked unreal, like walking into a film set. Dusk in a perfect street in a Walt Disney city.

I couldn't wait to get back and tell Fi and Lesley.

*

'Saw the light off the North Circular? It was probably a football match on at Wembley,' said Fi once I'd got home and told her all about the session. 'You can see the lasers all over London.'

My new-found peace of mind was disappearing fast, especially as she kept referring to the indigo as 'the indigestion', and laughing at her own bad joke.

'You just don't believe it's possible to have a spiritual experience somewhere as mundane as northwest London. You think you have to be sitting under a banyan tree in some romantic Eastern location.'

'You have no idea what I think,' she replied. 'But I will tell you this, there are a lot of charlatans out there who prey on the gullible.'

Francesca had prepared us for the reaction of know-it-all near-and-dear ones. 'The greater the light, the darker the shadow,' she had warned us before we left the meditation session. 'Expect hostility, expect rejection and rise above it.' I repeated it all to

Fi. 'It's your ignorance talking,' I explained, 'your fear of the unknown.'

'Fuck off,' she replied and left the room. She could be like that sometimes.

I went up to my room and reflected on how Fi treated me. She'd never taken me seriously. I was her kid sister and there was nothing I could tell her. Her flatmate Lesley was more open-minded. She came along to one of the meetings. I soon realized that she wasn't with me to listen to the teachings; she'd come along to see if there were any attractive men in the group. She only went the once.

Sara and Jo would have got it, I told myself. They were as open-minded as I was. Ally not so much. She always said that books and science held the answers. Despite our drifting apart, there were times when I still missed them, their feedback, their opinions and advice. I decided to call all of them. They needed to hear about this group. I was sure that they'd be more than interested and it might be something to bring us all together again. I remembered that they'd all moved on in their digs from student halls to shared houses so decided to call their parents to get their most recent numbers.

'Sara's in Bristol for the weekend, dear,' said Mrs Meyers when I called her parents' house. 'I'll let her know you've been in touch.'

'Ally's gone hiking in Cornwall with some friends,' said Ally's mum.

'I'll pass on the message when she gets back,' said Jo's father. 'She's at some music festival in Wiltshire.'

I wasn't going to give up. I found leaflets similar to the ones I'd been given in the first instance and posted them to their home addresses in Manchester. They'd get them when they went back to see their families.

I was so inspired, I even tried to get my parents on board, and called them in New Zealand. My father wasn't convinced. 'First you get pregnant, now you're preaching at us as if you're the first person on the planet to have a spiritual awakening. Call back and talk to us when you want to come and visit here and come to mass with us.'

A month later, I got a postcard from Sara with an Exeter postmark. She wrote the message that we'd always sent each other in our teens when we were apart: 'Weather is here, wish you were lovely.' No mention of the leaflet that I'd sent to her parents' address.

Chapter Twenty-Four

Sara

Present day, February

'Welcome to the big city,' I said to Jo when I picked her up from Paddington Station for our day visiting psychics. It was a few days after our Manchester visit and Lauren had lined up three mediums for us to visit in London. On the passenger seat was a carrier bag which I handed to Jo when she got in the car. 'For you.'

She looked in the bag and drew out a black and cream Jo Malone box. Her eyes teared up. 'Oh Sara.'

'I didn't know what scent you'd prefer, so I got one with five little colognes. You can try them all and see which one you like best.'

Jo opened the box, pulled out one of the bottles and applied the cologne to her wrist. 'Oh my god, that's divine,' she said as she sniffed and looked to see which scent it was. 'Dark amber and ginger lily. Hell, this beats bubble bath at £2.99. Thank you so much. This means a lot.'

'You're welcome, and I wish you many more gifts like this.'

'I might even buy some for myself,' said Jo. 'All those years of denying myself so that the kids had what they needed; from now on, I'm going to let myself have the occasional luxury.'

'Good. As you said, sometimes you have to learn to be your own best friend. I've added that to the list of rules.'

'So Ally's been staying with you since our trip up north?' I nodded.

'I feel jealous,' she said. 'You've been having sleepovers without me.'

'Well you're joining us now. We can do our hair and nails and talk about boys like we used to.'

'And make a plan for my future,' said Jo. 'A bucket list. There's nothing like a near-death experience for focusing the mind, I can tell you. You and Ally can do the same if you like. I mean, not wanting to be miserable, but after being confronted by my own mortality, it's made me think – who knows how long any of us have got left, so let's aim to make the most of it.'

'I'm with you on that. You've been running around after your family, I've used work as an escape from the emptiness in my life so yes, let's think about what we'd like to do.'

'My "to do" list was so boring – clean bathroom, buy new diet book, weed the garden, etc. I want my new "to do" list to be fabulous, luxurious, expansive. I want to experience life and all it has to offer.'

'Any ideas?' I asked.

'I'm not sure. Er . . . watch a sunset in a gorgeous location. Go to a smoky jazz club in Paris. Wear my pyjamas to go to the supermarket. Visit the meerkats at the zoo. Have filthy debauched sex with a man who worships me.'

'Spa weekends together.'

'Definitely together, all of it together. Travelling with friends.

And classes, I want to keep learning, maybe go back to my art. I've barely picked up a paintbrush since art college.'

'Painting weekends,' I suggested.

'Somewhere gorgeous, like Tuscany,' Jo added.

'Or Florence. We get a place to stay in some lovely old building, get up in the morning for a cappuccino and croissant in a café looking out on Ponte Vecchio—'

'Where we will eye up the local talent—'

'Then head off to a drawing class. Sounds bliss. I'm in, though I can't draw.'

We spent the rest of the journey chatting happily about what we'd like to put on our 'to do' list as we drove to our first port of call.

*

We arrived on the street in Kilburn where Ajay, the cameraman from Little Dog Productions was waiting for us. He waved when he saw us pull up.

'Do the psychics know you'll be filming this?' asked Jo as she got out her make-up bag and a mirror, applied red lipstick then twisted her shoulder-length dark hair into a knot at the back of her head.

'They're psychics. If they're any good, they'll have foreseen it. Joking. Yes, we've let them know. You always have to get permission on trips like this,' I said as I got out of the car. 'It will all be edited and some of it might not make the final programme, but all the people we'll be seeing were more than keen to be on TV. It's free advertising for their services.'

'Course,' said Jo as she followed me up the steps to the terraced house.

'Just act as if I'm not here,' said Ajay as he got out his camera and filmed us waiting for the door to open. 'Everyone inside has been briefed so just ignore me and carry on as normal.'

A pale gangly young man opened the door and flushed pink when he saw Ajay and the video camera. He introduced himself as Stevie then ushered us into a room where there were three people sitting with closed eyes. They were either asleep or in rapture after their session with Doris, the ninety-year-old medium we were meeting. The house stank of cats and on every surface was a crocheted doily or antimacassar. Jo and I sat down and waited in silence. After a few minutes, we were called to follow Stevie into a back room where a tiny old lady with her hair in a white bun sat at a table. Miss Havisham from *Great Expectations* came to mind; there was a look of decay about her as if she hadn't seen daylight for a long time. She indicated that we should sit on the two chairs opposite her. She nodded at Ajay, and Stevie went out and closed the door behind him. At her feet was a black cat; it opened a sleepy eye to watch us.

'How can I help?' Doris asked.

Jo took charge. 'We're looking for a friend, Michelle Blake, who we've lost touch with. We wondered if you could give us any clues as to where she might be.'

'Have you brought anything with you that belongs to her?' Doris asked.

We shook our heads.

'A photo, perhaps?'

'I'm sorry, no, we could have done if we'd realized we needed something like that.'

Doris sighed. 'No matter. Come closer and give me your hands. As you do, I want you to close your eyes and imagine your friend so that I can get a sense of her.'

We moved to the chairs nearer her and first she took Jo's hands in hers and then mine. She closed her eyes and took several deep breaths. After a few minutes, she opened her eyes. 'The day is for the living, the night is for the dead,' she whispered.

I felt a blast of ice-cold air to the left of me and the cat's ears suddenly pricked up as if it had heard or felt something. It sat up, fur rising, and stared in the direction that the sensation of cold had come from. Its head turned, its eyes watching as if something was moving from the left of the room to the right. I couldn't see anything. I glanced over at Jo. She raised an eyebrow.

'The spirits tell me that your friend has gone over,' said Doris.

'Gone over where?' Jo asked.

Doris closed her eyes. 'I'm looking, could be over the sea, could be that she's crossed the river we pass—'

'You don't mean she *died*, do you?' Jo asked.

Doris closed her eyes again; she began to sway a little. 'I must consult with the banshee—'

'Banshee?' I interrupted.

'They are the spirits who herald the death of a dear one. I feel one near,' said Doris, and began to moan softly.

Jo glanced over at me. She looked spooked and jerked her thumb at the door as if to say, let's get out of here. Doris suddenly stopped and her body sagged.

'When might this have happened?' I asked.

Doris opened her eyes. 'Time is not the same in the spirit world. Listen for the banshee.'

Jo stood up and headed for the door. 'Right. Listen for the banshee. Will do.'

'Do you wish to ask anything else?' Doris asked.

'Maybe another time,' I said and glanced at Ajay who was still filming.

'Can you edit this next bit out?' Jo asked.

'Sure,' he said.

Jo turned back to Doris. 'Will I have another relationship with a man?' she asked. 'Find love?'

Doris closed her eyes then began to moan softly again, as if in pain.'

'OK,' said Jo. 'No problem. In fact, that's how I feel when I ask myself the same question.'

I got up to join Jo at the door. 'Er . . . thanks for your time. Most helpful.'

Doris didn't answer. She stopped moaning and sat back in her chair and had fallen into what looked like a doze.

We heard a knock at the door and Stevie came back in. 'Your next appointment is here, Doris.'

We took that as an opportunity to escape. As we did, Stevie held out a donation box. 'How much is it?' I asked.

'Donations are voluntary,' he said.

I stuffed a ten-pound note in the box and we left.

'That was scary,' I said.

'And so cold in there. Do you think it's an act or genuine?'

'Don't know, don't care, maybe the cat's in on the act, but let's get out of here before the banshee gets us.'

*

The second session was above a health store in Kensington. A willowy woman in her thirties came out to greet us. She looked like Pocahontas, with long chestnut hair down to her waist; she was dressed in Hawaiian dress and had tattoos on her arms. She led us into a red room with soft lighting. Once we were seated, she introduced herself as Rain.

'What an unusual name,' said Jo.

'It's the one my spirit guide gave me,' she said.

As we had with Doris, we explained that we were looking for Michelle.

Rain nodded. 'We will try and make contact. I'd like you to sit and hold hands with me so we form a circle.' There were no chairs, only cushions on the floor, so we sat down and did as instructed.

'Now take three deep breaths,' said Rain. She then began to chant, which evolved into a sound as if she was being strangled in pain. Thinking she was having a seizure of some kind, I opened one eye at the same time that Jo opened one of hers. Rain was still groaning and swaying. I could see that Jo was already struggling not to laugh, which set me off. I quickly closed my eyes again as Rain continued with her strange wailing. I risked opening an eye a few seconds later to see that Jo's shoulders were still shaking in silent laughter, as were Ajay's.

I coughed.

Rain suddenly stopped her wailing. 'Stop!' she said. 'I have contact.'

'With Mitch?' I asked.

'No, with my spirit guide Orion,' said Rain.

'What does Orion say?' I asked.

'He says . . .' She began singing in a language I didn't understand. Jo and I looked at each other in puzzlement. Rain stopped again. She stood up, went to the corner and picked up a bottle of liquid that she proceeded to sprinkle over us whilst continuing her strange incantation.

'Er . . . should we join in the song?' asked Jo.

'Oh yes, please do if you know the words,' said Rain.

'But what about our friend Michelle?'

'She is no longer known as Michelle,' said Rain.

'Ah,' said Jo, 'that would explain why we haven't been able to find her. What is her name now?'

'Phoenix. She changed her name to Phoenix.'

Jo glanced at me and shrugged. 'Yeah. I can believe that,' she said, then turned back to Rain. Jo did a double-take. 'Woah! You OK there, Rain?' Rain had rolled her eyes back so far into her head that all we could see was white. It made her look like a zombie.

'Are you OK?' Jo asked.

'I am communing,' said Rain.

'OK, but where is Mitch, I mean Phoenix?' asked Jo.

'She will come to you,' said Rain.

'Where from?'

'Too many questions. Be still. Orion says she will find you.'

'So she's still alive?' asked Jo.

'Most definitely.'

'So why can't you tell us where?' Jo persisted.

'Seek and you will find,' said Rain.

'But you just said we should be still and she would come to us. So which is it? We stay still and she finds us, or seek and we will find?'

Rain collapsed down onto one of the cushions on the floor as if all the air had gone out of her. 'Any journey contains many contradictions. It is the task of the traveller to interpret these contradictions. Now I must rest.'

We took that as an indication that we should leave, so we got up and made our way out.

'Well that was weird,' said Jo when we got out onto the street, 'but kind of fun.'

'I'll kill Gary and Lauren. I swear they sent us there for a laugh.'

'Worth it just to watch your faces in there,' said Ajay and winked. 'See you at the next one.'

*

The third session was in a church in Muswell Hill and, as we had a couple of hours between appointments, Jo and I took a quick detour home to find a photo of Mitch.

Ajay was waiting for us when we got to the church. He was with a spindly, tall man with thinning hair, who introduced himself as Eddie, shook hands and led us inside where we sat on a pew at the back.

'You have come about your friend,' he said.

'We have,' I said as I handed over the photo of Mitch. 'We'd like to know if you could help us find her.'

Eddie glanced at the photo. 'What are the circumstances of her disappearance?'

Jo quickly filled him in.

'So you haven't seen her for forty years?' he asked.

We nodded.

'Have you tried the usual routes? Old contacts? Family? Other friends?'

'We have, but so far no luck.'

The man nodded, held the photo and closed his eyes.

'I sense your friend is still with us on this plane of existence,' he said. 'The energy around her is bright and vibrant.'

'That was Mitch,' said Jo, 'but can you sense where she is?'

The man shook his head. 'People often come to me when someone has disappeared, run away, been kidnapped or even been murdered. They come when other ways of searching have been exhausted. Sometimes I can feel the spirit of the missing person trying to reach me so that their story may be told. I sense no such urgency or distress with your friend, nor trauma. I sense she is no longer in this country but I suggest you search for her through the more traditional methods – records, schools, hospitals and, in this day and age, with DNA you may be able to trace her easily. I suggest you try those routes. I am sorry I cannot help you further.' He looked intently at Jo for a moment. 'You recently spent time in the spirit world, yes?'

'I . . . Yes, I did,' said Jo.

He smiled. 'Take heed of what you learnt there; such experiences are a gift.' Eddie got up indicating that the meeting was over, so Jo, Ajay and I filed back out onto the street.

'Of the three, Eddie was the most convincing,' I said.

'Shame he couldn't tell us more.'

'But he's right. I told Gary weeks ago that it was futile to go and visit psychics.'

Ajay grinned. 'TV gold, though.'

'I don't think so. Not one of them gave us a clue about where Mitch might be.'

'Maybe a banshee will come and tell us later,' said Jo.

'I really really hope not.'

'Me too.'

On the way back to the station, Jo attempted to sing Rain's song, and in the end I had to join in with her. Strangely, it made us both feel quite good.

'Eddie said she might not be in this country. Do you remember she went to India at one point? I don't remember much of what she did there, though. Maybe she went back there, which would explain why she's hard to trace.'

'Maybe.'

'And now to the commune,' said Jo as we got back into my car.

'Commune?'

'Your place. You, me and Ally all bunked up together. Maybe we're following in Mitch's footsteps after all.'

Chapter Twenty-Five

Mitch

December 1974

A short time after my meditation session, there was a trip planned to India to stay in the foothills of the Himalayas and to meet our guru, Sadhu Devanagari. He was to be staying in an ashram near the Ganges and would be giving a series of talks. It sounded so romantic. I saved every penny, borrowed a little from Tom and flew with him and a group of twenty other followers.

We arrived, hot, dusty and thirsty after a nine-hour flight and hour-long bus journey. Vans and coaches were pulling up and people of all races were spilling out, many greeting each other as long-lost friends. Our accommodation was not, as I had imagined, a room in an ancient and atmospheric monastery, but a sea of tents in a campsite at the back. I didn't mind. It was all new and exciting, and felt like an adventure far removed from the grey streets of England. The atmosphere was reminiscent of a pop festival, full of anticipation as the colourful followers, most of whom had adopted Indian dress of kaftans and kurtis, dyed in rainbow colours, settled in for the week. Some would sit chatting, smoking *bidi* cigarettes, others playing guitars or drums, other singing, others working in make-do kitchens preparing massive pots of vegetables and rice, enough to feed an army, always the scent of jasmin or sandalwood joss sticks wafting through the air. The overall mood was joyous; being there brought a tremendous sense of belonging to something bigger and better, and I began to feel I might be able to leave behind my recent personal pains and problems.

On the first evening, we gathered outside the veranda of the ashram and sat cross-legged on the blankets that had been laid out for us. A group of Indian men played sitar, tabla and sang, then there was silence as we waited for the guru. The air felt charged and there was a stillness in the crowd that was tangible.

After a short time, there he was. An elderly silver-haired and bearded man, dressed in white. He had the kindest face I had ever seen and a great serenity about him. He sat on the chair that had been set out for him, accepted a garland of flowers put around his neck by a lady in sari, then he gazed at the crowd, raised his arm in greeting and smiled, and such a smile, full of joy. We beamed back at him.

When he began to speak, it was in Hindi, but it didn't matter. The man exuded love and I was transfixed as layer after layer of pain and heartache melted away – my parents' disappointment, Fi's irritation, the loss of Jack, the separation from Sara Rose, and from my friends as Ally, Jo and Sara moved on without me; all the dark clouds I had been carrying suddenly lifted. I felt completely in the present moment, washed and cleansed of worry.

The conditions of the camp, however, were far from perfect. Finding my way to the foul-smelling camp lavs in the night was a hideous contrast to the divine rose garden and sandalwood-scented gathering I had just come from. Back in the tent, it was too hot to sleep and the mosquitoes had moved in with us.

In the day, I talked to many fellow travellers: Americans, Australians, Europeans; all high on being there, full of ideas and ideals about how we could change the world, how we had found divine love, unconditional, no strings, no letdowns. We would walk into town, buy samosas and delicious-tasting curry, peas and rice from roadside stalls, and talk about the meaning of life, the importance of being in the moment and the joy of living simply. I marvelled at the abundance of gurus on the streets. We saw one who sat smiling and naked under a tree. He looked as if he'd been dusted in talcum powder. Another, with garlands of flowers around his neck, stood on one leg and didn't move at all; another lay happily in a small white tent which stank of marijuana. Others were advertised in the many posters we saw around the shops and cafés: Bai jis, satguru jis, all promising peace of mind and the way to truth. As I took it all in, I found myself wishing my old friends were there to share it all with me. I felt disappointed that I hadn't heard from them after I had reached out. I told myself to let it go, let them go. They belonged to another era.

In the evenings, we would take our places under the night sky and listen to the guru and feel that just to be in his presence was a privilege.

Sadly the elation didn't last, as most of the group, probably about ninety per cent, came down with amoebic dysentery. Tom and I were two of the lucky ones who escaped, but that came at its own price, which was to tend to those who had been stricken, and were passed out between tent pegs. All talk of the pleasure of the simple life was forgotten as they clenched their aching stomachs and buttocks and longed for home. All efforts that had been made to aspire to being in the here-and-now were immediately replaced by an urgent desire to be anywhere else, preferably in the future, in a place with a proper bathroom with running water and a loo that flushed.

*

When we returned to the UK, I was invited to go and live in a house that Andrew – the sandy-haired guy who I'd first heard speak in the church hall – was planning to rent with some of his followers. It would be the second commune in the city. 'The more people who learn our teachings, the more peace and harmony there will be on the planet,' he told me. 'Meditation is only part of the way of life. We're going to change the world and you can be right here in the heart of it.'

I was torn, flattered to be asked, curious about how the commune would function and still inspired by the trip to India, despite the dysentery disasters. I told myself that there would be no harm in going to find out more.

*

'Are you out of your mind?' said Fi. 'Don't do it, Mitch, please don't. I know you; have known you all your life. You are someone who loves life too much. You mustn't shut yourself away and cut yourself off. I can't help but think you will regret it. This is just a phase, it will pass; don't give up your life for this. They've caught you at a vulnerable time. It will pass.'

'It's a commune,' I said. 'Just a few more people than there are here in your flat, Fi.'

'It's a cult,' said Lesley. 'You've been brainwashed.'

'A cult is an offshoot of a religion,' I replied. 'It's not a religion.

I haven't been brainwashed, I swear, at least that's what they told me to say.' They didn't laugh.

'Vegetarian?' Fi asked.

I nodded. 'I might even stop shaving under my arms.' She didn't laugh at that either.

I called Sara to tell her my plans and for once got through. I quickly filled her in, thinking she at least would share my enthusiasm. 'Don't you think it would be wonderful if everyone learnt to be more conscious, instead of rushing around so much, never experiencing the present moment? It could really change things.'

'I guess . . . but Mitch, is this really for you? You don't sound yourself.'

'I've never been more myself.'

'But is it necessary to move into this commune? Can't you practise whatever you've been taught at home?'

I could. I knew I could. Many of the members of the Rainbow Children lived normal lives; some were married with kids, had jobs, and they incorporated what they learnt into their everyday lives. But I wanted to do more. Fi and Lesley didn't understand. Sara didn't understand. We didn't talk for long. *What do they know?* I thought. They hadn't been there, under the stars, in what had been – until the Delhi belly hit – such an amazing, enchanted atmosphere. I didn't listen to them. I felt I had found my purpose, and that was to spread the message that peace was possible and change was coming.

Chapter Twenty-Six

Sara

Present day, February

The first few days of having Jo and Ally staying at my house were bliss. There was a lot of laughing over shared memories, terrible past haircuts and awful dress sense evident from the photos I pulled out from albums showing our teen years. We stayed up, feeling like teenagers, talking into the early hours of the morning, drinking wine, reminiscing.

'Remember the scarf incident that time we all got stoned?' asked Jo.

'Oh god yes,' said Ally. 'It was when we were in the sixth form and we'd been at a concert at UMIST and were walking home. Mitch was as high as a kite and convinced that her feet were making too much noise on the pavement and would wake people up.'

'She took her shoes off, insisted we did the same, then laid her scarf out on the pavement—' said Ally.

'And made us walk along it to soften the sound,' I said.

'And we did it too,' said Ally.

'And when we got to the end of the scarf, she picked it up and laid it down and off we'd go again. Tiptoeing our way home.'

'Took blooming ages,' said Jo, 'but it made perfect sense at the time.'

'We must have looked insane,' I said.

'And remember the time we were at that student house with Timothy Nash and all his mates?' Ally asked. 'We used to go and hang out there whenever we could . . .'

'I thought they were so sophisticated because they were in their first year at university,' said Jo.

'We all fancied Timothy,' I said.

'He looked like Marc Bolan but taller,' said Jo. 'He fancied Mitch, didn't he?'

'Everyone fancied Mitch,' said Ally.

'It was the burn-your-bra time and they insisted we took our bras off and be liberated women,' said Jo.

'Trying their luck, more like,' I said.

'I remember creeping around the house, hoping my mum wasn't up when I got home in case she noticed,' said Ally.

'And the time we took LSD . . .' said Jo.

'I didn't,' said Ally. 'Drugs were never my thing.'

I burst out laughing. 'Two times with Mitch and Jo. Mitch was so sure she'd found the secret to the universe the first time, but when the trip was over, she couldn't remember what it was. So a week later, when we took it again, I made sure she had a pen and paper and—'

'She wrote it down,' said Jo. 'I remember. We all gathered afterwards to read what she'd written. It was like a sacred moment as we waited for all to be revealed.'

'What was it?' asked Ally. 'I've forgotten.'

'The secret of the universe revealed itself to be . . .' I paused for effect. '. . . I was there and now I'm here.'

'Woah,' said Jo. 'Deep, man.'

We laughed. 'There is some truth in that, I guess,' I said.

'We used to be such ravers, didn't we?' said Jo. 'Curious and open to new experiences. I feel I've lost that somewhere along the way. God, I keep wishing Mitch was here. She ought to be here with us. We haven't been together like this since school and it just feels like someone's missing.'

'I don't think she's in the UK or even Europe,' said Ally. 'We'd have heard something, surely, if she was nearby.'

'The third psychic said he sensed she wasn't in this country,' said Jo.

'That's my gut feeling too – that she got married and is living abroad somewhere,' I said.

'Mine too,' said Ally. 'But where and doing what? That celibate lifestyle just wasn't her, not for ever. I really can't imagine her giving up men for all her life. Has she loved? Lost? Found The One we all used to talk so much about.'

'Maybe she felt that the three of us had let her down in some way, but it wasn't as if we were in touch with each other either, particularly in our twenties,' said Jo. 'We three drifted apart from each other as well as her.'

'I spoke to her when she joined the Rainbow Children.' I thought back to that conversation we'd had on the phone and remembered asking her if she'd really needed to do that, go to that extreme. 'She'd said she wanted more than just to practise the teachings at home, but when I think about it, she didn't really have a home. So maybe it was a place to belong for her, to be with like-minded people. I remember we finished the call quite abruptly, and I'd felt like I'd said the wrong thing. It was almost as if there was a part of her that had already made the decision to cut us out. Perhaps if I'd tried a bit harder, gone to see her at that time, things would have been different.'

'And it wasn't as if we were anti what she was doing,' said Ally, 'There were a lot of different groups doing it – some political, some spiritual – the Rainbow Children were just so all-consuming.'

'True,' said Jo. 'I do mindfulness now, though more often than not it's mind*less*ness – a good excuse to have a snooze.'

'I wonder if Mitch had kids,' I said. 'I sent her an invite to my wedding, to the last address I had for her in London, I seem to remember.'

'So did I,' said Jo. 'I was gutted when she didn't come because it was always the plan to have all three of you as my bridesmaids, ever since school.'

'She was down in Devon when you got married, Jo,' I said. 'I remember phoning her there to try and plan a hen weekend and she was quite off with me. Not in a rude way, more as though she just wasn't interested.'

'I called her too. She promised she'd come. Never did though, did she?' said Jo.

We were all quiet for a few moments as we thought back to that time.

'Where are you actually up to so far with the search?' asked Ally.

'Lauren, our researcher, is going the DNA route and looking into family connections to see if that provides a lead as well as contacting companies who claim to help you find missing people.'

'How do they work?' asked Jo.

'So much is on line now, I guess they start there – looking into companies who help people trace their ancestry as well as those who test DNA. A lot of people do it out of interest to find out about their roots and they make up family trees that they share on line. They may come up with something or someone.'

'Sounds more sensible than asking psychics,' said Ally. 'And I've got my sister in Manchester still doing a bit of scouring around behind the scenes.'

It felt good to have friends to share my space and, although I hadn't mentioned it yet, I wondered if Ally and Jo would be up for living together on a more permanent basis. It made sense. We were all older, all single, didn't want to be alone as we sailed into the golden season of our lives. Could we work out a way? Buy a big house? I decided to see how we got on and then I would put the idea to them.

Chapter Twenty-Seven

Sara

Present day, February

'Has anyone seen the bread knife?' I asked as I got out a loaf from the bread bin.

Ally pointed at the drawers next to the fridge. 'Second one down.'

'Why's it in there? It goes in the knife block,' I said as I pointed to the set of knives neatly stacked.

'Easier in the drawer,' said Ally. 'I've rearranged a few of your kitchen items, for ease.'

'I noticed,' I said. 'No need.'

'You'll find it works,' said Ally.

'I *had* a system that worked,' I said, then immediately regretted my tone. I wanted to make Ally feel welcome. She was still grieving and would be for a long time to come, but I wished to God she'd stop rearranging things and cleaning.

As the days had gone on, the initial exuberance of us all being under one roof had begun to fade. It was clear that we had very different ways of living. Ally was a control freak who liked tidy surfaces, not a cup or cushion out of place, whereas Jo couldn't care less and left mugs half full of coffee in the bedroom and bathroom, her shoes wherever she kicked them off, books and scarves on the table or chair. She left the milk out, the bread board covered in crumbs, a knife stuck in the butter.

I'd thought we'd be one big happy family, like the old days, but it was clear that – over the years – we had found our own routines, routines that clashed. When at school, we'd never actually lived together.

Ally was up at seven every morning and liked to chat. I was not a morning person and was quiet until I'd had at least two strong coffees. Jo slept late and, like me, didn't come around until mid-morning.

Jo liked the TV up loud and music on all the time; it was driving Ally and me mad hearing 'Bohemian Rhapsody' over and over again.

Ally liked the subtitles on TV and to watch political programmes that sent me to sleep. If we found a movie we liked, Jo talked through it, and she had a bad case of twitching leg that made it hard to focus, though she was completely unaware of it.

Jo liked to eat early whereas Ally liked to eat late (about nine).

When Ally cooked, the kitchen was meticulously clean afterwards, everything put away, in its new place. When Jo cooked, it looked as if a bomb had hit the room; she used every pan and utensil, which she then left out with a promise to clean up the next day. 'It's part of my new chilled persona,' she said if Ally started to clear up after her, 'leave it, it can be done in the morning.' I could see Ally begin to twitch then, unable to relax if everything wasn't immaculate.

After only a week, the saying 'guests are like fish, they go off after a few days' came to mind, and I found myself longing for some peace and quiet and to be able to find things where I had left them. The living-together idea was losing its appeal. How Mitch had done it, living in a commune all those years ago, I had no idea. In the meantime, neither Ally or Jo suspected I was finding it difficult having them, though I had a feeling that Jo shared my feelings and would have been glad to get back to her home and space as soon as she could. However, I could tell that Ally was loving having our company and someone to talk to, so I did my utmost to put on a cheerful face and keep chatting to her.

Ally

Present day

Get me out of here, I thought as I brushed my teeth. Who'd have thought it? My two best friends and they're both driving me mad. I love both of them, I do, always will, but that doesn't mean that we're good housemates. We're not. Living with Jo is like living with a chaotic teenager who never learnt to pick their socks up. Her stuff is everywhere! In the bathroom, in the sitting room. And what's hers is hers and what's mine is hers too. She's helped herself to my towel, my Clarins, my make-up, perfume. I even caught her wearing one of my tops yesterday. She has no sense of personal space. And Sara talks, from the moment she's had her morning coffee until the moment she goes to bed, and she follows me round the house to do so, appearing behind me in the bathroom when I'm cleaning my teeth. She doesn't talk *to* Jo and me, she talks *at* us. Maybe it comes from having lived on her own for so long, but I am out of here as soon as it's polite to take my leave. I'd give anything to know how Mitch managed in those communes she lived in. They were spilling out with people as far as I remember.

Jo

Present day

Hil-bloody-arious. The three of us, that is, sharing a house. Sara can barely contain her fury at finding things in her perfect home have been shifted. She never was any good at hiding her feelings. Her left eye begins to twitch if she's annoyed, and it's so obvious she is at the way Ally has rearranged her home. Ally has become more anally retentive than ever – she always was a born organizer but she's forever putting things away, in their place, tidying. I think she needs to chill and let go for a while. Doesn't really bother me, though. Personally I love it and don't miss home for one single second. I shall stay for as long as Sara will have me.

Chapter Twenty-Eight

Mitch

January 1975

'It's only temporary,' said Andrew when I returned to the house at Fairfax Street.

'And it will give you a chance to try our lifestyle and see if it's for you,' said Karen, a woman who appeared to be the housekeeper.

I'd paid a visit to the house where the commune members lived. Karen had greeted me and told me about the routine of daily life there.

'We work long days, starting at six a.m. with group meditation. We're vegetarian and we also agree to be celibate so we avoid the problems and distractions that relationships can cause.'

As she told me this, my heart had sunk – not about the celibacy rule, as that part of me had shut down after Jack had died, but I did like my lie-ins at the weekend. Apparently there were thirteen men and six women in three bedrooms, so there wasn't exactly room or privacy to hook up with anyone, in any case; it was more the lack of personal space that put me off.

*

A week later, I heard that Andrew and Karen were off to Amsterdam for a week-long conference and needed someone to look after the house and cook for those who were remaining while they were away. *I can do that, it's only for a short while*, I thought, and went back to Fi's to collect some clothes.

Fi shook her head. 'What's happened to you, Mitch? That you would seek a life of denial?' She'd heard all about the living conditions at the house and the celibate rule.

'I don't see it that way, Fi,' I told her, although there was a small part of me that heard what she was saying. 'It's only for a week, and something really big is happening. I want to be part of it.'

'There are other ways to change the world and do your bit, Mitch. You don't have to give everything up.'

'I won't. It's only temporary.'

'At least talk it over with your friends. Ally, Jo and Sara – what do they think?'

'Same as you, probably, though I'd hardly call them my friends anymore, we're barely in touch. They don't get what the Rainbow Children are trying to do and they don't get me any more.'

I asked my friend Tom what he thought. 'Give it a go. It's not a prison. You always have the option to leave.'

I gathered the few possessions and moved in with my new family.

*

The week that Andrew and Karen were away went by quickly; when they returned, it was taken for granted that I'd be staying on. It was easier to go along with it than object, plus, unexpectedly, despite the spartan conditions, I liked the camaraderie. For the first time in ages, I seemed to spend the week laughing. Plus I didn't really have any place to go to, apart from back to Fi's and she had a new boyfriend, so I'd been feeling more and more in the way there. Some distant cousin on my father's side still lived up on my parents' street, just down from the old family home, but she was a sour-faced old puss even though she was only in her thirties. She made her feelings very clear when I was pregnant and still living with my parents. It wasn't an option to ask her for any kind of help either. No. I'd do another week in the commune. I told myself I could always leave if I wanted to and, in the meantime, the endless tasks that needed doing in the Rainbow house went some way to filling the empty hole I felt inside at having given up Sara Rose. There still wasn't a day that went by when I didn't think of her, wonder what she'd be doing, how she'd look now, if she was being well looked after. I justified the lifestyle I had chosen by telling myself that I couldn't be a mother to her, but perhaps I could do something about the kind of world she'd be growing up in by giving my time to the Rainbow movement and furthering their message of peace.

At the commune, there was an infectious sense of belonging and purpose. I was one of them, and quite soon the thought of leaving and setting out on my own felt like a lonely place to go. The commune offered solace, shelter, understanding and, most of all, company, and so I became the seventh girl in an already crowded house.

'These will have to go,' said Karen after a few weeks of me living at the commune when she went through my few clothes and possessions. My jeans, jewellery, tops and make-up hit the box for the jumble, to be replaced with the commune uniform of Eastern-style tunics and long skirts, or loose trousers in rainbow colours. Although brightly dressed, we blended in with many of the hippies around the city who favoured tie-dyed clothes and the Indian look.

As there was no room for beds for everyone in the house, my given place to sleep was between the wall and the top of the one bed kept for travelling indigos. I had just enough room to lay out a sleeping bag. I soon got used to it plus, by the end of the day, I was usually so exhausted I'd be asleep in seconds. One night I needed to go to the loo at about three a.m., and it was like crossing a minefield, having to step over six humps of sleeping bodies without treading on any of them.

In the days that went by, I got to know my female roommates a little.

First there was Karen, who worked hard looking after the house.

Second was Gail, I called her Miss Prim. She had an air of disapproval about her and looked as if she'd just sucked a lemon.

Another lovely looking girl with long titian hair disappeared soon after I arrived. She couldn't get on with the 'up at six a.m. to meditate' part of the house timetable, something I also struggled with.

The fourth girl wasn't cut out for the lifestyle either, and always seemed to have some kind of mystery illness that excused her from activities. She was also on a macrobiotic diet and ate fried onions, rice, lentils and strange-looking things that looked like shrivelled bollocks – umeboshi plums, I think they were.

The fifth was a slender Indian girl who was always jolly, always laughing and easy to get along with.

And finally there was Rosie, a petite and pretty black girl with a wicked sense of humour. She soon became my friend.

The men were not stylish or cool, apart from Andrew and Nick. Most of them favoured open-toed sandals that they wore with socks, even in winter.

Two weeks later, I was washing those socks. I took up the challenge as best as I could and made bread, prepared pans of lentils and rice, red beans, mung beans, all cooked with consciousness, lentils with love. Sara, Jo and Ally would have died laughing if they'd seen me.

My morning tasks began with the opening of windows in the top bedroom where ten of the boys slept. We named it The Pit.

Andrew, Joseph and Nick were lucky to have escaped The Pit. They slept in the third bedroom that served as an office during the day. Andrew slept under the desk, Nick with his feet jammed up against a filing cabinet, and God knows where Joseph found a space.

On the girls' side, Rosie ran Rainbow Designs, making clothes for everyone. She had a jolly old time tie-dying shirts, scarves and jackets in red, green, blue, purple, yellow and orange, her hands almost permanently stained with dye. Everyone had a job that was Rainbow-related, from the Rainbow Wholefoods to the Rainbow hairdressers.

I learnt to be quick with my ablutions, a habit I never shook off. You had no choice when there were so many of you lining up and only one bathroom. If you stayed in longer than five minutes, your popularity faded fast. We'd stand in a line outside in the corridor, toilet bags in hand, legs crossed, waiting to get in. Everyone avoided going in after Ian. If you went in after him, you needed a can of air freshener and a gas mask. He was the house comic and musician and would entertain us, singing Bob Dylan-style, while we waited in line in the corridor.

I'm in Samadhi with my budgie,
My budgie's in Samadhi with me,
We meditate each day
And hope that in this way
We will finally be free.
And so on:
I'm in Nirvana with my newt,
My newt's in nirvana with me, etc.

'Not exactly The Grateful Dead, is it?' said Rosie one evening as we stood in line.

In those weeks that turned into months, I felt inspired, wanted, loved even, by my new friends. Everyone in the house felt their lives had been touched and transformed. Those who had been lost or lonely, confused or even suicidal had found a place, purpose and sense of belonging.

A new world was opening up to me. A new language, a new lifestyle. Fi dropped by a couple of times. She was appalled at the way I was living and begged me to leave.

'I'm happy here, can't you see that?' I said.

She refused to believe it. 'Can't you see? This place is an escape for you. I know life dealt you some hard cards, losing Jack and the baby, but you don't need to hide away like this, cutting yourself off in the prime of your life. Please at least stay in touch with your old friends. There must be other ways to move on from your bad experiences.' She gestured round at the room and house. 'This has provided an alternative family, and the people who run the movement are kind parent figures to replace our old grouchy ones, but it doesn't need to be like this. It's like you're punishing yourself for something, doing some kind of penance, or that you don't believe you deserve to be truly happy.'

Her words probably had some truth, but I asked myself: what was wrong with the lifestyle I had chosen? I'd made the biggest mistake of my life in letting go of Sara Rose, so maybe Fi was right, and living the way I did was a self-imposed penance of sorts, but the Rainbow Children was a good cause. What did I have going for me otherwise? Parents who'd moved as far away as possible, a sister who didn't really want me around? Friends who'd moved on without me. No. I'd stay where I was, where I was wanted and I could contribute something.

'We want to bring peace,' I said.

'Idealistic bollocks,' said Fi as she rolled her eyes and made for the door. 'Good luck with that.'

Chapter Twenty-Nine

Sara

Present day, February

'Rebecca's arriving later this afternoon,' said Katie Brookfield, 'so come down early and we can show you round our living arrangements. Do bring Ally too.'

'And our friend Jo? Do you mind if she tags along?'

'The more the merrier,' Katie replied.

Filming for programme one – 'Let's Hear It for the Girls' – had been moved forward because Katie Brookfield had been in touch to let us know that they had planned the celebration for their friend Rebecca's birthday. It was to be held in a hotel close by to the village where Katie lived just outside Bath, and the party theme was Holy or Whore. 'We love any excuse to dress up,' said Katie. 'I'm going as Lord Shiva with a blue face. It will match my veins.'

It was too good an opportunity to miss and would be, as Gary frequently liked to say, 'TV gold.'

*

Jo, Ally, Ajay and I travelled down by train to Bath first thing in the morning, then took a cab to Katie's house in the village where she and the other Bonnets lived.

'Remind me of their names again,' said Jo as we left the main road and drove down a country lane into a picturesque village. The houses were built with soft honey-coloured brick which gave the whole area a golden glow.

'Katie, Bridget, Gabrielle and Jenny,' said Ally. 'All in their eighties now. As you know, Sara, Katie is my author, Bridget used to run an advertising agency, Gabrielle was an actress and Jenny was a dress designer.'

'Creative bunch,' said Jo.

'Like us,' said Ally. 'And Rebecca was a playwright – she's the one coming over later today from Italy.'

'We're meeting at Katie's house to do a short interview with the first four,' I said, 'then a quick tour of where they live.'

'Great,' said Jo. 'I love having a nose into other people's homes.'

We stopped on a quiet street with a row of houses with picket fences and small front gardens on one side and a large green verge on the other.

'This is Katie's,' said Ally, as she pointed at a double-fronted cottage with a wooden porch and bay windows painted a soft grey-green. The door opened and a black dog rushed out, followed by Katie, who greeted us warmly before ushering us inside. She was a striking woman, her posture and mobility giving nothing of her age away. I loved her style too. She was wearing a scarlet velvet tunic dress, ropes of amber necklaces and brown leather boots. Her soft brown hair was cut in a neat bob just above her shoulders, but it was her eyes that drew attention, sharp as a bird's. I got the feeling she missed nothing. Katie introduced the dog as Doodle. 'He's a labradoodle, hence the name, and is an absolute sweetheart.'

We were soon ensconced in a charming red snug with comfy tan sofas, floor-to-ceiling curtains, and book-lined walls. It had the feel of an old-fashioned library and reminded me of Ally's sitting room.

'So this is home,' Katie told us, as she settled herself on the sofa. She was soon joined by Doodle who put his head on her lap. 'The others will be along in a moment. If Gabrielle's been baking, be polite, her cakes never rise. I've taken no chances and bought some scones from the farm shop in case anyone's hungry.'

Katie lifted up an album from the coffee table that contained photos of The Bonnets. One showed them all dressed as nuns outside a pub. On the back, someone had written – How Do you Solve a Problem Like O'Mara?

'That was for Bridget's birthday,' Katie explained. On another photo, the women were dressed as though for Ascot in huge hats. On the back of that one was written: Ascot Gavotte for Gabrielle's birthday.

'We sang "My Sweet Lady Jen", to the Rolling Stones song, "My Sweet Lady Jane" for Jenny's birthday, all dressed in Renaissance gear. I can still remember the lyrics.' Katie launched into them, her voice as clear as a bell.

> Our great matey Jen *(that's you Jenny)*
> A birthday again
> Your best friends are we
> Although we're a pain.
>
> Our great matey *Jen*
> Spends too long in the can
> Problems with her bladder
> Have made her go madder
> Golden years are here my dear,

But never fear my dear
We'll all be here for matey Jen

Oh, dear matey Jen
We're all on our knees *(and not sure we can get up)*
For time's running out *(not a moment too soon)*
For your dear pals and thee.'
So let's drive fast cars dear friend
And burn our bras dear friend
And make the most of, matey Jen.

We all laughed. 'Love it,' I said.

'On one of Katie's big birthdays, they dressed in silk dressing gowns and long blonde wigs, including the husbands. They sang the Beatles "Paperback Writer", all dressed up to supposedly look like Katie. I was there for that one,' Ally said.

'I was so touched by their efforts.' Katie smiled as she closed the album and placed it back on the table.

Moments later, the doorbell rang and three elderly women entered. Each of them looked sprightly and vibrant and, like Katie, younger than their years. Gabrielle was willowy and elegant with white hair and was dressed in pale lavender and grey. 'I brought cake!' she said as she produced a cake tin.

'Oh, how lovely,' said Katie, then winked at Ally when Gabrielle wasn't looking.

Bridget was colourful in a dark red and maroon calf-length dress and bright purple Indian scarf, Jenny in a mustard tunic and olive green leggings and matching scarf.

After introductions had been made, everyone seated, tea made, cake offered and refused by Ally and me (Katie was right, it looked flat and unappetizing; only Jo, too kind-hearted to refuse, took a piece), we got started.

'First of all, thank you so much for agreeing to take part in the programme,' I said. 'As you know, it's about friendship, and I'd like to ask you about yours.'

'Good lord, what on earth makes you think we're friends?' said Gabrielle. 'I can't stand any of these women.'

Katie, Jenny and Bridget laughed. 'Likewise,' said Bridget. 'I only spend time with you because you've not got long to go and I feel sorry for you.'

'How long have you been friends?' I asked.

'Forty, fifty years,' said Jenny.

'Forty for Jenny, Gabrielle, Rebecca and me,' said Katie. 'Bridget came along later.'

'And there's been no getting rid of her,' said Gabrielle. 'Try as we might.'

'How did you come up with your Bonnet names?' I asked.

'My husband and I were christened Lord and Lady Muck because we were moving into rather a grand house when we arrived in the area,' Katie said. 'I added the name Ebaynia to become Lady Ebaynia Muck when eBay began, because of my talent for finding a bargain on there.'

'I chose to be Lady Bottom,' chimed in Bridget. 'We added "the finest seat in the county" because I lived in a place called Rowbottom.' Her eyes twinkled mischievously. 'Rebecca became The Duchess because of her love of quality.'

'And I became Lady Eyre.' Gabrielle wafted an imaginary fan and fluttered her eyelashes.

'She signed her name differently in all the letters, sometimes Lady Eyre, sometimes LadyEyreinmytyres or Lady EyreonaGstring or Lady C Eyre if she was at the seaside,' added Katie. 'A dry wit, our Gabrielle.'

'And I was simply known as Rosamund, "arbiter of taste and decorous fashion",' said Jenny.

Katie informed us that there were two other Bonnets but they didn't live in Bath. They were known as Lady Sew and Sew and Lady Burble. Lady Sew and Sew studied tango for years and still practised enthusiastically.

'And what is the key to your friendship?' I asked, as Ajay found the best position from which to film the interview.

'Knowing they can take the piss out of you and it makes you laugh because you know they know you so well and you love them for it,' said Bridget.

'Mutual support,' said Katie.

'Sara's compiling a list of rules,' said Jo as she turned to me. 'You could add some of these.'

I gave her the thumbs up.

'Loyalty, trust,' said Gabrielle. 'They have to know you've got their back in every circumstance.'

'Listening as well as talking,' said Katie.

'Enjoyment. I like their company,' said Bridget.

'Discretion,' said Gabrielle. 'You have to trust each other with your secrets.'

Bridget tapped the side of her nose. 'And we've certainly had a lot of those over the years. Also shared interests and a sense of adventure. What I like about these women is that they still have a curiosity about the world which makes them interesting company.'

'You will be on their side and support them, whatever, against anyone,' said Jenny. 'You feel their pain as your own and you are genuinely pleased for all good news that comes their way.'

'They know and forgive you all your faults,' said Katie, 'without saying they're doing it. They know when you're kidding yourself, boasting, exaggerating, deluding yourself.'

'They never, ever bore you, and there's always, always something to talk about,' said Bridget. 'We never seem to run out of things to say to each other, whether it's discussing the news, sharing gardening tips, or looking at new movies.'

'And it's good to have a clear-out of friends every now and then,' said Katie, 'like you do with your wardrobe. Those who you no longer have anything in common with and have outgrown, let them go.'

'Or those who bore the pants off you,' Gabrielle added, 'and you only see because you feel obligated, let them go.'

'Those who bring you down with sarcasm or cutting comments, who are judgemental or moaners and your heart sinks when they get in touch,' said Jenny, 'let them go.'

'With a cheery wave,' said Katie, 'let them go and stay with the ones who bring something to the party. Some friends are for ever, some are not.'

I marvelled as they chatted on, each with something to say. I'd done thousands of interviews in my time and seen people go blank in front of the camera or become inarticulate when asked a question for TV. These woman were naturals.

'We've seen each other through illnesses,' said Katie, 'the death of friends, parents, siblings; through money worries, loss of jobs, and through good times too, but we never take our true friends for granted. Don't let them go and make the effort to keep them in your life. Good friends are a joy and never, ever an effort.'

'Apart from Gabrielle,' said Bridget, 'who, to be honest, is bloody hard work.'

Gabrielle blew Bridget a kiss.

I thought about me, Ally, Jo and Mitch. Did we have what it took to end up like these inspiring ladies? We hadn't done a very good job so far, but I hoped we'd turned a corner.

'And you chose to live near each other?' I asked.

Jenny nodded. 'There were times in our friendship when we

lived in different cities, and even periods when we didn't see so much of each other over the decades, but as we began to age—'

'And bits began to drop off,' said Bridget.

Gabrielle sighed, 'And people began to drop off, pass away, our dear husbands among them, one after the other, we got together to see if we could devise a plan to live nearer—'

'Possibly together,' said Bridget, 'though that idea soon got thrown out.'

'Why's that?' I asked.

Bridget rolled her eyes. 'Friends we might be, but under one roof and there would have been mass murder.'

'Yes, we're a bunch of difficult old moos,' said Gabrielle.

'We're all very independent,' said Katie, 'and we like our own routines.'

'Stubborn and fixed in our ways you mean,' said Bridget. 'Katie never stops talking and *always* has to have the radio on; Gabrielle's a ditherer; Jenny's so noisy and opinionated . . .'

'And you're perfect, are you?' Jenny asked.

'Yes. Always right, too,' said Katie with a grin.

I glanced over at Jo and Ally. Jo raised an eyebrow back at me in recognition.

'Jenny has a huge family,' said Bridget.

'Eighteen when we're all together,' said Jenny. 'That was never going to work if we'd bought a house together and I had family over.'

'And Bridget's a mad cat-lady whereas I like dogs,' said Gabrielle.

'So yes, we had our differences, but we wanted to be close, there to support each other,' said Katie.

'Have company if we were feeling lonely,' added Gabrielle.

'So we came up with the idea of buying in the same village,' said Katie. 'It took a while, a number of years while we waited for the right properties to come up, and then we had to sell our previous places . . .'

'This village was perfect, close to a city but far enough away to be quiet,' said Jenny. 'We were on a local walk about eight years ago when Katie spotted this house. She was first to move, then I came the following year.'

'I sold my house in Wales but nothing came up here so I moved in with Bridget,' said Gabrielle, 'and we waited until something we liked near here came on to the market. It took over a year.'

'Year of hell,' said Bridget.

'And *voilà*, here we all are, within five minutes' walk of each other. Independence maintained, company when we need it. And the village has everything we need – a pub, a vet, a local shop . . .'

'A doctor's surgery, a good bus service into Bath,' said Katie.

'A field full of llamas down the road,' said Bridget. 'Not ours, but we do like to go and look at them.'

'It's peaceful,' said Jenny. 'Wonderful views and walks.'

'What about at night?' Ally asked. 'Don't you miss someone being in the house then?'

'Part of the reason we chose this village is that the houses aren't isolated, the neighbours are a call away,' said Gabrielle. 'And I have my dog.'

'Who sleeps on the bed with her,' said Jenny and pulled a face. 'Ew.'

'We all have pets for extra company and friendship,' said Bridget. 'You'll meet them all later.'

'And we keep our phones close to our bed,' said Katie. 'If any one of us feared an intruder, one call and The Bonnets would be here en masse armed with—'

'Spades and baseball bats,' said Bridget, 'and actually Gabrielle and I live right next door to each other and we have one inter-connecting door upstairs.'

'We see each other pretty well every day. Monday, we do a cookery class at Jenny's – she has the biggest kitchen – then eat what we've made for lunch. Tuesday we walk – there are so many lovely places near here.'

'Wednesday morning we do art,' said Gabrielle. 'Katie and Jenny are quite good. Bridget and I are rubbish.'

'Thursday is Pilates,' said Jenny. 'Saturday we do yoga and once a month we have a film night.

'And a book club once a month,' Bridget added.

'Wine tasting most nights,' said Katie. 'At least, that's what I call it.'

'I call it hitting the bottle,' said Bridget.

'And we plan theatre outings, garden visits, attend lectures and tours. We get together once a month with all the "what's on" magazines and book up what we want to see or where we want to go.'

'Sounds idyllic,' said Ally.

'It is,' said Katie. 'I couldn't ask for more, like our own tailored retirement community where we get to choose the other residents.'

'And Rebecca? Why did she leave?'

'She's always loved the sunnier climates,' said Katie, 'so after a few years here, she chose to move away, but she still has a cottage here. She rented it out so that she didn't burn her bridges in case she ever wants to come back.'

'Which I am sure she will in time,' said Jenny. 'You need friends around you as you get older. We're throwing her a huge party – of course she couldn't resist and was persuaded to travel back for it. Our parties are legendary.'

'Yes, we're planning a humdinger this time. Anyhow, would you like a tour?' asked Gabrielle.

Ajay nodded, and soon we were being escorted around the various houses. Gabrielle's cottage was like her, elegant and tastefully decorated in pale pastels. Even her dog was elegant – a silver-grey whippet called Lola. Bridget's home was similar to Jo's, a colourful, cosy space with riot of artifacts and artwork on every wall. There we met Maisie, a tabby Maine Coon and a silver-grey Norwegian Forest cat called Barney. Both big animals that were clearly adored by their owner.

Jenny lived in a lovely manor house around the corner. Her pet was a moggie called Sam. 'He just appeared at the back door one day about four years ago, looking thin and hungry, and he's stayed ever since. I bought this place because as well as being near my friends, I needed spare rooms for when the family descends – which is often,' she said as she showed us around what appeared to be the perfect country residence, with ancient flagstone tiles and wood panelling in the hall leading to a light sitting room with French doors opening onto a court-yard garden.

'I know the feeling,' said Jo. 'My lot moved away, then years later, they all came back.'

*

Seeing The Bonnets' homes and animals gave me an idea. Once Ally and Jo were settled back at the hotel where we were staying for the night, I went back with Ajay to talk to The Bonnets about their pets as friends. We could use their comments and enthusiasm about their cats and dogs as part of the programme about pets.

Overall, their living situation was inspirational and gave me food for thought. It was obvious that they all looked out for each other and lived full and happy lives. Maybe not yet, but sometime, Ally and Jo might be up for something similar. Like The Bonnets, it was clear that it wouldn't work if we lived under one roof, but several roofs in a location of our own choice, near a city, maybe . . .

Chapter Thirty

Sara

Present day, February

Back at the hotel, I called Lauren at Little Dog Productions. 'How's the search through the missing person's agencies going?' I asked.

'We've some news that might be a lead, we're not sure yet. The agency focused on family trees made by people looking into their DNA and have come up with a name. A David McDonnell.'

'Why might he be a lead?'

'Often when people have their DNA tested, they also compile a family tree to which they can add other relatives they know about who have died or who haven't had their DNA tested. The marvel of it all being on line now is that family links can easily be found. This David McDonnell was linked to the Blake family and the name Michelle Blake was on one of the family trees as a distant cousin. We have David's number. I was going to call him but Gary said it should be you.'

'OK. So what do you know?'

'Only that he's in Inverness. Will you call him?'

'What, now?'

'No time—'

'Like the present. Yes. And say what?'

'Ask if he knows anything.'

I took down the details then, when Lauren had hung up, I called the number she'd given me. The phone rang a couple of times, and then a male voice answered. 'Hello?'

'Hello. My name's Sara Meyers and I'm looking for David McDonnell.'

'This is he.' He sounded elderly.

'I got your name from a site where one can register to explore DNA . . .'

'Oh yes, the Ancestry one?'

'That's it. I hope you don't mind me calling.'

'Speak up, lass; I'm hard of hearing. Is it Lisa again?'

'Lisa? No. My name is Sara.'

'Oh, right, Sara. How can I help?'

'I'm looking for an old school friend called Michelle Blake and I believe you were related?'

'Ah, I canna help you there, lass. I did discover that we were related somewhere down the line, but I didn't know her or any of that clan. Lisa was looking for her, too.'

'Lisa?'

'Michelle's daughter.'

'*Daughter?*'

'Yes. I couldn't help her. I did the DNA test to see about my heritage, not to find anyone in particular like she did. She told me that she did the test in order to find her mother and my name came up as a distant relative. We're fifth cousins or something.'

'Daughter? Did you say daughter?'

'Aye. Michelle Blake's daughter.'

'So why didn't she know where her mother was?'

'You tell me. I've no idea. People lose touch. I didn't ask. I only told her that I hadn't known the Blake family. It was a branch of the family that we up in Scotland never met.'

'I don't suppose you have any contact details for her.'

'Now that I do. She asked me to take her email and number in case any other family members got in touch. None have – apart from Lisa. But you never know. The website for the DNA testing sends me names of distant relatives almost weekly, people all over the world. My son tells me it's becoming more and more the thing to do and he's been busy putting together the family tree which is where I believe he found the link to the Blake family. Just wait a moment and I'll get the number for Lisa.'

I was stunned. David came back to the phone a moment later and gave me an email, a phone number and an address in Camden Town. I wrote them down in a daze. 'Is there anything else you could tell me?'

'I told Lisa all I knew. It was an interesting test. Tells you about genetic ethnicity. I always thought we were Scottish all the way back but it seems we're a real mix.'

'I mean about the Blake family. Michelle had a sister too.'

'I know nothing about her. As I said, we're a separate clan, her name might be on the family tree but Lisa would never have found me if I hadn't been given the DNA kit for Christmas.'

'Is there anything else you can tell me about Lisa?'

'We had a good chat. She sounded a nice lass. She wanted to fly up and meet me but I said no point. I couldn't help her find her mother. It would have been a wasted journey, but she seemed eager to meet any relative.'

'Did she tell you anything about herself? Like how old she is?'

'She's in her forties, married, was a dancer before she had

children, now she works as a . . . oh, what was it? My memory's not what it used to be. Teacher, I think, or was it therapist? I can't remember. You'll have to ask her.'

'In her forties?' I sat down as the implications hit me. 'Er . . . David, please can I leave my number with you in case anyone else gets in touch with you?'

'Aye. I can add them to my collection,' he said then chuckled. 'My wife will be getting suspicious of me having my list of young ladies' numbers to call.'

I gave him my number, hung up the phone and went straight to Ally's room where she was having a cup of tea with Jo.

'Seems Mitch had a daughter called Lisa,' I said, and filled them in on my conversation with David. 'I've got her email address.'

'No! Wow,' said Jo. 'So she must know where Mitch is.'

'Ah . . . not necessarily. It doesn't sound like she does, anyway. She was trying to find her, that's why she got in touch with David McDonnell.'

'So what do you have?' asked Ally.

'Name and address. Lisa Wilson, about forty, lives in Camden Town. Oh my god, this is amazing. Remember when we went to Manchester and knocked on all the street doors, that distant relative we found, Eileen – she was going on about Mitch being pregnant. We thought she'd got her wires crossed, that it might have been Fi or someone else. Maybe she hadn't been confused after all. Seems Mitch did have a child. Shall I go to the address? Or email? Or phone?'

'I'd suggest email in the first instance,' said Ally. 'You don't know who she is or what the connection really is and we don't know why she did the DNA test. We don't want to scare her. Some people do it purely to find out about their heritage, not because they're looking for anyone in particular.'

'David did the test to find out about his heritage but, from what he told me, Lisa sounded as if she was looking for someone in particular, that person being Michelle.'

'But that's odd, isn't it?' said Jo. 'Not to know where your own mother is? Unless . . .'

I nodded. 'Exactly – unless she was adopted. She's in her forties.' I felt as if a blast of cold air had hit me. 'In that case, Mitch would have had her when she was around nineteen or twenty. No way, no. I would have known, surely?' My mind was reeling. 'Lauren said they're looking into the birth, death and marriage records too. If Mitch had Lisa in this country, they should be able to find her birth certificate, and that might give us some clues.'

'Now we're getting somewhere,' said Ally.

'Yes but . . . I can't believe Mitch would have had a baby and not told us,' said Jo.

'Me neither,' said Ally. 'We were her closest friends.'

'And if Lisa is forty then that means—' Jo said.

'Exactly, that Mitch had her *before* she went into the commune,' I said.

'No! I feel heartbroken and *guilty*,' said Jo. 'I wonder what the hell happened. Did we let her down? Too caught up with ourselves, busy busy with our own lives, university.'

'We were twenty, Jo,' said Ally. 'You're meant to be busy busy with your own life at that age, everything opening up in front of you. Don't beat yourself up. She could have told us. It was her choice. For some reason, she didn't.'

All of us were silent for a moment.

'Even those Bonnet ladies said that there were periods in their lives when they weren't in touch so much,' said Jo.

'I know,' I said, 'but do you think she tried to contact us, tell us? It's so long ago, but I seem to remember there were times when it felt as if we were missing each other's calls. It's not the sort of message you leave over the phone, like, hi, Mitch here, give me a call back and, by the way, I'm pregnant.'

Ally nodded. 'She'd call and I'd be out or I'd call and she'd be out.'

'Let's think. She moved to London to live with Fi,' said Jo. 'I wonder if that's when she had the baby.'

'I wonder who the father was,' said Ally. 'And when she met him. I can't believe she didn't tell us.'

'Maybe she tried to and we *did* speak in the first year, we did, we just didn't see much of her so she might have been pregnant one of the times we spoke on the phone,' I said.

'If she had told us, we would have been there for her, wouldn't we?' I asked, thinking about those brief phone calls. I couldn't now ignore the feeling that there was some subtext or unspoken message from Mitch that I'd missed.

'Maybe that's why she didn't come to my wedding,' said Jo, 'me being pregnant and her not having kept hers. God, there's so much we don't know.'

'Nor her about us,' said Ally. 'Don't forget, it works both ways.'

I smiled. 'Always the voice of reason, Ally.'

She shrugged. 'It hasn't always been easy for any of us. We've all had our rollercoaster ride. You with your divorce, Sara, Jo with Doug. We don't know the whole story about Mitch yet.'

'So let's find out,' said Jo. 'Sara, what do we do next?'

'Email Lisa and then we wait,' I said as I sat at my desk, opened my laptop and went to mail. 'Should I say we know you're looking for your mother?'

'No,' said Ally. 'Tell her our side and then see how she responds.'

I started typing:

Dear Lisa,

I hope you don't mind me contacting you but I am trying to find an old friend of mine called Michelle Blake. We were at school together, and I and two other friends who knew her, have been trying to find her. I managed to track down a relative, David McDonnell, through DNA records and, from talking to him, I believe you may have some connection to the Blake family. I wonder if you would mind getting in touch if you have any news of Mitch or her sister Fi's whereabouts. If you do, I would very much appreciate it,

With best regards,
Sara Meyers

I pressed send and off it went.

'There. Done. I didn't put that we think she is Michelle's daughter because you never know who is going to read the email.'

'Good call,' said Jo.

I left my laptop open and all of us kept glancing at it as Ally poured us a glass of wine. 'A watched laptop never pings, or whatever the saying is,' she said.

We didn't have to wait long. Half a glass of wine later, and my laptop pinged, alerting us that an email had come back. We gathered round to read.

Dear Sara,

!!!! Great to hear from you. Oh my god! I'm so glad you got in touch. I'd reached a dead end. Please can we meet? You must be wondering who I am or what my connection is to your friend. You may already know this but I was adopted at birth and Michelle Blake is the name on my birth certificate for my mother. My adopted parents gave me the birth certificate when

I was fourteen and I asked about my real parents. I do hope it is the same Michelle you knew, in which case I would love to meet you and your friends and hear whatever you can tell me about her. I have been searching for her but with no luck. Maybe we can share resources? Do you have photos of her? I am dying to see what she looks like and hear anything you can tell me about her.

    With best wishes, in anticipation,

    Lisa

We stared at each other in shock.

'Wow,' said Ally.

'Exactly,' said Jo. 'Wow.'

'As we suspected, she was adopted at birth,' I said.

'Maybe that musician guy was the father?' said Jo. 'He's the only boyfriend I can remember her talking about. Can anyone remember his name?'

'I can't,' said Ally. 'The band was . . . Rose something, no, Wild Rose.'

'Black Rose,' said Jo.

'I think he was Jack or John or maybe Jake,' I said. 'I could kick myself for not asking about him more at the time.'

'I wonder why Mitch gave Lisa up for adoption,' said Ally. 'Whatever the reason, it must have been painful. Maybe that's why she took the route she did, as some kind of escape.'

'Like I did after Charles left. I threw myself into the world of TV. As long as I was working, I didn't have time to think about it too much. It gave me a sense of purpose and belonging.'

'We all need that,' said Ally. 'And, in my own way, I did the same; not so much as an escape, but when I went into publishing, the people there became my family, my universe. Later, when I started in a literary agency, that was another small family and

I made it my business to get to know everyone in that world. I think we all need a sense of belonging.'

'And the Rainbow Children provided that for Mitch,' said Jo. 'I bet she was hurt after giving up her child.'

'In the meantime, we have two leads,' I said. 'Lisa and the band Black Rose. We can see if they're still around and if the guy she was with remained in contact at all.'

'He might not be the father,' said Jo. 'We don't know anything about Mitch's love life at that time, or he might be the father but Mitch never told him.'

'True,' said Ally, 'maybe Lisa could tell us. If Mitch's name was on her birth certificate, the name of the father might be on there too.'

'OK, let's check that first, then if it is the guy from the band, we can contact him,' I said.

'Why wait? We could at least google them now,' said Ally. 'Put Black Rose in search.'

'Good thinking.' I went to Google and typed in Black Rose. Hundreds of pages came up. 'Oh look, they have their own Wikipedia page.' I clicked on the link and up came the page. We read down, Jo and Ally peering over my shoulder.

'Oh no,' said Ally as we reached a paragraph about the founder members of the band.

'Jack Saunders,' I said. 'That was his name. I remember now.'

Jo read the page out loud. 'In 1973, Jack Saunders, original band member, was killed in a motorbike accident.'

We were all silent for a few moments. 'Do you think . . .' Jo started.

I nodded. 'I do. Poor Mitch. The dates add up, unless she had some other boyfriend around then, but I only remember her talking about the one in the band, Jack. She said something about getting us together to meet him, that was just after we all went to college, but then when we met in the summer, she didn't mention him as far as I recall.'

Ally nodded. 'I wonder if he knew Mitch was pregnant?'

'Or . . . if his death was the reason Mitch gave up her daughter,' said Ally.

I was stunned by the revelations, and sad. How could I not have known my friend had been going through so much, and why oh why had she kept it from us?

'Email Lisa again,' said Jo. 'Ask if there was a father's name on the birth certificate, then tell her we'd all like to come and meet her.'

'Will do,' I said, 'chances are, if she only had his name, that she doesn't know that he was in a band. In the meantime, let's have a good look through my old albums for photos of Mitch so that we can take some for her when we meet up.'

Another email pinged. 'Lisa again,' I said as I looked at the inbox. It was as if she was sitting at her laptop, as eager to find out about Mitch as we were. She'd written: My father's name: Jack Saunders. Musician. I know he's deceased. Did you know him too?

I wrote back: So sorry, none of us knew him, but we do know he was in a band called Black Rose. Let's meet soon. Sx

Chapter Thirty-One

Mitch

June 1975

Spring turned to summer as weeks and months passed by in the commune in a haze of early mornings, early nights interspersed with cooking, washing, ironing shirts, studying, meditating.

Life felt like one long camping trip with a big, happy family, and I'd made good friends: Rosie, Andrew and Tom Riley from The Seventh Star, who'd finally succumbed and moved into the commune. We talked about the Age of Aquarius and thought we were bringing it in with bells on. In the times when I needed space, I'd take myself off to the allotment and dig the vegetable patch.

Tom didn't last long. His love of marijuana, women and cheesecake won the day and he headed back out, but we stayed good friends. He went back to his flat in Notting Hill with an open invitation to hang out there if I wanted to get away.

Occasionally we'd have a visit from a travelling indigo sent to inspire us, keep us on the right track and teach us a new form of meditation.

'We are all prawns in the chess game of life,' said Aadir, an Indian indigo, which caused Rosie and me to do the silent shoulder-shake of laughter at the back of the room. It reminded me of being back in chapel with Ally, Jo and Sara.

One evening, Andrew came in and told me that there was a phone call for me. I went upstairs to the office. 'Mitch, got you at last.' It was my old friend Sara Meyers. 'Where are you?' she asked. 'Where have you been?'

'Me? Where have *you* been? I tried to get in touch a few times.'

'Fi said you're living in some kind of commune.'

'I am. How did you know I was here?'

'Fi gave me your number, she's still at the flat in Notting Hill. When can I see you? Are you ever back in Manchester? Or in the southwest?' Her words were slightly slurred, as if she was drunk.

'Not these days. You sound pissed.'

She laughed. 'I am a bit, celebrating a promotion, we opened a bottle of bubbly.' She chatted on, filling me in on the past years. She'd finished university, was living in Plymouth, got her first job as a researcher/runner at a TV station, was with a man called Tim who was doing his PhD and was madly in love. Her life and lifestyle seemed a million miles away from mine. 'What are the men there like?' she asked.

'Men? Sweet. Not your type – or mine.'

'Fi said you are all celibate? Why? Are you mad?'

'It makes things easier when there are so many of us living together. If someone wants to be with someone, they can always leave but, to be honest, the celibacy rule? If you saw the men here, you'd realize it's a blessing.'

Sara laughed. 'But . . . you're Mitch Blake, boy magnet. I can't see you living that way. I don't get it.'

'I love it. I feel part of something big.'

Sara went quiet on the other end of the phone. 'Mitch, I'm worried about you. You don't sound yourself.'

'You said that last time. You don't sound yourself either. Look, I'm fine, I really am. The world needs to change, needs peace. You ought to come and check it out, maybe even join yourself.'

'Me celibate? Not likely, thanks.'

'You don't have to live in the commune.'

'Not for me, Mitch. There are other ways of changing the world, all sorts of ways – writing, journalism – you don't have to live as you're doing and to miss out on relationships.'

'It's my choice, Sara . . . It sounds to me that all you think is important is finding a man. I doubt if that's going to change the world.'

'Hey, that's harsh, just because I haven't joined some evangelical group.'

'Is that what you think? That I've become evangelical?'

'Yeah, a bit.' There was an awkward silence for a few moments. 'Let's not quarrel. Will you stay in touch, Mitch? Write to me at least? Let me know how you're doing? I do care about you, you know. And if I come to London, I promise I'll look you up.'

I felt angry but took a deep breath. 'Yes, do, come and check us out. I'd love to tell you all about it. I promise I haven't become a religious maniac.'

Sara laughed but it felt hollow, and she didn't sound enthusiastic about coming to check out the movement. All the same, I gave her the address and assured her that I'd write. Or maybe I'd wait until she came to visit. But what would she make of it? Maybe I wouldn't show her round. Like Fi, I was pretty sure she would be appalled if she knew exactly how I was living, and I wasn't sure I wanted the judgement, the criticism. She also seemed so far away, part of a past I no longer belonged to. I put down the phone and went back down to my new housemates.

In the meantime, the group was expanding, more people wanting to be a part of it, and the few small communes that had been set up were full to bursting, so more were opening nationwide. I got my marching orders and was sent to Devon.

Chapter Thirty-Two

Ally

Present day, Febuary

Rebecca's party was well under way by the time, Sara, Jo and I arrived at the hotel where it was beng held. It looked as though we'd walked into a madhouse, with people dressed as vicars, priests, a couple of popes, a cardinal, a group of nuns. Then I spotted The Bonnets by the bar and burst out laughing. Apart from Katie who, true to her word, was dressed as a Hindu god with a blue face, the others were dressed in wigs and trashy outfits worthy of Hollywood divas. Gabrielle was wearing a long blonde wig and a leopard-skin dress, Jenny a red curly wig and a long sparkly silver dress. Bridget was in a pink wig and pink dress and Rebecca in a turquoise dress and black Cleopatra-style wig.

'Nice legs,' I said to Gabrielle, who was at the bar and was wearing the shortest dress. She did, too, toned and with great ankles.

'If you've got them, flaunt them,' she replied. 'Don't we look awful?' She handed me a glass from a waiter passing with a tray. 'Here, have a glass of bubbly, I have to go and change.'

I was about to ask why she was changing her costume when Rebecca came over and hugged me. 'Darling Ally. I heard about Michael. I am so sorry. How are you coping?'

I shrugged. 'Good and bad days.'

She hugged me again. 'I know.' She indicated The Bonnets. 'We've all been through it. It's hard.'

'It is.'

She indicated her friends again. 'If it hadn't been for this lot, I think I would have gone under. You must lean on your friends, let them help you. Of course there will be days when you want to hide away, but I remember Michael well from the times I met him. He wouldn't want you to be unhappy.'

'I know.'

'Life goes on whether we like it or not . . . I would imagine your house feels very quiet.'

'It does.'

'Make the changes you need to and try your best to embrace a new life. Fact: we're born alone, we die alone, and in between we're bloody lucky if we have someone to mooch along with. They will come and go, but it's not over yet for you, Ally. There will be happy times again.'

I laughed. Rebecca had always been one to speak her mind, and actually I didn't mind. I liked the fact that she spoke so directly instead of walking on eggshells like so many of my friends back at home. She was right. Like it or not, Michael had gone. I was still here. 'So . . . who are all these people?'

'People from the village, old friends, new friends, and these are two more Bonnets,' she said as two elderly nuns wearing scarlet lipstick came over. 'Lady Sew and Sew and Lady Burble, meet Ally.'

At that moment, there was a scuffle, and Bridget, Katie, Jenny and Gabrielle disappeared.

'Oh god,' said Rebecca. 'Here we go.'

'Here we go what?' I asked.

'You know the tradition? We all do a song for birthdays. God knows what they have lined up for me.'

A few minutes later, the lights dimmed and the opening chords of the 'Dance of the Sugar Plum Fairy' began to fill the room. Gabrielle came in first dressed as a fairy in a white tutu and tiara. She danced around like a professional ballerina, then stopped and indicated a door with a graceful arc of her right hand. The door opened and out came Katie (still with a blue face), Jenny and Bridget. They were dressed in pink tutus and were wearing wellies on their feet. They went into a comedy routine with Katie and Jenny dancing perfectly in time, Bridget missing every beat, turning when she wasn't supposed to and not turning when she was. Beside me, Rebecca guffawed with laughter.

At the end of the dance, they lined up and bowed to great applause from the gathered guests. One of the party went forward and offered a bouquet of flowers to Gabrielle, which she accepted and held, until Bridget whipped them away and the others began to fight over them as they made their exit.

'A triumph, darlings,' Rebecca called, then turned back to me. 'I wondered what they were going to come up with. Thank god there was no singing this time. They really sound dreadful when they do that, me included.'

Sara and Jo were chatting to some of the guests across the room and Rebecca was soon called away to talk to one of her friends. I was alone for a moment when I felt someone touch my arm. I turned to see that it was Lawrence.

'I thought you might be here,' I said.

'And Katie told me that you might be coming,' he said. 'I'm glad you made it. I know it's tempting to hide away after losing someone.'

I pointed over at Jo and Sara. 'I've been staying in London with friends.'

'Good, and you have an open invitation to come and stay with me, too, any time. I think it's important to stay connected.'

'Katie and Rebecca said the same. I will.'

Jo and Sara came over to join us and Lawrence drifted off to talk to someone else.

'So?' said Jo.

'So what?'

'Who's he? He's very handsome.'

'Stop it. I've known Lawrence for years. We're just good friends and you know I am not, nor ever will be, looking for a replacement for Michael.'

'I'll have him if you don't want him,' said Sara. 'I like a tall man, plus he still has hair—'

'And his own teeth,' said Ally.

Jo laughed. 'God, listen to us, we're like three fifteen-year-olds.'

'Not when we're discussing if a man has his teeth,' I said. 'And I can tell you Lawrence isn't looking for a replacement for his late wife either. And . . .'

'Yes?' chorused Jo and Sara.

'There's no chemistry either, never has been.'

'I'm definitely having him then,' said Sara.

'Not if I get in there first,' said Jo.

'Oh, grow up, the pair of you,' I said, but as I watched Lawrence chatting away to one of the guests, I could see that he'd have appeal. He had an old-fashioned elegance about him and I thought it was a shame he wasn't my type. He was alone, I was alone, but no, it was too soon to even consider such things, not just with him, but with anyone – not now, not ever.

Chapter Thirty-Three

Sara

Present day, Febuary

Back in London the day after Rebecca's party, we arranged to meet Lisa in a café just off Camden High Street. As we made our way there in the taxi, I got a call from Gary at Little Dog Productions.

'I hear you're going to meet Mitch's daughter. I could send Ajay down,' he said.

'No way, we'd scare her off,' I said. 'Let Ally, Jo and me go in the first instance, then if she agrees to being filmed at a later date, maybe. We'll do this part away from the cameras.'

I could almost hear Gary pouting at the other end of the phone. 'Could be TV gold,' he said.

'Tough,' I replied.

*

When we reached Camden, we got out of the taxi and made our way over to the café near the bridge. Just as we got there, I noticed a slender, graceful-looking woman on the other side of the road. She had dark hair piled loosely at the back of her head and was dressed in Indian clothes in reds and pinks. I knew immediately she was Mitch's daughter and my eyes welled up. She saw us, waved and came over.

'Are you Sara, Ally and Jo?' she asked.

'We are, and you must be Lisa,' said Jo and embraced her. 'How did you know it was us?'

'Three of you, about the right age and . . .' She turned to me, 'I recognize you from the TV, Sara.'

Jo introduced herself and Ally and we went inside the café, got seated and ordered coffees.

Lisa looked nervous. 'I didn't sleep at all last night. I can't tell you how long I've waited to find someone who . . . you're the first people I've met who knew my mother so . . . What was she like? Do I look like her? Were you around when she was pregnant with me? Do you know what happened?'

Ally smiled. 'We brought photos. Yes, you definitely have a look of her around the eyes, and her lovely heart-shaped face, though she was blonde. And what was she like? She was great, one of life's forces.'

I got the envelope out of my bag and handed the photos over to Lisa. She took them, took a deep breath, then studied each one carefully. When she came to one of the four of us taken at school, leaning against the wall, she gasped, her eyes filled with tears and she took a deep breath. Jo reached over and squeezed her hand.

'I don't need to ask which one she is,' said Lisa, as she reached into her bag, got out her phone, opened it and scrolled through her photos. She held up the screen to show us one of a pretty blonde girl pouting at the camera; she had a ring through her nose and was dressed in short denim cut-offs showing off long slim legs. Next to her was a sweet-looking boy with a wide grin. 'My children, Liam and Scarlet. Liam's twelve, Scarlet's sixteen. Seeing that picture of you all, Michelle as she was then—'

'Scarlet's the spitting image of her,' said Jo.

'Totally,' I said as I looked at the picture.

Lisa kept looking from her phone to the photo of her daughter. 'It's amazing. This is amazing. I'd begun to think I'd never . . . So what happened?' She took a gulp of air and looked as though she was about to cry. 'Do . . . do you know why she gave me up for adoption? Do you know where she is?'

Jo shook her head. 'No to both questions. I am so sorry, we don't. We think she must have got pregnant just after we three went to university and left Manchester. Why she didn't tell us, we have no idea.'

'It really is a mystery,' I said, 'we were close but . . . we did lose touch—'

'With each other as well as Mitch,' said Ally. 'It wasn't a conscious thing, just life in our twenties took over.'

'Mitch,' said Lisa. 'You call her Mitch. So – if you all lost touch, how come you three are here with each other now but you don't know where my mother is?'

'Over the years,' I said, 'we kept in touch with each other's news, although we lived in different parts of the country. We met up occasionally but Mitch . . . she disappeared completely in our mid-twenties. We think she must have gone abroad at some point. We've been trying to find her.'

'But why now? Why try and find her now?' Lisa asked.

I quickly filled Lisa in on the concept of the programme I was working on. 'So you see, it's all about looking for long-lost friends and it seemed like the perfect opportunity to try and find Mitch – actually, not only that, I got to a point in my life where I was reviewing so many things, friendships in particular, and I realized I missed my dearest oldest friends, and that got me thinking. I contacted Jo and Ally but it also gave me the idea for the programme.'

'But now more than ever,' said Jo, 'having found you, we must track Mitch down.'

'When exactly did you last see her?' Lisa asked.

'In the summer after our first year at university,' said Jo.

'She went to university?' asked Lisa.

'No, sorry, we did, at least us three. Mitch put it off for a year . . .' Ally filled her in on what we knew, ending with what we knew of Mitch's involvement with the Rainbow Children.

'I've never heard of them. Were they a cult?' Lisa asked.

'Not exactly,' said Jo, 'at least I don't think so, more like a positive-thinking group.'

'Cult,' said Ally. 'She became evangelical for a while.' She shrugged her shoulders. 'Sorry, but true. On the occasions we did contact her, she tried to enlist us too. The way of life she chose was close to monastic.'

'How long was she involved?'

'That we don't know,' Jo replied. 'A good few years.'

Lisa stared back down at the photos we had brought. 'What was she like? As a person?'

'Mischievous, always one step ahead of the rest of us,' said Jo.

'Endlessly curious,' said Ally.

'Stunning looking,' I said. 'The coolest girl in school.'

'Scarlet is too,' said Lisa. 'She's going to break a few hearts.'

'So did Mitch. She had her pick of the boys,' said Ally.

'What about you, Lisa?' Jo asked. 'Were you happy? Placed with a good family?'

'I was, yes,' said Lisa. 'I couldn't have asked for better. I have one sibling, a brother, older than me. He wasn't adopted but, after he was born, my mum – that is, my adopted mum – was told she couldn't have more children. She wanted more, which is why they took the adoption route.'

'Are your adoptive parents still alive?' I asked.

'They are,' said Lisa, 'here in London, and they are completely supportive and understanding of me looking for my birth mother. When I was about fourteen, they told me that I was adopted. I was surprised, but I should have known. I don't look anything like the rest of my family.'

'When did you start looking?' I asked.

'Not for a long time after Mum and Dad told me about the adoption. It rocked my world at the time, I can tell you, finding out that I wasn't who I thought I was. At first I felt angry with Michelle, Mitch, angry that she'd given me away. I thought how could she do that? Just discard me? Because of that anger, I didn't want to know, I didn't even want to look at my birth certificate, which my parents said I could see any time I wanted. I didn't want to. I felt if I read it, it would make it real, and only make me feel more at sea. Also, I didn't want to upset my adoptive parents. I adore them. They couldn't have been more loving, and I didn't want them to feel that they had been lacking in any way. But as the years went on, it niggled: who were my physical parents? I knew I could have started to look for them when I turned eighteen but part of me was afraid – what if I found out something terrible? What if I didn't like them? What if they were a pair of losers? An unwanted pregnancy and child. What if I was the result of a one-night stand or even worse . . . I let it go, it wasn't as though I was desperate to find out because I had plenty going on in my life.

'The turning point came later, much later, when I had children of my own, Scarlet and Liam, and I could see myself and my husband in them. I began to wonder again. Do I look like my parents? What was their story? I became addicted to that programme on TV, you know the one, *Long Lost Families*, and then it became an obsession, I *had* to find them. I asked my adopted parents for my birth certificate and it named both parents. My father Jack was easy to trace and I soon found out that he was deceased. Did any of you meet him?'

We all shook our heads. 'We didn't, and as Mitch didn't mention him after a while, we, or at least I, assumed that they'd broken up.'

'We had no idea that he'd been killed until we saw it on Wikipedia,' said Ally.

'Did you know he played in a band?' I asked.

Lisa nodded. 'Oh yes. Black Rose. I've got all their music and history and some images of him from the Net and old music magazines. I even met one of the former band members, guy named Lou. He told me all about my dad. He didn't know much about my mother, said he only met her once or twice. My son Liam's very musical, so I wonder if he got that from his grandfather. I suppose Michelle gave me my second name Rose in memory of Jack and the band Black Rose.'

'Lisa Rose,' said Ally.

'Oh no,' said Lisa. 'The name on my birth certificate was Sara Rose. My adopted parents named me Lisa.'

'Oh . . .' I let out a soft moan as the implication hit me and felt sudden tears prick the back of my eyes.

'You OK?' Jo asked.

I nodded. 'I . . . Remember? Mitch and I promised that if we ever had girls, I'd name mine after her and she'd name hers after me. She kept that promise and I . . . knew nothing about it. I just . . . I don't understand.'

Jo put her hand over mine. 'I *do* remember.'

'From the research I did,' Lisa said, 'I gathered that Jack'd died about seven months before I was born.'

'*Before* you were born?' asked Jo. '*No*. We didn't know that either. So—'

'This is all a lot to take in,' said Ally as she took a deep breath.

'I know. Maybe that's why she gave me away,' said Lisa. 'Couldn't face being a single mother. Who knows? I've imagined every scenario under the sun. After hearing of his death, maybe she couldn't manage? Went into a decline and got depressed? But . . . if you were so close, how come none of you knew she was pregnant?'

'That's exactly what we've been asking ourselves over and over since we discovered she'd had you,' said Jo.

'I seem to remember, when she first mentioned him, she was really head over heels,' said Ally, 'and we made her promise to bring him to meet us next time we were in Manchester.'

'But it never happened,' I said. 'We thought nothing of it because we all dated men for a short while in those years – we were young, it wasn't time for settling down. I assumed Mitch moved on from Jack. The next thing we heard, Mitch was in London, living with her sister, working in a hippie shop. That was about the time she got involved with this group, the Rainbow Children and, to be honest, that's all she ever talked about.'

'And that's the last you heard from her?'

'Not exactly,' I said. 'There were phone calls after she'd moved in the commune—'

'And I visited her once,' said Ally, 'but she'd changed. It wasn't a comfortable meeting. I guess we thought it was a phase, and that when she came through it, she'd be in touch again . . .'

'And I got married young, had children, and that took over,' said Jo.

'To begin with, I think I was vaguely aware of where she was,' said Ally, 'just as I vaguely knew where Sara and Jo were.'

'London, then Devon, then I seem to remember her saying she was moving back to London, and after that, nothing,' I said.

'And she's not on Facebook or social media now,' said Jo. 'We don't know where to go next.'

'Has she got other family? Siblings?'

'One sister, Fi. We've been trying to track her down too. We do know that her parents are dead. They moved out to New Zealand in the 1970s.'

'What were they like?' Lisa asked.

I glanced at Ally and Jo. 'She . . . er . . . wasn't close to her dad—'

'He was a miserable old sod,' said Jo, and Lisa laughed. 'He was critical and scary. We rarely used to hang out at her house because there was always an atmosphere.'

'Her mum was sweet enough,' said Ally, 'but very much in her husband's shadow.'

'And her sister? Was she close to her?'

'Not really,' I said. 'They were like chalk and cheese. Mitch was such a bright spark; her sister was intense, political—'

'Not a barrel of laughs,' said Jo.

'I'd love to see photos of them too,' said Lisa. 'Do you have any that were maybe taken at her house that have her family in them?'

I shook my head. 'We don't, but my TV production company have got a couple of agencies working on looking for Mitch. They claim to be able to find anyone anywhere in the world, so maybe they will trace Fi.'

'What school did you go to?' asked Lisa.

'St Mary's Convent in Manchester,' said Jo.

'Have you looked on Facebook for your old school page?'

'We have. No joy,' said Jo. 'It's a sixth-form college now and all the posts are from recent pupils.'

'I know what else you could do,' said Lisa, 'it's obvious. If your last point of contact was this group, the Rainbow Children, you need to track them down. If my mother was involved for as long as you say, she was bound to have made friends there. Maybe some of them are still around. Have you looked?'

'No. We haven't. Why didn't I think of that?' I said. 'Lisa, you're brilliant. We're not very good sleuths, are we?'

'The Rainbow Children may have a website,' said Jo, 'although I don't think they exist as a group any more. I haven't heard anything about them for years, decades.'

'Let's google Rainbow Children, see what we can find,' I said.

On cue, we all bent down and pulled our phones out of our bags.

Jo was the fastest. 'There are lots of pages about the Rainbow Children,' she said a moment later.

'Try Wikipedia first,' I said.

Jo did as instructed. 'Got it.' Four heads bent over so we could all see.

The Rainbow Children. A movement started in 1971 in San Francisco by John Reed, Robert Sanders, Debra King and Maya Hayes, inspired by the teachings of Guru Sadhu Devanagari. Dissolved 1977.
- Commune members lived a monastic lifestyle.
- Community members lived a normal life and supported the movement.

The movement expanded globally in the 1970s and ended when the founders closed all the communes and disbanded what was left of the movement in 1977. Robert and Debra now run a lifestyle coaching retreat in California. John made his fortune when he developed a meditation app called Peace. Maya died in 1984 after a short illness. Guru Sadhu Devanagari died in 1978.

Surviving members of the group went on to found Rainbow Foods store, which changed its name to Harvest in the 1980s.

'So it was dissolved in 1977,' I said. 'That's about the time we lost track of her.'

'Wow,' said Jo. 'So it is no more.'

'Apart from Harvest foods,' I said. 'I know the shop well; they took over the premises where The Seventh Star used to be.'

'Maybe there are some of the old followers there?'

'Worth a try, but we're talking forty years ago. I often go there to buy bread and most of the staff are in their twenties.'

'Maybe there's a link for old members on the page for the Rainbow Children?' said Ally. 'There often is for these types of groups, those who want to stay in touch, share memories.'

Jo scrolled down. 'You're right. There's a heading saying "Members".' She read the page. 'There are a few links here. If there are any contact details for them, maybe one of them could tell us what became of Mitch. I'll do some more research when we get home.'

'Put Rainbow Children into search and click on images,' said Ally.

Jo did as instructed, and we all huddled together to look. Jo pointed at a photo of four hippie types that was repeated many times on the page. 'They were the Americans who founded the whole movement.'

'What were they hoping to achieve?' asked Lisa.

'Promoting a more caring world,' said Jo, as she continued to scroll through the pages, 'that's what I understood, anyway.'

'Sounds cool,' said Lisa.

'Stop!' said Ally, and pointed at the screen. 'There, that group there. I'm sure that's Mitch.'

'Zoom in,' I said.

A photo showed a group of about fifteen people, some standing, some sitting, all beaming at the camera. Underneath it said: Indigo Group, 1976.

'Indigo?' asked Lisa. 'What was an indigo again? It said something about them on Wikipedia.'

'They were the travelling teachers,' said Jo. 'I remember Mitch telling me about them. They needed them because there were only four of the founders and they couldn't get around everywhere as the movement grew. It was before FaceTime and Skype and all the global links we have now. Some of the followers who'd been around a while were trained to pass on the teachings and they went around from place to place.'

'Like sales reps,' said Lisa.

'Sort of, I guess. Looks like Mitch became one,' said Ally.

'Or maybe she was just photographed with them,' I said. 'I can't see Mitch becoming one of them; they really were like travelling monks, from what I remember her saying about them. I reckon she just happened to be in the photo.'

'She looks happy there,' I said.

'I wonder if she was,' said Jo, 'or if she ever had times when she wished she'd gone a different route.'

'Let's get to the office and print out the photo,' I said, 'then if we can find an ex-member, we have a visual as well as a name to jog their memory. Mitch was involved from the beginning, so we're bound to find someone who knew her. This is brilliant, Lisa. At last, we're getting somewhere.'

Chapter Thirty-Four

Sara

Present day, February

Ally, Jo and I set off for the Little Dog Productions office to see if Lauren had any news for us and to update Gary on the latest. I could see it the moment he and Jo set eyes on each other through the glass partition in his office. Ding-dong. Chemistry.

'Give me five minutes,' I said. 'I just need to talk to Gary a moment.'

Jo and Ally sat on chairs in the reception area as I went into Gary's office.

'*Who* is that gorgeous woman?' he asked as I'd shut the door.

'The taller or smaller?'

'Taller. Looks like an exotic goddess.'

'That's Jo. She's my old school friend, I told you about her. I'll introduce you.'

I beckoned Jo to come into Gary's office and, when she did, he blushed and looked at his shoes, looking every bit the love-smitten teenager.

I offered to make coffees, and as Ally and I busied ourselves in the small kitchen at the back, I could hear Gary in his office roaring with laughter. When we went back in, Jo was regaling him with stories about her livestock and tales of Jonathan Livingston Chicken (after Jonathan Livingston Seagull), who was always escaping and how he'd ride on Jo's shoulder back to the coop. And Rambo the smiley-faced sheep who'd follow her around like a dog. 'They're spoilt, they have a sheep shed,' Jo said, 'a field to themselves, Wi-Fi with Netflix. *Shaun the Sheep* is their favourite movie.' For a moment it looked as if Gary believed her about the Wi-Fi, but then he cracked up laughing.

'We must feature Jo and some of her menagerie in the programme about animal friends,' he said when Jo had nipped out to use the cloakroom. 'Sounds like she's pals with all her animals.'

'That's Jo.'

'Is she single?' asked Gary.

'She is.'

'Do you think she'd have dinner with me?'

'What are we, Gary? Fourteen? Ask her yourself.'

'Out of practice. Can't you ask for me?'

'I think she'd have dinner with you.'

He grinned. 'Seriously? Excellent.'

'And make sure you tell her how gorgeous she is.'

'I will. She is. In the meantime, I hear you have a lead on finding your friend.'

'We do. That's why we came into the office, to do a bit of research and printing out.'

Gary left us to it for the rest of the afternoon. The link that the Wikipedia page had provided for old members of the Rainbow Children led to further links. One had a phone number that I tried immediately.

'Hello,' I said, 'I got your number from Wikipedia. I'm looking for previous members of a group called the Rainbow Children.'

'Can't help you,' said the voice on the other end. 'We're a life insurance company.'

The next number led to a dull tone telling us that the number was no longer in service.

'What about the food chain? What was it called?' Ally asked.

Jo checked the page again. 'Rainbow Foods then became . . . what was it Sara?'

'Harvest. It's just down the road from where I live, about a ten-minute walk but, as I said, all the staff are kids.'

'Try phoning,' said Ally. 'Ask who the founding members were and if any of them are still around. You never know.'

'Good idea,' said Jo, and googled for the phone number. 'Got it,' she said a few minutes later.

'Put it on speaker,' said Ally, as Jo punched in the number and a moment later, a woman answered.

'Hi. I'm looking to track down an old friend and believe one of your founder members there might know her or someone who knows her. Is there anyone who works there who was involved in the Rainbow Children, a group who were around in the—'

'Yeah. I know who they were,' said the woman. 'You need to speak to Tom Riley.'

'Is he there?'

'Not often these days, and he's on holiday in Goa at the moment.'

'When will he be back?'

'Next week some time, I think.'

'Can I leave a message?'

'You could. He's pretty hopeless at returning calls, so I suggest you come in and try and catch him. What's the name of the friend you're tracking?'

'Michelle, Mitch Blake.'

'Nah. Don't know her.'

'Is there anyone else there who was involved with the Rainbow Children.'

'Nah. Don't think so. Only Tom.'

'So near but so far,' said Jo after I'd switched off the phone.

'At least we've got a lead,' said Ally. 'We just have to wait.'

'So what's next?'

'Meeting Ajay, then out onto the street to further our research into what makes a friend,' I said. 'This time we'll be asking the public.'

*

Half an hour later, we'd met up with Ajay and were busy filming sound bites on Ladbroke Grove. Some people were happy to be filmed, others shied away from the camera.

'Do you have any rules for your friendships?' I asked a white-haired elderly lady who was waiting at a bus stop.

'Stay in touch,' said one old lady. 'And if you choose your friends wisely, they'll last a lifetime.'

'Don't talk about your friends behind their backs,' said a teenage girl who was standing behind her. 'It always gets back to them.'

'Keep your mates' secrets. No exceptions,' said her friend.

'Be kind and show your appreciation,' said a lady on her way into the chemist.

'Accept your mates for who they are, even if they're mad,' said a teenage boy.

'Be loyal and don't post rubbish pictures of them on

Instagram,' said another teenage girl, 'or they might do the same with crap photos of you.'

'Tell your friends you love them,' said another elderly lady. 'It can cheer them up no end. We all need a bit of love in our lives.'

I turned the camera on Jo. 'Be a friend to yourself,' she said.

I looked over at Ally. 'Be yourself with real friends,' said Ally. 'And what about you, Sara?'

'Er . . . listen as well as talk,' I said, and Jo and Ally laughed. Cheeky sods.

We got some good stuff, which could be edited to use interspersed throughout the series as well as added to my list of rules for friendship. *All in all, a good day*, I thought when we finally headed home.

Chapter Thirty-Five

Mitch

Summer 1975

On the journey down to Devon, I discovered that the latest in the Rainbow expansion was to be a school. Many parents involved in the movement felt that state schools didn't always provide what they wanted for their offspring. These were children of the golden age and their parents wanted their education to reflect that.

A friendly bearded man called Derek drove me from London to the southwest.

'And what's my role to be?' I asked.

'Domestic cocoordinator,' he replied.

'Cooking?'

He laughed. 'More than that, a *lot* more than that. There are about forty people living in the area where the school's to be. Three different groups and no one to oversee them.'

My alarm bells began to ring. 'Why are there three different groups?'

'The people who want to live the commune life, then there's

the teachers and their families and, lastly, the others who work the land.'

'So where do they all live?'

'At the moment, some inside, others are in caravans on the site and some are in the outbuildings. Problem is, there's one big kitchen area but everyone is preparing their food and eating separately. No one's sure of anyone's role or whose food is whose or when they can get in to cook. It's a mess, so they need someone to pull it all together. That will be you.'

I felt a rush of panic. I could cook but organize forty people? I wasn't sure I was up to the task. However, my anxiety soon lifted as the scenery began to change. Ahead, I could see miles of coastline stretching in front of us, the sun sparkling on the sea and I felt my spirits rise despite my apprehension.

Derek took a turn off the main road, drove up a narrow lane, turned right through an open gate and came to a stop outside a grey brick farmhouse on top of a hill. 'Home sweet home,' he said as we got out of the car. 'This is Hazelmere House.' I looked around. The views were stunning. At the bottom of the hill, I could see a bay surrounded by dense woodland; nestling on the shore was a village with rows of cottages painted ochre, blue and pink. I breathed in the fresh air. 'I feel like I've landed in heaven,' I said.

Derek grimaced. 'Best wait until you've seen the set-up before you make claims like that.'

A spindly man with glasses and thinning hair came forward to meet me. He introduced himself as Geoffrey Brown, the headmaster.

'Thank God. I'm *so* pleased you're here,' he said as Derek got back into his car and drove off. 'Come on, put your bags down and let's show you round, then you can get started. The building has two floors and a loft area.'

As I followed him inside, I noted the exposed brick walls everywhere and overhead beams. 'On the first floor are the teachers' rooms and classrooms and this is my office,' Geoffrey continued as he opened a door into a large sunny space with a study which led into a double bedroom and bathroom.

'Very nice,' I commented. I was eager to see where I'd be staying. If the girls' room was anything like this, it would be wonderful.

He looked pleased. 'Isn't it?'

'And where are the people who opted for the commune life to sleep? Maybe I could leave my bag there.'

'Ah . . . There aren't many of you and one left yesterday. The men, Bruce and Jerry, have opted to live in one of the outbuildings. I'll show you where the women are.' He led me to the back of the building where he opened a door into a corridor that led to a bathroom. 'This is where the women will be. There are only four of you, so we've put you in here.'

'What? I . . . but this is a corridor?' No windows, no natural light, no drawers or cupboards, just a hard floor and bare walls and a pile of sleeping bags rolled and stashed in the corner.

Geoffrey looked uncomfortable. 'Only in the daytime. No one comes through at night apart . . . er to get to the bathroom,' he said as he pointed to the stairs, 'and there's a couple upstairs in the loft. I . . . er, there was nowhere else to put you.'

'But . . .' I was shocked, lost for words, part of me wanted to laugh, say, 'you are joking, right? Now show me where I'm really to sleep.' But Geoffrey wasn't laughing and was moving on. I followed him, wondering how to deal with him. I was about to object but then held back. Perhaps this was part of the mess that I'd been sent to sort out. I'd hold my tongue until I got a better idea of the lay of the land and then I'd begin to make changes.

'I'll take you to what will be your domain,' said Geoffrey as we left the corridor and headed for a stone stairway, 'it's the barn area downstairs which serves as a kitchen, dining room and laundry.'

'I was told that there are forty people here – where do they all sleep?'

'Some of the teachers have found places to rent in the village down by the bay. My wife and I have to be on site, plus a couple of teachers and the women, like yourself, who want to live the commune lifestyle. And there's Hugh, he's our handyman, he and his girlfriend are up in the loft. He does his own thing.'

We reached the lower level, where Geoffrey opened a door into a large barn full of wooden tables and chairs on the right and an open kitchen area with a large fridge and two stoves on the left. The area was full of people, many who looked harassed as they tried to prepare food or to quieten squealing children. Everyone appeared to be in everyone else's way.

'As you can see, we share the kitchen and dining facilities, which is why you're here. So . . . yes, I'll leave you to it.' He gently pushed me forward then disappeared. I stood there looking around. A few people gave me a cursory glance but no one took much notice of me. They were all immersed in their individual tasks, chopping, feeding, frying, eating, but no system or method to the chaos.

I realized I was shattered after the travelling so I made my way up to my new luxury guest quarters. I entered the corridor, rolled out my sleeping bag and made myself as comfortable as I could.

A moment later, a big bear of a man with shoulder-length hair and a beard came into the corridor. 'Oops, sorry, I didn't realize anyone was here,' he said, although he made no move to leave.

'I'm Mitch. Just arrived.'

'Oh yes. Hi. Welcome. I'm Hugh. I live upstairs.' He held out his hand for me to shake. 'Sorry about having to go through your room, but there's no other way up to the loft.'

'Maybe you could knock on the door then. Just in case anyone's changing.'

'Sure. Sorry, though most of the girls change in the bathroom.'

I looked around. 'Yes, I can understand why they'd do that. So what do you do here?'

'Whatever's needed. Grow vegetables so that the school can become self-sufficient, any DIY around the place. Let me know what you need and I'll do my best to keep the kitchen supplied.' He seemed friendly enough and I found myself warming to him.

A moment later, the door opened again, and in came a stunning Scandinavian-looking blonde girl. 'This is Minna,' said Hugh as he put his arm around her. 'She looks after the office here as well as . . . other things.' He grinned. Minna gave me a smile then disappeared up the stairs to the loft.

'Bit shy,' said Hugh as he went to follow her. 'So, yeah, let me know if you need anything, and don't let the bastards grind you down, especially that tosser headmaster.'

I grinned back at him. I'd found a friend. I knelt back down on the floor and got into my sleeping bag. I had just fallen into a doze when the other girls began to arrive. I pretended to be asleep and watched through half-closed eyes so I could check them out.

As I settled back down to try and sleep, I became aware of sounds coming from the loft above, thumps, creaks and moans. 'Oh god, Hugh, ohhhhh . . .'

Geoffrey, the headmaster had said that Hugh did his own

thing. From Minna's groans, it sounded as though he did it quite well. I made a note to get some earplugs.

*

The following day, I was thrown into the daily life at the farm. Slowly I got to know the individuals among the mass of anonymous faces, and I didn't have time to be unhappy or alone because there was so much to do – an endless round of shopping, cleaning, cooking and washing up.

One afternoon, I was called to the office by Minna.

'Phone for you,' she said as she handed me the receiver then made herself scarce.

It was Sara Meyers. 'Mitch, I'm in London, but you've gone again. I've been into that shop where you used to work and someone there, Lesley I think her name was, said you're in Devon now. You do get around. Listen, I've been in touch with Jo and Ally and we want to come and visit. It's been way too long. Road trip. What do you say? Is there a beach nearby? We could have a picnic, stay in a B and B.'

I felt a rush of panic. No way could they come. They'd want to see where I slept, where I lived. I could just imagine their faces when they saw I was sleeping on a wooden floor in a corridor. And when they saw me. I hadn't had a decent haircut in ages, hardly thought about what I wore to do my work in. It would be a disaster. I wasn't ready. They'd see me as an unpaid servant, which I was, dressed like a bag lady in bright rainbow colours. I felt torn. Part of me wanted to see them. Should I risk their disapproval?

'Mitch, are you still there?'

'Yes, yes, but don't come here.'

'Why not? I'm dying to see where you are and I love Devon. We have so much catching up to do.'

'Yes, but the thing is, I'm not staying here long. Er . . . probably returning to London any day now,' I lied. 'Everything's up in the air at the moment. Can I let you know?'

'Sure.' Sara sounded hurt but we chatted generally for a while and I did my best to enthuse about the school idea. She didn't sound impressed and filled me in about her work and what Ally and Jo were doing. Ally had got a job to start in September in a publishing house, Jo was temporarily back in Manchester. I felt a moment of confusion. Part of me missed them, part of me felt I'd moved on.

'Mitch, we really would love to see you,' said Sara. 'Please let us know where you are. Friends for life, remember? We've all been a bit crap at it, but we can change that.'

'Sure, course,' I said.

'And between us, I think Jo's going to be getting married soon, within a year I'm guessing. You know she'll want us all as bridesmaids.'

I smiled. 'That was always the plan, wasn't it? We'd be each other's?'

'I thought we could combine the trip with a sort of hen night or weekend. What do you say? The Fab Four back together.'

'Sounds a plan.'

'I know. Overdue. So stay in touch, OK?'

'I will, I promise.'

*

Jo called a week later.

'Mitch, is that you?'

'It is. I've just been thinking about you.'

'Me too, about you. God, you're hard to track down. I've called a million numbers, then Sara told me I'd find you here. Guess what? I'm pregnant! I know. Up the duff. Would be me, wouldn't it? Predictable to the end, but Doug, he's the father, he's asked me to marry him and my parents are being great . . . God, so much to tell you. Mitch, you there? Say something.'

'I . . .'

'Obviously I want my friends to be bridesmaids, you, Ally and Sara – I think Sara may have mentioned it to you. They've said yes. Will you? Please say you will? Remember how we all talked about it in school? How we'd all be each other's bridesmaids? Will you come? It's in about six weeks – better do it before I have to waddle up the aisle like a big fat whale in a wedding dress. It's all planned. It wouldn't be the same without you and I know I haven't been in touch and I'm sorry about that but this is something I really want to share with you all.'

'Of course I'll come, Jo,' I said, though my mind was already presenting negatives. How would I get there? I had no money. Where would I stay?

'Brilliant. You've made my day. Write this down, hold on a sec.' The line went quiet, then she returned and gave me the date and an address of a church up near Manchester. 'Call me in a few days because we need to sort out dresses and so on. I'm so *so* happy you're coming.'

'Me too. I've got to go, Jo, I'm manning the office and the other line's going,' I lied, 'but I promise, I'll be there.'

'Can't wait. We have so much to catch up on.'

'We do.'

I stared out of the window. Jo's news had hit me like a thunderbolt. She was pregnant, about to be married, everything I'd hoped would have happened to me with Jack. I decided I couldn't face her or Ally or Sara. Neither could I summon the courage to call and say I wouldn't be there, hear the disappointment in her voice. I felt ashamed. I was going to let her down. If she knew the whole story, she might have understood, but it was too late to tell her and I couldn't cast a shadow over her happiness with my tale of woe. She'd always been so soft-hearted; she'd have wept for me and I couldn't do that to her at the happiest time of her life. No. Best I stayed away, I convinced myself, kept my story buried. All the same I felt guilty as hell. I sent a card to the address she'd given me, apologizing but explaining that I couldn't get away at present, nor for the coming weeks. I knew it was a pathetic excuse.

*

As the weeks went on, there was little time to dwell on Jo or missing her wedding and, after a month, Hazelmere House was unrecognizable. I'd created order out of chaos and there was some satisfaction in that. I'd saved the day and discovered I had a skill. I was a born organizer. Who'd have guessed it. Once my plans had all been set in motion, no one had too much to do or too little.

But the accommodation was still a problem, the commune life no longer provided the escape it had back in London and I began to feel an overwhelming sense of loneliness. I missed the atmosphere of inspiration in London, and I missed my friends there. It felt like all work and no play where I was. For the first time, I had a chance to think about all I'd given up and realized that I missed my home comforts. I wanted a bed to sleep on, not a floor with no mattress. I wanted a lie-in, a decent cup of coffee and some less worthy company. The longing for a home became a physical ache in the pit of my stomach. But where was home? I didn't have one. Maybe now would be a good time to leave and start a new life, I told myself, still supporting the Rainbow Children but not living in the commune.

Making plans to leave filled me with hope and a sense of relief but then came a call from Andrew . . .

'We need you here, Mitch,' he said. 'As you know, the movement is expanding so we need a central office. I'm setting it up and getting the gang back together. Rosie's already here. Pack your bags and get up here.'

I found out later that the school at Hazelmere House never did open. The teachers couldn't decide on policy and, in the end, most of them left disillusioned and disappointed. Some left to take jobs in the nearby villages, and the farmhouse was taken over by Hugh and Minna, who went on to run it as a very successful B & B.

Chapter Thirty-Six

Sara

Present day, March

A week later, I called Harvest again and, happily, we heard that Tom Riley was not only home from his holiday, he was at the shop that very day. Without wasting any time, Ally, Jo and I headed along to the food emporium. It was a vast high-ceilinged place selling fresh and packaged food, the accent being on local and organic.

Ally went over to the nearest counter and spoke to the young man with a goatee beard who was serving there. 'Please could you tell us where we might find Tom?'

The man jerked a thumb towards the back of the store. 'He's in the office, past the bread counter, right-hand corner.'

We made our way through, found the office and knocked on the door.

'Come,' said a voice.

I opened the door. Inside was a tiny office crammed full of shelves laden with files, books and paper. An attractive older man with a mane of grey hair wearing a Mexican shirt and jeans was sitting behind a desk.

His face lit up when he saw me and he stood up. 'Sara Meyers, well I never. I've seen you on the telly. I loved the series you did on health spas last year. I saw every one. How can I help?'

Jo stepped forward. 'I'm Jo and this is Ally. We're looking for a friend of ours and wondered if you knew her.'

'Name?'

'Michelle Blake. You might have known her when she was a member of the Rainbow Children.'

'Mitch, course, we were mates. I remember her well.'

'Do you know where she is?' Jo asked.

Tom shook his head. 'Ah, now of that I can't be sure, it's been a while, a long while. I'm sorry but I have no idea where she is.'

'Do you know anyone from the Rainbow days who might still be in touch with her?' Jo asked.

Tom thought for a moment. 'Maybe Rosie Mason. They were good friends back in the day. They may well have stayed in touch.'

'Do you have a number for her?' I asked.

'I might have, though I haven't seen her for years either. Give me a moment.' Tom opened a drawer and rummaged through, pulled out a shabby-looking address book and flicked through. 'Yep, here we are. Rosie, Muswell Hill, here's the last number and address I had for her. No idea if she's still there.'

Jo wrote down the details he gave and moved towards the door. 'Thanks so much and, just before we go, can you tell us any more? I know it's a long time ago, but how was Mitch when you last saw her? We lost touch with her in the Rainbow Children period.'

'Friends of hers were you?'

We all nodded. 'School friends,' said Ally.

'Mitch was a bright girl, had an edge,' said Tom. 'We were

friends in the early days when this place was called The Seventh Star but, as I say, it was a very long time ago and everyone went their separate ways when the movement folded.'

'Was she happy in the communes?' asked Jo.

'I think so. I don't recall her not being. She struck me as self-contained, kept herself to herself a fair bit.'

'Were you in the commune?' I asked.

Tom laughed. 'Short time. The lifestyle wasn't for me.' He gave me a mischievous look. 'I couldn't do the celibate part.'

I raised an eyebrow and smiled. 'Don't think I could have done either.' Hmm, if I was not mistaken, there was a bit of flirting going on here.

'If you speak to her, tell her I say hi, and hi to Rosie too.' He smiled in recollection. 'I always remember Mitch as being very upbeat and committed. She was good-looking too, and a real grafter. All the blokes in the commune had a crush on her.'

Ally laughed. 'So some things didn't change.'

*

We made for the juice bar in Harvest and ordered carrot and apple. Once we were settled on stools, we took turns in calling the number that Tom had given us for Rosie.

'No answer,' I said after I'd tried. 'So frustrating. After all these years to get so close and then a phone that rings and rings.'

'We could always go to her address,' said Jo.

'That's if it is still her address,' I said. 'Tom said he hadn't been in touch for years, and people do move.'

'It's all we've got at the moment,' said Jo.

'And if she is there, it might be a bit much, all of us arriving out of the blue. Best find out if the number is still current before we think about turning up on her doorstep,' said Ally.

'She could be away on holiday,' I said.

'She could be anywhere,' said Ally. 'Out working, visiting a friend.'

'Talking of which, I have to leave soon,' said Jo. 'I said I'd go and help Gary sort through some of the material he has for the programme in the series about animals being people's best friends. He said they have a surplus and hasn't a clue where to start, so needs a fresh pair of eyes to help him sift through.'

'Sure,' I said. 'Though you know that really it's just because he fancies you.'

Jo looked coy. 'He did ask me out for dinner afterwards. My first date with a man in years.'

'Nervous?' asked Ally.

'A bit. It's the taking my clothes off that worries me.'

I laughed. 'I thought you said it was dinner.'

'You'll be fine,' said Ally. 'Like riding a bike—'

'Cheek,' said Jo.

'OK, wrong metaphor,' said Ally. 'Just go, have a glass of wine, enjoy it and don't worry how you look.'

'And don't sleep with a man on your first date. How old are you?'

Jo laughed. 'But there is chemistry there. I get the feeling it will be on the cards sometime.'

'Gary probably can't believe his luck. He thinks you're gorgeous.'

Ally sighed. 'I suppose it's only a matter of time before people start trying to pair me off with widowed or divorced men. Why do people think you'd even want to replace your partner?'

'Because some people do,' said Jo. 'Some people don't want to be on their own. What about you, Sara? That Tom Riley chap back there clearly fancied you.'

'I got the impression he's fancied a lot of people in his life. I wonder if Mitch ever got involved with him.'

'Hopefully we can ask her soon. Let's try phoning Rosie again,' I said.

Once more the phone just rang and rang.

'Still no reply,' I said. 'Maybe she's out of the country.'

'Or it might not even be her number any more,' said Jo. 'Tom did say he hadn't seen Rosie in ages. She might have moved.'

'Then we'll find her. I'm not giving up on this lead having got so close,' I said. 'We'll try again tomorrow.'

Chapter Thirty-Seven

Mitch

October 1975

I was looking forward to being back in London, OK, maybe not my old stomping ground in Notting Hill, this time I was to be in the south somewhere, but this was a city that I knew, and to be back on familiar turf and be with old pals would be a welcome change to the disaster that the Rainbow school had turned out to be.

Andrew came to collect me from the station and it was a joy to see an old friend after living with virtual strangers.

'A lot going on,' he said as we drove south. 'Big changes. We're getting a new indigo. American chap. Adam Sorkin. You can meet him this afternoon.'

'And what am I meant to be doing?'

'Personnel. We need someone to oversee the communes. That will be you.'

'But . . . I'm not sure I want to live this way any more,' I said. 'I'm done. I've had enough of sleeping on floors. The girls' sleeping area at the school was a corridor. I want a *home*. I want a *bed*. I want some *space*. I know we're trying to make the world a better place and all that, but I just don't think I'm up to it any more. I've tried the monastic life, been there, done it – now where's the nearest fecking bar?'

'But don't you see, Mitch, that's why you must stay. We're evolving as a group. You're right, a lot of things need to change and you're just the person to do it.'

I laughed. 'Ever thought of going into politics, Andrew? You'd be good. But I'd prefer to leave making the changes to someone else. I really am done.'

'Don't make up your mind just yet. *Please*.'

'OK,' I agreed, though I had no intention of hanging around.

We drew up in front of a Victorian semi-detached house on a tree-lined street and got out. Before we got to the front door, it was flung open, and there was a very welcome sight. Rosie. She ran down the steps and gave me a huge hug. 'Thank God you're here. I'm so glad to see you.'

'I have to warn you, I'm not staying long.'

'Give it a chance here at least. I know your last placement was crappy, so was mine in Newcastle. The thing is, as people are wanting to join, almost as many are wanting to leave, and who can blame them? Conditions have been rubbish, but *we're* going to change that. We'll make people feel more wanted and appreciated. No more crowded rooms – and we're going to get beds!'

'A few weeks,' I agreed, 'and that's mainly so I can hang out with you for a bit. Then I am gone.'

*

Adam Sorkin hit the UK like a gale-force wind. He arrived on a mission to whip all the communes into shape and make them more habitable. In the months he was there, he toured the country with lightning speed, familiarizing himself with who was living where as there were communes in every major city, with over three hundred people living in them. He was aghast at conditions, and standards began to improve under his guidance. All commune members had a bed, no one slept on the floor any more, people felt more valued.

That done, he called a meeting for everyone in the communes. On the allotted night, he strode to the front of the hall, ready to address everyone. A tall man who radiated energy and was impeccably dressed in the American preppy style. I looked down at my scuffed sneakers and made a note to look for some decent shoes in the jumble. He began by saying how much he liked England, talked about the Rainbow Children, what we were trying to achieve, the ups and downs. He made us laugh, and had us all eating out of his hands, then he let rip.

'You're out of touch and it shows. Read the papers, listen to the news, get with it. And, no doubt, you're all dedicated people, but who's going to want to join us when the women look like bag ladies and the men look like unwashed peasants. Seriously, guys, you all need to shower more.' There was a collective sharp intake of breath in the hall as he continued.

His speech was followed by a shocked silence. We weren't used to that kind of talk. We were used to quotes from the Scriptures, inspirational sayings, fables from the East, Buddhist sayings; no one had ever said we looked like bag ladies before. I glanced around at the women present. Adam had a point.

He certainly livened things up and he influenced many in the communes, who tried to gear up to become more socially acceptable. The women started taking better care of their appearance, wearing make-up, getting their hair cut properly. The men smartened up too and, although everyone still dressed from the

Rainbow jumble, clearly an effort was being made to be more selective.

We also started reading the papers again, watching the evening news, attempting to join the changing times we were living in. His visit moved things forward for us as a group and we became less cut off from what was happening in the rest of the world. As part of that, I tried to contact my sister, Fi. I wasn't sure where she was living any more and had got no reply when I'd tried the last number I had for her. I wrote to Mum in New Zealand to ask her for the latest, but knew it would take weeks before I got a letter back so I went into The Seventh Star to see if anyone there knew of her. Lesley greeted me with a warm hug. 'Didn't you know? Fi's not in London any more. She went travelling with Jacob. Last I heard, they were in India.'

I also tried Sara Meyers and called her old home in Manchester. 'She's working in Bristol,' her mum told me. 'Do get in touch; I know she'd love to hear from you. She's working for a TV company there.'

I took her contact details and meant to get in touch, but life took over again. Changes were happening in the communes and it was hard not to get caught up in the buzz. People were falling in love, left, right and centre. Those who'd opted for the celibate life were agonizing over the battle of the senses, between desire and a life of celibacy. There were late-night confessions over toast and tea, breakdowns, tears. Many couples left, others stayed and were miserable as they tried to go beyond their sexual longings; others sneaked out at night for illicit rendezvous in secret places. Rosie was one of them. She'd fallen in love with Patrick Mason, a tall, handsome man who helped run the London branch of Rainbow Foods with Tom Riley. They'd sneak out and meet in the park in the evenings.

Not me. I couldn't have been more uninterested in men. There wasn't anyone who turned my head. I had no need for a man, nor was there anyone I even vaguely found attractive. I had purpose, a position and a renewed sense of belonging. I was beginning to feel that I was in it for life again.

And then a second visitor arrived.

Chapter Thirty-Eight

Jo

Present day, March

A week of romance: Monday. The preparation.

I had my dinner date with Gary and we got on like a house on fire. I liked him *a lot*. It had been a long time since a man had been so attentive and made me laugh. We'd seen each other most days because he wanted my input into the programme about animals being best friends. I had a good idea that it was just an excuse to see more of me, which was very flattering, plus I was enjoying doing something different. Gary was an animal lover too and had a brown Labrador called Dudley that he invited me to go and meet. His way of saying 'come and see my etchings', I reckoned. When the time was right, I got the feeling some hanky-panky would be on the cards. The idea made me feel slightly panicky, but Ally said it would be like riding a bike, cheeky madam.

So. Underwear. Oh dear. Not good. Not sexy. I'd gone for comfortable and functional in the last years/decade. Who cared when it was only me that ever saw it? Another thing to change,

I realized. Not just for Gary, but for my own self-esteem and part of my new attitude to life. *I shall spend the kids' inheritance on silk knickers and sod them*, I thought.

Off to the department store, found the lingerie area.

'Your bra size, madam?' asked the matronly assistant.

'Oh, not sure, thirty-eight something.'

'When were you last measured?'

'Er . . . never.'

She had a cursory glance at my chest, did a quick measurement with a tape, tutted. Then she led me into a changing room and told me to strip off my top layer. In the meantime, she disappeared, reappearing soon after with armfuls of lace bras.

'Let's start with this one,' she said as she separated a jade green one from the pile. 'Now bend over.'

'Oo-er,' I said. She didn't laugh so I did as I was told and she stood behind me, fastened the bra round my rib area then cupped and scooped my boobs one by one into the bra cups. 'Excuse me,' I said. 'We haven't even had dinner and a date. I don't even know your name.'

Again she didn't laugh. 'It's Stacey,' she said with one last shove into the cup. 'Now stand.'

I stood, looked in the mirror. 'Wow. Perfect,' I said. 'Size is spot on. It feels supportive too.'

'Thirty-four double D,' she said.

'Never.'

Stacey softened, proud of her work. 'Most women are going round wearing the wrong bras. Now, would madam like briefs to match?'

'I would. High leg.'

This time, to my relief, when she returned, she passed them through the curtain. Beautiful gossamer-thin bits of loveliness.

I put a pair on. They fitted fine but the lace trimming around the edges of the legs was trimmed with black furry stuff that didn't look so good. My pubes had a life of their own. God, when had I last had a bikini wax? Back in the Stone Age.

I bought two sets, one ivory silk, the other pale duck egg, and hastened to the beauty salon on the fifth floor.

'A leg and bikini wax,' I requested at reception.

'Hollywood, Brazilian or standard?'

'What's the difference?'

'Hollywood's all off.'

'All off? That's a bit creepy, and I fear I'd look like a plucked chicken . . .'

'Brazilian is where you leave a landing strip . . .'

I started to laugh. 'Landing strip? Like at the airport? Can they coat it in luminous gel or something so you can see it in the dark? Be like guiding a plane in.'

Cheryl didn't react. 'Nah, we don't do luminous, but we do sell glow-in-the-dark condoms.'

'You do? Excellent. I'll take three,' I said. 'Sounds like hours of fun.'

'We do flavoured ones too – strawberry, apple or tropical fruit.'

'How about menthol for when you're not in the mood but don't want to use the headache excuse?'

'Nah. We don't do menthol.' She handed me a card with all the treatments listed. I glanced down.

'What's a vajazzle?'

'It's when you decorate the area where the hair's been taken off with glitter, crystals, rhinestone and sequins.'

Ah, so she did have a sense of humour. I laughed but she handed me a brochure showing lady parts where they'd had the Hollywood (the lot off), and had patterns of stars or flowers made of tiny crystals put in its place.

She wasn't joking. Where had I been the last few decades? When I was still in the game, a trim with a pair of scissors, a slap of hair conditioner and I was ready to party.

'And do you do specials for Christmas?' I asked, thinking I was making another of my hilarious jokes.

'Oh yeah. You can have your pubes shaped into a Christmas tree and the little silver sequins dotted about like baubles. S'very popular for a bit of a festive feel.'

Clearly I'm out of touch when it comes to lady-garden styling, I thought as I pursued the options. *What would Gary like?* There were many: pubes shaped into hearts, flowers, bats – the flying kind, ice-cream cones, butterflies.

'And a vagacial? What's that?'

'Like a facial but for your vagina.'

What!!? 'Of course. And how do you do that?'

'We have a throne you sit on and it steams warm air and herbs up your – you know what.'

'Up your Watford tunnel. Fascinating.' I settled for a standard bikini wax, refused the additional butt wax, but bought a pot of glitter on the way out of the store to have ready as well in case the mood called for it. With all that and the luminous condoms, I was ready for anything.

*

Tuesday night: Ally and Sara had gone to see a movie and agreed to stay out of the way if I wanted to invite Gary over. I did. I cooked a moussaka dish with baked aubergines. Halfway through the meal, Gary did a bolt, and moments later I could hear him throwing up in the cloakroom. *Oh my god, is my cooking really that bad?* I thought as I waited for him to return. He came out looking green. 'So sorry, I'm allergic to aubergine,' he said, and opted to go home for an early night and some Milk of Magnesia. Who said romance is dead?

*

Wednesday. Gary invited me over to his. I met Dudley the dog, we got a takeaway, watched a movie, then kissed, lovely slow-building kisses with a promise of things to come. After a short while Gary got up, took me by the hand and led me to the bedroom.

'I just need to use the loo,' I said. Once in there, I realized I wasn't ready. I might have my pot of glitter in my bag to bedeck my lady parts, but now it was happening, I was seized by panic. I went back into the bedroom where Gary had stripped off and was sitting up in bed. He looked more nervous than I was.

I sat on the end of the bed. 'Truth is, I haven't done this for a long time and wondered if we could slow things down a little. Maybe just cuddle then sleep together, get to know each other a bit better.'

Gary visibly relaxed. 'Great plan.' He budged over in the bed and patted the pillow next to him. 'That sounds perfect.'

It felt lovely to do just that, to lie in his arms and not have to worry about what to put where and when and how. Both of us were asleep in minutes.

I awoke the next day to feel an arm softly tossed around me. Still feeling sleepy and warm, I caressed the arm, noting how thin and bony it was. *Shame*, I thought, because I liked a bit of muscle on a man, *but it feels nice, silky even*. In that not-quite-awake-yet state and without opening my eyes, I turned a little so that Gary could lean in and kiss me if he wanted. He began to lick my face. *OK, bit weird*, I thought as the licking got more intense. *Just go with it*, I told myself, *this phase is all about learning what turns each other on but this . . . ew, isn't exactly doing it for me.* My right ear and my cheek were getting a good wash; in fact, the sensation was altogether too wet, not sensual at all, nor was the smell of his breath. Added to which, despite our agreement to take things slowly, Gary was pushing against me with a mounting passion. I opened my eyes.

It wasn't Gary. It was Dudley the Labrador.

I yelped. Dudley yelped. Gary came running in. He burst out laughing when he saw Dudley trying to hump me through the bedclothes. 'One night together and already you're being unfaithful,' he said as he pulled Dudley off and I sat up.

'Is that what people mean when they say they like it doggie-style?' I asked as Gary led a disappointed Dudley out of the room.

*

Thursday evening: back at Gary's. Dudley was locked in the kitchen. He wasn't happy and, before Gary shut the door, he looked at me with the great sad eyes of an unrequited lover.

Safe from disturbance, we ate, we drank, we adjourned to the bedroom.

Happy days are here again.

Chapter Thirty-Nine

Sara

Present day, March

Ikept trying Rosie's number but no joy, the phone just rang and rang. In the meantime, an interview had been scheduled for the 'Let's Hear It for the Boys' programme. This time I was on my own because Jo was going to be busy 'helping' Gary with the animal programme, and Ally had gone to have lunch in Soho with her old friend Lawrence Carmichael, who was up in London for the day.

Lauren had come up trumps in finding our celebrity Simon's friend Steve and they had been successfully reunited weeks ago. The idea was to film Simon and Steve away from the Little Dog office telling the story of their reunion and doing the sort of thing that they enjoyed doing together now. Simon said that they both loved looking at art so had suggested meeting at the Royal Academy in Piccadilly.

I was well prepared with my questions so set off with Ajay to meet them.

Both were already there, waiting in the foyer, when we got

there. I was struck at once by how handsome Simon was, drop-dead gorgeous, in fact, and beautifully dressed; a tall, dark man with an athlete's physique. Steve was smaller, broader, with glasses, brown hair and an intelligent and friendly face. I warmed immediately to both of them, particularly to Simon, and made a note to self to check out if he was still single.

'You must be Sara,' he said, 'and this is my long-lost friend Steve.'

Steve put out his hand to shake mine. 'Charmed to meet you. We must thank your company for reuniting us.'

'And thank you for agreeing to take part,' I said. 'As you know, we wanted to focus on men's friendships for our second programme.'

'Fine by us,' said Simon.

'Shall we chat as we go round an exhibition or get some coffee in the café?' I asked.

'Oh coffee, I think,' said Steve. 'You can film us perusing the paintings later.'

Pleasantries out of the way, we went into the café, found a table and Ajay got out his camera. 'So . . . first off, how do you think men's friendships differ from women's.'

'Oh . . . right,' said Simon. 'What you do you think, Steve?'

'I thought you might ask that so I've given it some thought. Many of the men I know, particularly those who are married, might keep up with one or two good old friends but rely mainly on their partners for their social life. Generally I think men aren't as good as women at keeping friendships up.'

True, I thought. When I was married to Charles, it was always me who organized the dinners, the outings, booked weekends away with friends. I wondered if Ruth did the same now that she was with him, then pushed that thought away. 'Why do you think that is?'

Simon shrugged. 'Maybe men are more self-contained, or lazier . . .' As he spoke, I noticed his hands, long fingers and perfectly manicured nails. I looked back at his face – denim-blue eyes, a wide, sensual mouth. I felt a tug of desire, something I hadn't felt for a long time.

'But men need friends just as much as women, don't they?'

'Definitely,' said Simon, 'but when my wife was alive, I was the classic example of letting her keep up the friendships. I suffered because of that when she died – I found myself quite lonely. I have my work friends, but they are more acquaintances than true mates. I realized that we all need company, someone to share life's experiences with, someone to watch a sunset with, cook a meal with, watch a good film with, appreciate a good piece of art. Those who have your back and you have a shorthand with when it comes to communication, they are rare and precious.'

I could watch a sunset with you, I thought as I gazed into his eyes.

'Indeed,' I said, 'there are the friends you get squiffy with after work, those you go and see a movie with, but those who really know you and you them, they're more valuable than rubies.' I decided to let it drop that I was single in the hope that Simon would pick up on it. 'When I separated from my husband, I realized I'd become very dependent on him, to the exclusion of others, and then I threw myself into my work to disguise the fact that I didn't have anyone to share my life with. Big mistake. Realizing the need for friends is what inspired this programme.'

Simon took the bait. 'How long ago did you separate?' he asked.

'Ten years ago.'

'And have you a partner now?' he asked.

I shrugged. 'Still single but open to possibilities.' *Great*, I thought, *he's asking all the right questions*.

'Choice, or the right man just hasn't come along?' Steve asked.

'A bit of both,' I replied whilst looking straight at Simon.

'I also think that men don't tend to confide in each other about anything negative or difficult that they're going through in the way that women do,' Steve said. 'I don't know whether that's a throwback to when we were hunter-gatherers and it was in our blood not to show any sign of weakness, but I have noticed that men don't tend to share failures—'

'In fact, they're more likely to talk to a woman about anxieties. A more sympathetic ear, perhaps?' Simon added. 'Is that a generational thing? Maybe you need to talk to some younger men and see if they share their feelings and doubts more than men our age.'

'I always noticed that men have an ability to compartmentalize worry better than women,' I said. 'If I needed to talk to my ex about concerns, his reply was always to turn the page, not dwell on things, whereas I needed to talk things through in order to move on.'

'I'd agree with that, I bury the hard stuff away,' said Simon, 'and the men I know also tend to hide behind humour if they're worried about something, make light of it, but that's not always the best way. Worries can eat you up if not shared but – going back to what Steve said – men rarely let on if they're in trouble for fear of it being seen as weakness. They tend to talk things up instead.'

We chatted on about how they'd met at university, stayed in touch for a short while after, before work had taken Steve abroad to Hong Kong and Australia. I found myself increasingly drawn to Simon. He was articulate, appeared to be emotionally intelligent and thoughtful. Charles had been 'The One'. Simon could be 'The Next One'. I hadn't felt such an attraction in a long time. I could see us dating and I imagined long conversations over dinner, a bottle of wine, a weekend away . . .

'And now where do you live, Steve?' I asked.

'I'll be returning to the UK in the next few months and I'm going to settle back here,' he replied, and smiled over at Simon. Simon reached out and put his hand over Steve's. *Woah. Hold on a minute, have I missed something here?* I asked myself as I watched the two men look at each other affectionately. 'Simon here was the great love of my life when I was in college—'

What!?

'And after a brief and clandestine affair, we went our separate ways,' Simon continued. 'My career took precedence and I blocked off the fact I was gay. I let Steve go, something I regretted with all my heart, but back then I wasn't ready.'

'Nor me,' said Steve. 'In fact I got married—'

'As did I, and I was happy with my late wife,' said Simon. 'However, when you contacted me about your programme, I thought now is the time to look for Steve again, to reconnect, find out if what we once had was still there but I had no idea where to begin looking. Thanks to your research team, Lauren in particular, I didn't have to wait long to have Steve's contact details. Now we're together and I no longer want to hide who I really am, or my sexuality, and I can honestly say I've never been happier.'

'That's wonderful,' I said.

Damn damn damn it, I thought as I gave them both the Sara Meyers wide dazzling smile and crumpled inside.

Chapter Forty

Mitch.

December 1975

It must have been like every man's dream come true. Easy pickings. Like walking into a hothouse of luscious, ripe blooms all wilting from lack of water. We were all in our early-twenties by the time Alec arrived. The other men in the group were not exactly a great temptation in their open-toed sandals and duffle coats, with as much sex appeal as a friendly Old English sheepdog. Then Alec flew in from California one morning in December, dark brown eyes twinkling with mockery for our high ideals, a devil in saint's clothing. Out of the blue: a man who with a glance reminded me that I was female – that sex and sexuality existed and I wasn't getting any. The other men in the group called us their sisters. Love, peace and the brotherhood of man. We were one big family out to make a better world. What I felt for Alec was far from brotherly; the first man I'd found attractive since Jack. It came as a shock. What was I supposed to do about it? I was supposed to go beyond it, wasn't I. I was supposed to have higher matters on my mind, but in the space of a few weeks, my peace of mind and sense of purpose went out the window.

The first meeting with him was scheduled at the Highgate house. All of us from the office were there, scrubbed and punctual, wondering who and what to expect from the new arrival. Alec was already there, sitting back in a chair, arms above his head, as if he was some superior being, watching us all settle as he chatted to Andrew. He had a slim build, silky dark hair brushed back from a high forehead; he was tanned, dressed in jeans and a T-shirt. When everyone was seated, he stretched lazily and leant forward. *Arrogant prick*, I thought as I took an instant dislike to him.

'Alec Curtis. English. Went to public school. Lived in the States the last ten years. Been sent over to shake things up a bit. I'm going to be taking over from Adam.'

I exchanged a look with Rosie. *Oh God, what are we in for this time*, I wondered. As he spoke, I took in the fit-looking body, broad shoulders, long legs, noting nice hands, good shoes. He saw me watching him and he tilted his head back and considered me in much the same way. I felt he was laughing at me, blushed and cursed myself for doing so. He turned his attention away as swiftly as he'd turned it on and asked everyone to say a little about themselves. He didn't ask me.

After the meeting, we trooped out for coffee in the kitchen and he came straight over.

'So you were a public schoolboy, huh?' I asked. For some reason, I doubted it.

He raised an eyebrow in surprise then his features relaxed into a look of pure devilry as he turned me away from the others, leaning in so they wouldn't hear. I caught the clean scent of soap, lime and sandalwood. 'I *did* go to public school, honest . . . at least it was open to the public.'

I laughed. Maybe it would be refreshing to have someone with a sense of humour around. 'So, in this shaking up of things, what role would you like me to play?'

Again, the raised eyebrow, the look of amusement. 'You?' He looked at me hard and long. I met his gaze and, in doing so, felt a tug inside at the frisson of electricity. He felt it too, his eyes narrowed, crinkled a little and he looked away. 'What role would I like you to play? Hmm . . . How about Hamlet?'

I rolled my eyes. 'Alas poor kciroy, I knew him backwards.'

Alec cracked up. 'Yorick. Backwards. Funny.'

'I did *Hamlet* for A-level. My school friends and I used to say that line.'

Alec's expression became serious. 'So Mitch. Why are you here?' I knew he meant what was my position at the office, but chose to ignore that. He wasn't the only one who could be elusive. 'Why am I here? That's the big question,' I replied.

'I mean where are you from?' he asked.

'Ah. Another big question. Isn't everyone trying to find the answer to that too? Why am I here? Where have I come from?'

He laughed. 'I meant where in the country, not in the cosmos.'

'I know what you meant.' *Hark at me*, I thought. *Flirting. And there was I thinking I'd got rusty.* Then I remembered what I was wearing. A shapeless old top and cheap jeans, no make-up. I hadn't had a decent haircut in weeks, despite Adam's advice that we should be more presentable. 'I'm originally from up north but haven't been back there since I left school.'

'And what do you think needs to change around here?'

I thought for a moment. 'People need some personal space. I know I do. I'm done with sharing a room and sleeping on a lumpy mattress for a start.'

He laughed again. 'Well Michelle Blake, I look forward to

working with you,' he said, then turned and went back into the meeting room.

*

'So what do you think of the new wonderboy?' Rosie asked later that night, as we undressed ready for bed.

'Arrogant. I don't like him at all.'

'Really?' Rosie looked surprised.

'Why? Do you fancy him?'

Rosie shook her head. 'Not my type, but I think you should give him a chance. He looks like fun to me. Just what we need.'

I wasn't so sure. Fun? To me, he looked like trouble.

*

As the weeks went on, Alec began to make his mark. He was worldlier than any of the other people who had been sent over and he wasn't an indigo as Adam had been. Whereas they had advised more meditation, more discipline, Alec encouraged loosening up on all levels.

He liked going to the movies, he liked late-night pizza, he read all the daily papers and told us to do the same in order to keep abreast of the times.

When he spoke at meetings, people lapped up his humour, charisma and charm. 'Who said we have to live like hermits?' he'd ask. 'Come on people, get real. We've grown stuffy and, if I'm honest, a tad worthy here and there.'

He brought with him a normality that had been missing. He had no time for anyone who was holier than thou – and there were many of those. I was still wary, though, and felt suspicious of him – there was something about him I didn't trust. Having cleverly won over Gina in accounts in the first week, he had the old office banger replaced with a sleek black Saab. 'If we're to make an impression, we can't look like a throwback to the Woodstock days,' he said. I noted that he was looking at me when he said that. 'The right image is everything. If we're to attract people with half a brain, we have to look as if we're living in this century.'

Alec rented a house to serve as his base and handpicked his fellow housemates, Rosie amongst them, soon followed by po-faced Gail, who I'd lived with in the first commune. Gail was to be his personal assistant. Lastly, I was invited to join the household, where Alec made sure I had my own room. On my first night there, I noticed an envelope on the bed with my name on it. I opened it to find a postcard showing a princess with flowing hair lying on top of twenty mattresses. I knew the illustration; it was by Edmund Dulac for 'The Princess and the Pea'. On the back was written: Sweet dreams, princess. No more lumpy mattresses. I hope you enjoy having some space in here. AX

So he'd taken note of what I'd said. Bah, I thought. *He might think he could win the others over with his charm but not me.* I put the card in the bin.

I retrieved it an hour later.

*

The following day there was to be a conference held in Bristol. Alec came into the kitchen. 'Gail, I want you to go with Andrew and Rosie. Mitch will come with me.'

For a second, Gail's tight self-control wavered. I could see she was disappointed, but she quickly pulled herself together and started fiddling with a briefcase.

'And on the way, Mitch,' Alec continued, 'I want you to fill me in on all the personnel, starting with Gail.' He gave her a cheeky grin.

She flicked her hair. 'Oh you,' she said coyly. She looked worried all the same.

Once in the car, Alec drove in silence until we hit the motorway. 'Tell me about you,' he said eventually. 'What's your story? How did you get involved? How's it been for you?'

No one – apart from Rosie – had expressed any interest in my personal life or thoughts for years. With his encouragement, I told him about my life before joining the Rainbow Children, my family, my old friends, and how we'd drifted apart to the point of no contact now. I omitted the part about Jack and Sara Rose. I hadn't told anyone about them, not even Rosie. Alec listened, asked questions, and seemed genuinely interested and friendly, and I began to think maybe I'd been wrong in judging him as arrogant. I was seeing another side of him. It was only when we got out of the car that I realized he knew almost everything about me but I knew nothing about him.

My impression of him only improved during the conference. I noticed how he went out of his way to acknowledge any effort anyone had made, something that had been sadly lacking up until his arrival. No one had been praised or singled out, and he had a way of making people feel that they were of value, with something to contribute. I could see he was winning himself a loyal team of supporters, and I was beginning to join their ranks.

On the way back, it was dark and wet outside. We roared up the motorway through the rain, a CD of Jean-Michel Jarre playing at full blast. I was seated low in the passenger seat, enjoying the sensation of sound and speed, watching the lights from cars and houses flash by. Suddenly I became aware of the proximity of him. His hand on the wheel, the scent of leather, his cologne – a masculine, woody scent. The atmosphere felt warm, erotic and intimate. I closed my eyes and imagined how it would feel to have the weight of his body on mine, him lying on top of me, nudging my legs apart with his so he could lie between. How would that feel? I wondered how the skin of his naked chest, hard, would feel against mine, soft. I—

'I suppose people assume that we're getting it on,' he remarked.

I woke from my reverie. 'What? Why? Why would anyone think that?'

'Arrived together at the conference. Left together.'

'Don't be ridiculous.'

He laughed. I was flustered and he knew it; he was enjoying my discomfort. I opened the window and let in air. *Be careful*, I told myself. I must never let go like that again. Nothing good could ever come from it. Although my impression of Alec had changed, I instinctively felt he was not a man to be trusted when it came to my heart. He struck me as the kind of man who liked the conquest, and he already had Gail and half the women in the communes in love with him.

We spent the rest of the journey in silence, and when we got back, I went straight to my room. Despite my warning to myself, it was too late; Alec'd got his hooks in. In the next weeks, I found myself listening out for him, for his car, his key in the front door. The air seemed brighter when he came into the office and I knew I perked up. The air felt charged if ever we were alone. I was over-aware of him, who he was talking to, who was waiting to see him; too aware of his physicality or proximity.

One morning, Gail told me he wanted to see me. I went into his room where he was lying on the bed, wearing a grey silk dressing gown open to his waist. *Didn't get that in the jumble*, I thought as I looked away and studied the carpet. He was going through post, sipping coffee from a tray that Gail had brought up earlier. He motioned me to sit on the end of the bed.

'Adam Sorkin's returning for a brief visit,' he said. 'We need to make some space for him.' I could feel the pressure of his bare leg against the fabric of my jeans as he spoke.

'So you want me to move out?' *Actually, that would be a relief,* I thought. *I don't think I can bear much more of this loaded atmosphere.*

'Only for a short time. So we won't be living together but . . . hey, we probably would have done if it wasn't for this saving-the-world malarkey, wouldn't we?' He looked directly at me and, as when we first met, I felt the sweet sensation of chemistry.

'Wouldn't we have what?'

'Lived together. Don't you think?'

I laughed. 'Bit presumptuous, Alec. What makes you think you'd be my type?'

He shrugged. 'Unspoken but not unknown,' he said, then he smiled and went back to his mail, but kept his leg pressed against mine.

I moved away. 'Is there anything else?'

He didn't look up, just continued reading. 'Nope.'

I got up and left the room feeling confused. Nothing had been said, but there was no doubt I felt something. Was he saying he felt it too and was sincere when he said we'd have lived together if things had been different? Or was he just playing with my head? Attempting to win me over, as I'd watched him do to so many others since his arrival. I tried to convince myself it was harmless, but the sensations and emotions he'd awoken and aroused in me were overwhelming. I was still in my twenties, hadn't been involved with anyone since Jack.

I thought of the others I'd pitied when they'd fallen in love. I felt ashamed that I'd judged them from the lofty heights of spiritual arrogance and now, here was I, falling for a man who was probably sleeping with the housekeeper, his secretary and God knew who else.

Chapter Forty-One

Jo

Present day, April

Well, blimey O'Riley, my life has changed. Gary and I were now an item, going steady, or whatever it is that people said these days. My kids kept calling and asking when I was coming home, so I took a quick trip back to pick up some clothes and check that my animals were being cared for – a lady from the village was going in daily to take care of all their needs. Like me, she was an animal lover, and I trusted her completely.

'When are you coming back?' asked Kirsty.

'Soon, not sure, I'm having such a good time. I really only came back to check the animals were OK.'

'*Animals?* What about us?' asked Kirsty.

'You're old enough to take care of yourself now,' I replied. 'It's about time you lot all started fending for yourselves.'

'But I'm exhausted, Mum,' said Kirsty. 'No one does anything around here.'

I didn't care. The house was a mess and I could see it needed a good clean and the fridge restocking, but I took a deep breath, let it go and headed back to London, leaving Kirsty looking gobsmacked.

*

Sara and Ally were beginning to lose heart about our Rosie lead, but I was determined to keep trying. On the weekend, I decided to give it one last go and pressed in her number for the umpteenth time.

The phone rang and rang then I heard, 'Hello?'

'Oh! Sorry, I wasn't expecting anyone to answer. Is that Rosie Mason?'

'That's me.' Her tone was cautious.

'Don't worry, I'm not selling anything. Tom Riley at Harvest in London gave us your number. I'm trying to trace an old friend of mine and I believe you knew her. Her name's Michelle Blake. Tom said you might know where she is.'

'I might. How did you know her?' asked Rosie.

'We were at school together. My name's Jo.'

'Jo. Right. I remember Mitch talking about you.'

'Do you know where she is?'

'I do. I had an email from her only last week.'

I felt a rush of adrenalin. 'You *did?* So you know where she is?'

'I do.'

'Could you tell me where?' I asked.

'I could but . . . I don't want to hand out her contact details just like that. I'd need to ask her if it's OK – or maybe we should meet first. Sorry to be cautious, but you really could be anyone and I'd need to check with Mitch if she'd be happy to let you know her whereabouts.'

'Great, of course, that's fine. Yes. Thank you.'

We arranged to meet the following Saturday and I went running in to tell Sara and Ally in the kitchen.

'Result. I spoke to Rosie and she wants to meet us at the weekend.'

'Does she know where Mitch is?' Sara asked.

'She does . . .'

'So she's alive?' Sara asked.

I nodded and Sara beamed and punched the air.

'Oh thank god!' said Ally. 'What else did she say?"

'She wants to give us the once-over first, in case we're lunatics escaped from the asylum.'

'So she didn't tell you where Mitch is?' Sara asked.

'Not yet, but I think she will.'

Sara got up and hugged me. ' 'Excellent news. I can't wait.'

'Me neither,' said Ally. 'This calls for celebration. Let's open some bubbly.'

'On its way,' said Sara as she headed for the fridge.

Chapter Forty-Two

Mitch

February 1976

Rosie, Andrew and Gail were chatting at the kitchen table one morning. 'Have you heard?' asked Gail when I went to join them. 'The reason for Adam Sorkin's visit is because there's going to be a new training programme to make more indigos, and he's going to make some more changes.'

Even Alec was unsure what these changes would mean for us – both our roles were in limbo – but strangely this meant we were relaxed about the future and more at ease than usual. We walked in a nearby park, talked about dreams, people we'd known, how our lives might have ended up if we hadn't got involved with the Rainbow Children. We went to a movie, where once again the proximity of him in the dark, arms touching, felt as charged and erotic as if we were in bed, lying entwined.

At the end of the day, we went back to the house, to our separate rooms, but it felt as if our connection had become stronger. I decided that it was time to open up to Alec, voice the feelings that were unspoken but not unknown.

First I needed to talk it over with Rosie.

'Hmm,' she said. 'How does he feel about you?'

'I suppose I could be imagining the whole thing. I have no idea really.'

'He's a flirt, Mitch. He's an attractive man who likes to know he is. I'd forget him if I were you.'

I wished it were that easy. I was thinking about him all the time, wanting him. He was an ache that hurt.

After a bad night's sleep, I decided to make my feelings known. I went to his office and knocked on the door. He looked busy, and Gail was hovering by the desk sifting through papers.

'Can I speak to you for a moment?' I asked.

He barely looked up. 'Can it wait?'

'Not really.'

He sat back in his chair. 'OK. Go ahead.'

I couldn't tell him how I was feeling, not with Gail there. She'd love that.

'It's private. Can I see you . . . er, alone?'

'Alone? Why? There's nothing we have to say that Gail can't hear.'

Ah. I felt my heart sink. I saw Gail's smug expression. I got the message. He knew what I wanted to say. He just didn't want to hear it. 'Er . . . it was just, if I have to go and get a job, do I need to explain my filing system to anyone?' I'd made the question up on the spot – anything to get me out of there.

He half smiled. 'Don't worry, we'll manage.' His expression became cold as he went back to whatever he was doing.

I got out, closed the door, and cursed myself for going in there. Stupid. Stupid. I'd been like a lovesick schoolgirl with a crush. I'd known men like Alec back at school, boys who liked the dance. They'd show an interest, be charming, seductive, and the minute you responded and moved forward, they'd take a step back. Conquest made. Alec was one of those. I used to be wise to his type. Used to spot them a mile off. I should've known better. How embarrassing, how humiliating.

I felt a fierce resolve grow in me. I'd forget about Alec. I didn't want him or the confusion he caused inside me. I'd been agitated, restless, unhappy since he arrived. I wanted my peace of mind back.

I made another decision, though. I was out, out of the commune lifestyle. Definitely this time. The attraction to Alec had one positive. It had shown me that the part of me that wanted to love and be loved hadn't died when Jack had. It had been buried for a while – months, years. Not all men were like Alec. Maybe there was someone out there for me. I would leave the commune, stay with Tom for a while and, for starters, see if I could get a job back at The Seventh Star. I'd support the movement from the outside. I was done with rules and denial.

I felt brilliant. I felt liberated.

*

The next day I went to clear my desk. It was a Sunday so there was no one around. The phone rang as I put my belongings into a box. It was Adam Sorkin.

'I'm sorry Alec's not here,' I said. 'I can leave a message on his desk. This is Michelle Blake.'

'Just who I was looking to speak to,' he said. 'I need to get hold of three people in the UK. I know you know where everyone is. They're to start on the indigo training programme on Monday with others from Europe. Can you let them know? Michael Harris. Nick Jenson and the third one is . . . Michelle Blake.'

'Michelle Blake?'

'Yes. You. You ready for the challenge?'

'I . . .'

He didn't wait for an answer, instead he gave me details of the programme and told me to get packing.

I put the phone down. Me? Become an indigo? *Me?* I felt flattered, it was quite an opportunity but . . . I was about to leave the movement, wasn't I?

Chapter Forty-Three

Sara

Present day, April

The third programme in the series about animals as friends was well under way. Lauren, Gary and Jo had spent hours trawling footage on the Internet and YouTube to find clips from all over the world, and we gathered at the Little Dog offices along with Ally to review what they had. The first thing that was apparent was the easy relationship between Gary and Jo. Although still based at my house, Jo was spending more and more time over at Gary's, and it was lovely to see how she had blossomed and was growing in confidence. It also meant that life at my house with just Ally and me there was quieter, and we'd begun to muddle along quite well. She'd stopped trying to organize me. I'd learnt to give her space.

'We've a surplus of material,' said Gary, 'and there's no doubt about the fact that people's pets provide companionship and comfort for many.'

'We've divided what we've got into sections and this first one is about people with unusual pets,' Jo explained as she showed

Ally and me some of the clips they'd chosen. There was footage of people who kept spiders (*wargh!* not for me), sheep, llamas, alpacas, ducks, and one man who kept a crocodile. *He'd be an interesting man to have as a boyfriend*, I thought, *like – come and meet my pet. Mind your leg if you want to keep it.*

There was a moving story about a man who had rescued a baby hippo and, even after he had let it go into the wild, it would return and lie at its rescuer's feet. *Whatever floats your boat*, I thought as we watched the screen.

'The second section is about individual animals who have their own unusual friends,' said Gary as we went on to the next section. There was the alpaca who had a rabbit as his pal, a polar bear and a piglet curled up asleep together, a rhino and sheep cavorting in a field like gay young things in love, an orang-utan grooming a very patient dog, a goat and an elephant, cats and dogs cuddled up together, a cat and a crow playing chase, a gorilla gently stroking a kitten, a horse running in a field with pygmy goats on its back, and on and on the clips went. 'I can see why it's been a task choosing which to include,' I said as I watched further clips of a monkey and kitten play, a squirrel and cat charging around a garden, a bear and a tiger, deer and monkey, all so gentle with each other.

'We could learn a lot from animals about getting on with people who are different to us,' Ally commented.

'And for a few laughs, we thought we'd include these clips,' said Jo as the footage moved on to show a dog that liked to sing along when his owner played the piano, a cat that went through a series of yoga exercises with his owner, mimicking the moves with great precision as they both lay on the floor; but my favourite was the black and white cat that appeared to pole-dance on a broomstick when its owner played soul music.

'We can cut some of these clips down to make a montage,' said Gary, 'but I think we have to include them.'

'Absolutely,' I agreed.

'Next on the agenda is the filming we've done with pet owners and their animals. No one will ever love you like a dog,' said Jo.

'Hey,' said Gary. 'Although I don't like to leave you and Dudley alone too long.'

Jo laughed. 'You know what I mean – they're always pleased to see you, give unconditional love . . .'

'So do I,' said Gary.

'Early days, mate,' said Jo, but she was smiling. 'There are inspiring stories of animals alerting their owners if there's a fire . . .'

'Dogs that can smell when their owners need insulin,' said Lauren.

'Or even has cancer,' said Jo.

'And so many examples of cats and dogs comforting someone when they are ill or grieving.'

'Have you got any footage of dogs as hospital or care home visitors,' I asked. 'When my mum was in the care home, a lady used to bring her yellow Labrador in once a week and the residents loved him. A furry presence of warmth and affection. He brought great comfort, and many of them responded to the dog more than human visitors.'

'We'll make a note of that,' said Lauren. 'So far we haven't but I think we should.'

'We do have one heartbreaking clip of a dog whose owner died,' said Jo. 'After the funeral no one could find him, people searched everywhere. He was eventually found lying on his owner's grave, with his head down between his paws.'

'Oh god, that's too sad,' I said.

'Include in the programme or not?' asked Gary.

'Include,' I said. 'We'll have laughter and tears. There can be both in friendships.'

'But what's the reunion story?' asked Ally. 'I thought every programme was going to be about someone getting back together with an old friend.'

'We're filming that early this afternoon, then there will be some time in the studio. All sorts of people are bringing in their pets,' said Gary.

'Including your Bonnet friends,' said Jo. 'They've hired a minivan and are coming up for the day with their dogs.'

'And my agent Nicholas is bringing his dog Atticus in,' I said.

'And my son is driving up some of my animals,' said Jo. 'Including Rambo my sheep.'

'Good luck with that,' said Ally.' I hope you have some animal minders on hand to keep the animals under control.'

I noticed Lauren and Gary exchanged glances. Clearly not.

*

'How long has your husband been away?' I asked Maggie Mitchell as we sat in her light airy kitchen in north London that afternoon. Ajay and Gary had come along, ready to film the return of Colin, her soldier husband from Afghanistan.

'He's been away four months and Alvin here has been pining. From the moment we got him as a wee puppy, he was Colin's dog, his constant companion and best buddy. He sleeps on his side of the bed.' She indicated the black German shepherd lying under the table.

A car had been sent to pick up Colin from the airport; about fifteen minutes before it was due to arrive, Gary got a text to say that they wouldn't be long. It appeared that Alvin got a psychic text of his own, because he suddenly perked up and ran to the front door, his tail wagging. There he sat, as if he knew Colin would be back any moment.

'He used to do that whenever Colin had been out without him, like to the gym or the supermarket. It was as if he had some inner antennae that alerted him to Colin's movements.'

'I've heard of cats doing that as well as dogs,' I said as Ajay got up to film Alvin waiting by the door.

A text announced Colin's arrival, and the rest of us trooped through into the front room to watch as the car drew up. Already Alvin was barking in the hall. A tanned, fit man with short brown hair got out of the car and approached the door. When Maggie opened it and Colin walked through, she barely got a chance to greet her husband. Alvin went ballistic, delirious with joy, paws up at Colin's chest, dancing on his back legs. Colin dropped his gear, got down on the floor with him and Alvin gave him a good licking before flopping down into his lap and looking up at him adoringly. Colin laughed. 'Some homecoming – guess I was missed, hey?'

Alvin gave him an extra lick as if to say, yes, yes, you were, and at last Colin could get up to hug his wife.

We were all wiping our eyes as we watched.

*

After a bit of chat to camera about Colin's friendship with Alvin, Gary, Ajay and I got back in the car and headed for a studio that had been booked in west London for the afternoon.

We walked into pandemonium. Dogs barking, cats meowing, a llama in the corner, various I-don't-know-whats in small cages. I wouldn't be going near those in case any contained spiders. There was a pot-bellied pig running around being chased by a pygmy goat, a parrot with Tourettes in the corner, whistling then shouting obscenities: 'Bugger off, vicar, bugger off.'

'Marvellous,' I said as I spotted Nicholas. 'What's the saying? Never work with children or animals?'

'I'm leaving,' said Nicholas, 'Atticus is getting distressed.' At that moment, Atticus cocked his leg and peed on Gary's shoes.

Over in the corner, The Bonnets were gathered with their dogs, so I went over to speak to them. 'Everything OK over here?'

'Just about,' said Katie. 'We think we might just escape for a while, though, because Doodle has spotted the cats and wants to play. They don't. Good job Bridget didn't bring her cats. They'd be on the ceiling by now if she had.'

I went over to where Gary was now chatting to a man with a snake around his neck. Ajay started filming as the man lifted the snake and put it around Gary's neck. Poor Gary went white as the snake wound its way down his back then its head reappeared between his legs in Gary's crotch. 'Well, hello sailor,' I said.

Everyone in the vicinity cracked up laughing, apart from Gary who looked as if he was going to pass out.

The snake owner managed to detach the snake and Gary stumbled off in the direction of the gents.

Jo was fantastic. With help from some of the crew, she went around talking to owners, separating people and their pets into areas divided off with chairs and tables that were stacked at the back of the hall. Peace was restored, apart from a frisky ferret who escaped from his owner, found a lady nearby and disappeared into her shirt.

'Happy days in the TV business,' I said to Gary, who'd reappeared but was hovering as close as he could to the exit.

'Yes, happy days. Let's just do some interviews, get out of here to the nearest pub and down a few large glasses of red wine. Animals might well be a man's best friend but don't ever ever put them together in one room. Lesson learnt.'

Chapter Forty-Four

Mitch

1976

On a Monday morning in March, I found myself sitting in a conference room with twelve others from different parts of Europe. The air was thick with anticipation and no one spoke. I felt nervous and excited to meet the founders of the Rainbow Children, unsure how to be with such celebrities – relaxed, cool, respectful, how? It was a bit like meeting royalty.

Finally the wait was over, the door opened, and there they were, John, Robert, Maya, Debra, and so began the most intense few weeks of my life. As they expanded on their plans to spread the message of peace, I felt that all the doubt and sleeping on hard floors had been worth it. It seemed to have been leading to this place, to be here, at the centre.

The movements' founders were charismatic, radiant, funny, intelligent. They made all of us feel special, accepted, like we had something to contribute, and that drew me in. I badly wanted to contribute and feel that my life had some kind of purpose. Another plus was that as the weeks went on, I found I had made new friends as well as colleagues.

We learnt how to present ourselves in public, walk tall, to look people in the eye, shake hands firmly, be positive, and to practise positive thinking at all times.

We were taken shopping and bought new clothes, had our hair professionally styled. Mine was cut just below my shoulders. We were polished on every level – the spiritual, the mental, the physical, until we shone and were ready to go out into the world.

They ran through the life plan that we would be sent out to teach, emphasizing that we mustn't try to interpret the message or add our own angle, that we were to keep our talks free of politics and religion. 'Like water,' said John, 'keep the message pure. Don't add your own flavour.'

'If you're to do this,' said Debra, 'you must have no desires, no attachments. If you're sent to New York and your heart is in London, you're no use to us. There is no room for pretenders or those who feel this is the slightest sacrifice, no room for martyrs here. This work has to be your whole life. If you have the slightest reservation, then leave now.'

No one did. There wasn't the slightest doubt in me that here lay my destiny.

I hoped that once I'd finished the training that I'd be sent far away from the UK. I knew that some of the new indigos had been sent to Australia, New Zealand, South Africa, Europe; it was part of the job – to always be on the move. Hopefully, I could leave the UK, forget about Alec and any future I might have dreamt I'd have with him, forget about my past and the child I still thought about daily.

At last came the day when we heard our assignments. John

came in and read the list and where around the globe we were all going to be sent. Then they came to me.

'Michelle – South Africa.'

Excellent. A new start, I thought. I was ready for it.

Chapter Forty-Five

Sara

Present day, April

The fifth programme was going to be an interesting one. How friends can hurt as well as heal. For this one, our celebrity was a successful singer-songwriter in her early twenties called Luca. I met her in a hotel room in Piccadilly. I liked her style. Skinny with dyed green glossy hair cut to her shoulders, silver rings through her ears and one through her lip, tattoos up her arms and wearing sweatpants and a cut-off T-shirt. After introductions and thanks for taking part, we got down to the nitty-gritty.

'I was bullied at school,' she said, 'never one of the popular crowd. I never fitted in, so yeah, I can tell you about how friendships can hurt. I hurt a lot. I was isolated, humiliated, called names, laughed at and lonely. Girls can be mean. It's not fist-in-the-face bullying like it often is with boys, it's more subtle with girls – texts, false rumours spread, comments on social media. I came off all of it after getting slagged off on Facebook. Basically my first years at secondary school were crap.'

'All the way through?' I asked. I thought about how wonderful my school years had been, knowing that was down to having Ally, Jo and Mitch. I felt for Luca that she hadn't had the same.

'Things changed in Year Thirteen. Along came Jenni Barnes, we're still mates now. You mentioned friends who hurt and heal. She healed because, up until then, I thought there was something wrong with me, that I was the problem because I was different, not invited to parties, not included in the gossip. She made me look at things differently. Jenni was different too: a chubster, so she didn't fit the mould. I was a skinny round-shouldered thing, didn't fit the teen dream either.'

'So what happened? I mean, look at you now.'

'Everything changed when I met Jenni. I had someone to talk to, someone to hang out with. Us against the world. We thought the same, read the same books, liked the same music; we were smart too, worked hard. But what changed was this. I'd gone into victim mode before Jen came along. Poor me, why me? Crap me. One day I realized I had a choice – sink or swim – and I thought fuck it, I'm gonna swim. I could have gone on forever feeling sorry for myself but yeah, fuck that. It's all how you look at it. I could look back and think the worst but, actually, I choose to see that all that happened made me who I am; it made me strong, independent, self-sufficient. It's choice, innit, not chance that determines what you make of your life, and I chose to move on, be myself, be proud of who I was. It's not what life throws at you that makes you who you are, it's how you react to those things. I started writing songs about everything I'd been through, not in a "poor me" kind of way, more in a "let's celebrate me" kind of way. So I don't fit the popular mould – that's because there's only one of weird-and-wonderful me, and that's OK. I started playing locally and yeah, people liked it, it took off, got spotted by a producer and yeah, look at me now.'

'Have some of the girls from your old school been in touch?'

'You bet. They all want a bit of it, a bit of me now that I'm famous, but no way. Not no way in a nasty way. I choose love, but they're not coming in my space.'

'And friends now?'

Luca shrugged. 'Some other musicians who get the life. Jenni still as well, though I haven't seen her in person for a while now she's living in Goa. Your programme researchers said they'd fly her over so we could do the big reunion; that will be cool, though we regularly FaceTime. And course there are the hangers-on. People just want to know me because I'm famous, but what's that about? Sometimes it's hard to know who to trust in this business. But there are other people I've met, successful in their own right. They're not envious and they don't measure what they've got with what I've got because they've got their own.'

'Equals.'

'Yeah. Equals. How about you? You're successful. Sara Meyers. You got good friends?'

'Ones I've been rediscovering. I get what you're saying about the people who you're unsure why they want to be friends with you. My real friends go back a long way, knew me before I was Sara Meyers, TV star, etc.'

Luca held up a fist, I did the same and we knocked knuckles. 'Sweet,' she said.

'Sweet.'

I liked Luca a lot. A wise head on young shoulders. She was a great role model and her songs were inspirational.

'So what advice would you give to anyone who has been hurt by friendships? Someone who, maybe like you were, is being bullied.'

'Talk to someone about it. Being strong doesn't mean not asking for help. You have the power to change things. Learn to love yourself, that's a good starting point. Treat yourself the way you'd like others to treat you. Do not go into victim mode, it's a waste of time and the only person who suffers is you. You have the power. Look at the support sites on line. Don't engage with bullies, don't try to win their approval, most of them are cowards anyway. Don't stoop to their level. Be yourself and proud of it. It's never too late to change and live the life you know you really want.'

'And for making friends?'

'Don't hide away. Get out there, meet people, go to things. There's always stuff happening somewhere. Find your tribe. Don't focus on the negative, what you haven't been invited to. Go to somewhere, something where everyone's welcome and doing something you like – music, art, books, travel; whatever is your thing. And get a dog. I got my boy Baxter. Best friend a girl could have after Jenni.'

I laughed and told her about our programme featuring animals.

'Wish I'd been there,' she said. 'I'd have brought Baxter.'

'I'd love to meet him, and look forward to meeting Jenni too.'

I left the hotel an hour later, feeling inspired by Luca, plus she'd given me more good rules for my friendship list. She made me think. No doubt about it, I'd spent many years feeling sorry for myself about Charles and how my best friend Ruth had betrayed me. 'Choice, innit,' Luca had said. 'Not what life throws at you but how you react.' I nodded. I'd been so hurt by Charles and Ruth, two of the people closest to me, so I'd reacted by not letting anyone get near to me in case they did the same. Work had been my refuge. It was time to change that and embrace life outside a career again. Travels, fun, leisure time and, with

Jo and Ally, I had just the people to do it with. If we could just find Mitch, our old gang would be complete.

*

Back at the office, I had a meeting with Gary and Lauren about what else to use in the programme. Luca had been so upbeat, I didn't want to bring down the tone of the programme with stories of revenge, betrayal and jealousy, even though there were plenty of those. The musician whose agent and friend robbed her of all his money, lied about it and left her bankrupt; women like me who had been betrayed by friends taking their husbands, untrustworthy people, people who didn't communicate or brought you down or put you down; friends who abandoned friends after a divorce or separation when they took sides with one of the people involved. There were plenty of examples, but I wanted to highlight the fact that we always had choice. Sink or swim. Hide away or embrace life's endless opportunities to change. Trust or be bitter and suspicious. Choose to fight for friends.

'I reckon, with Luca's help,' I said, 'we could turn this programme into a positive one instead of a downer. It's all down to what perspective we take.'

'Good thinking,' said Gary. 'All the other programmes have been upbeat, there's no reason this one can't be as well. We won't shirk the truth that friendships can hurt but we can emphasize that that needn't be the end. Life goes on.'

'Life is what you make it, innit?' I said. I put out my fist to bang knuckles as I had with Luca. Gary and Lauren stared at my hand, unsure what to do.

Chapter Forty-Six

Mitch

April 1976

Rosie and Andrew drove me to the airport and, as we said our goodbyes, Rosie gave me a letter. 'Alec asked me to give you this,' she said. 'If I were you, I'd bin it.'

'I might well do that,' I said as I heard my flight being called.

As soon as the flight took off, I got out the envelope that Alec had given me and read his note.

You know you have my fondest love and deepest affection. Let's get married next time round. Yours truly, Alec. X

I ripped it into small pieces, glad that his words had no effect at all.

As the plane rose into the sky, the city beneath grew smaller until it looked like a toy town. Roads, cars, houses, green fields receded until they were gone and there was just a snowy white mass of clouds underneath us. *And that's the end of you Alec*, I thought. *You're a dot on the landscape far below*.

'You heading for Cape Town or Jo'burg?' asked the man I was sitting next to. I hadn't really noticed him when I took my seat on the plane but, turning to look at him, I saw a man, probably in his thirties. He had an open, friendly face, tanned and glowing with health, and looking as though he spent a lot of time outdoors.

'Cape Town,' I replied.

'Home, business or pleasure?'

'Business mainly. You?'

'I live near there so I'm heading home. Your first visit?'

'It will be.'

'It's a beautiful place. Make sure you see all of it, and especially Stellenbosch, that's where I live. I know I'm biased, but I believe it's the loveliest part of South Africa. I hope you have a good stay. I'm Rob, by the way.'

'Michelle, but everyone calls me Mitch.'

He didn't chat much more than that and I was thankful. Hostesses brought food, drinks, a movie started up, lights went down, and soon the man next to me was asleep. I glanced at him as he snoozed. He looked a kind man. I thought about what Alec had said to me once back in England. 'In a different life, we'd have been together.' That was never going to happen. *Maybe in a different life I'd have met this man next to me, had a romance, got married.* I laughed to myself. *As if.* I genuinely didn't care any more. Flying above the clouds on a twelve-hour flight, I felt as if I had stopped for the first time in years. I thought about my past and my mind turned to my old school friends. We'd all moved on, but I felt that I'd let them down, especially Jo by not attending her wedding. Would it really have been so difficult to have been a bridesmaid for her? I realized that I'd been so caught up in feeling sorry for myself and my losses, I hadn't allowed for the fact that they too might have been fighting their own battles as they made their way out in the world. They hadn't the slightest notion what I'd been through with Jack and the baby. I'd broken all the rules of our friendship, the main one being to trust each other always. *I'm sorry, Jo, Sara, Ally. One day you might understand*, I said to myself. *One day.*

I must have fallen into a deep sleep because the next thing I knew was that the flight was beginning its descent. As I looked out of the window, I saw the ground beneath; it looked dry, dusty and red, so different to the green fields I'd left back in England.

'Have you got a lift?' Rob asked as the seatbelt sign went on.

'Thank you. I'm being met.'

'Friends?'

'Not yet, but I hope they will be.'

'Ah. You're going into a new situation?'

I nodded. 'New chapter.'

He reached into his jacket and pulled out a card. 'In that case, can I give you my card? My family has a hotel over in Stellenbosch. Should you ever be visiting the area, please give me a call and come and check us out.'

I took the card. 'Thanks and I might just take you up on that.'

I put the card in my wallet and thought no more about it.

*

The Cape Town commune members were a mix of wonderful characters, all in their twenties and, just as the followers back in the UK, eager and enthusiastic about spreading the message. They gave me a warm welcome at the white colonial-style bungalow where they lived, and I felt at home there from the moment I arrived. It had a garden on all sides, a veranda where we'd eat breakfasts of mango and pawpaw, drink rooibos tea and gaze out at the garden of bougainvillea and pink hibiscus. It felt wonderful to have constant days, that turned into months, of good weather, and to feel the warm sun on my skin after the long cold winter in the UK.

Jonas, who was in charge of the commune, was a tall blond Afrikaner, and he insisted on showing me around the country. I grew to love our excursions out to locations such as Constantia, where I was surprised to see many areas as green and lush as the southwest of England, I particularly loved the stunning coastline to Hout Bay with its sandy beaches; we even took a trip up Table Mountain from where the views of the coast were spectacular and we could see the range of mountains called the Twelve Apostles stretching out before us.

'Whatever mood you're in, we have the landscape for it,' Jonas told me one day as we drove out to Cape Point at the tip of the peninsula, a journey that was interrupted along the way by baboons jumping up on the car bonnet and peering in at us in the hope of some food. 'We have the rocky untamed beaches on the Atlantic side, the warmer Indian Ocean on the other. There are mountains to climb, pine forests if you fancy that, and the national park to roam in if that's where appeals – all within a short drive.'

'What about Stellenbosch?' I asked.

'That's a town in the west of the Cape,' said Jonas. 'We can go there if you like. It's grape-growing country – very lovely; in fact when the Dutch first arrived they claimed it to be paradise, the land of milk and honey, because, with its climate and scenery, it's about as close to that as you'll find. I'll take you.'

True to his word, we made the journey the following week and I fell in love with the place at first sight. In later weeks, we travelled to Durban and Johannesburg. Along the way, we watched sunsets that took my breath away, vivid in purple, gold and scarlet, different and stunning every dusk. The surroundings seemed brighter, more vibrant – the red earth, the endless blue skies, the beauty of creation evident everywhere I looked. As the months went by, I felt the power of Africa, magical and ancient, reach inside and heal my heart.

A letter came from the founders of the Rainbow Children after I'd been in Cape Town just under a year,

Dear Indigo (Michelle),

Pardon the formal nature of this letter, but as there are so many indigos now around the world, we have had to contact everyone by post, giving a telephone number – which you can find at the end of this letter – for you to call if you have any questions.

There are to be a few changes in how we run things. I hope you understand and will be happy with how things are to go forward. We've been reviewing everything in the last few months and decided that we have to halt the direction of the movement. Looking at how we appear to the general public, it has been noted that many believe us to be a cult. Being a member of the Rainbow Children, you know that this is not true as we are not a religious group, far from it, but in view of this feedback, we are implementing some changes to make the teachings more user-friendly. We will be dissolving the communes and encouraging all those who live in them to go back to their lives, find jobs, find homes and continue with the teachings in their everyday life.

We are also letting go of the indigo system of spreading the teachings. It has been noted, since their numbers have grown, the message has been diluted, as individuals added their own personal beliefs – some politics here, a sprinkling of a religious belief there. It was inevitable that this might happen but, in order to keep the teachings simple and clear, we are working towards using other methods of spreading the message and we will be creating videos, films and reading material that the public can access when they wish.

We would like to thank you for your efforts, time and energy on our behalf and wish you all the best for your future.
In love and peace John, Robert, Maya and Debra.
Any questions, please call: 00 0786999

Just like that, it was over.

It felt as if someone had poured a bucket of cold water over me. I was shocked. Although I'd had times of wavering about the lifestyle back in the UK, I'd been happy in South Africa, and had begun to think my commitment to the Rainbow Children would be for life, like a marriage. Suddenly I'd been informed that, out of the blue, there was to be a divorce.

As the implications hit me, so did a sense of panic. Where would I go? What would I do? I was twenty-three. I had no money, no savings, no job experience to speak of; nothing to put on a CV. The reaction in the commune was mixed. Shock, some relief, some anger. Some left the same day, some the day after; some were anxious about where they were to go. Like me, they had given their time and energy to furthering the teachings.

By the end of the week, besides me, there were three left in the commune. Jonas, Peter and Susan.

'Talking about rats deserting a sinking ship,' said Jonas, as we watched another housemate get into a friend's car and drive away.

'What will you do, Mitch?' asked Susan.

'No idea. Maybe return to the UK. I don't know. I have to speak to someone back in the UK, see if there is any kind of plan in place.'

'But what do *you* want?' asked Jonas.

I laughed. 'Me? I've no idea any more. Being part of the Rainbow Children has been my life for so long, it's hard to know what to do or where to go.'

It felt strange to have been given my freedom. It felt like teetering on the edge of a precipice.

That night, after I'd gone to bed, I closed my eyes and it felt as though the last few years were playing like an inner movie in my mind. Ally, Jo and Sara, where were they now? Should I reach out to them if I were to return to the UK? Send postcards. What would I write? Sara Rose. Where was she? Why had I let so many in my life go? Pushed them away; shut them out in my pursuit of a high ideal.

As I stared up at the ceiling, I felt something shift inside me. It was as if I was suddenly remembering who I really was and that there was a world out there, waiting to be explored. I felt that, on some level, I'd been asleep for years and was awakening after a long winter hiding away in hibernation. Something was stirring deep inside, wanting to grow, put its tips up and out into the sun. It was a desire to come out of hiding and really live. Being with the Rainbow Children had provided a safe place to shelter, with not many questions asked about who I was before. I thought back over all the places I'd lived, the communes and the weird and wonderful people in them, and now I was off into another unknown. I could go anywhere in the world. But where? I was rootless, had no ties anywhere. Maybe I'd get on another plane. Just fly away. Go anywhere. America, Europe, Australia. Back to Devon? I'd liked it there and could hook up with Hugh and Minna. Or India? I'd liked it there too. Maybe New Zealand – visit Mum and Dad?

*

I spent the next week in a daze, at sea, without a rudder. As long as I was with the Rainbow Children, I'd had a purpose, a direction. Now that was all gone.

I finally got through to the number the founders had provided on the letter.

'You'll be sent a plane ticket back to the UK,' a girl told me.

'But what do I do when I get there?' I asked.

'Do you have family or friends?'

'No family. A few friends.'

'Then I suggest you look them up,' she said.

'I have no money.'

'Ah yes, that. As you can imagine, we can't hand out funds to everyone who was involved. You'll have to get a job. See it as a challenge.'

She sounded as if she didn't give a damn.

I decided to call and ask Rosie if she knew what had happened to Alec.

'Alec? Oh Mitch, he was one of the first out of here, first plane out back to the States. Please don't tell me you still hold a candle for him.'

'Not really. I . . . oh, I don't know, everything's up in the air now isn't it? I thought he might have been in touch. We were close.'

'You and about a dozen other women. Gail's in pieces, not to mention a good number of others. He had his own private harem all convinced they were special to him. You have to let go of him, Mitch. Brutal though it is to say it, there were a number of women he was involved with, all thinking they were The One. He strung you all along. Forget about him.'

I laughed. 'I will. I was just considering my options and that one has just been deleted from the list,' I said. *Forget about him. Wise words Rosie,*I thought after she'd hung up. Let him go. So he'd sent me the note saying let's get married next time around. He'd probably sent the same card to all his admirers. I'd been stupid to consider him even for a moment. *So what are my other options?* I asked myself. I didn't have any. I went to my room and wept, not for Alec but for everyone I'd had to let go in my life – Jack, Ally, Sara, Jo, Sara Rose, my mum and dad, Fi. I was alone in a strange land with no family or friends. What was I to do and where should I go?

*

A week later, I was packed and ready to return to the UK. I'd decided there was nothing for me in South Africa and it would be best to return to the land I knew. Andrew was going to meet me at the airport and Tom had offered to let me stay at his place until I decided what I wanted to do.

Jonas drove me to the airport, where he dropped me off at the departure lounge.

'You take care,' I said and gave him a final hug.

'You too. It's been short but sweet, but new chapters beckon for both of us.'

I'd grown fond of Jonas and was reassured he had a place to go back to with his family in Durban.

I picked up my bag and walked into the airport where I joined the queue for UK travellers. I'd only been in the line a few moments when someone tapped me on the shoulder.

'Hey you.'

I turned to see a face I recognized, kind eyes smiling at me. I smiled back at him. 'Hey yourself. Fancy seeing you here.'

Chapter Forty-Seven

Sara

Present day, April

We were finally meeting Mitch's friend Rosie.
En route we dropped into the office to see how things were progressing.

'All looking good,' Gary glanced at Jo. 'A lot of editing to do – you're going to continue to help me sort through what to keep and what to throw?'

'Sure,' said Jo. 'Maybe we could link to some of the pet rescue places and feature animals in there. It could be a real boost for them, help them find homes.'

'Excellent idea, Jo,' said Gary. I knew for a fact that Gary had already got Lauren and the researchers on the case looking into the rescue centres. He was asking Jo for her help as an excuse to spend more time with her. *Good for him*, I thought. He was a nice man, generous and kind. I hoped it worked out for them, Jo deserved a good man.

'Programme Four is pretty much well in the bag with Luca. We also have a short piece with friends who have felt thwarted or left behind as others moved on without them but, as you requested, we've tried to keep it positive and have got a great section on how to deal with bullies at school and in the workplace.'

'We need some men in that one too,' I said. 'Maybe focus on how if men don't nurture friendships, they can end up lonely – so not how friends can hurt, but how *not having them* can hurt.'

'Sure, good idea, we'll add that in,' said Gary. 'Programme five, friendships across the cultures, is also pretty well sorted. We also thought that in this programme, we'd feature ideas of where you can make friends.'

'Where?' asked Ally. 'I'll need to make some new ones, especially if I move.'

'You've got us,' said Jo.

'Yes, but you're not local. I need friends who'll drop in on me and I on them; people with whom I can do things in everyday life – have a coffee, go for a walk – all the mundane everyday stuff.'

'Research is showing shared interests are a great way to meet new people – book groups, walking groups, wine-tasting evenings,' said Gary. 'Whatever floats your boat. Anything that gets you out mingling with people. Then, of course, programme six is your story, Sara. I hear you've made some headway at last and have a contact with an old friend of Mitch's.'

'Yes. We're meeting her this afternoon.'

'You are? No one told me. It's a bit short notice to send a camera crew but . . .'

'Yes, about that Gary. Ally, Jo and I have talked about it and decided that we want to meet Rosie on our own, and if we do find Mitch as a result, we want to meet her on her own too. I think it might feel too intrusive if we take a camera crew along, plus if Rosie does lead us to Mitch, and it sounds as if she knows where she is, Mitch might think that the only reason we've been trying to find her is because we want material for a TV show.'

'She could be very offended,' said Jo. 'As if we're trying to capitalize on the story with little thought about her reaction.'

'Especially now we have the news of her daughter looking for her too,' said Jo.

'Mitch was part of the reason that the idea for the programme came about,' I said, 'but now we're so close to finding her, I don't want such personal and private moments filmed for the whole world to see.'

Gary groaned. 'But it could be TV gold, really emotional stuff. Audiences will love it.'

'Tough,' I said. 'I remember working on a programme once after a fire in a school. I had an earpiece in, connecting me to the producer. I was interviewing one of the mothers whose child had been injured. She was barely keeping it together when I heard the producer's voice in my ear whispering, 'Get her to cry, we're going to zoom in for a close-up shot.' Heartless. I didn't do it and I swore I'd never be involved in that kind of programme-making again.'

Gary looked sheepish. 'It's the world we work in. Our job is to get good stories.'

'But not to take advantage of people at their most fragile or vulnerable moments. We still don't know why Mitch gave up her daughter but, whatever the reason, I doubt if it's something she'll want broadcast to the public.'

Gary sighed. 'Point taken. It's your series so you call the shots but don't rule out the cameras completely. At a later date, Mitch might agree to being filmed. Her daughter Lisa might agree too.'

'Maybe, but first we have to arrange their reunion and then

put them in the picture. If they don't want to be a part of the series, I'm sure we could find someone else for the last programme. Maybe we could keep the material on where to make new friends for the last programme so we'd end on a really positive note. We can easily find people who've relocated and have good stories to tell about how they made a new social circle, that sort of thing.'

Gary put his head in his hands and sighed. 'Fine, just keep me in the picture.'

'And we can bring everyone from the series together, a big party, a sort of summing up. As well as how to make friends – we could get some experts in to give examples and advice. Go back to some of our celebrities; they can talk about how they made friends, how they sustain them, and we could incorporate those rules of friendship I've been working on'

Gary lifted his head. 'Could work, I guess, but I'm not giving up on the idea that you and your pals will be there too, including Mitch and her daughter.'

*

Later that day, Rosie Mason greeted Ally, Jo and I like long-lost friends. She was a petite and attractive black lady, her hair braided in cornrows, and she was dressed in a leaf-green tunic and jeans and silver jewellery. She had the look of an artist or designer and exuded warmth and a sense of calm. I liked her immediately. She welcomed us and ushered us into her cosy sitting room. 'I have news for you, but first get settled and I'll make tea. Builder's, camomile, green, peppermint, ginger, chai? We have the lot here. Remember back in the days when a cup of tea was a cup of tea; now it's like a complicated question-naire – and don't even get me started on coffee.'

'Earl Grey,' said Jo. 'We all like that.'

'Women after my own heart. Now get comfy and I'll be back in a jiff.'

She returned soon after with a tray laden with cups, teapot, and what looked like home-made cake.

'Lemon drizzle,' she said. 'My husband Patrick made it this morning. Who wants a piece?' Rosie proceeded to cut generous slices of cake, put them onto plates and handed them out to all of us.

'So you knew Mitch when she was with the Rainbow Children?' I asked.

'That's right. We shared a room many a time.'

'And you're still friends?' Jo asked.

'We are, but first I have to ask you, why now? Why look for Mitch now after so long?'

I quickly filled her in on the programme idea.

Rosie looked thoughtful. 'Ah, so you want to contact her for your series?'

'Yes and no,' I replied. 'It started out that way. I came up with the idea to make a series about looking for friends because I'd been thinking about them, the importance of maintaining contact with the good old ones and realizing that I'd lost touch with mine. That led me to getting back in touch with Ally and Jo. We were all close at school, and Mitch was one of our gang too.'

'I think she might be hurt if she thought the only reason you were getting in touch was to make good TV,' said Rosie.

'I agree. We agree. Exactly what we thought and, in fact, we have just told the producer that. I don't care about the TV programme; no, that's not true, I do. I'll be presenting it and I still feel passionate about exploring the theme of friendship, but we won't use the search for Mitch as part of it. It's started to feel too personal now.'

'We just want to reconnect,' said Jo. 'I want to talk to her about some of her experiences in meditation when she was with the Rainbow Children. When she used to tell us about it all, I didn't get it, but I think I do now.'

'Why's that?' Rosie asked.

'Sounds mad. I had a near-death experience recently, out of body into the tunnel, into the light. I've never felt such peace.'

'Sounds amazing,' said Rosie, 'not mad at all. I've read a lot about people who've had similar experiences.'

'It sure shifts your perspective on things,' said Jo. 'I remember Mitch saying she'd experienced a light when she was meditating. I always thought she meant the light of clarity, but now I realize she saw actual light.'

'Me too,' said Rosie. 'Not every time I sat to meditate, but enough times to know that there is an energy or force inside all of us and it makes you feel very peaceful to connect with it. But we were striving for much more than that. The idea was that the more people who felt peace in their lives, the more peaceful they would be in their everyday lives and so it would spread.'

'Why was the movement called the Rainbow Children?' I asked.

'Rainbows are a universal symbol for peace and harmony, and that's what the group was all about,' Rosie replied.

'Is there anything left of the group?' Ally asked.

'Not really. It all dissolved around 1976. Some followers tried to keep things alive but it had lost momentum. I still meditate and use a lot of what was taught – kindness and respect for others and the planet, and we still do what we can to promote awareness of climate change. So much of it was good common sense, but a lot of us realized that we never really knew the teachers behind it all. They were always at a distance from us, like rock stars: tiny figures on a stage. Who knows what they were like in their private lives.'

'I went to one of the meetings,' said Jo.

'You did? And?' asked Rosie.

'I liked what they were saying, but didn't think you had to live in a commune as Mitch chose to.'

'You didn't. Only a handful, couple of hundred, maybe more, chose to live in the communes in the UK. That's where Mitch and I met. We recognized each other as kindred spirits from the off, but the members in the communes were only a small percentage of the overall followers. Most people carried on normally and incorporated the teachings into their daily lives and, like me now, probably still do on some level.'

'I felt there were other groups saying very similar things,' said Ally. 'The Rajneesh, the maharishi, the Hare Krishnas; back then there were so many gurus around, all saying we have to look inside to find peace.'

'Absolutely. We weren't saying anything new, just trying to work towards a kinder, more caring world, and it's interesting to see how much of it has become more popular now – like mindfulness, eating fresh organic food, caring for the environment – all the stuff we were into.'

'I just want to see Mitch again,' said Ally. 'See where's she been and, of course, let her know that her daughter's been looking for her.'

Rosie looked shocked. 'Daughter? What daughter? What do you mean? Looking for her?'

'She has a daughter, Lisa,' said Ally. 'Didn't you know?'

Rosie looked stunned. 'No. She never said anything about a daughter. Now I'm confused. Maybe my Mitch is a different one to yours. How old is Lisa?'

'In her forties. We didn't know about her either, until recently.

We discovered that Mitch had a daughter who she gave up for adoption, probably just prior to joining the commune. She wants to meet her mother and has been looking for her.'

'Are you sure? She never told me, never breathed a word.' Rosie didn't say anything for a while. 'What about the father?'

Jo filled her in on what we knew about Jack and the timing of his death.

Rosie let out a deep breath. 'Wow, that's so sad. I knew about her family, her sister, and even about you three. I thought I knew everything about Mitch, but clearly not.' She was quiet for a few moments as she took in what we'd told her. 'What you've told me explains a lot. In some respects, Mitch wasn't like the rest of us back then, in that some of us, many of us, in the commune were bouncing off the walls trying to live the celibate life and go beyond desire in our pursuit of a goal of detachment. We were all in our twenties and not many of us were truly cut out for the life of a monk or nun, which was virtually what we were. Mitch was different. She was much more focused than I ever was, which is probably why she was chosen to be an indigo. You had to be detached to live the way that they did.'

Ally, Jo and I glanced at each other. 'Indigo?'

'Yes. She was chosen to be one. It meant giving everything up.'

Ally let out a deep breath. 'That wasn't the Mitch we knew. Yes, she was endlessly curious about life, vibrant and open to experiences, but she was the last person on earth I would have said would go the way she did. She was a boy magnet at school, and way ahead of the rest of us in terms of experience; always in love or dating someone, which is why we could never understand why she cut herself off from mainstream life and gave up so much.'

'I think we know why now,' said Rosie. 'Losing Jack, and then whatever happened with her child must have hurt her badly. I guess the Rainbow Children provided a safe haven for her, and a purpose in life. And yet, you must believe it wasn't all sacrifice. Yes, it appeared we gave up some aspects, but there were years when things were buzzing, the communes were happening places to be, and I don't think I have ever laughed as much as I did in those years. We were going to change the world, were having great experiences; we were young and inspired.'

'And there were no men she was interested in?' Jo asked.

Rosie laughed. 'Only one, but nothing came of it because he was a Casanova with a capital C, the kind of man who likes the challenge and the chase, then would lose interest. She did consider him for a nanosecond but she wised up pretty fast as to his true nature. Will you tell her about her daughter?'

'Of course,' I said. 'But where is she? We're dying to know.'

'South Africa. Stellenbosch. She's been living there since 1977. She was sent out there as an indigo just before the movement folded. She grew to love the country and stayed on.'

'South Africa?' said Ally. 'No wonder we couldn't find her.'

'And of course she goes by her married name now,' said Rosie.

'She got married?' asked Ally.

'Yes, to a lovely man, Rob. She met him on her flight out to Cape Town, then bumped into him again just as she was about to leave. Great timing! Her husband's family had a hotel and vineyard in the Stellenbosch area which he inherited. I've been over there to stay a few times . . .'

'How is she?' asked Jo.

'Great, really happy. She loves it out there and, I have to say, I have been tempted a few times to go and live there myself, but I'm not sure I could deal with the political unrest.'

'Children?' I asked.

'Two boys, all grown-up now with kids of their own.'

Jo laughed. 'So she's a grandmother. I don't suppose you have any photos?'

'Loads,' said Rosie. 'Want to see them? The place where she lives is absolutely beautiful and the hotel so much more than that. With Mitch's input, it's a centre for well-being and they run all sorts of courses where people can go and stay, either to chill in the spa or do various classes; and her gardens, wow, you should see those. The centre has acres of land so, as well as the grape growing, Mitch has herb gardens and vegetable plots; everything's fresh when you stay there.' She got up, found her laptop and we all gathered round. Moments later, we were looking at photos of an attractive couple standing in a sun-filled garden with two yellow Labradors by their side.

Jo's eyes filled with tears. 'She looks fantastic. To tell the truth, we had even considered the idea she might have died, so it's so good to see her looking so . . . so alive.'

'She does look good, doesn't she?' said Rosie. 'The location and lifestyle out there suits her. All the knowledge of planting and the land that she'd learnt while with the Rainbow Children was put to good use. She fell in love with Rob and he with her and they were married a year after they met at the airport.'

'It's a real happy-ever-after story,' said Ally. 'I'm so glad things worked out for her.'

'Me too but . . . how are we going to do this?' I asked. 'Will you tell Mitch we've been here?'

'Of course,' said Rosie. 'But whether to call her . . . or maybe, if she agrees to it, we could set up a Skype or FaceTime call so you can all see her and she can see you.'

'Or do we go over there in person?' Jo asked. 'And what about Lisa? At what stage do we tell Mitch that her daughter has been looking for her?'

'And how's she going to feel about that?' I asked. 'We still don't know what happened, nor if Mitch wants to reconnect.'

'And how's Lisa going to feel when she finds out she has two brothers and nephews?'

'Nathan and Leigh and their kids Callum and Josh,' said Rosie.

'If Mitch does want to meet Lisa, it might be better for them to meet in person,' I said.

'Ask her what she wants,' said Jo, 'then we can take it from there.'

'Sounds like a plan,' I said. 'I can't wait.'

Chapter Forty-Eight

Ally

Present day, May

Rosie tried to reach Mitch a few times but the phone just rang and rang. In the end, we had things to do. I was going to watch the filming of the *Long Lost Friends* series so far with Sara, and Jo was meeting Gary for a drink. Rosie promised she'd keep trying and call us all as soon as she had news.

As the time grew closer to reaching Mitch, I found I had more and more concerns. 'We hadn't been able to trace Mitch until now,' I said to Sara, 'but if she'd chosen to, I'm pretty sure that over the decades she could have found one of us. There has to be a reason why she hasn't, doesn't there?'

Sara nodded. 'I've been thinking the same. Is she angry with us? Or just plain not interested? I'd envisaged the big happy reunion, but now I wonder if that's going to happen.'

'Maybe we've left it too late,' I said. 'One of us could have tried to find her before. I reckon we're all as guilty as each other.'

'Guess all we can do now is wait and see, though I must say I feel a certain trepidation.'

Part of the reason I wanted to go along with Sara was not just to watch the footage so far, but also because Katie Brookfield was coming in to watch with us. I'd been thinking a lot about how I wanted to live in my future, and the living situation Katie'd created with her Bonnet friends had appeal. I wanted to chat more to her about it.

'I'm having the most marvellous time, Ally,' said Katie when we met in her hotel in Kensington during a break, and Sara was off editing her to camera shots. 'The crew are treating us like stars.'

'Well you are a star,' I said, 'and after seeing how you live with your friends, I wanted to ask you a few things off camera.'

Katie looked at me affectionately and reached out and took my hand. 'I wondered how you'd been coping since Michael passed. Is that why you want to ask?'

I nodded and felt tears well up. 'Amazing how your life can change in a minute. All Michael and I built together just doesn't work any more – the house, the lifestyle. I don't like being there on my own. The house is too big just for one and, although I know it's a contradiction, the silence is loud.'

'What about your own Bonnets? I mean, your own close friends like mine? Sara? Jo?' Katie asked.

'Yes, but they're at a distance. I have great friends near where I live but they're all in couples; not that they mind me being the single amongst them, but I do. And I've only recently reconnected with Sara. I'm not sure that, with Jo, we could live together as you do with your friends.'

'But you've been wondering about it?'

'Yes and no. We get on, but it's pretty clear we'd drive each other mad if it were a permanent arrangement. We all have our own ways of doing things.'

'That's exactly why my friends and I opted for close but independent housing. It's important to have one's own space as you get older.'

'True, but I also want company. That's why I asked about how you all felt at night.'

'Of course, that's when you feel it the most. I'd drop the idea of sharing a house, just as we did. Besides the need for independence, etc., there would be the questions of – for instance – are you going to have one big communal kitchen, shared bathrooms, TV – and if so, who has the remote? No, in the end, we realized it wasn't going to work if we lived in the same house, which is why we came up with the arrangement as it is now. We're within five minutes of each other. We all live the way we want to, decorate the way we want to but, if we want company, we're there, and as I said when you came to meet everyone, at night we're only a telephone call away.'

'Sounds perfect. I might look into that if the others are open to it.'

'Something else you may need to consider, Ally, is that – as you get older – you'll find that although in one sense you might feel that you need people more, you also have to do a lot of letting go and learn not to need. You won't survive otherwise.'

'Why?'

Katie sighed. 'Because things shift and change all the time. It's true that friendships are precious but, in order to be happy, you must learn to let go, have no expectations and to become self-sufficient. Your friendship circle will reduce, not through fallings out or any wish to lose them or be alone, but circumstances change. Some people leave the party altogether . . .'

'You mean die?'

Katie nodded. 'Harsh fact of life. You will lose friends, people you have relied on, especially as you get older. I know, you've just lost Michael. It's tough. Some friends will also pass, others will disappear into a renewed family when their children have grandchildren and suddenly that takes all their time and energy. They have their own family bubble. You will be happier if you can learn not to need anyone and curiously, in doing so, people will be more attracted to you.'

'How am I supposed to do that?'

'Meditate, fill your house with books so that in every room there are unwrapped gifts to be opened, do classes, keep learning so that you may occupy your time if friendships do change. Learn to like your own company. How many of you are there in your group of single women?'

'Three, four – no, three. There were four of us, but Mitch, the fourth of our group, disappeared when we were in our twenties. We've just discovered that she's in South Africa and are hoping to speak to her on Skype or FaceTime, if not today, then in the next few days. We also discovered that she had a daughter when she was nineteen or twenty. I never knew about that, nor did Jo or Sara. Her daughter's been looking for her.'

'Sounds exciting. Have you told her daughter yet?'

'We have, as soon as we discovered where Mitch was. She wants to come out to South Africa with us to meet her but, understandably, is cautious – so many emotions there and I guess the fear of being let down if it doesn't work out.'

'And you have to consider that your friend Mitch may not want to be found by her, or by you. There may be a reason she disappeared.'

'True, and exactly what Sara and I were just saying, but that's what makes it all the more intriguing. What has she been doing all these years? Why didn't she tell us, her oldest friends at the time, about her child? I share her daughter Lisa's apprehension. Mitch might be angry with us for not having been there for her in a time of need. Who knows? Really none of us knows how it's going to turn out.'

Chapter Forty-Nine

Sara

Present day, May

Rosie called at eight thirty the next morning. She sounded as high as a kite. 'Good news. I've been in touch with Mitch. She was very surprised to hear from you all after all this time.'

'Surprised-happy or surprised-shocked?'

'A bit of both, if I'm honest. I told her how you'd tracked her down and found me and she was more surprised-shocked and did ask why after all this time. Of course, I couldn't tell her, nor do I want to be the one to tell her about Lisa. I think that must come from you.'

'Will she talk to us?'

'She will; she's as curious about all of you as you are about her, and said she will be at her computer at midday today if that suits.'

I breathed a sigh of relief. 'It does, that's fantastic news.'

'I could come to you if you like.'

'Great, see you then,' I said, gave her the address and went to tell Jo and Ally.

*

Rosie appeared on the doorstep just before midday with a bunch of tulips and a home-made carrot cake. 'How you all feeling?' she asked.

'Bit nervous,' I said. Ally nodded.

'I can't wait,' said Jo. 'Who's going to tell her about Lisa?'

'I think you should, Sara,' said Ally. 'You started all this.'

I set the laptop on the island in the kitchen, we gathered round, and Rosie gave us details to get through to Mitch. Moments later, I pressed connect and there she was, Michelle Blake, looking into the screen. She looked as anxious as we all were.

I felt a rush of affection. 'Hey you,' I said as I tried to take in that the woman on the screen was the one I had known. The Mitch I remembered had been in her early twenties and, unlike with Jo and Ally, who I'd seen through all the decades, it was a shock to see her face looking lined and older. As I looked more closely, though, I could see that she'd aged well and had a different beauty to the girl of so many years earlier: more mature, obviously, but still with the fine bone structure and slim figure.

Jo was jumping up and down behind me and waving. 'Mitch, hey, hi.'

'Hi Mitch,' said Ally. 'It's me, Ally. Bet this is a shock. Do you recognize us?'

'Of course, though I still remember you as girls,' said Mitch as she stared at us all, 'but . . . you've hardly changed.'

Now we were face to face, or rather FaceTime to FaceTime, I

suddenly felt lost for words and slightly awkward. I'd envisaged us leaping up and down with joy as Jo was, but seeing Mitch after so long, I suddenly felt shy, unsure how to be with this person I had known so well but didn't know any more.

'I . . . I can't believe it,' Mitch continued. 'Let me look at you all. Sara hi, Jo, Ally. How the hell are you?' She was dressed in a blue shirt and jeans, and her hair, white-blonde with silver streaks, was cut into layers and fell just past her shoulders.

'You look bloody amazing,' said Jo. 'Like some American country and western star – Emmylou Harris.'

Mitch smiled. 'You look pretty good too, my old friend.'

'Less of the old,' said Jo.

Jo was right, she did look amazing, her skin tanned and glowing with good health. *They say that in later life, you end up with a face that shows the life you have lived. Mitch looked serene,* I thought, *as though she'd lived a happy life.*

'So, where have you been? What's been happening?' said Mitch. 'Hell, so much to catch up on.'

I searched her face to gauge her true feelings. It was hard to read what was really going on. She seemed pleased to see us, her manner friendly and polite but slightly stiff, which could be nerves or could be that she felt, as I did, that the distance and years had made us into strangers.

'I'm sorry we've left it so long,' said Jo. 'Why did we do that?'

'Me too,' said Ally. 'Good to see you, old friend.'

'Yes, you too, long time, long *long* time. I hardly know what to say or where to begin . . .'

'We should get together properly, don't you think?' asked Jo.

Mitch hesitated for a moment. 'Get together? Er . . . I suppose we could.'

'We could come there,' said Jo.

Mitch looked surprised and caught off guard. '*Here*? Come out and stay? Well, we have the space, that's for sure, I . . . I suppose you could. We have a hotel here and a spa; let me think about it, talk to my husband. You could all have your own lodge in the grounds.'

'Lodge in the grounds? Where *are* you?' said Jo.

Ally laughed. 'And how do you/we précis forty years?'

'We meet up. We must meet up in person,' said Jo. 'So. Who goes first? Where have you been for forty years? And what's been happening?'

'Jo. My dear sweet Jo,' said Mitch. 'Where have *you* been? I tried to contact you all a couple of times, you know I did, but I didn't know where you were. Then after I met Rob, he's my husband, life took over, children, looking after this place . . .' She held up her arms and indicated her location. She was sitting on a wooden veranda with jacaranda bushes in the background. It looked like paradise.

'Us too, we tried to find you,' I said, 'but you'd gone from London, and no one at The Seventh Star knew where you were. I did go in to try and find you.'

Mitch studied me closely. 'The Seventh Star? Oh my god, that's a long time ago – in the hippie days.' She looked at all of us. 'Are you guys married? Have children? Where do you live?'

'I'm in Wiltshire, widowed,' said Jo. 'Two children, four grand-children.'

'Oh, I'm sorry you lost your husband, Jo, and . . . I'm so sorry I never made it to your wedding.'

Jo shrugged. 'No need, he turned out to be an arse, though you might have spotted that if you'd come. You might have saved me.'

Mitch laughed out loud.

'I'm in Devon, also widowed recently, husband not an arse,' said Ally, 'two children, one grandchild.'

'Oh Ally, I'm so sorry,' said Mitch, 'about the widowed part. How are you doing?'

Ally grimaced. 'Adjusting.'

'Then you must come and stay out here, definitely, it's a very restful place. Seriously. You'd be so welcome. What about you, Sara?'

'Divorced. I married a man who ran off with my best friend—'

'Wasn't your best friend then,' said Mitch. 'What an idiot.'

I shrug. 'History. I'm over it.' I felt Mitch staring at me again and I glanced away. I'd forgotten how she could zone in on a person as if looking right into them and seeing all their secrets.

'And you?' asked Jo.

'Very happy. I love it out here. I found my place. Married with two lovely boys, though hardly boys now as they're both grown-up with their own kids.'

'Mitch, before we go any further, we . . . er . . . we have something to tell you,' I said.

'OK. Oh. Looks serious. What is it?'

'I . . . well, while we were looking for you, we met someone else who has been trying to find you—'

'Not the tax man, I hope . . .'

'No, not the tax man – your daughter. Lisa.'

Mitch appeared to freeze on the screen. 'Daughter?' she whispered.

I nodded. 'Lisa. She's in her forties and wants to meet you.'

Mitch's eyes filled with tears. 'Oh my god, how did you . . .? How did she . . .? Lisa? So that's what they called her. You know about her.' She was quiet for a few minutes, clearly trying to digest what I'd just told her, and I felt so glad I'd insisted to Gary that this was all to be off camera. 'How did she – Lisa – find you? Or me? Where is she? I tried to find her. I hoped that when she was old enough to look for me that she would, but nothing ever came of it so I told myself I had to let go. Some adopted children don't want to ever find their birth parents. I guessed she didn't want to know me. The adoption agencies said that can happen sometimes but . . . I always hoped . . .'

'It's true. She didn't want to look for you in the beginning,' I said. 'She said she had the best parents and after she'd found out she was adopted, she didn't want to upset them . . .'

'When did they tell her? What age?'

'Fourteen, I think,' said Jo.

Mitch nodded, taking it in.

'She said that at first she was angry,' I said, 'upset that she had been discarded, abandoned—'

'Oh no, it wasn't like that.' Mitch's eyes welled up with tears and she was clearly finding the conversation difficult.

'I am sorry to spring this on you, Mitch, but . . .'

Mitch took a deep breath as if struggling with an avalanche of emotions. 'No, no. I want to know, tell me everything. So she didn't want to find me then?'

'Not at first. She said that everything changed when she had children of her own, then it became a compulsion. She had to know why you had given her up.'

Mitch nodded again. 'Makes sense. I thought she might not want to know me when she heard that she was adopted but people change don't they? I should have updated the agencies as to where I was, never given up looking for her. I guess I got good at shutting some things away and once I was settled here with Rob, my previous life felt further and further away and I told myself I had to let it go.' She looked overwhelmed and sad. 'How is she? Where is she?'

'She's here in London. She's great, vibrant, she has two children . . .'

'One of them is the spit of you, Scarlet, she's sixteen,' said Ally. 'Lisa had a career as a dancer before becoming a mother, but now she teaches dance. Remember how you wanted to go to dance college back in the day?'

Mitch took a few more deep breaths. 'I do remember wanting to dance. I'd love to meet Lisa. I must tell her how it was when she was born. Does she want to meet me or just call and ask her questions?'

'She wants to meet you, very much,' said Jo.

'But how would you like to do it? I asked. 'On FaceTime, Skype or in person?'

'Oh. Phew. Let me think about that. Maybe both? I'll talk to Rob. He knows all about her.' Suddenly she smiled. 'I named her Sara Rose, you know. Remember, Sara? We promised each other that if we ever had girls, you'd name yours Michelle, I'd name mine Sara. And Rose was—'

'After Black Rose, Jack's band,' I said. 'I know. Lisa told me. Mitch, I was so touched by—'

Mitch looked shocked. 'You know about Jack too?'

'We do, or at least we know a bit now, that he died . . . but what happened?

'He died on his way to see me. Does Lisa know that?'

'She'd worked it out,' said Ally, 'though not the details.'

'We'd planned to get married and were about to tell my parents. I'd cooked, it was to be a great celebration, but Jack never made it.'

'You must have been devastated,' said Jo.

'I was, but more angry and confused at first. It was a hellish time. You see, I didn't know he'd been killed on the motorway on his way north. I thought he'd done a runner, abandoned me, left with the band for their tour of America then Europe. I hated him for it. I'd given my heart and believed that he felt the same way, but then I thought he'd just deserted me. Of course he hadn't, but I only found out a year later that he'd died, and by then it was too late. I'd given Sara Rose away.' She gulped back a tear, the memory still clearly raw, even after so long. 'My parents took it badly. I lived with them for a time while I was pregnant, but it was awful. You probably remember my dad . . .'

We all nodded. 'Scary,' said Jo.

'Strict,' said Ally.

'Disappointed,' said Mitch, 'so I moved to London and stayed with Fi. That was only marginally better, but at least she didn't judge.'

Ally, Jo and I glanced at each other. 'So Jack never knew that you were pregnant?' I asked.

'Oh yes, he did know, he was over the moon. No one else knew, no one in the band. We planned to tell my parents first then let the band know. Truth is, the band didn't know how serious we were about each other. We'd planned to break it to them gently.'

'Christ, Mitch, that's tragic,' said Jo. 'Why the hell didn't you let us know?'

Yes why? I thought, as we waited for Mitch to reply.

Mitch hesitated. 'I tried to,' she said finally, 'I left messages for you all at your various universities—'

'Not saying you needed help,' said Ally.

Mitch looked wistful, 'It's not the kind of message you leave with some stranger in your digs who happened to pick up the phone.'

'You could have said *something* to indicate what had happened,' I said.

There was an awkward silence as each of us struggled with

our feelings; for me it was a mix of shame, guilt, and frustration that I hadn't known the facts.

'I could have,' said Mitch. 'Why didn't I? I was so mixed up back then. I was numb for a long time, my confidence, my reality had taken an almighty knock, I felt I'd got so much wrong. Fucked up, big time. Part of me withdrew to some place deep inside and closed the door. When I discovered that Jack had died, I regretted with all my heart that I'd given Sara Rose away. I thought she would be a reminder of his abandonment when actually she would have been a reminder of a man I'd loved and lost. I put it all in a place inside and locked it away, put a wall up to protect myself; didn't want to talk about it or even think about it. I hid behind that wall for a long time but, in keeping the hurt out, I kept some of the good stuff out too, and I guess that includes all of you as well, my old friends.'

I wished I could reach out and hug her. 'I understand, Mitch,' I said. 'I understand all about hiding behind a wall. Sometimes it's not even a conscious thing, more like self-preservation.'

Mitch nodded, smiled sadly and glanced at Jo. 'I think that's partly why I couldn't face your wedding Jo. I felt bad about that. And I don't doubt that you would have been there for me. I'm sorry, but what could you have done? We were all so young. I was nineteen, thought I knew it all but of course I didn't. I feel bad about the way I acted, and letting go of Sara Rose was the biggest regret of my life. After all this time, years, there hasn't been a day when I haven't wondered where she is, what she looks like—'

'We have a photo of Lisa if you'd like to see it,' said Jo.

Mitch caught her breath. 'I would.'

Jo dived into her bag, pulled out her phone and found the photo we'd taken of Lisa. She held it up to the screen so that Mitch could see. She studied it for a long time in silence then suddenly she disappeared from the screen. We all looked at each other as we could hear the sound of her sobbing.

At our end of the call, Jo, Ally and I looked at each other. *Had this been the wrong approach?* I wondered.

'Mitch, are you there?' I asked after a short while.

Finally a red-eyed Mitch returned to our screen. 'Woah, sorry,' she said as she sat down and faced the laptop camera again. She smiled weakly, 'And the wall comes tumbling down. Lisa looks so like her father. I can see Jack in her face.'

'Mitch, we so wish we'd been there for you. I am so sorry I wasn't,' I said.

'And me,' said Jo,

'And me,' said Ally.

Mitch nodded. 'And me,' she said finally.

'She's a beauty, isn't she? Your Lisa,' said Ally.

'Have you any more photos? What part of London does she live in?'

'Camden,' I replied. 'Mitch, I know it's a lot to take in all in one go but, if she agrees, she could come out with us and she can tell you herself.'

'Yes. Of course, I'll pay,' said Mitch. 'Tell her I'll cover all the costs.'

Rosie had stood to one side for most of the call, but now she moved closer so that she could be seen by Mitch as well. 'And why didn't you tell me about her?' she asked. 'I thought we told each other everything.'

Mitch sighed. 'Wow, this is some phone call, isn't it? Dear Rosie, what can I say? I owe you an apology too. Why didn't I tell you? I'd let go of the old Mitch when I met you, buried her. It was so painful, I made myself move on, reinvented myself. If I'd talked about what had happened, about Sara Rose, it would have made her real, kept the pain of losing her alive, and yet there was nothing I could have done, having signed all the adoption papers. I wanted to move on, so I threw myself into the Rainbow Children way of life and, in a way, that was my salvation.'

Rosie nodded. 'I understand.'

'Thank you.'

'But no more secrets, OK?' said Rosie.

Mitch smiled. 'Sure. But you guys – Ally, Jo, Sara – have you been in touch all this time? And why contact me now?'

I filled her in on the TV programme idea and how that had led to reconnecting with Ally and Jo, 'and of course, we had to find you.'

Her face became still, betraying no emotion. 'Ah, so I was the fourth one?' said Mitch.

'We don't want to film,' chorused Jo and I.

'Not any more,' I continued. 'The TV programme was the catalyst to finding you, but they can find someone else for the sixth programme, I've already told them that. The important thing was finding you, and we would have done that regardless of the TV series.'

Mitch hesitated. 'Let me think about it, Sara. You've given me a lot to take in, I can't think straight or make any decisions. But yes to meeting Lisa. So she knows that you're contacting me today?'

'She does,' said Jo. 'She's at home, waiting to hear how you want to take it from here.'

'We thought it would be too much to have her here today as well,' I said.

Mitch nodded. 'You're probably right, although I can hardly wait now that I know she wants to make contact. Oh, dear girl. Please tell her what I've told you. I wish I hadn't had her adopted. I think about her all the time and would love to meet her, more than anything. Please ask her to forgive me.'

'We will,' I said, 'and I'm sure she'll understand.'

Mitch sighed then sat up straight and smiled. 'Onwards, amigos.'

'Onwards,' said Jo. 'I want to climb into my computer screen and give you an enormous cyber-hug.'

'Me too. Blue skies? Sunshine? Mitch?' said Ally, and turned to Sara and me. 'Road trip, ladies?'

Jo laughed. 'More like plane trip. I'm in.'

'Me too,' I said. 'We'll set it up, Mitch. Watch this space.'

Chapter Fifty

Ally

Present day, May

Flights have been set up for a week's time. South Africa here we come. I was grateful because it would be a further distraction from the empty house that awaited me back in Devon.

As I busied myself with picking out summer clothes, choosing photos to show Mitch of the last forty years (we'd all agreed to take a selection), I had two interesting invites.

One to stay with Katie Brookfield at the village just outside Bath, or alternatively to rent the cottage owned by Rebecca – aka The Duchess – whilst she was still in Italy. I liked the set-up Katie had going with her friends, but I knew I wasn't ready for that yet. Katie and her friends were in their eighties, I was almost twenty years younger. I would go and stay with her, though. Those old ladies were a lively bunch and time spent with them was always reviving.

The other invite came in a letter out of the blue.

Dear Ally,

I have a proposition! Nothing ventured, nothing gained as they say, whoever 'they' are. You may balk at it. You may not. I'm hoping not. I'm writing in the first instance so that you can have a think about what I have to say and I will call in a few days to hear your initial response.

You have lost Michael. I lost Emily. It's crap, isn't it? All those well-meaning friends and their invites, but you and I both know someone is missing and it will never be the same again. It won't. We're on our own. We return after the dinner party to a silent house. We wake in the morning, or middle of the night, in an empty house, and all the invites and friends dropping in during the day can't prevent that.

So. Rambling a bit.

I have a house in Sussex. You have a house in Devon. If you're anything like me, you're rattling around in it. What are our options? I'm sure you've been considering a few. Live with one of the kids in a granny or granddad flat? No thanks. Retirement village or apartment? I'm not ready for that, and who knows what the others there would be like? We could take in lodgers? Airbnb so that there's life in the place? Don't think so. I don't think I could do the breakfasts with a cheery smile. I'd be Basil Fawlty personified.

Here's what I'm proposing. We've always got on. We've holidayed together without falling out. I'm not looking for love. No one will ever replace my darling Emily. Nor am I looking to replace Michael for you, and I'm pretty sure that's the last thing on your mind, anyway: I know what you two were to each other. What I am suggesting is this – we share a house. Mine, yours, or we pool resources and buy something together where we both have our own space or wing or whatever, separate bathrooms definitely, kitchens too if you'd prefer that, but a house where I'll be around somewhere in the background, mowing the lawn in the summer, and you'll be around doing your thing too, pruning roses, reading or cooking. I know you like to cook. We'd have someone to go on a city break with, travel with. We'd have someone to ask, 'Fancy a movie or a walk or a meal out?', without having to phone around. That's one of the things I miss, that ease I took for granted of being able to walk into the next room and say, 'Hey – the sun's shining, let's go for a hike.' Or, 'Just seen in the paper that there's a Hockney exhibition on. Get your coat.'

What do you think? Our beloved partners have died, gone and aren't coming back, but for us, life goes on and we don't have to be alone. We could be companions. You might meet someone else in time, you might not. If you do, I'd get out of the way but, in the meantime, we're still here, there's a lot of living to do and it would be nice to do it with a companion, a friend.

What say you? We know each other well enough to be completely honest, so if your reaction is – Are you out of your mind? Bugger off, you daft old idiot, then say that. But if any of this appeals, let's get together and discuss practicalities. I've given it a great deal of thought. I think it could work.

I'll call in a couple of days.

Yours respectfully and hopefully,

Lawrence

X

PS: If nothing else, if we did shack up together, it would at least put a stop to my friends trying to pair me off with their single/widowed/divorced friends. I really cannot do another one of those awkward dinner parties.

His letter made me smile. He was one of my oldest friends, as well as Michael's. I'd always liked him, not fancied him, nor he me, but I did enjoy his company, his dry sense of humour. Like Michael, he had a fine mind, was kind and was a true gentleman. He'd make a great travelling companion.

Two days later, I picked up the phone and dialled his number. 'Deal,' I said. 'Friends who live together.'

I could feel him grinning at the other end of the phone. 'Friends.'

For the first time since Michael had died, I felt a glimmer of hope for the future. I went into the kitchen to make a celebratory coffee and there on the floor was a large white feather. OK, so yes, the wind might have blown it in but, as with the kamikaze pigeon, the timing was uncanny. I smiled as I picked it up. I felt Michael was nearby, watching over me, urging me to go ahead.

Chapter Fifty-One

Sara

Present day, May

The aeroplane landed at Cape Town International Airport to a cheer from the passengers, and soon we were up, gathering our belongings and filing towards the exit sign. As the door opened, we were hit with a blast of heat as if someone had opened a hot oven.

'Sunshine, yay!' said Jo as she got out her sunglasses and we began to alight onto the tarmac where a bus was waiting to take us to the main building.

After the usual queues for passports and luggage, we were finally on our way into town. Lisa had been very quiet on the flight out and was now dozing in the back of the taxi. Despite her confident mask, I could see the vulnerable little girl inside, unsure about how meeting Mitch would be and what she'd feel.

After dumping our bags and a quick shower at our hotel, Jo and I headed off to Mitch's. She'd wanted to come and meet us at the airport, but Lisa wanted to meet her in a more private space, so the plan was that Jo and I would go out in the first instance and Ally and Lisa come out later.

Our journey from the hotel in Constantia took us through the most stunning countryside, away from the coast and mountains towering behind us, and it felt wonderful to have the car window down and a gentle warm breeze blowing through. I wondered how to be and whether to bring up our past, or would it be inappropriate? Today was all about Mitch meeting Lisa. All the same, it felt as if a lot needed to be said and the air to be cleared.

We'd been in the car about an hour when Jo pointed. 'There it is.' We looked to our left to see a sign saying 'Rainbow's End'. Our driver turned into the drive and soon we could see through trees in front of us, an old white board house built in the Dutch style with a veranda at the front. There, at the top of the steps, was Mitch, dressed in a simple blue linen dress, her hair caught up at the back.

As soon as she saw us, her face lit up. 'There you are!' she said as she came forward with a big smile on her face. She looked more relaxed than last time when we'd had our FaceTime call. Understandable. We'd sprung a lot on her. Jo embraced her first, then it was my turn to give her a long hug.

'Look at you two, you've hardly changed.'

'Hah, well that's rot for a start, but you?' said Jo. 'You look fantastic.'

'So do you. Come in. God, where do we start? How are you? How was your journey? I've been counting the days, the hours.'

'My lord, you landed on your feet,' said Jo as she took in the tropical garden and fields stretching out behind, mountains in the distance. 'This is like *Out of Africa.*'

Mitch laughed. 'Well, we are *in* Africa so that's hardly surprising. I know. I've been very lucky – mainly in meeting

Rob and his family, who embraced me as one of their own. This has been a fantastic place for the boys to grow up. Rob will be back later. He took himself off into town with the dogs to give us some space. Want to look around?'

'You bet,' I said.

As we walked around the grounds, we did a bit more catching up. It was great to see Mitch in her environment, clearly happy, clearly self-sufficient, but I sensed that there was still a tension between us and, despite Mitch's warm greeting, part of her was reserved.

'Strange,' she said, after showing us a large vegetable and herb garden, 'after growing up in a city, as we all did, I found I love the countryside and don't miss the urban life at all. I've become a real country girl. My days here are tending the land, walking the dogs, reading, swimming, horse riding.'

'Sounds idyllic,' I said.

'A girl after my own heart,' said Jo, 'though not the horse riding part. But back home I have some land, nothing like the scale of this; just a small menagerie of chickens, cat, dogs, sheep.'

'Have you ever been back to the UK?' I asked.

Mitch shook her head. 'I haven't. There was nothing there for me apart from Sara Rose – sorry, I mean Lisa – and I wasn't sure where she was in any case; her adopted parents could have taken her anywhere. My parents moved to New Zealand, as you know, and Fi eventully moved out there too. We were never that close, anyway, as you probably remember.'

'Have you seen your mum?' asked Jo.

'Oh yes. She's comes out every other year and I've been over to her. She's happy where she is and, with Fi and her family nearby, she has someone to make sure she's OK.'

'And did you ever think of us?' asked Jo.

Mitch thought for a minute. 'I did, of course I did.'

'But you never tried to get in touch, not after the Rainbow Children,' Jo persisted.

'Nor did you. I know—'

'Are you angry with us?' Jo asked.

Mitch looked at the ground and shifted on her feet, clearly finding the conversation difficult. 'Are *you* angry with me?'

'I was,' said Jo, 'my wedding and all that, but hell, that's a long time ago. Even after the Rainbow Children group dissolved, though, you didn't make any effort to get in touch.'

'I know. I could have but so could you, any of you.'

Ah, I thought, *so she was angry with us, possibly still is, and who can blame her?*

'I guess one of the things about friendship is that it needs to be fed,' Mitch continued as she indicated the land, 'like a plant that needs sunshine, food and water, friendships need to be nurtured.'

Should I say something? I asked myself. I didn't want our time together to be unpleasant, taken up with old resentments or miscommunications. 'How do you do that?' I asked. 'Nurture friendship?'

Mitch was quiet for a few moments. 'Shared experiences. Making sure you spend time together in person. When we were at school, we did things together, classes, all the exploration of teenage years and, in doing that, we discovered we were kindred spirits, that we reacted the same way, we understood each other. It's complicated. I suppose I felt that none of you got what I was into when I was with the Rainbow Children and then . . .'

'We were no longer kindred spirits?' I asked.

Mitch nodded. 'For a time, no we weren't. The movement was important to me, but none of you got it or really tried to. Plus so much had happened to me that I couldn't share, didn't want to. But . . . how were you to know? You didn't, so I have no right to be angry with you. As I said, it's complicated. I put that wall up and moved on from my former life and you girls were part of that.'

'I can totally relate to that,' I said. 'Different circumstances, but I did something similar myself. After a rough time, I hid away and, as you said when we FaceTimed, put up a wall to keep the bad out, and in doing that I also kept the good out and let my friendship with Jo and Ally fade. I hope to remedy that with them and with you too.'

Mitch studied me for a long while, as if searching for something or someone. 'We did have a bond, didn't we?'

'We did, we *really* did. And we could get into blame and accusations about who should have made more effort to stay in touch and all that, but the truth is, we're all as guilty as each other. I wish I'd done many things differently but I can't go back forty years. I can, however, go forward. We let something precious die, but I for one am hoping it can be resurrected.'

'Me too,' said Jo.

Mitch considered what I'd said. 'I hear you, but I'm not the girl you knew any more, Mitch from the old days . . . I have a lifetime of experiences behind me that neither of you were any part of.'

'As do we. I'm not that young girl you knew any more either . . .'

'We've all had our share of successes and losses,' said Jo, 'big and small, but there is a part of me that is still Jo, the girl you knew; older, not much wiser, but in essence still there.'

Mitch was silent for a while and we continued on our way around the grounds.

In bringing up the past, have Jo and I ruined the moment? I asked myself. *It was naïve of me to have thought we could just turn up and we'd be back as we were, at that bus stop so long ago, promising that we'd be friends for ever.*

'I guess, like in any relationship,' said Mitch finally, 'you can get it wrong, make mistakes.'

I nodded. 'I know I did, but mistakes can be remedied. It's never too late.'

Mitch reached out, took my hand and squeezed it. 'Let me think about it. It's all been so much to take in.'

'Can you forgive us?' Jo asked.

'Can *you* forgive me?' Mitch asked.

'We were young, so much to learn,' I said. 'We have to forgive ourselves too.'

Mitch laughed. 'When did you get so wise, Sara?' she said.

'Me wise? I don't think so.'

Mitch looked at me with kind eyes. 'I guess we all broke the rules of friendship.'

'Forgot them more like, but I am relearning them and the importance of old friends and you are up there with them. There's a lot I regret. I could, should have made more effort to come and see you while I was at university, called more often.'

'Goes both ways. I could have too,' she said as she checked her watch and I realized that she was anxious about Lisa's arrival. We began to walk back towards the house and no more was said, but we'd made an inroad into talking about the past, we'd broken the ice and hopefully there would be other times, more appropriate times, when we could pursue it further. For now, the most important thing was Mitch reuniting with Lisa.

'What time is the cab bringing Lisa and Ally?' she asked.

'Soon. They should be on their way. How are you feeling?'

Mitch let out a deep breath. 'Nervous, like I'm going on a first date or something. More than that, I feel terrified. I've been waiting my whole life for a day like this, hoping, but never imagining it would happen and now . . . What if she doesn't like me?'

'Course she will,' said Jo. 'She's as nervous as you are, and probably thinking the same thing. Come on, let's go inside and get something cool to drink. I'm roasting.'

'The house looks old,' I said as Mitch led us up the steps to the veranda at the front of the main house.

'It dates back to the 1600s,' said Mitch as we went inside to a hall with a dark wooden floor, rugs and antique furniture and white walls. It was a cool contrast to the blazing heat outside. Mitch fixed us drinks in a tall kitchen, then we headed back out to the veranda to await Ally and Lisa.

'We'll make ourselves scarce when Lisa gets here,' I said. 'Private moment.'

Mitch took a few more deep breaths. 'You don't have to. Whatever you think best. Oh, I don't know. I'm so excited to meet her, and agitated at the same time. I'm finding it hard to breathe. I hope they come soon.' Five minutes later, we glimpsed a black car advancing up the drive and she stood up. 'Oh god, here they are. Oh . . .'

Jo and I stood up, ready to go inside. 'No, no, stay, please,' said Mitch.

Jo put her arm around Mitch and gave her a reassuring hug.

Mitch made her way down the steps ready to greet the car and, moments later, Ally and Lisa got out.

Mitch only had eyes for Lisa and looked at her searchingly, as if unsure who should make the first move. Lisa looked shy but smiled at her mother who then stepped forward, embraced her and, for a while, they held each other in silence.

'You're so beautiful,' said Mitch when they finally let go of each other. 'Oh god you look like Jack, your father. I'm so *so* happy to meet you. I'm sorry I'm crying. I'm so happy.' She then turned and embraced Ally who had been standing to one side. 'My lovely Ally. God, I feel emotional!' Mitch returned to Lisa and put her arm around her shoulder. 'I . . . er . . . How about we take a walk and catch up a little then come back and join the others?'

Lisa nodded. 'I'd like that. I don't know where to start. I can't stop staring at you. Sorry. I mean, you're my actual mother, my physical mother, it's weird.'

Mitch smiled at her. 'It is, isn't it? But pretty marvellous too. Here I am, I know, I live in a place that is as close to paradise as anyone could ever find, I have a lovely husband and two beautiful boys, your brothers who will come and meet you later; but there was always something missing for me, not something, someone – you.' Her eyes shone with affection as she spoke. 'I never stopped thinking of you, Lisa, and wishing I'd never given you away. I had nothing, you see, when you were born – no home, no money; nothing – and I thought Jack had abandoned me as well. I only found out when it was too late that he'd died, too late to get you back. And when you were old enough, I tried to find you, but there was never any news of you. I thought I had to leave you be, that you didn't want to find me. I tried to understand that, could understand that, but you've always been here in my heart, I'm so sorry . . .'

We were all in tears as Lisa hugged her mother. 'No need. Don't be sorry. It's never too late and look, here I am and here are you.'

'Hey,' said Ally, 'remember the secret of the universe? Remember, Mitch? We were in sixth form. One day you told us all you had the secret and had written it down – I was there and now I'm here. Well now it's true, everything passes. You were there and now you're here.'

Mitch looked utterly bewildered. 'Are you on drugs, Ally?'

Ally cracked up. 'No, but you were,' she said quietly.

Mitch took a deep breath and laughed. 'I have no idea what you're talking about but I don't care.'

Mitch fussed around for a few minutes, making sure Ally, Jo and I had everything we needed, then she led Lisa away. Ally, Jo and I lay on the loungers on the veranda sipping cool drinks, chatting and dozing, while Mitch and Lisa walked around the grounds. I watched them in the distance, heads bowed, occasionally stopping to face each other and talk further.

After an hour, we stood up as Mitch and Lisa returned, both looking a lot more at ease and peace.

Mitch skipped up the steps towards me. 'This is the happiest day of my life. Thank you. Thank you, Sara, for finding Lisa, it's the greatest gift anyone could have given me and I have this to say . . . OK, so we weren't there for each other as friends for so many years, but you came through and did this, this is the best present a friend could ever give me.' She looked fondly at Lisa then turned to Jo and Ally. 'Thank you all for coming out here and giving me a second chance.'

I felt ridiculously, overwhelmingly happy. To have been part of their reunion and, although it was clear we needed to have further conversations of our own, to have found a dear old friend again too. I looked at Ally and Jo and we were all tearful again.

'Group hug,' said Jo, and we gathered together in a huddle, arms wrapped around each other.

'Friends for life,' I said when we stood back.

'Friends for the *rest* of life,' said Mitch, then her eyes twinkled and I caught a glimpse of the teenage girl I'd loved so much. 'Stand on one leg.'

Ally, Jo and I immediately recognized the command from our spot at the bus stop forty years ago and did as we were told.

'Deal,' said Mitch.

'Deal,' we echoed as I wobbled on one leg.

'Amen,' said Mitch.

'Amen,' we chorused, and I knew we were going to be OK. The Fab Four were back together again.

Epilogue

So, what happened next?

Well, the *Long Lost Friends* series was a resounding success, with over ten million viewers each programme and a second series already underway. Mitch and Lisa agreed to take part in the last programme, but only in the background talking about the importance of friends. Ally, Jo, and Sara featured too, talking about the importance of doing things together and making plans for future adventures, travel and time together.

Rhys Logan, Sara's arch rival, was last seen in a *Big Brother-*type house. He was first to be voted off.

Lisa is a regular visitor at Rainbow's End in South Africa, and Mitch has been over to the UK on a number of occasions to meet Lisa's family. Mitch stays with Sara, and Jo and Ally join them for sleepovers. Jo and Mitch have had many long talks about seeing the light. It hasn't stopped them enjoying a good glass of Chablis at the same time.

Ally and Lawrence bought a house in Devon, near Ally's old one so that she could stay in touch with her friends in the area. Ally and Lawrence divided the new house into two parts, one side for him, one side for her. They were last seen heading off on a trip to Indonesia.

Jo married Gary from Little Dog Productions. He treats her like a goddess. They have moved into a house in the same village as Ally and Lawrence, with a field at the back to accommodate their many animals. Jo's children regularly come to visit, but Gary and Jo have stipulated that they only stay three days at a time, quoting the 'guests are like fish, they go off after three days' line to support their rule.

Sara Meyers became established as the face of the over-fifties on TV, which sorted her finances out. With the help of friends, she completed her book on the rules of friendship, with case histories from people involved in the show, illustrations by Jo, and for which Ally found a publisher. It was a great team effort and was on the non-fiction bestseller list for eight weeks, until knocked off by Katie Brookfield's *The Real Bonnets of Bath*.

The press are still unaware that Sara is actually mid-sixties. She never went back to full-time employment, preferring to work two or three days a week so she can spend the rest of the time reconnecting with old pals. She went from being a crap friend to an ace friend and has never been happier. She purchased a two-bedroomed cottage in the same village as Ally and Lawrence, which she rents out occasionally. At other times she uses it as a second home, with a view to moving there later in life. She has recently been seen out with one of the founders of Harvest food, Tom Riley. She insists that they are just good friends.

The Rules of Friendship by Sara Meyers and assorted chums

Sara

- Keep your promises to friends.
- Friendship is a two-way street. Both make an effort. You get in touch, they get in touch.
- Friends who want to stay in touch, do. Those you never hear from, unless you call or text, don't feel the same way about you, so let them go.
- Listen as well as talk, especially if your friend is going through a rough patch. Snoring is optional but not advised, nor is checking your mobile whilst they're baring their soul.
- Friends share the organization of outings, meals out, walks, holidays or theatre visits. Don't leave it to the same person each time.
- True friends don't assume they know what is happening in a friend's life, they find out the reality. It often isn't what was imagined or presumed.
- Don't neglect a friend when a new relationship, project or a demanding job comes along. If you're having a mad busy time, say so – even a text like: 'will be in touch when I resurface' will help maintain the bond.

- Friends embrace opportunities to let their inner child out, laugh their heads off and act like idiots. There are far too many times in life when you have to be serious and responsible.
- It's never too late to connect up with good friends you've lost touch with. Don't let guilt or embarrassment about not having been in contact get in the way.
- Be generous and show your appreciation to your friends. They're worth it.
- Friends support each other and feel safe to tell each other anything without being judged.
- Take the time to work through misunderstandings or miscommunications with people you value.

Nicholas (Sara's agent)

- If you want a friend, be a friend.
- Don't waste your time with fake friends who have an agenda for spending time with you. I get a lot of this being an agent: people who appear to want to be my best pal but all they really want is for me to get them a deal. Harrumph and bugger off, I say. I choose my friends wisely.
- Be aware of friends' or in fact anyone's finances when dining out and splitting the bill: not everyone can afford bottles of Bolly. Always reimburse swiftly if a pal has booked theatre tickets, etc., so that they're not out of pocket. It's only polite.
- True friends are genuinely glad about your successes and don't measure them against their own and feel envious. Jealousy can kill friendships.
- Be prepared to do the 'organ recital' and talk about medical ailments with older friends. Limit time as you go round the

group, i.e. John, you've got five minutes to talk about your hip replacement, Eddie's next to talk about his heart bypass and what meds he's on, then Jacqui's going to entertain us with details of her haemorrhoids. Hours of entertaining fun. Not. Keep it short.

- True friends will speak out when a friend is deluding themselves or talking tosh.
- Good manners. Be on time, not just for friends but for everyone, as being regularly late indicates that other people's time isn't as valuable as yours and makes you out to be a thoughtless pillock.
- Be aware if a friend is lonely and do something about it, especially at times like Christmas.

Jo

- Be your own best friend and kind to yourself.
- True friends don't let distance get in the way and pick up the phone, as nothing beats a proper chat or, failing that, send the occasional text or funny photo of yourself looking your worst whilst having your highlights done or when you've overdone the eyebrow dye and ended up looking like Groucho Marx. FaceTime, Instagram, emails, a card just to say I'm still here and thinking about you.
- True friends don't let friendships drift because they don't get on with your partner, dog, parrot or pet llama.
- Friends trust each other, are discreet and keep secrets.
- Friends don't judge each other – no, that's a lie, they do, but they don't say it out loud or to others. It's OK to tell the cat, though.
- Friends have your best interests at heart and will point out

food spilt down your chest, prominent chin hairs (not on men, obviously), and spinach or lipstick on teeth. Same goes for unflattering clothes, haircut or make-up. On the other hand, they will also notice the good physical changes and compliment, whether it be a new top, great haircut or pair of earrings.

- Friends think about what they can do to help in the future when a friend's current position is rocky.
- Friends are genuinely glad when a friend has good news, even if they are getting everything you wish you had. Life is a rollercoaster for all of us, so celebrate the good fortune of those you care about.

Ruth (Sara's ex friend)

- Don't sleep with your best friend's husband or partner.

Katie Brookfield

- Friends are happy to dress up, help you pick out a hideous fancy-dress costume and act the fool for a friend's big birthday – or any time really.
- Friends remember birthdays. Presents, cards and cake, depending on what your agreement is and finances allow.
- Friends encourage each other to do their best, follow their dreams, take up the challenge and fight the good fight.
- True friends can take the piss out of each other and have a good laugh because they know you well and you love them for it.
- Friends share new experiences. Apart from enemas – those are best done alone.

- Time with friends is never an obligation, so ditch the ones who bore the pants off you.
- Having good friends is the most precious thing in the world. Cherish them.

Ally

- Friends listen with an open mind when their friend comes out with ideas that might seem far-fetched. White feathers left by those who have passed away, the need to juice copious amounts of celery or move into a commune. Some of the most brilliant and innovative minds were at one time considered crazy.
- Cultivate local friends if geography distances you from your old dear ones. It's never too late to make new friends and it's a pleasure to have someone call and say – fancy a coffee tomorrow? See you at the deli.
- Friends are sensitive to their friends' way of doing things in their own homes, so don't rearrange a friend's kitchen or their furniture, for example, without permission.
- Friends surprise you with good ideas to make your life better.

Philippa (Ally's friend)

- At times of crisis, don't ask, do. Practical actions. Take a casserole, give a lift, do a grocery shop or the washing up – whatever needs doing.
- If a friend has a serious hospital appointment, go with them if you can, so they know that they're not alone in facing whatever comes up.
- Be there in person, if you can, at times when a friend has

been thrown one of life's curve balls and their familiar landscape has shifted.

Lawrence

- Friends spend time together but also give each other space; they care but don't smother.
- Friends 'get' each other, always have lots to talk about and can be completely themselves with each other.
- Friends don't try to pair single friends off with every available man/woman available unless they're asked to.

Tom Riley

- Keep phone numbers and addresses of old friends: you never know when you might need them or what they might lead to.

Gary

- Don't let your furry best friend sleep on the bed on the first night sharing it with a new partner.
- Don't put your furry best friends in the same room as other people's pets unless you want trouble.

Simon and Steve

- Men need good friends as much as women.
- Don't let your partner make all the social plans. Share the organizing as your partner might not be there to do it for you for ever.

Luca (singer-songwriter)

- Respect a friend's privacy if they don't want to appear on social media, on Instagram or Facebook falling out of a car pissed as a fart, looking their worst or snogging the waiter, no matter how hilarious it seemed at the time. Especially if they're married and were supposed to be somewhere else.
- Find your equals.
- True friends are loyal and always have your back. They don't stay silent if others are criticizing, slagging off or gossiping about a friend. Friends stand up for each other.
- New friends can be found through exploring like-minded activities and interests.

Mitch

- True friends can be vulnerable and completely honest with each other. They don't have to put on a brave face or down-play their fears. A friend can only help and show care if they know what's really going on.
- Friends do interesting, challenging and new things together, except maybe bungee jumping or taxidermy.
- You have to nurture friendship, with time and attention for it to grow and blossom in the same way you care for a plant.
- Be open to letting go of past mistakes with friends you care about.
- Many friendships dip in and out over the years, but the true ones stand the test of time and will come through in the end.

ACKNOWLEDGEMENTS

As this book is primarily about girlfriends, first of all I'd like to thank mine for being there through the various chapters of my life. I feel truly blessed to know you – some are old friends, some new but all have enriched my life and continue to do so – Annie, Nicky, Liz, Sarah, Greta, Jude, June, Carole, Caroline, Carol, Rosie T, M and B, Charlie, Beth, Teresa, Helen, Debbie, Laura, Janet, Sonia, Marion, Mary, Jenny B and F, Sue, Jess, Lily, Jane P and R, Mary, Val A and new ones: Suzie, Val L, Joanna, Lyn, Angie, Sharon, Claire, Maria, Fi, Marilou, Sarah C, Marion, Jill, Fran, Celia, Bridget, Sandy, Trish, Mairiona, thank you, thank you.

Thank you to my husband and friend Steve for your endless support and encouragement through this book and all the others. You've been a rock.

I've also been lucky to have the best of agents, people who have become friends, so thanks to Christopher Little, Emma Schlesinger and Jules Bearman for everything you've done for me over the years. Truly appreciated.

And not forgetting the editor Kate Bradley who I've had the pleasure of working with at HarperCollins and am very glad to have in my corner. Thank you for your persistence, insightful advice and refusal to give up on working on this book, even when I was ready to jack it all in and go into recluse in the Himalayas. Also, to Penny Isaac for her eagle eye and constructive advice at the copy editor stage and to Claire Ward and Caroline Young for their wonderful covers. Behind the scenes is the wonderful and enthusiastic team at HarperCollins. Thank you all. It's been a blast.